SYMPATHY F

During the mid-1980s Howard Marks had forty-three aliases, eighty-nine phone lines and owned twenty-five companies trading throughout the world. At the height of his career he was smuggling consignments of up to thirty tons of marijuana, and had contact with organisations as diverse as MI6, the CIA, the IRA and the Mafia. Following a worldwide operation by the United States Drug Enforcement Administration, he was busted and sentenced to twenty-five years in prison at United States Federal Penitentiary, Terre Haute, Indiana. He was released in April 1995 after serving seven years of his sentence. His autobiography, *Mr Nice*, was first published in 1996, and has been published in nine languages. The film of *Mr Nice*, starring Rhys Ifans, Chloe Sevigny and David Thewliss, was released in 2010.

ALSO BY HOWARD MARKS

Mr Nice
Howard Marks' Book of Dope Stories
Senor Nice: Straight Life from
Wales to South America

HOWARD MARKS

Sympathy for the Devil

VINTAGE BOOKS

London

Published by Vintage 2011

2 4 6 8 10 9 7 5 3 1

Copyright © Howard Marks 2011

Howard Marks has asserted his right under the Copyright, Designs
and Patents Act 1988 to be identified as the author of this work

This novel is a work of fiction.
Although loosely inspired by the disappearance of Richey Edwards from
the Manic Street Preachers, all characters and events described in this book
are the product of the author's imagination. Any resemblance to actual
persons, living or dead, is entirely coincidental.

First published in Great Britain in 2011 by
Vintage
Random House, 20 Vauxhall Bridge Road,
London SW1V 2SA

www.vintage-books.co.uk

Addresses for companies within The Random House Group Limited can be
found at: www.randomhouse.co.uk/offices.htm

The Random House Group Limited Reg. No. 954009

A CIP catalogue record for this book
is available from the British Library

ISBN 9780099532736

The Random House Group Limited supports The Forest Stewardship
Council (FSC), the leading international forest certification organisation. All
our titles that are printed on Greenpeace approved FSC certified paper
carry the FSC logo. Our paper procurement policy can be found at
www.rbooks.co.uk/environment

Mixed Sources
Product group from well-managed
forests and other controlled sources
www.fsc.org Cert no. TT-COC-002139
© 1996 Forest Stewardship Council
FSC

Printed and bound in Great Britain by
CPI Bookmarque, Croydon CR0 4TD

Wrth fargeinio gyda'r hen ŵr,
Nid oes diben cynnig dy enaid,
Fe piau hwnnw eisoes,
Rhaid I ti roi'r hyn sy'n agosach i'th galon.

To bargain with the old gentleman,
No point in offering your soul,
He already owns that,
You must give him what's closer to your heart.

A Book of Witches. Anonymous. Welsh, 19th century

They are at the door.

The two men again.

She can hear the slapping of their palms on the walls, out in the passage she has never seen.

This is her sign. She must kneel now, put her face to the wall. Close her eyes, not look back as they enter the room.

For one bright moment, as the door opens, she can smell the mildew of long-abandoned houses by the sea.

On the wall over her head – their silhouettes, the vague shapes of the bundles under their arms.

From the cupboard in the corner where they leave the school books, the taller one takes out her mask again.

He is putting on the buckles at the back of her shorn head. He pulls the straps tight.

Their hands are moving on her gently. They must feel she is broken now.

She knows what is coming, she tries to feel nothing.

No anger, no fear, this is her resistance, not to feel.

1

They guide her again to the reclining chair, to the leg straps on either side.

In the shuttered half-light she sees their perching shapes, shifting, spreading. Over their eyes are mirrors. She tries to close her eyes, but she cannot. They are taped open.

One is beneath her, the other above and over the walls run shadows of her twisting in their hands. She tries to turn her head away, but she cannot.

The first one's skin is calloused, knotted with muscles, the other's younger, soft almost as her own. She sees the staff again, thick with ancient carvings.

She waits for the pain. She tries not to make a sound, not to cry. This is her resistance. It makes the pain worse, not making a sound, but still she does not.

She knows she's always been here, it was the before that was unreal.

She waits for it to end, for it to begin, for it to end. This is the only clock she knows. One is beneath her, the other above and light shimmers in the mirrors over their eyes – an old light, like a deep winter dawn – and by it she sees everything that is done, and she remembers.

PROLOGUE

IN THE CITY
FEBRUARY 1998

Of all the moments in her life, this was the one Catrin would most like to have back.

It was the night when news of the rock star's suicide at the bridge broke. Not that she thought that had anything to do with it; nothing, not at first. Like the rest of the city, she was huddled over a television, watching the shocking events unfold live. In her arms was her man Rhys who meant more to her than the rest of her meagre life put together. More than life itself, it felt like. But for once her eyes were not on him, but trained on the flickering screen.

It had been a bitter, fog-bound February, the first winter Catrin had made detective: a suit, not that she ever wore one. That night she was in her old joggers, Rhys sprawled naked over her. The room was dark, the furniture barely visible. But they hadn't switched on the lights, hadn't even gone to get their smokes. They weren't moving from in front of the set.

On the screen the stage was lit by a single spotlight beam. In and out of it a lone figure was swaying in silhouette, his narrow shoulders hunched. The light created a pale halo around his head. It was the last song of the set, the torch song, and creeping into the darkness came a faint glow from thousands of flickering lighter flames.

The spotlight found the singer again, his shirt ripped open now over his chest. It was narrow and lined with horizontal cuts, the stains darkening it. The rest of the group were behind him in the shadows. His face was soft, dreamy, his eyes half closed behind dark smudges of make-up, and all around him pulsed a strange, low trance-like beat.

As his arm began windmilling over his guitar, his forearm appeared to be painted in bright red letters. The camera panned in closer. *Owen Face* the letters read. They looked as if they had been freshly carved into his flesh with a knife.

As they saw this, people in the crowd tried to run towards him. But the black-shirted security men were already closing in, holding them back. From the front a fan in a velvet cloak reached out his arms, shouting something, his words lost in the wail of feedback. The singer was staggering back now out of the spot to the back of the stage.

'It's so they know who I am.' The singer's words came out in a single, slurred rasping sound. He seemed about to lose his footing, more men in black shirts were rushing in around him and he disappeared from view.

'This is the last show, folks.' From behind the row of bulked-up figures his words came whispered, like a prayer, the mike only just catching them. 'See you all in a better world.' If he said anything further it was lost in the sound now filling the hall, a sound that seemed almost biblical, the sound of thousands gasping and weeping, and mingling with it came the whine of approaching sirens. The stage was dark again, the only lights tracking the bodies of those who'd fainted over the heads of the crowd back towards the exit doors.

The round-the-hour news coverage flicked back to the live-time shot at the top of the screen. Out of the fog loomed the outlines of towers and arched span of the old Severn Bridge, the country's favourite suicide spot. Overhead choppers were still circling, their beams crossing the surface of the waters below. The channel was using night-vision cameras to try to penetrate the banks of fog, the scene bathed in an eerie greenish light. At the edge of the water Catrin could just make out police barricades, the crowd a heaving mass of black leather and spiky Goth cuts. In the strobing lights she glimpsed white mask-like faces running with make-up, others bleary with shock and tears.

The windows shook with the thrum of a chopper

passing low overhead. She pushed the volume right up, but they could no longer hear the set.

'Search and Rescue must be looking for his body down on the mudflats. That's where the jumpers usually wash up.' Catrin glanced down at Rhys, his cheek nestling between her small breasts. His eyes were fixed on the screen, the light from it running over his gaunt face.

'The tides are still up.' Rhys was almost shouting, something he very rarely did, so she could hear over the roar of the chopper. 'So these must all be press choppers – it could be the biggest rock 'n' roll suicide since Cobain.'

'Sure, Face was rock royalty. But what do you mean *could* be? Face said his goodbyes at the gig, drove to the bridge and jumped. It's a done deal.'

'No body yet though. They found his car at the jumpers' bridge, but no body.' Rhys slipped his head into the toned hollow of her belly, his hand resting on her thigh. 'On the way here I could hardly get past the three-hut circus at the docks. There were BBC, Sky OB units along with a crowd of ghouls and rubber-neckers. Even saw foreign units down there, CNN, Fox, RTL.'

'But it looked like all the action was at the bridge. Why the party at the docks?'

'There was a body sighting there. Turned out to be

a shop dummy dressed up like Face in leathers and a black wig. Some sicko's idea of a joke.'

'Right,' she said, 'events like these always bring out the artists.' She let her fingers drift down the side of Rhys's hair, to rest on his small, elfin ear. Overhead the sound of the chopper was fading. She turned back to the screen.

One half was still showing the spotlights and the fog and the dark, choppy waters under the bridge. The other half, a montage of recent clippings from the tabloids. A pack of paparazzi, standing on ladders with long-lenses outside the wrought-iron gates of a private rehab clinic. Cutting to Face in striped pyjamas, sitting on a sofa for a photo shoot, his head shaved, his forearm lined with tidy horizontal scars, his cheekbones sharp enough to poke through the skin.

'I'm surprised no one tried to stop him.' Catrin was pointing at the scars on Face's arm. 'Self-harming. In and out of clinics for depression, starving himself. The classic tells of a suicide plastered over the red-tops for months, but no one tries to stop the bloke going for the exit.'

She saw Rhys was pointing at the image of the press outside the private clinic. 'They may be barking up the wrong tree there. That wasn't one of the clinics he attended. Face was always a very private man.'

She glanced down at Rhys but he wasn't looking

up at her. 'Maybe Face should have gone to a clinic. Maybe that would have saved him. Looks like the bloke was completely out of control,' she said.

'You're wrong, Face was never out of control. Everything he did was planned.' Rhys was staring intently at the carpet, his fingers slowly moving over its blank surface. 'This could've been some kind of stunt, maybe one that went wrong.'

'But stunts weren't Face's style.'

'No, you're right, they weren't. Face had the balls to cut himself on stage, why not finish it there. Instead he drives down to the bridge.'

'Oh please, don't start with theories. He was hardly going to off himself jumping into the mosh pit. And nothing's worse for the image than a suicide that goes idiot wrong.' She watched as Rhys got up, a look of puzzlement on his face. He stepped into the bathroom. Through the door came the swish of the shower curtain, then the sound of water flowing. She stood, sensing Face's gaze still flickering across the room as she went over to the window.

The outlines of the city had disappeared behind the fog. She looked out, seeing nothing, her heart thudding. The streets were silent. Everyone was huddled around their TVs or gone to join the crowds at the waterside. The only sound was the faint trickle of a radio somewhere playing one of Face's old hits. It didn't sound like music, more like someone moving something heavy around her head. Dropping it, dragging it, then dropping it again.

She closed the curtain, let her hand rest on the shelf. There were no books there, only the delicate origami birds Rhys made. Swans, owls, ravens, others she didn't recognise. Imaginary creatures, perhaps. It was a habit he had, working with Japanese paper during long undercover stake-outs around the city, the ones she sometimes joined him on. When he was bored or just watching he made swans and owls and other birds; alone he only ever made ravens, the paper's tip folded out into hooked beaks. The birds weren't something he showed around: as soon as he made them he tore them up. She'd been the one to save them, display them in this neat line on the shelf. Made the place feel like a nest, he said; she wasn't sure if this meant he liked it. Maybe it was just his way of saying he wasn't ready for anything permanent yet, his way of telling her not to take anything about him for granted.

She was only trying to make their bare flat a little nicer, not just a place they crashed between shifts. Putting a few pretty things on shelves didn't mean she was thinking of vows and wedding bells. She never thought that far ahead, took each day at a time. In the mirror over the shelf she caught a brief glimpse of herself, and quickly turned away. She didn't like what she saw, her eyes too wide and staring like a child's. She wondered again what Rhys had ever seen in her, someone to protect, a duty, a responsibility, or was it something more?

She heard him coming out of the bathroom, the clatter of the wardrobe as he pulled out some clothes. She didn't have to turn to see him. He was there always scored behind her eyes. Like the afterglow of a too-strong light. His snake hips and narrow chest, pale as the sheets they'd lain in all weekend, his eyes like some damaged poet's eyes and nothing like a fellow officer's.

It was at moments like this she wondered why she needed him as much as air and water. There was what he had done for her in the woods of course, his saving her. But that was only the start of it. It was the sense of a pain in him, that he was keeping locked away, something she couldn't reach. Whenever she thought she'd found the door to it, another closed in her face. To understand him she needed to open all those doors. But there was always a risk in that: to understand a man like this might be to lose him.

Whatever it was, it was eating him up. She felt it in the knotted muscles in his back when he should've been spent and empty in her arms. She saw it in that stoop he'd begun to walk with. It was like something loaded on his shoulders he couldn't shake off. She heard it in his voice, the dryness in his throat. And it was there in his eyes. The way they didn't lose themselves in hers any more, how tight they'd gone at the rims and the irises shrunk and pointed like pinpricks.

She went down the cold passage into the tiny kitchen. From the shelf she took down an onion, peppers, lemon grass, and laid them on the board. She took a knife, began chopping. When had they last had a proper meal together?

'I'm not hungry.' Rhys was standing by the door. 'Late for my shift at that crack pitch in the docks.'

'But the docks are overrun tonight, you said it yourself. Why go?'

He didn't answer. She watched him take his keys from the bowl, a Marlboro soft pack from the carton next to it. She pushed the chopped food off the board, down into the sink. 'I'm coming with you,' she said softly.

Later she'd wonder why she went with him. Maybe things would have been different if she hadn't gone. Maybe if you don't see something in some way it never happens. Like trees falling in the woods. If no one was there to hear them falling maybe they never made a sound.

She glanced at Rhys, but he remained expressionless. She sensed he was thinking of a reason to go on his own. He was taking his time putting on his puffer jacket, his black wool cap.

If she didn't know him, had just passed him in the street, she'd say he looked like a dealer, street, no different from the types he busted every week. He fitted in well among them, maybe too well. But behind the hardness she sensed a strange purity there, almost other-worldly, as if he were on a sacred mission he kept strictly to himself. He didn't share his colleagues' interests in sport or banter or drink with them. Very little out in the world ever seemed to interest him, only her and his work. When he ate he liked to eat in silence. When he listened to a track, he left half an hour of silence either side. If she put on music, he switched it off; scented candles, he snuffed them out. When he touched her he did just that: nothing else seemed to exist for him, just those simple moments between them. Everything he did as if for the first and last time. It was intense, as if he believed the time he had left was limited and he wanted to strip everything down to the essentials. But maybe that was just how he looked at things. If he'd believed he was in some sort of danger, he would have told her, wouldn't he?

She followed him down to the car. It was cold, the heater blew freezing air around her feet. They drove without talking through the terraces of Bute towards the waterside.

At the lower crossroads Rhys began tracking along the radio dial. All the stations were playing Face's old hits, the talk shows going over what had gone down at the gig and the bridge. When Rhys hit the end of the dial he turned it off. Catrin could hear snatches of Face's low, murmuring voice still playing through her head. She began humming to shut the sound of it out.

She turned to Rhys in the darkness, put her hand lightly on his thigh. 'It's there in Face's lyrics,' she said. 'What he did tonight, it was like a self-fulfilling prophecy.'

'Which lyrics?'

'That one about the snow. *I'll walk across snow without leaving footprints*.'

'That could just be a reference to his anorexia.'

'Anorexia? It's an unusual condition for a man.'

'Well, Face was an unusual man.'

As they got closer to the water they passed several BBC vans down from Broadcasting House in Llandaff. Beside them Catrin recognised the Asian reporter from Sky News, his scarf the only point of colour among the columns of black-clad Goths silently filing past. On both sides of the road were more OB vans, their satellite dishes silhouetted in the dim light of the candles cupped in their hands by the crowd.

As they neared the block where Face had lived the bodies tightened around the car. The headlights picked out a flash of feather boas and sequins, some girls rushing forward, their make-up smudged with tears. Locals from surrounding pubs were waving their arms at each other, bobbing forward in the quickening flows of the crowd. For a moment the road ahead appeared blocked by some form of queue. A man was standing in a doorway, letting in one person at a time. There was a glimpse of a stairway up to a flat, a view down onto Face's street and the waterfront.

'Typical. The guy's only been gone five minutes and already someone's making a few quid off him.' Rhys held his warrant card out of the window, his hand on the horn. They passed a couple of uniforms standing beside some transparent evidence bags. Inside Catrin saw the limbs of a shop dummy, the type that would be light enough to float, a black leather jacket and wig. But no one seemed to be paying the find any attention. The crowd was pushing forward towards the end of the street. All eyes were focused now on a slim female figure standing on something raised behind the cordon.

In the roped-off rectangle in front the press were gathered. The woman's face was hidden by the mikes clustered around her. But Catrin already recognised the lean, taut figure and rod-straight black hair. It was Della Davies, the senior press officer from Area Headquarters.

The woman rested one hand on the hip of her tight

ski-pants, her patent jacket glinting in the lights. She looked like she was striking a pose at the end of a runway rather than briefing on a dead man.

Catrin felt a sudden surge of anger. She'd heard the talk around the station, that Della had her eye on Rhys, that there was something between them. The call was that Della was the sort who always got what she wanted in the end, always got her man. Or woman: she walked both sides of the street. And at that moment Catrin didn't want to look at Rhys. She didn't want to see what his face might betray.

Against the Dellas of the world she'd never stood a chance. She'd been brought up by a chaotic hippie mam, whose idea of beauty was henna, patchouli, tie-dye smocks. Scratch the surface, she was still gawky, childlike, that tomboy who never wore skirts, hid herself behind boys' kit. Any man who stared at her too long, she thought there was something wrong with him, didn't trust him. But Della – Della soaked up men's gazes like it was her birthright, always looked like she'd just spent the last five hours in a day spa. Her effect was sleek as a doll, a perfect shiny shell but what was inside no one seemed to know.

'Yes, for the last time, I can confirm Mr Face's body has not yet been recovered.' Through the freezing air Della's throaty voice carried over the hushed crowd.

The Sky reporter was jostling his way to the front, holding a mike up under her plumped-up lips.

'So when the tides go out, where do you expect the body to be lying?' he asked.

'I can't speculate on that. We've got some of the strongest tides in the world here. Sometimes it can take several months before bodies are found.'

'Then why not let us through, what are you hiding back there?' The voice was American this time, young and reedy.

'We're not hiding anything, sir.' Della cast a disdainful glance in the direction of the voice. She ran her long nails briefly along the top of the panel. 'These cordons are purely an issue of crowd safety.'

The Sky reporter still had his mike in her face. 'Any other possible explanations for Face's car being found abandoned at the suicide bridge?'

'Nothing has been ruled out at this stage.' For a moment Della lightly stroked the shaft of the mike before pushing it away. 'And I'd remind you that the bridge is still open to traffic and can be popular with visitors taking in the views.'

'But Face wasn't a visitor, and since the new bridge was built, no one drives that way. His car was found after dark, so he was hardly going down there for the view. Are you saying the police are pursuing a line of inquiry other than suicide?'

'No further comments.' Della abruptly ducked away among the uniforms. As Catrin turned she noticed Rhys was staring at the spot where Della had disappeared.

'Della's certainly enjoying her fifteen minutes,' he said.

'Knowing Della, she'll make it last longer than that.' Catrin kept her eyes straight ahead as Rhys edged the car up to the cordon. He held up his card, the panel was lifted by a young WPC and they passed through. As they drove on into empty streets the hum of the crowd soon died away behind them. The only sounds were the lapping of the waves against the front, and out in the channel the chug of a motorboat, its dim form ghostly behind the banks of fog.

Rhys's surveillance point was down the other end of the waterfront, but he didn't seem in any hurry to reach it. He was slowly doubling back around the block into the street behind the cordon. All the time Catrin could hear the smooth whirr of a large car behind them. They were moving slowly, but it didn't pass, just kept a steady distance behind.

In the rearview Catrin saw the car pulling up about twenty yards back on the deserted street. 'Looks like someone wants you to stop,' Catrin said quietly. Rhys's shoulders tensed. He had slowed to a crawl, not looking round.

They waited, but no one got out from the car behind. She noticed Rhys checking the rearview for a moment before he opened the door. He said nothing. He was walking back into the headlights. Catrin turned and watched him disappear behind the glare.

Catrin saw only a single figure in the car. It was difficult to make out much, but she could see long straight hair, a jacket with a sheen to it. Whoever it was had left the headlights full on so they couldn't be seen clearly.

Rhys was leaning through the window now. She thought she saw him putting something in his pocket. Then he was half running back through the glare as the other car revved, swerved off at speed towards the cordon.

Catrin caught the faint scent of a woman's perfume as Rhys closed the door.

'Who was that? Della?'

He shook his head as he settled back in his seat. 'Nothing to worry about.' He started the car, his eyes straight ahead as he moved towards the surveillance point.

Thirty yards further along he turned next to the pavement along the dock. To the right a small pontoon provided berths for four small boats, all of which looked in need of repair and a coat of paint. On the other side was a clear sightline up to the door of what had once been a late-night drinking club.

The place had been closed for months. Most of the local landlords had sold their leases to the seafront development companies. This whole area was a ghost town now, every building around them marked out for demolition.

Catrin watched as Rhys lifted the night-sight Bushnells and camera into place on the console, focused on the front of the empty club. The lights were off above the doorway. Usually there'd be a couple of Somali lads just out of range of the CCTV above. Occasionally cars would pass or lads with heads down under their hoodies to buy a stone or a sixteenth, moving off into the alleys behind. But tonight with the cordon in place the pitch was deserted, no sign of passing trade.

It was the watching unseen that had first turned Catrin on to police work, that and seeing patterns where there didn't seem to be any at first. But now there wasn't much for them to look at, just the fading posters on the wall, the view across the bay shut out by the fog. She reached her hand across in the darkness, held Rhys's, letting her face rest against his chest. He opened the glove compartment and took out a tube of Fruit Pastilles.

'Want one?'

She took a lime one, slipped it in her mouth without chewing.

'You knew there'd be nothing here tonight,' she said. She held the pastille against her cheek with her tongue. 'Why come down? What were you expecting to see?'

Rhys lowered the binoculars.

'I don't know. I'll only know when I see it.'

A few insubstantial flakes landed on the car window, melting almost immediately. Catrin shivered, hunkered down inside her parka. Only ten minutes had passed, but her feet already felt cold.

'This is all just bullshit.' She pointed at the empty street. 'You came down because you knew *she* would be here.'

'Who's she?' he said casually.

'Oh please.' Catrin put her hand in Rhys's pocket, and felt his hand on her wrist. She thought he was going to stop her, but he didn't. At first her fingers found only the little folded papers he used to make his origami birds. Immediately she began to feel ashamed for doing this, for doubting him. She laid the papers out on her palm. A swan, an owl, a raven. Then she felt something else, wrapped in cellophane. She knew what it was before she even took it out.

'What the fuck's this? Why isn't it in an evidence bag?'

He shrugged, said nothing. It would have been so

easy for him to lie, but he just said nothing. She held it closer to the light. It was a wrap, just as she'd thought, the cellophane transparent, burnt at the corner to seal in the brown heroin powder.

'Della gave this to you, didn't she?'

Rhys was looking away down the street, avoiding her eyes. She felt a pain now in her temple as at the onset of a fever, a sudden emptiness in her stomach, that feeling she had whenever she looked down from heights and there was nothing dividing her from the fatal emptiness beneath.

She touched his cheek, tried to make him look at her. 'What's so bad,' she said softly, 'that you have to do this to yourself? Is it a case? I thought we shared everything.'

He remained still as a stone, staring out into the night. She tried to force herself to think positively. *He's never lied to me. He could have, but he didn't. Maybe he wanted me to know, maybe he was just waiting for this to happen. Maybe he couldn't bear to hide it from me any more.*

'Whatever's hurting you, I can handle it,' she said. 'You don't need to protect me, not any more.' He still said nothing. She heard her own voice trailing off. Sometimes the truth couldn't be sugar-coated. He'd been using and she hadn't even seen the signs. She'd been trained to read those signs, but so had he, he'd known how to cover up. He'd committed original sin for a drugs officer, and what was worse he hadn't turned to her for help, he'd kept it hidden.

She tried to swallow her anger but couldn't stop herself. She heard her heels on the pavement, the slam of the car door behind her before she was even aware she was moving.

She walked fast through streets she had known all her life. She could have kept her eyes closed and still found her way home. On the other side of the street she saw a solitary figure, a young girl. A stray from the crowds at the docks maybe. It was late for her to be out. The child was doing everything to avoid drawing attention to herself, head down, taking fast, small steps. Catrin wanted to follow the girl to make sure she was safe, but already she was losing sight of her. The girl broke into a run, weaving between the pillars of the low-rise flats then disappearing into the blackness.

Around one corner, then another and Catrin passed a barber's pole above a charred hole in the brickwork, then under the shop sign over another boarded-up front. Most of the houses beyond were covered with metal sheets to keep squatters out, awaiting demolition. These streets would disappear soon to make way for the new waterfront developments, and for a moment her mind was filled with a vision of all the lost souls who would continue to pace them in their dreams until their dying days.

The curtains were pulled across the windows of her mother's house, no lights visible from the street. The fairy lights still not taken down from previous Christmases, now a permanent feature, gave out not even a flicker. Catrin went down the path to the back door. She moved quietly up the steps between the troughs that had once held pink flowers she'd never known the name of. She was aware her mother might already be sleeping, and didn't want to wake her.

Catrin was trying hard not to think about what had just happened, but the harder she tried not to picture it, the more it ran through her mind. Maybe it hadn't even been Della in the car behind. She had to hang on to that possibility. Maybe Rhys had just forgotten to slip the wrap into an evidence bag. There could always be innocent explanations for things. If you looked at them in a certain way, didn't look at them too long. The trick of making life bearable, a life like hers where she was paid to think the worst of people.

Through the hallway she went into the kitchen. She could hear the sound of a television from the next room, and out over the water the sound of the choppers just a distant thrumming. She stood at the door, but the room was empty. The light flickered over a tracksuit hung over the back of a chair. It was one of the wooden dining suite her mother never used. Her mother didn't come downstairs often now, and when she did she always ate her meals on her lap on the threadbare sofa that faced the television.

Catrin stood at the sink and ran the water until it was so cold it seemed to burn her fingers, then she went upstairs. When she flicked the switch the hallway remained dark. The bulbs hadn't been replaced. In the street light she could just make out the patch on the wall where the Salem picture had hung, the proud old woman at chapel with the devil's face showing in the folds of her shawl. Dust-sheets covered the furniture waiting for the council to take it to the sheltered housing where her mother was being rehoused.

The door to her mother's room was closed. She stood with her ear to the peeling paintwork, could hear nothing within. 'Mam,' she whispered. But there was no reply. Through the crack came the flicker of the gas fire. She opened the door silently and peered in. Her mother lay unmoving on the bed, her chest slowly rising and falling. Her face in the glow of the fire looked hollowed out, pale from all the medication and so many months indoors.

Catrin went over, drew the blanket gently up to her mother's neck. When she bent and kissed her forehead it felt cool, dry, as if it had been buried in parched earth. She wondered how long her mother had left now. She'd asked the doctors enough times and always they'd said the same thing. They didn't own crystal balls, they couldn't see into the future. It sounded as if they were trained to say it.

Even in the dimness she could make out the marks where the cupboard and armchair had stood, and where the rug had lain for so many years. Beside the bed the packing case was covered with her mother's cigarettes, her blister packs of pills, her many lighters and dog-eared Mills & Boons. Catrin tried the lighters one by one, but they were all dead.

Beside her she heard the shallow rasp of her mother's breathing, her eyes half open but seeing nothing. In her sleep her mother was rolling over, her arms reaching around the pillow, cradling it close to her. Catrin drew back the tie-dye cloth hung over the dusty window and looked out into the night.

In the moonlight the frozen grass glistened. The clothes hanging on the makeshift line should have been brought in hours ago. When she goes to bring them in in the morning they will be stiff as cardboard, Catrin thought.

At the bottom of the yard a cat moved among the bins. In the window opposite an Asian family were eating their dinner together, they could not see her watching them. Like everything that night they felt like something glimpsed on a distant screen.

SEPTEMBER 1998

'Catrin.'

She opened her eyes. It was dark still, but she could make out a vague movement near the door.

What time was it? Morning? She turned and looked at her alarm clock. Two a.m. No wonder she felt strange, she'd only been asleep an hour.

She could make out a man crouching by the door.

There was something in his hand, something long and dark. He was wearing a loose tracksuit, the hood pulled up. He was still, absolutely still, and he was watching her.

'Catrin.'

Her heart leapt. That's what had woken her, the sound of Rhys's voice. He'd come back to her. She waited for him to hit the switch, then opened her eyes again slowly.

'Oh Rhys,' she said, 'you look terrible.'

He hadn't come home for two weeks and now she noticed all the things she'd got used to when she saw him every day. The state of his clothes and the way they hung off his body, the state of his skin, the pallor, the dullness of his eyes. The drugs and the not eating: his life was destroying him from the inside out. He's come back because he knows I'm the only one who can save him, she thought.

He was only thirty-five after all, there was plenty of time for him to change. She wasn't the innocent kid she'd been when they first got together. She was twenty-two years old now, a serving Drugs officer, just like him. She was going to save him.

Then she noticed the suitcase, lying on the floor at his feet.

'What's that?' Her voice was small and scared. 'What are you doing, Rhys?'

It was obvious what he was doing. He was taking his clothes from the cupboard and he was putting them in the suitcase.

'I'm sorry, Cat,' he said.

She got out of bed, hoping that the sight of her fit young body would be enough to give him second thoughts. Fat chance. He didn't even look at her. He just kept stuffing his things into the case, and all at once she felt self-conscious in her nakedness, and aware that he was no longer hers. She quickly pulled on her joggers and T-shirt.

'Where are you going, Rhys?'

His eyes gave him away, flickering towards the

window. She crossed the room and opened the curtains a crack, just enough to see the street outside. There was a car parked there, a long, dark, expensive-looking coupé. A woman stood next to it, smoking and looking straight up at her.

She's standing there so I can see her. The bitch, she's relishing this. Even in the half-light Catrin saw how slim, how lithe she was. She was dressed in a tight shiny dress with a snakeskin pattern, and heels, as if she'd just left a glamorous club or party. Catrin shivered, closed the curtains again.

'It's that bitch. Della Davies,' she said.

'Yes.' Rhys was closing the suitcase, moving away towards the door. 'Don't tell me you didn't know.'

Had she known? Of course she had, but increasingly she'd hidden it from herself. When the gossip in the station had stopped, a part of her had so much wanted to believe it was over. All at once it hit home, how terribly young and naïve she'd been. What could she offer him now that would make him change his mind? She felt a rising panic.

'Please,' she said. She needed urgently to get away from the flat, from the place they'd shared. 'Let's take a walk, talk for a minute.'

Catrin moved her hand to touch his cheek. Rhys didn't look at her but nodded. She sighed with relief. He still cared enough to do that for her. She left her fingers there, drew them softly down to his neck. She slapped him hard where she had just stroked him. He didn't move. His eyes were still, expressionless.

'Hey,' he said, a tiny smile playing around his chapped lips, 'that's no way to say goodbye.'

She couldn't help smiling back. They both loved Leonard Cohen. Did Della Davies love Leonard Cohen? She couldn't imagine it. She put her trainers on, and they walked out of the house together into the mild night.

She kept her eyes straight ahead, looking away from where Della was standing. She caught a brief flash of stretched halter-top, big gold jewellery, deep fake tan. The light from the street lamps glimmered over the car behind her. It was a late-model Mercedes, looked as if it had just come from the showroom.

That's an expensive car to run on a press officer's salary, she thought. But then she'd heard the rumours around the station, that Della had some line on the side. What this line was, no one really knew. Some said she worked as an escort for wealthy businessmen, and that she offered unusual, very specialised services. Others that she ran an agency for officers moonlighting in the shadier end of the private-security game. There were other rumours, even more bizarre. But no one had ever backed up a single rumour with a single fact.

She's the sort of woman who knows about everyone else's business, but nobody knows about hers, Catrin thought. And she's too smooth an operator to let that change.

Rhys was leading Catrin down the street now. He was heading towards the park, the stretch of empty lawns behind the trees. He walked to where the ruins of a small bandstand were circled by railings overgrown with ivy. The floor of the shelter was littered with cardboard where rough sleepers had been; tall beeches hid the place from the lane.

She saw the glow of Della's cigarette behind the trees, and Rhys glancing back towards her as if at a view of something indistinct and far away. Catrin nodded towards the trees. 'She's just a user, she wants you for something. After that, she'll treat you like you never existed.'

'This isn't about her,' he said slowly.

They stood there, six foot apart. Catrin wanted to close the gap but knew she couldn't. For the moment they were like opposing magnets. She waited, watched Rhys make the effort to start saying what he had to say. Finally, he was ready.

'Cat,' he said. He paused, took a deep breath, carried on. 'You know about the tests?'

She nodded hesitantly. Rhys had been drug-tested at work a month back. He was a DS. Undercover on the Drug Squad. Of course – the tests. She felt a sickening lurch in her stomach. He moved forward, held her by the wrist. She felt their pulses collide, weirdly out of sync.

'They'll question you first,' he said quietly. Although she could not see his eyes she knew he was watching her closely. 'That's the way Internals and DPS always do it. They start with who they think is the weakest link.

'Say nothing,' he said in the same level tone. He'd taken a soft pack of Marlboro from his pocket, was tapping one out into his hand.

'I don't know anything.'

'It's all right. I know.' He lit a cigarette and she caught a glimpse of his sunken cheeks, his clouded eyes. Still, betraying nothing.

'But you've heard rumours, haven't you?' he said.

'What's been going round the station. Nothing more.'

He'd raised one hand, opened it as wide as it would go and closed it again.

'These rumours. What have you heard?' He glanced back towards the lane.

'Only the same talk that's been around for months. That the squad's dirty, and it's down to you.'

'Well the results came back. On the back-up test as well. I'm fucked.'

She stepped back, feeling confused, slightly faint now.

'But I thought you always carried a vial of clean.'

'I forgot it that day.'

For the first time that night he was looking straight into her eyes.

'It's simple. If I stay, you'll always be under a cloud. You could go down with me. But if I leave, you've still got a chance.'

'I don't care.'

'You will, Cat. Area has got you marked down for great things. Don't let this screw it up for you.'

She reached around his waist and grasped at his belt, trying to pull him back. She could feel how loose the belt was on his hips as she drew him closer. He was pushing her away.

'But you're still a good officer. You took down Angel Jones, Angel of Darkness Jones.' She heard the desperation in her voice. 'That has to count for something.'

She gripped his belt harder. But he turned away.

'Oh, that.' He seemed hardly to be listening, as if she was talking about something someone else had done, not the man standing in front of her.

She saw he was no longer trying to find her eyes in the dimness.

'That counts for nothing any more.' He was backing away from her towards the entrance to the shelter. 'A

Drugs officer with a habit, they need that like a hole in the head.' She saw he was looking again towards the lane.

'So this is where the bitch in the Benz fits in, is it? A sugar mummy for when you're out of the job? She's playing you, and you can't even see it.' She was crying now, damn it. Such a fucking girl.

'No, you've got that wrong.' She saw he looked pained now, he could never bear to see her cry. 'She has connections. She can help someone like me.'

He'd let her pull him back against the railings. But he was straining against her grip. Something small and white had fallen from his pocket to the ground.

'Look at me, Cat,' he said. He moved her hand down so she could feel how thin he was, pushing her fingers over the ridges of his chest. 'I can hardly look after myself.'

As she pulled her hand away, he broke from her, moved out onto the leaf-strewn grass. She went after him, ran ahead, blocked his way. 'Rhys?'

'Please,' he said, 'for your own good, never try to follow me. Never contact me again.'

He walked away, the dead leaves swirling behind him. This time she let him go, crouching with her back against the damp railings. She picked up what had fallen.

In her fingers there was a paper bird, half torn, an

origami figure with a long bent beak. It was a raven, a good likeness of one.

She watched as Rhys made his way through the trees to where the lights of the passing cars merged with the glare of the night sky.

Then she sank, very slowly, to her knees and started punching the railings. She did it methodically, right left, right left, till her knuckles were bleeding and her blows started to skid and slide off the surface and then, only then, did she stop.

PART ONE

2010

I

It was a dry cold January evening. DS Catrin Price was looking out of the window of the Future Inn lobby towards what had once been the docks.

The motel hadn't been there when she'd left all those years before. Nor had much of what she could see over by the water. The glittering copper dome of the Millennium Centre opera house, the glass and steel structure that housed the Welsh Assembly, the lights of new hotels and waterfront apartments. 'Cardiff Bay' everyone called it now. No doubt she'd get the hang of it soon enough.

She glanced down into the street. A man was getting out of a grey Audi, which he'd parked at the entrance of the brightly lit drive-thru pizza opposite. That hadn't been there in the old days either. But the man walking towards her from the car, he'd been there. DS Jack Thomas. Obvious copper even in his smart casuals. Fortysomething, clean cut, a little grey around the temples, a self-satisfied grin. He'd been tasked with showing her the ropes her first week back before she was assigned to one of the DI's teams.

'You ready then?' he called out chirpily.

He hasn't aged much, the bastard, she thought. He still walked with the old swagger, his broad chest moving through the air slightly ahead of him. If anything the walk seemed to have become more pronounced with the years.

'Maybe we could cover another sector tonight?' she said. His grin was still fixed on his face.

'The way this works, love –' there was a slight edge to his voice now – 'you shadow me, not the other way around.'

Catrin nodded, without looking up at him. She'd have to toe the line for this first week: what other choice did she have?

Thomas was walking ahead of her back to the car. 'My report will go to Human Resources. The various DIs in Major Crimes, they'll all see it, decide which is the right team for you.'

It was something he had over her, for these first days at least. After that, she'd make sure he never had anything on her ever again. He opened the car door for her, and held it as she got in.

'I heard you used to be on the Drugs Unit,' he said, 'back in the day?'

Didn't Thomas remember her then? If he did, he

was making a good show of disguising it. He was treating her as if they'd never met before. She saw him glance briefly at her legs before closing the door.

She remembered him well enough. He'd been CID intake three years ahead of her, before that a sergeant based down in Butetown, the old docks. Always used to give her little looks whenever their paths crossed, the sort of looks that made you check all the buttons on your blouse were done up. Was it her imagination, or hadn't he had a bit of a thing for her? He'd had a habit of turning up in places just before her, as if by chance, or perhaps it had been chance. And then there'd been that night they'd got drunk together, and what had followed. She felt a little inward shiver of shame at the memory of it. Maybe he was embarrassed. Maybe he'd genuinely forgotten. Men can be like that, she thought.

Had she really changed that much? Catrin looked briefly into the passenger mirror, pushed her hair away from her face. Though her hair was longer, her make-up more rigid, it was not a face someone would forget that easily. Childlike still, a little weird, the features not quite spaced right, as if once they had been pulled apart and they'd never been put back quite right, and dark in that Celtic, almost Romany way. And the way she dressed hadn't changed. It wasn't a look you forgot in a hurry either, at least not on a plain-clothes. More like a reject from a biker gang than a cop, everything black, leather, heavy eyeliner, black tatts on her arms, and on a lot of other places. But then, twelve years was a long time to have been away. Twelve years working in London and Reading. Twelve years since her mam died. Twelve years since Rhys and all the pain and confusion that she had coped with in her own strange, stubborn ways.

'Why did you come back?' he asked. She pretended not to hear, focused on the radio.

Why was she back? She'd asked herself the same question enough times, not found an answer that made sense yet. On one level she knew. It was a decent opportunity for her, a promotion. But there were other jobs out there. If she'd been more patient she could have held on for something in her home force in Reading. She'd had a life there, she'd felt safe. And instead she'd taken Cardiff, where there were nothing but ghosts. Or maybe that was the reason why. Maybe it was time to lay the ghosts to rest.

As on the three previous nights, their brief was to follow up on some minor complaints from members of the public. It was midweek, and cold. The streets in the centre of town were quiet. Thomas drove first to an alley near the station. There'd been reports from a residents group that a gang of Kosovans was using it to sell drugs to passers-by.

'So what are we looking out for?' she said. He hadn't even had the courtesy to brief her.

'The obvious. Anyone loitering.'

But both corners were deserted. The only sign of life was a small late-night store, dim lights bleeding from behind its metal blinds.

They waited in the car for a few moments in an uncomfortable silence. There wasn't much to look at, and no one passing. Thomas seemed bored already, drumming his fingers on the steering wheel.

'Looks like a false report,' he said at last.

He told her the next stop was another alley, on the far side of Caroline Street. There'd been some muggings a couple of months back. Since then, it had become a regular stop-off point for night patrols with time on their hands.

He drove past the mouth of the alley without stopping. It looked quiet also, and dark. There were no obvious signs of suspicious activity. The only figures visible were a couple of elderly rough-sleepers, pulling a trolley piled with bin bags.

This time Thomas parked two streets away, and they approached on foot. She followed a couple of paces behind to discourage conversation. He was taking the route down Chip Alley, fifty yards of kebab shops and curry houses, the haunt of after-pub stragglers. But it was still only Wednesday, and hardly anyone was about braving the cold.

Glancing at the neon of the shopfronts, memories of her teenage years came flooding back; ending up here at the end of a big night out, some boy who couldn't hold his cider chucking up in the gutter while the rest of them threw chips at each other and wondered what might happen next.

But the city she grew up in had a yeasty, comforting smell. This new place smelt like plastic, and something else. There was just a hint of vomit in the air, not strong but lingering in the background like an unpleasant memory that refuses to fade.

Thomas had slowed his pace, was following her sightline towards the kebab and curry houses.

'Brings back memories, does it?' He said this without the earlier edge in his voice. 'This is one of the parts that hasn't changed much.' It was an unusually sensitive remark for Thomas, but she ignored it all the same.

They had come back to the mouth of the alley. The rough-sleepers and their trolley had gone now. The shops were closed, blinds down. The place was dark, empty of human life.

At one end of the alley there was a CCTV camera on a high metal pole. These had been placed at all the city's trouble spots, but the alley was so poorly lit the thing was next to useless. Thomas was waving into the lens. Maybe he'd check the footage later, she thought, see how effective it was. Maybe he was just clowning about.

'There's fuck all here,' he said.

She noticed he was stifling a yawn.

'What next?' she said.

He didn't answer, just drove away, circling the block. He wasn't even bothering to look at the figures walking on the pavements. He seemed to be marking time.

Then his phone went off, the ringtone from *The Pink Panther*. He cracked the window, leant away, so she couldn't hear, but she could of course.

'A floater?' he said. 'At the tidal barrier? Are you sure about that?' He didn't sound too excited, but she saw his legs jerking, as if to some fast, inaudible rhythm.

She remembered the term floater from the old days. The strong tides brought bodies from all the way down the coast into the bay. The bodies would turn up every couple of months, drunks and suicides off the Severn Bridge usually. Some things obviously didn't change.

'Keep the press away,' she heard him say. 'We don't want another scrum. No, doesn't matter if it is or it isn't – either way we don't want them within a mile of this.'

'What's all that about?' she said.

'You'll see, love,' he said, the irritating smirk back in place. 'You'll see very soon. We're taking a little trip down the bay.'

They drove down Bute Street, past the Butetown housing estate, the shadowlands where the last remnants of the old Tiger Bay were still clinging on. It looked every bit as dilapidated as Catrin remembered. At the end of Bute Street came the grand Victorian commercial buildings, left over from the years when Cardiff was the world's premier coal port. It was in these buildings that the world's price for coal had once been fixed, and the first cheque for a million pounds written. But not even ghosts seemed to remain there now, just smoke-blackened walls and a labyrinth of mouldering inner passages and yards where it always seemed night.

Thomas took a right onto the flyover and crossed to the western side of the bay. Once there he turned again and headed along the dark riverbank. They came down to the edge of the tidal barrier, a vast, black, grid-like structure that lay across the mouth of the river. Within it, a series of gigantic locks blocked off the Taff estuary, separating it from the tidal chug of the Bristol Channel. From above, it looked like a huge piece of wreckage dropped from space.

In the car park there were already three squad cars, lights flashing, and an ambulance with all its doors flung open. Without a backward glance to see if Catrin was following, Thomas had jumped out of the car, zapping the lock before she'd got out. Wanker, she thought, as she hurried after him.

A couple of uniforms stood to one side of the blue-and-white crime tape, and on the other was a small but noisy crowd of youths. Most were dressed identically, clones of each other in black leather jackets with long, raven-dyed hair. It was nearly impossible to tell the boys apart from the girls. There was something vaguely familiar about the general look of this crowd, she wasn't quite sure what it was. Some of the youths were holding hastily made placards. *No Cover-Up!*, one said, and another *Truth Will Out!*

Heading for the centre of the action, Thomas went straight past the crowd, a huddle of people up on the barrier where the lock gates opened to let boats in and out. Catrin stopped to talk to one of the uniforms.

'What's with all the youths?' she asked him.

'They hack the police radio frequencies.'

'They?'

'They're Owen Face fans, the new generation. Every time a body's washed up, they come to see if it's him. Barmy after all this time, but there you are.'

'They believe after all this time there will be anything left of him?'

'They're obsessed.'

'Sounds like people round here should get out more.' The uniform was peering at her, but she wasn't going to try to explain herself. She turned away, looked at the growing line of officers blocking the way down to the barrier.

She still remembered the night it all began of course, the events that would later fuel the myths. For a long time, the story had been the only reason the city ever made the news. It was the nearest thing the place had ever had to an international mystery. Owen Face had been the front man of the city's biggest indie-rock band, Seerland. After his farewell concert, his car had been found at the Severn Bridge, a notorious suicide spot. But no body had ever been recovered. And for a while the case had become a magnet for every media wonk and wacko with a conspiracy theory to peddle.

But that had been over twelve years ago. The story had long gone stale, everyone had lost interest apart from a few late-night radio jocks and diehard fans in the chatrooms. Then a few months back, a skeletal foot had turned up in the bay. It had been wearing the brand of trainer Owen Face used to wear. The story had gained second wind as all the local channels and many of the internationals, CNN and BBC World covered it again.

To Catrin the whole business reeked of a publicity stunt – his band getting themselves a lot of free airtime every time a body washed up anywhere in South Wales. There'd been another a month or so back. A body had pitched up on the Newport mudflats. The press were all over it as some pathologist refused to rule out the body being Face. Then, a couple of days later, they found out it was just a sixty-year-old alkie. Publicity whores the lot of them, these days: coppers, rock stars, even bloody coroners.

One of the youths had got through to the other side of the tape. A young girl, no more than fifteen or so. She was standing alone, biting her nails, crying. The girl's coat swung open to reveal a T-shirt bearing a photo of Face, all snow white skin, jet black hair and red lipstick. It was the iconic shot, frozen in time, every Goth girl's dream boy.

'You think they've really found him this time?' the girl asked one of the uniforms. But no one was paying attention to her. The crowd's focus was on the crime tent set up on the tidal barrier.

Catrin began to move towards it, straining her eyes to get a better idea of what was happening.

'You can't come through, dear – only authorised personnel beyond this point,' the uniform said to her with a self-important sneer. Another young male PC throwing his weight about, he looked barely out of police college.

It was a mistake she was used to, of course. She

didn't look anything like a police officer, more like one of the crowd with her heavy make-up and black leathers. Her eyes had a half-closed look about them, like a cat's sometimes. People often thought she wasn't the brightest branch on the tree. But she'd topped exams nationally in forensic computing and digital surveillance for three grades above her present ranking, and under the layers of black was a fit, natural athlete's body trained in martial arts so exotic most people had never heard of them. They'd been a study in self-discipline. She wasn't an aggressive person, she hated and feared any type of violence except with consent in the bedroom – that she needed from time to time. But she could have had the little runt in seconds.

She flashed her warrant card, and he let her pass.

She walked over to the lock gate and joined the huddle of police and medics. She heard the buzz of excitement as she approached. The group was tightly packed and all she could make out, as she peered between the shoulders of two PCs, was the bottom end of a body laid out on a stretcher. It was too dark to see much more. A couple of medics were struggling to rig up arc lights and she stepped back, to wait until she could see better.

Catrin was standing back from the body as DS Thomas caught her by the arm. She turned to face him.

'Had a look yet?' she asked.

'Nah, not yet.' He shrugged, his earlier excitement apparently all gone now. 'Just waiting for the medics to do their stuff.'

Then he pointed to the other side of the marina. There was a fire guttering beside some sort of beach hut.

'I'll give you long odds body's come no further than from over there,' he said.

She looked over at the bleak stretch of moonlit pebbles beyond the barrier. The hut seemed to have been an ice-cream stand, but it was now covered with strips of corrugated iron and hardboard. There were smaller shelters built along its sides, their walls blackened by previous fires.

'It's where junkies and rough-sleepers doss down,' he said. 'We get their bodies turning up here every couple of months or so.'

She looked over at the shelters, but there was no movement. In the gloom she could just make out a security camera over the shingle. The place seemed deserted.

'How come they get in the water?' she asked.

'The tides come up. The junkies light their fires, fix up and drift away. Sometimes literally. We must've recovered half a dozen bodies here over the years.'

He gave Catrin a look then.

She said nothing. It was quite a distance from the beach to the barrier. She wondered if Thomas wasn't being a little premature in his assessment of what had happened. Maybe trying to impress her, show her how much catching up she'd have to do. Before she could feel it was her turf again.

She saw him following her look, reading the scepticism in it. He was nodding down at the black, frothing base of the barrier beneath them. The arc lights came on. Thank Christ, she would have kicked him if he'd said another word.

As she got close there was a gasp from the watching huddle. She pushed to the front and saw the skeletal-thin body lying on its front. It was dressed in Face's trademark black, from biker boots to leather jacket, and it had the coal black hair of the missing rock star.

Catrin turned to look at Thomas, expecting some signs of his former excitement. But he was still looking bored, detached from it all, as if he knew something the rest of them didn't. She turned back to the body, wondering at the adrenalin that was coursing through her veins. After all, it wasn't like she was ever that fussed about Seerland. As for Owen Face himself, she could understand why the little Goth girls loved him, but personally speaking, she could never get past all that lipstick and make-up. One of the medics approached and without ceremony, like a butcher with a side of beef, flipped the body over.

Another gasp from the onlookers but this time of

disappointment. It wasn't Owen Face. For one thing this man couldn't have been in the water for more than a few hours. Secondly he was a good ten, maybe twenty years older than the missing guitarist. Thirdly – oh sweet Jesus, she knew who it was.

Catrin reeled away from the crowd, walked fast towards the barrier and stood looking down at the black waters. She was trying hard to take deep breaths and not throw up.

'You all right?' said Thomas, joining her, still with the air of being one step ahead of everyone else that made her want very much to punch him.

'Yeah, no. I don't know,' she said, sounding like an idiot but not caring, past caring. Then taking another deep breath, composing herself.

'I know who it is,' she said.

Thomas didn't respond for a moment, lit up a cigarette, and offered her one. She hesitated, then almost snatched it from his hand.

He waited till she'd taken a couple of drags then said, 'Yes, I thought you might do.'

'What d'you mean?' said Catrin. 'You know who that is?'

'Course,' said Thomas, smirk still in place, 'Rhys Williams. He used to be a copper. He'd been hanging with the junkies here for years. It was an accident waiting to happen.'

'You . . .' she said, then stopped before she could get herself into trouble. She turned away, didn't want him to see the confusion and anguish distorting her face. 'How did you know I knew him?'

Thomas dropped his fag to the ground, stubbed it out with his heel. 'You do have a file, love. And I do have a memory.'

Catrin stared at him, trying to hold onto her anger as it seemed to be keeping the nausea at bay.

'You're not even going to bother to spend time on this, are you?' She looked down so he couldn't see what was going on in her eyes.

He spoke more softly now.

'There's nothing here, love. It was an accident. Either that or he just jumped off the barrier. Couldn't stand the sight of himself any longer.'

'You really are a bastard,' said Catrin.

Thomas looked at her carefully. 'There'll be an inquest of course. We'll go through the formalities. One dead junkie fallen in the water. He wasn't the first out here, won't be the last.' He paused. 'Why all the attitude anyway, love? What did he ever do for you?'

'What did he do for me?' she said. 'He saved my fucking life.'

2

It was over a week since the body had washed up, and Catrin still felt disorientated, her mind in a fog. Partly it was the diazepam, of course, doing its numbing work, keeping the panic at bay. As she went down the steps to the pathologist's office, she clutched the rails to keep her balance.

From the window there was the view out over Cathays Park. A lane between the formal gardens, the pavements covered with black leaves from the beeches and horse chestnuts that overhung the unlit paths. A vague memory was floating to the surface of her mind. DS Thomas standing there among trees, watching her.

The truth was she couldn't be sure if it was real, and even if it was, that was what men did sometimes, she knew that, quite ordinary men. They waited for women, and watched them. That he might or might not have been there, it probably meant nothing. She was over-reacting, sweating it, she needed to get a grip.

The front office of the pathologist was filled with the usual police-issue desks and chairs, the walls blank except for some postcards stuck to a board. She sat opposite the biggest desk, which he was gesturing her towards.

'Hi Cat, heard you were back.' He shook her one hand with both of his. They felt cold. That's how a priest does it, she thought.

He was a tall man in late middle age, pale ginger hair matching a puce bow-tie. Emyr Pugh. They'd exchanged Christmas cards every year, the lines inside getting shorter with the years. She'd known him since she was a teenager, since he'd lived next door to them in Bute and dated her mother for a couple of years. And this being Cardiff, less a city than a giant village, that was how things were, only two or three degrees of separation, and everyone related and knowing each other's business. He'd made a point of coming to see her and say hello her first day back on the job. But she'd been out and he'd left her another card, a short note inside. Just reminding her he was there if she wanted to talk about the old days, which of course she didn't. She hadn't called him on the number he'd left, felt bad about it now. He was probably just lonely: his wife had died a few years back, she'd heard.

He looked older of course, but different in some other way she couldn't quite put her finger on, more reserved, as if with the years he'd grown in on himself.

'You know I can't show you the body.' His tone was grave, apologetic, that hint of the priest again, as if he was apologising for all the sins of the world.

'Oh?' She pretended to sound surprised, but of course she knew the rules.

'Not family, and it's not your case.'

She looked up at him, held his gaze.

'But the autopsy, your report notes?'

'I can show you those.' He reached down, opened a drawer. 'But they're not of any interest.'

He spread some discs over the desk, and a file, without opening it. He was smiling at her, a soft, lopsided smile she remembered from the old days.

'Every few years, I'd run into Rhys, usually down at the riverside, where they found him.' Pugh sounded as if he was reminiscing about something that was sad but already ancient history. 'Every time he'd look a little worse, more gaunt, more run-down.'

'He was ill?'

'No, just the classic symptoms of long-term heroin abuse.'

He turned, pointed at the tidal barrier on a map of the City.

'The place where they found him,' he said. 'It's where quite a few junkies from those shelters have washed up in the past.' He indicated the strip of shingle where the shelters were. 'The reason the junkies and dealers like this part,' he said, 'is that you can only get there on foot. They can see who's coming.'

She nodded; nearer the water the shingle would be rougher. Above it was a slope a car couldn't handle. It would be difficult for officers to get there quickly. That's why the cameras and lights had been put there, to deter drug-taking, soliciting, fly-tipping. It was official Area policy at every known crime point in the city, an unofficial saving on police man-hours.

'Any witnesses?' she said.

'We've got better than witnesses.' Pugh turned again, to a monitor on the desk. 'I shouldn't show you this,' he said. 'But we have a record of his movements before he went under. And it isn't pretty.'

She recognised the street immediately. It was the alley she had checked with DS Thomas earlier the same evening, and she was watching footage from the CCTV camera on the pole. The alley was empty, but there was light coming from one of the broken, lower windows. Two figures were standing there: a man and a woman.

The man was Rhys. The woman looked slim, attractive, was dressed in a dark, well-cut trouser suit. Catrin couldn't see her face. There seemed to be some sort of struggle going on, the man pushing the woman back against the wall.

He was slapping her face, his other hand running over her thighs. There was no sound on the film, but the woman's head was thrown violently back, her mouth open wide. As Rhys moved away the woman relaxed her stance, slumped back against the wall. Her face was still unclear.

'It's an area known for muggings.' Pugh had picked up a Biro and was pointing at the screen. 'Look at Rhys's right hand as he leaves.'

She could see Rhys was holding some notes now, maybe a couple of twenties. He was hurrying away out of shot, down towards the water.

'Has the woman come forward?' she asked.

'No, but that's not so unusual. The muggers usually pick on women who've been drinking heavily. Seventy per cent of these type of incidents never get reported.'

She knew he was right, she'd seen CCTV of city-centre muggings enough times to know that's probably what she'd just watched. Younger junkies usually shop-lifted; the older ones who were too well known, barred from shops, tended to house-break and do muggings. After closing hour, with lone drinkers wandering about, that was when most of the incidents were caught on camera.

He flicked the control again. The next sequence showed the shelters on the beach. It had been filmed from some distance above, by the CCTV camera on the slope above the shingle.

Unlike the earlier footage, this was a series of stills,

a couple of seconds between each, the movements of the figures jagged like a primitive cartoon.

This time Rhys was approaching a man standing by the door to the ruin of the beach hut. The man passed over something, a bag of drugs it looked like. Rhys gave him the twenties that were still clasped in his right hand.

Then Rhys was hesitating, backing away a few feet. He was holding something long and jagged. It seemed to be a broken bottle.

The second man was turning now, trying to enter the hut, Rhys moving in behind him. Rhys was pushing the bottle at his back, once, twice. The second figure was falling inward, face first, disappearing from view.

'Who's the second man?' she asked.

'Another local junkie, a dealer.'

She sat back, shuddering slightly. She was grasping for alternative explanations, anything to show Rhys in a better light, but the more she thought about it the worse it looked for him.

'That was a serious assault. Why hasn't this been investigated?' she said at last.

'No hospital admissions fitting the description of the victim. No body – no crime.'

Pugh played the last sequence again. She could see the man lying motionless on the floor of the hut.

'But why does Rhys attack him? He'd already scored his shit.'

'It often happens. Law of the street. The stronger junkie takes the weaker's stash. Most of it was found on Rhys's body when it was recovered from the water.'

'And the twenties?'

'Back on Rhys's body.'

Pugh crossed his arms. His smile was there again, warm but subdued, like a hearth seen through thick glass. He was trying to reassure her, but about what she couldn't imagine.

'The sad truth is that's what Rhys had become, I'm afraid. Just another mugger, just another street junkie.'

The final footage showed him heading down the beach, away from the hut. It was clear he'd had his fix now. Rhys was moving slowly, stumbling at times on the pebbles. He looked like a clown in an early silent movie. Then he lay down, on the strip of pale pebbles by the dark water.

The water was covering his shins. He didn't seem to notice. He just lay there, motionless, his eyes closed. The last frame showed the waves breaking over empty pebbles.

'It was painless, at least.' Pugh was getting up, his eyes no longer on the screen. 'There are many worse ways to go.'

She nodded. Rhys hadn't looked in any condition to get up. It seemed the obvious explanation of what had happened.

Pugh went into the next room, she could hear an electric kettle begin to boil. She stood up in front of the monitor. Moving fast, she fed a customised memory-cuff into the side of the hard drive. In less than fifty seconds she'd got everything she'd just seen.

She sat down again, as Pugh brought through two City mugs. He passed one to her, his smile gently indulgent, as if at a child who was finally accepting the obvious.

She put the tea down without sipping it.

'And the autopsy?'

He opened the file on the desk.

'Just what you'd expect.'

'In the tox report, no other incapacitants?'

'No,' said Pugh, the merest trace of impatience in his voice now. 'It's all straightforward enough. High levels of opiates consistent with long-term addiction. No surprises.'

'The tests are clear on that?'

He glanced at the notes. 'His urine was significantly positive for opiates, though that's not the only measure used.'

She remained silent, waited for him to go on.

'Heroin is metabolised to 6-monoacetylmorphine, then to morphine in the blood. It's not like alcohol testing. You can't get a definitive reading from the urine. But the level of morphine there shows he'd been heavily exposed to opiates prior to the test.'

'You measured sweat levels?'

'Positive again.'

'Hair?'

'Of course. Everything consistent with long-term use. No sudden spike at the end.'

'Saliva?'

Pugh sighed, barely hiding his impatience now.

'Positive.' He looked back down at the notes. 'The legal limit of plasma morphine from OTCs, codeine and the like is twenty nanos per mil, equivalent to ten nanos per mil in blood. Rhys's levels were about five hundred nanos per mil. That's exactly what you'd have expected of a long-term user.'

She waited, hoping there would be a 'but' some-where, a catch that would open the situation to some new, healing light. But she already sensed there wasn't going to be one coming. This was a case where things were as they seemed.

Pugh was smiling wryly, sympathetically.

'There's no mystery here, lovey. It's obvious what happened to the poor bastard. He'd just fixed a gramme of seventy per cent pure Afghani brown into his groin. He then passed out, as you saw, and drifted out on the tide.'

He switched off the computer, and gathered his papers.

She picked up one of the pictures from the file. It was a shot of Rhys lying there in his black jacket and biker boots. His eye sockets were empty, just blank slits in the pearl-grey skin, but otherwise the body looked perfectly intact.

She didn't ask about the eyes. She knew the fish ate them, it almost always happened, even if a body had only been under a few minutes. She glanced again at the picture, at the jacket and the boots.

'His clothes look good quality,' she said, 'not charity shop stuff.'

'They were traced to a new shop on the arcade, they'd had some lifted.'

She knew that was the likely explanation. Street junkies were all expert shoplifters. She guessed Rhys was barred from most shops so would've targeted anywhere new opening up.

Pugh closed the file.

'Could Rhys have known I was back?' she asked.

'Doubt it.'

She saw Pugh was looking dismissive but in a kind way. She suspected he'd already guessed what she was thinking, that the place where they found Rhys was about half a mile from her motel. But it was a small town, this meant little in itself. It was the time factor that niggled with her a little. Not that it meant anything sinister had occurred, Rhys could have been intending to see her, just out of curiosity, then OD'd in the meantime. But the likelihood was he hadn't known she was back. Out on the streets he'd hardly be plugged into the police grapevine.

Pugh turned and took down something from the wall. 'If he knew you were back, which I doubt, he'd have wanted money off you.' He was smiling to himself at the thing from the wall. 'He'd not have wanted to upset you turning up unannounced. He'd have called first, but you never heard from him.'

He glanced at her. He was looking at her kindly but with detachment. She thought she could read that look. He wanted to help with her grief but he didn't want to encourage her to believe anything insubstantial. He knew that would just cause her more hurt. She looked at him and nodded, as if to signal she accepted there was nothing more to it.

'It's common for the bereaved to feel connected to what happened, that they could've prevented it, you know that,' he said. 'But Rhys was a junkie. Junkies die young, you just have to try to accept it.' He'd taken down a photograph from the board. It was of a cottage with rolling hills and fields in the background.

'It's my holiday place up Monmouth way,' he said, a hint of pride in his voice.

She took it, without looking at it. 'Must be nice to

have something like that. Not one home, two,' she said.

The picture had fallen through her fingers onto the floor. She crouched down, reaching for it. She realised she was sobbing, warm fat tears dripping down on the linoleum, staining the picture. She struck the ground, with a sudden simple force. He was trying to stop her, but she wouldn't let him, she kept hitting the ground, then abruptly she stopped.

She didn't like to show emotion like this, not in front of someone she hardly knew any more. She stood up quickly, composed, like an actress who'd just finished her scene. He took her arm, guiding her out into the fresh air of the stairwell.

She looked up to see the Chief Constable, Geraint Rix, wearing a Hawaiian shirt. Some office clown had hung the poster there, almost life-size. Not Pugh, it wasn't his style. A joke for the benefit of the coppers trooping through. All Rix's time, she'd heard, was spent on the media circuit sharpening his image for a safe Liberal seat at the next election. Being head of the Gay Police Association had given him a national platform, but he was the straightest-looking gay man she'd ever seen. Being gay in the force did that, she guessed.

As she turned away from Rix's blokey grin she felt Pugh press something into her hand. She looked down.

It was a bunch of keys, the ring a miniature silver copy of the cottage in the picture.

'Stay as long as you like, you need a rest,' he said gently.

Outside, she sat on her bike after he'd closed the door, not moving, staring out at the trees in the park. Then, after how long she didn't know, she started the engine and pulled out into the traffic.

Catrin wasn't paranoid. She knew dealers so wacked out they thought they were being followed by bendy-buses, the numbers on the buses sending them personal messages. Now that was paranoid, but working ten years in Drugs, most of it under, still does things to a mind.

Along City Hall Road, keeping a few cars behind her, she saw a dark van move out into the traffic. The same van had been there on her way in, parked up across the square. She noticed things like that. As she swung into North Road, it was still following four cars behind. She doubled back towards the public gardens. The van was keeping to the end of the dimly lit streets, not closing the space between them.

She checked her rearview: it looked like a woman at the wheel. Well-cut jacket, big bouffant hair, almost like a wig. But it wasn't close enough, it was too dark for her to get the number.

She did a full circle, along Park Place down into City Hall Road. She waited but it didn't reappear. She'd lost it, no chance to run the tag on the PNC. She waited to see if it would come round from the north. But nothing else passed. Through the trees she saw the lights of the empty offices.

She rode east for half a mile, then pulled over. She took out her phone, logged on to the South Wales Police network, went into Human Resources and filled out a compassionate leave form. She copied it to Occupational Health. Then she switched off her phone. She didn't want to have a mast signal for the location of what she was about to do.

She rode on to the Newport Road and found an internet café in a side street. Unlike in the city centre, there were no cameras outside; none inside as far as she could see. The terminals were in booths for privacy. Keeping her helmet on, she took a booth at the back.

The thought that Rhys had been so close to her, it wouldn't quite let go yet. In her heart she wanted it to, but even if there was one per cent of doubt she knew she'd have to keep turning the stones. It was selfish of course, she'd be doing it to put her own conscience at rest. Not for him at the end of it, that's what made her feel sick at herself.

He'd been scoring, no doubt about that from the film, none at all. But junkies scored like a car takes on fuel. He'd have needed to score just to keep moving. There were places he could've scored nearer the alley where he'd snagged the twenties. But he hadn't, he'd come down to the water. Was that his destination, or had he been on his way somewhere else, up to the streets around her motel? Or was he just going nowhere?

She booted the drive, waited for the monitor to come to life. The place she was going to find an answer, if there was an answer, was in the case notes. She had no authorised access; only the SIO and the other officers assigned to the case had. She'd have to improvise a little. All the time she'd put in moling at the Hendon Data Centre had taught her how to do that without leaving footprints. She didn't find hacks interesting in themselves, not at all, they were just a tool. A digital picklock. She was good at hacks because she was curious, and she was curious because she was one of those people who needed to know the truth about things, and in her experience the truth tended to get hidden.

Shadowing Thomas around the offices of Major Crimes, she'd noticed that South Wales Area had recently upgraded to Niche One-Sign, a single sign-on system for all applications. Previously officers might have to use ten separate passwords to access the HOLMES enquiry system, National Criminal and SPIN intelligence and all other databases on the national mainframes and back-up servers. Now, for everything, they just needed a single seven-digit password, and an ID. But any security system was only as secure as its weakest link, and in this instance that link was DS Jack Thomas. He'd told her enough times to come up close, watch what he was doing over his shoulder.

She logged in his password and within less than a minute she was into the case file. She noted the case hadn't been rated important enough to attract the attention of a major rank as SIO. As senior officer on the scene Thomas had been responsible for uploading all the notes. And there wasn't much to see.

She copied everything onto a Zip file, encrypted it with her PGP key, then sent it all to an anonymous account on a server in the Ukraine. That way she wouldn't ever need to carry the data on her, could access it from anywhere. She clicked out of the Area system, back into the case notes. Looking closer, there was even less to see than at first glance.

Thomas had played it by the book. The coroner's inquest determined only how a subject met their death, not the whys and wherefores. In the file there were no witness statements, nothing relating to Rhys turned up by searches onshore. Only the CCTV footage, the pathologist's tox data. Exactly the same data she'd already seen. No next of kin or associates interviewed, as there weren't any. Played like this, the coroner's verdict was a foregone conclusion. Category One, Death by Drug Dependence, Solitary.

The rest of the notes took up less than a page. The wallet found on the body had led to a room in a derelict council block in Riverside, the place Rhys had called home in his final weeks. There were some photos included, a list of contents. It was a short list. A life come down to nothing, just a backpack full of Oxfam clothes and three battered books of poetry. And a single origami bird they'd found in the fireplace. She stared at it, couldn't even make out what type of bird it was.

She felt the warm tears beading her cheeks, gathering against her collar. But she was wearing her visor still, the place was empty, no one could see the tears.

3

It was the first time she'd heard the sound in over a week. Somewhere at the edge of her consciousness a phone was ringing. Catrin pushed her head further down under the cold pillow, but the sound didn't let up.

The ringing was coming from under the pile of dirty clothes in the corner. Shuffling unsteadily across the room, she reached down, felt through the pockets and, without looking at it, switched the handset off.

She'd woken late at Pugh's cottage. It was almost ten, the light outside was the ash grey typical of a Welsh winter. She went through a shortened version of her morning routine. First, a glass of tap water. Then she stretched through the twelve sun salutations from the Hatha, the only habit she'd kept up from her mam and her hippie hangers-on. Then half an hour of tae kwon do on an empty stomach, kicks and jabs. Krav maga, wing chun ending with regular squats and crunches.

She worked up a sweat, tried to push some of the anger and sickly guilt out, but found she couldn't. At the end the sweat stung her eyes and tears still blurred them. She hated herself when she cried, it was something she thought she'd trained herself not to do any more. She took a long cold shower, focusing on a square of tile, nothing else, trying to make her mind go blank. Only a single image was left there. Floating up over the tile. Rhys's face at the window of the dojo where she'd trained as a girl. His eyes watching her as she practised alone. He'd thought the tinted glass hid his face. He hadn't known she could see him there. Of all the images of him this was the one which came back to her.

She went down to the kitchen for yoghurt, oats and frozen berries, then through to the living room. She didn't pull back the curtains, made for the worn sofa.

She curled up a strip of card, adding a paper and some tobacco. Feeling through the pockets of her joggers, she found her bag of kanna and crumbled a pinch in. She'd switched to it from weed like others in the force since the new random testing had come in. An African herb used by Khoi tribesmen for hunting, it didn't show up. It had much the same effect. The floor around the sofa was covered with empty smoothie bottles and all her notes. It took her a couple of minutes to find the remote.

Out of the darkness emerged the image of the alley.

She saw the lights in the broken, lower window again. The two figures standing there, Rhys and the woman.

There was the struggle, Rhys pushing the woman back against the wall. Then he was hurrying away out of shot, down towards the water.

She ran it slowly, three more times, then frame by frame. She'd done this many times already, and as she closed her eyes she could see each frame as clearly as if it was still flickering in front of her.

She switched the remote to the next sequence, the shelters on the beach. Again she ran it slowly, then frame by frame.

Rhys approaching the man at the hut. The man passing over the bag of drugs. Rhys giving him the twenties, still clasped in his right hand.

Then Rhys hesitating, backing away, holding the broken bottle.

The man turning, Rhys moving in behind him, pushing the bottle at his back. Then the man falling inward, face first, disappearing from view.

After a few minutes she sat back, put her Mac on pause, stubbed her roll-up. The truth was she was seeing nothing new in the film. In fact, each time she watched it, she felt she was seeing slightly less. This wasn't going to be one of those cases where a detail in the background would reveal some sudden unexpected truth.

The film showed exactly what it appeared to show. A man mugging a woman, assaulting another junkie, then passing out on the beach. Pugh and the others were right, there was no mystery here. She was wasting her time. You get exactly what it says on the tin with this one, she thought.

She lit another cigarette, opened the window a crack, then lay back on the sofa. There was only one detail that had struck her as odd in all her viewings of the film. It was not enough for her to doubt the basic truth of what she had seen. But it was a detail that didn't entirely make sense all the same.

Before assaulting the second man, the other street junkie, Rhys had handed him the twenties. Why had he done this, if he was about to assault him? Why hadn't he just assaulted the man from the outset? Why bother to give the twenties first?

Rhys had backed away a few paces, she'd noticed, before he had begun the attack. As if something the man had done had triggered what followed. But in the stills the second man had not altered his posture, had not even opened his mouth. It was an entirely unprovoked attack, or appeared to be.

Of course, not everything a junkie did would make sense. Maybe Rhys had only decided to attack at that moment, or had given the twenties first to put the man at ease. There were explanations, rationalisations, there always were. But something about this detail didn't feel quite right to her.

She picked up her phone, dialled DS Thomas's number. 'The man in the hut, the street junkie,' she said. She didn't bother with greetings. He'd know what she was talking about straight off.

'Yes? What about him?'

'Has he been seen since the attack?'

'No, nothing.' He wasn't showing any signs of caring she'd seen the tapes. He sounded relaxed, slightly bored with the topic. 'We're not seeing him as a suspect, if that's why you're asking.'

'No?'

'We have officers who saw him lying in exactly the position you see in the film. And that was after Rhys's body had been found.'

'They didn't try to rouse him, call for an ambulance?'

'They didn't see signs of injury. Just thought he was a dosser sleeping it off.'

She pondered this for a few moments. 'So he can't have been that badly hurt, if he then got up and made off?'

'I guess not.' He was yawning now, not trying to hide it either. There was a tinny bleeping noise. It sounded as if it was coming from a computer game.

She thought she saw why Thomas wasn't interested: if the man had been badly hurt he'd have turned up in an A&E somewhere along the coast by now. Most likely he was just lying low, not wanting to get involved in something he'd had nothing to do with.

'No one seems to care that much,' she said.

There was silence, he'd switched the game off.

'It doesn't alter what happened to Rhys, does it,' he said. 'Rhys may have committed an assault before he died. But his death was still an accident.'

It was difficult to argue with this logic. That was the problem with Thomas, he was detestable but he was logical.

'So you don't want to know why Rhys assaulted the man?'

Thomas was sighing, it was obvious the matter didn't interest him in the least.

'Rhys was a street junkie,' he said, 'assault is what street junkies do.' He paused. 'Rhys committing an assault before he dies, it's about as significant as an average bloke having a couple of pints.'

She hung up. Though she hated to admit it, she knew he had a point. It was probably a routine enough act for Rhys. Not pretty, but not significant. She had been letting long-obsolete images of the man cloud her judgement.

There was an old telly in the corner. She switched it on, flicked the channels until she found tennis. A tournament somewhere hot, where the palm trees were casting shadows over the clay.

She'd played when she was younger, still played in her head sometimes. They'd said she could've been a champion, but tennis had been thought soft at her school. She'd had to play on the sly, in a park at the far end of town where no one had seen her. She didn't follow the game closely now, but liked to watch when she could, found it therapeutic, a physical version of chess. Like the drink and the kanna, it helped to take the edge off things.

The taller player was serving. He was using a slice technique, hitting the ball into the outer corners, throwing the receiver way off the court.

Once he'd served, the taller man rushed the net, volleyed the return down into the opposite corner. It was a crude but effective tactic. At least it appeared so at first. The receiver was small, agile, but he couldn't get back in time to reach the ball. When he did the shots went wide or were easy prey for the taller figure at the net.

She clicked into iTunes on her Mac, the tick-tock lilt of the Velvets' 'Sunday Morning' filling the room as the tennis players moved in and out of time to the beat.

She watched three games go with serve, each player using the same basic tactic. It was now five games all. The taller man was serving. He whipped the ball down into the left corner, as before. This time, however, the receiver was already off court, waiting. His return was low and fast, down the line, passing the man rushing to the net.

The next serve was an ace. She found herself rooting for the smaller man. But not passionately so. She preferred to watch the game for the artistry, the tactics. It was never a matter of supporting one player blindly for her.

The receiver seemed to fret about at the far end, as if waiting for something from the crowd, but what she couldn't understand. The server was in position, tossing the ball into the air.

But then, as if from nowhere the receiver was back at the place where the serve fell. It had been a feint, he had pretended to look unprepared. But he had known where the serve would land and was waiting for it. His return was low, precise, brutal. The server did not even reach it.

In the final game the shorter man won every point, the taller one's fight seemed to have gone out of him. In a couple of minutes it was all over. The coverage on the channel changed abruptly to bowls.

She lit another cigarette. Everything can turn on a single point, she thought. The other player was the stronger, had all the natural advantages, but he hadn't had the moral fibre to accept his own moment of weakness, and so he'd lost.

As she switched off the set, she noticed how pale her hands were. She hadn't intended to become a recluse, but the weather had been so foul she hadn't even walked out to the farmhouse down the hill.

The cottage was geared for summer renters. There wasn't much in the way of home entertainment, just a row of paperbacks on the shelf, a couple of games, the old television under the window. On the sill was a picture of Rix, smaller this time, in the loud Hawaiian shirt. She turned it over: there was nothing on the other side. She wondered why Pugh had it, laddish humour wasn't his style. She drew back the curtains. Outside was a long barn. Its doors were closed, but on previous evenings as the light faded she'd seen the farmer come that way on his muddy tractor.

All along the track, the dull sky hung low over shallow puddles where cows had trodden the grass into the earth. It could have been anywhere. The place wasn't familiar to her, and so it didn't feel like a home-coming – it felt like unknown territory, and all the better for that.

Her thoughts were interrupted by a loud clanging noise coming from the empty hall. She hadn't realised there was a landline in the house. But now she saw the phone, a black Bakelite up in a niche by the door, covered in dust.

'Catrin?'

She recognised the voice at once, though it had been many years since she'd last heard it. Catrin said nothing at first, she'd been caught off guard. But somewhere at the back of her mind she'd known all along this moment would come. She'd been waiting for it ever since her return.

'It's been a while – hasn't it?'

The words came out in one of those Welsh purrs that could make the most innocent comment sound like an indecent proposal. Catrin still said nothing. She heard her heart beating but it sounded remote.

'It's Della, dear. Della Davies, remember me?'

'How did you get this number, Della?'

In the background Catrin could hear bracelets jangling. Then silence. She'd never liked Della. And not just for the obvious reasons. She was the type people probably imagined first when they thought of a successful media operator: no cracks showing through her hard shell, all side. She'd heard Della had done well for herself. She had her own press agency now, and a celebrity column in the *Echo*.

'You sound well, Cat?' the soft voice said at last.

Catrin was aware she'd hardly spoken yet.

'Anyone say I wasn't?'

'Right as rain – that's what I heard.'

Slowly Catrin leant back against the wall. 'So why

do I feel you're about to tell me something that'll stop me feeling that way?'

'Still the sharp one, eh Cat?'

Catrin could hear faint music now, as if playing on a car stereo.

'I don't think I want to talk to you,' she said.

The music stopped. Down the line came a low rustling sound.

'It's about Rhys.'

The gentle purr again. It was still a voice that sounded as if it was used to getting what it wanted.

'Oh.'

'We both knew him, I thought you'd want to talk about it. That's all.'

Della held the pause a moment. Catrin kept her silence, hoped Della would just hang up. But she didn't.

Catrin was intrigued, she had to admit it. Why was this woman calling her after all these years? It certainly wasn't for sentimental reasons.

'They've closed his file, I suppose?' the soft voice said.

'Yes.'

'Accidental Death no doubt they called it.'

'They did, yes.' Catrin held the phone a hand's length from her ear; she could hardly bear to hear the voice, its gentle, wheedling sound.

'What if I told you Rhys was working a case when he died.'

Catrin laughed. She couldn't help herself. There was no joy in it though.

'Working a case? He wasn't working anything except a needle into his arm.'

'Yes,' said Della, 'he was doing that all right. But it didn't mean he didn't have a brain. Did you ever know anyone smarter?'

'No,' said Catrin, her voice suddenly weaker, 'no, I didn't.'

'Well he didn't lose that, no matter how much shit he took. And he was working a case.'

'How do you know?'

''Cause he was working with me on it, that's how. You want to know what it was?'

Catrin kept the phone raised, and waited.

'It was the Owen Face case. Remember, the bloke from Seerland?'

Catrin let out a humourless bark. 'Oh for fuck's sake. That's just junkie bullshit. That's not a case.'

'There'd been a new sighting.'

Catrin gave another dry laugh. 'But that's just a tabloid myth, like Lucan. No one actually takes that stuff seriously.'

There was another pause, longer this time. For a moment she thought the line had cleared.

'What if I told you that I'd seen something that would make you change your mind?' the voice said at last.

There was a metallic scraping sound in the background Catrin couldn't place, then a sharp intake of breath.

'Rhys had some photos, some new evidence.'

She noticed Della spoke more quietly now.

'New evidence, eh? Another loser's staggered out of a pub, skinful of Brain's Bitter, and had a close encounter with Face – this sort of nonsense has been going on for twelve years. Next you'll be telling me Elvis is running the gift shop on Barry Island.'

'I thought you were a fan?'

'No, I was never a fan.'

'No?'

Catrin paused, her attention distracted by a spider's web in the corner of the hall. 'Rhys was a junkie. He fell in the water. It happens. Whatever he was working on, it's not important.'

'A bit strange, don't you think. First time you're back for twelve years, and he winds up dead. You were even there on the scene, I heard.'

'What do you think you know, Del?'

'Meet me, let's talk about it.'

'We never liked each other, Del. Why would I want to do that?' Catrin sat down on the ledge, took a deep breath, then laughed dismissively. 'It's not possible anyway,' she said, 'even if I wanted to. I'm in the middle of nowhere.'

There was a background rustling, like leather brushing over leather. 'I know. You're in the cottage near the top of the hill. I can see it from here.'

Catrin felt a sudden clamminess.

'Where are you, Del?'

'I'm down in the village, at the Red Lion. I'll be waiting for you.'

Catrin put down the receiver, then bent down and pulled the wire from the wall socket. Sitting back on the cold floor, she ran it through her fingers.

Outside the window she could just make out the track disappearing over the brow of the hill towards the village. The forms of the trees were barely visible through the rain, the lines of the hills lost in the low clouds.

Catrin eased her old Laverda through the muddy track, and out along the lane. The bike was jittery at low revs. She had to hold on hard to stop it losing grip. It wasn't more than a mile to the village. She could easily have walked, but the clouds had darkened, promising sleet, perhaps snow.

Briefly she checked her reflection in the side mirror. Her jacket was fraying, her hair hung down limply, almost obscuring her face. Her T-shirt was stretched tight over her small breasts, the words THE BAD SEEDS faded to a blur.

The hedges along the road were threadbare, wearing winter colours. The lane came down to a fork, then ran between some firs towards a solitary pub. Its narrow drive was empty apart from an ancient van and a black Range Rover with a Cardiff dealer's plate. She parked her bike beside it.

The pub's interior was dark, the walls covered with the usual horse brasses and prints of hunting scenes. In front of the bar three men were standing. All were dressed in corduroy trousers, thick jumpers, green wellington boots. They'd been talking to the barman and stopped when they heard Catrin enter. She walked around the corner, into the snug. At first sight it seemed to be empty. The walls were covered with more hunting prints. Beyond the last of these, she saw a woman sitting in the corner. Her back was turned to the door, a Bloody Mary, half empty, on the table in front of her.

In this light, she thought, Della looked younger. She was wearing a pair of white Diesel jeans that showed off her pared-down figure, and a skinny leather jacket, the sort that doesn't come under a grand; a matching Chloé buckle bag took up the whole seat beside her.

Della was standing now, her smile revealing ice-white veneers where once there had been gaps and angles. In close-up, her lips were plumper than Catrin remembered, her forehead smooth and free of wrinkles. When Catrin gripped her upper arms, partly to steady herself, partly to keep her distance, she could feel the muscles shifting beneath her hands.

Della moved her phone and handbag, patting the seat beside her and waiting for Catrin to sit. Catrin remained standing, resting her hands on the table. She looked straight into Della's eyes, which were narrowed, slightly bloodshot, tired. Nothing like she remembered. She was looking at an entirely different woman from the one who'd taken Rhys from her all those years before.

'Did you love him?'

'Jesus, Catrin!'

'Did you kiss him behind the ear, that sweet spot he had there?'

She saw that Della was staring at her like she was looking at a madwoman, and maybe she was.

'Yes,' she said softly, 'yes I did.'

'Yeah?' She was sitting down now, still looking Della right in the eye. 'And after he came, when he was lying on top of you, did he cry just a little bit?'

Della shook her head imperceptibly, broke eye contact.

'You fucking bitch.'

Catrin felt a moment's triumph then a giddying swing down into pure self-loathing.

'Yeah well,' Della said, 'I stole him from you, didn't I?' She stood up. 'I'll get you a drink.'

Catrin nodded and sat back. In the background, Nick Drake was singing 'Time of No Reply'. She still couldn't believe that Nick Drake was a popular act and not the secret treasure he'd been half her life, the discovery she'd made, hidden at the back of her mum's stack of old vinyl. She'd always thought Rhys looked a bit like Nick Drake, a bit too sensitive for this world. She'd never told him that, wished she had now.

Della put two brandies on the table, large ones. Then she sat down beside her on the bench, closer than before.

'There was something you didn't let me get to on the phone,' she said quietly.

Della was lifting a manila envelope out of her bag, placing it on the table.

'The day after Rhys died this arrived in the post.' Della had opened the envelope just enough to reveal some black-and-white photographs. As she pushed the envelope closer, Catrin smelt her perfume. Rive Gauche, a clean but not especially feminine scent. Della spread the photographs out on the table.

They looked blurred. The light was too low to make out anything more than a series of tree-like shapes over on the right side. Catrin turned over the first photo and saw a sticker with the address of a photographic shop near Fishguard way out west, in the wilds.

In the next picture she was able to make out a little more. There were figures in hooded robes dancing around a fire.

'Looks like a bunch of location stills from *Blair Witch*.'

'Keep going,' said Della.

When Catrin came to the sixth or seventh photo she stopped, held it up to the light and scrutinised it carefully. The shot appeared to have been taken with a telephoto lens. A man stood in a cloak and hood, but his head was turned to the right, as though he half suspected he was being watched. The figure had the same hollow cheekbones and gaunt features as the late Owen Face. The resemblance was undeniable even to the most sceptical eye.

'Oh,' she said.

'Yeah,' said Della, 'that's the one got me going as well.'

'But what's to prove it wasn't taken years ago? Could be a still from one of those old videos Seerland used to do.'

'Could be,' said Della, 'only they were developed last week, according to the camera shop stamp.'

Catrin put down the photos, pushed them back towards the middle of the table.

'But it could just be an old roll of film someone passed off on Rhys?'

'Yes,' said Della, 'the thought occurred to me too. Only thing is, Rhys called me two weeks ago, said he'd tracked down Owen Face and was sending proof.'

Catrin sat back. The whole thing had the smell of a scam about it, but who was working who? That she couldn't get a handle on yet. If it was a scam it was a slick one and it had taken money and organisation, more than Rhys would have had.

But looking again at the picture, she wasn't sure. Something about it was drawing her in; it looked and felt right. She'd developed a sense over the years, knowing what was real and what wasn't. The truth was she couldn't understand any of it yet, and wasn't sure she even wanted to.

She only had Della's word that Rhys had any connection to the photos, and Della's word counted for nothing.

'How do you know he wasn't playing you?' she asked.

'What? Rhys?'

'Mocking stuff up to get more money from the client?'

'Rhys wouldn't have risked playing me,' Della said. 'I owned him, he got every penny he ever earned through me. I was his meal ticket.'

Della moved her hand up to the stem of her glass, was touching it gently. 'In any case, he still loved me.'

Catrin kept her head down, focused on her drink, she wasn't going to rise to this. 'But even if Rhys believed the shots were genuine, it doesn't exactly give them credibility. Rhys was a street junkie.'

'That's how he looked on the outside, maybe, but he was still as smart as they get. A bit like you, eh?'

Della leant forward, smiling thinly, tight leather rustling like a lizard through the undergrowth. Gently she put one hand on Catrin's: it felt soft, moist with some expensive lotion.

'You and Rhys, you're very alike, aren't you?'

Catrin could feel the heat gathering under her collar, making her skin prickle. She wanted to reach up, loosen her shirt.

'What do you mean?'

'You act like a rock chick, hard living, but underneath you're all steel and muscle and alpha-plus brains.'

A compliment of sorts. That meant Della was trying to sell her something, and whatever it was Catrin wasn't going to buy it. She'd hear her out, pick up any useful information, then leave and hope never to see the woman again.

'How did Rhys seem to you when you last saw him?' Catrin asked.

'A mess as usual, just looking for money for his next fix.'

'Was he still doing his origami? Those little birds he made?'

Della shrugged. 'So far as I know, why do you ask?'

'Because if you were still close to him, you'd have known that.'

A brief image flickered through Catrin's mind of the photos she'd seen in the case notes of his desolate room in Riverside. The backpack full of Oxfam clothes and three battered books of poetry, and that single origami bird they'd found in the fireplace.

'Look,' she said, 'how about you fill me in on some ancient history. Last I heard of Rhys was twelve years ago. He takes himself off in the middle of the night to live with you. Haven't heard a word from either of you since.' *Haven't spent a day since without thinking about Rhys either.*

Della slid closer along the bench so that their thighs touched briefly. She lowered her voice, though there was no one else in the room.

'We split up after a few months, I'd begun walking on the other side of the street if you know what I mean.' She was so close now that her breath tickled Catrin's ear. Their thighs were touching again. The bitch is actually getting off on this, she thought.

'So how come you were still even in contact? You a successful media type, him a street junkie.'

'Over the years he'd been getting by on scraps I fed him to pay for his habit.' Catrin was pretending not to look too interested. She was good at that.

'As he went downhill, he just got the shitty stuff, sitting in dives eavesdropping, going through people's rubbish. Doorstepping, that kind of thing.'

'So how did this lead to the Owen Face job?'

'Six months back I got a call from a documentary maker, he was asking for leads on Owen Face. Like you, I thought it was a waste of time, nut job material.'

'Why involve Rhys?'

'This film-maker was spreading a lot of money about. And I mean a lot, all up-front, with big bonuses for any sort of result. So I put everyone I had on the case. It just happened Rhys was the one who came across the photos.'

'Documentary makers don't usually have a lot of money to spread around,' Catrin said.

'This one's rich, a multimillionaire, made his money in commercial TV. The film is his personal hobby horse. The Owen Face mystery is something of a life's obsession for him, apparently.'

Catrin drained her glass, took her bike keys out of her pocket. She'd got it all now, the whole thing had been a set-up from the start.

'This doesn't have anything to do with Rhys, does it?' she said.

'What do you mean?'

'You want me to work for you. Rhys was just a hook. He never even had anything to do with those photos, did he?'

Della picked up a book of matches and struck one, touching it to her menthol.

'You're a quality investigator, top two percentile nationally in all your exams. You'd be a real asset to me.'

'So this whole thing has just been a play for getting me to work for you?'

'Well, you were hardly going to if I'd asked you nicely.'

Della held up the envelope with the photos in it. She lifted the edge to show a fat wedge of fifties.

'The cash is a cut of your up-front fee,' she said softly.

Della was smiling. She took a deep drag on her cigarette, exhaling slowly through her nostrils. 'Come on, lighten up. The pay is hardly much at your grade, you could do with the extra.'

Della crossed her legs and folded her hands across her lap, her right foot gently swinging, as if marking time. Catrin got up, reached over for her bag.

Della nodded towards the wedge of notes. 'The

client's willing to splurge, has the funds to do so. He's an obsessive millionaire, about the best sort of client you could wish for,' she said. 'You'd do well out of this, and there'd be plenty more work to follow.'

As Catrin picked up her bag, Della leant over, touched her arm just below the elbow, leaving her fingers there.

'No hard feelings then, Cat.' Her voice had softened to a whisper.

'Del, you're even lower than I thought.'

'I've done my research, Cat. I know who you are. You want this.'

'This was never even connected to Rhys.'

'I still know things about him.'

'Bullshit. You probably haven't seen him for years.'

Catrin was backing away, but Della's arm still gently rested on hers. Catrin could feel the heat from her fingers. As Della leant closer, her jacket rose to reveal a wide tan belt, a glimpse of starved abs. Her face was inches away now. Catrin could see the paleness under her tan and the fine, determined lines around her lips.

'We can make a night of it, if you want, Cat.'

Della's bag lay half open now. Above some papers was a baggie containing pills, a couple of glass phials. As Catrin looked up she saw that the pupils of Della's eyes were dilated, the whites bloodshot and dark and there was something lonely and desolate there.

Catrin gently drew herself back, then Della glanced down at the face of her man's watch, looked up and smiled demurely. She moved out from behind the table and, picking up her bag, began to walk towards the door. Catrin remained seated at the table.

'You've left your pictures behind,' she said.

Della turned to face her again, but didn't pick them up. She dropped a business card on the table. Her company phone numbers were in steelpoint lettering in the centre, but no address. She walked back through the bar, and out to a black Range Rover on the drive.

Catrin heard the wheels spinning on the damp gravel as it reversed. The car barely slowed as it moved out of the blind turning and down the lane. She went though the bar to the door. The rain was heavier, the light fading. The lamp in the pub's entrance behind her bled yellow onto the ground as she wrapped her arms around herself against the cold.

She looked at her watch. Nearly four o'clock. In less than an hour it would be dark again.

4

They are at the door.

The two men again.

The taller is kneeling over her, and from the cupboard in the corner where they leave the school books, he takes out her mask again.

She cannot move her hands to feel it. He pulls the straps to. In the close air behind her, she hears the swish of their clothes falling to the ground, a muted tinkle like distant wind chimes.

Over their eyes are mirrors. She tries to close her eyes, but she cannot.

She sees herself in their painted arms. Her bound, parted body painted like theirs. She tries to turn her head away, but she cannot.

All her limbs are aching. They feel hot with fever. Over them there's a stale, clammy sweat.

It's all she can smell, her fear quickening around her now.

She prays it will be the same as last time, no worse than that. She will not cry out. She does not want to give them that pleasure. She hears the squelching of the oil in their palms, she feels the rub of it between her limbs as she becomes all surface to their touch.

Catrin woke, shivering. It was the old dream again. The one she'd had ever since Rhys had found her in the woods all those years ago. She sat up and turned on the light.

She shook out two diazepam, crunched them in her teeth so the effect came on quicker. She lit a cigarette, stared at the carpet for what seemed an age.

This much she knew. When she was fifteen years old she had been walking home from the city centre, half-six on an ordinary autumn evening. As she passed through the car park, next to the football pitches on Llandaff Fields, a car had pulled up next to her. And then nothing. Nothing till four days later when she woke up in a hospital bed in Cardiff, her mother holding her hand and Rhys, a young handsome, clean Rhys, sitting there at the end of her bed, the first time she'd ever set eyes on him.

Over the next few days she found out a little more. Rhys, a detective searching for a drug lab way out in West Wales, had found her wandering in the woods, hypothermic, heavily drugged. She was wearing a skirt she'd never seen before and a man's T-shirt. No underwear. She had been recently bathed. Her hair, and this had really terrified her, had been cut short and freshly washed. She had absolutely no memory of any of it. As to what she had been drugged with, the police lab said they had simply never seen anything like it before.

At first they believed she had been raped. She'd been examined while still unconscious, and there was no obvious sign of sexual assault. And that was it. No arrests were ever made, no suspects identified, even. Who had abducted her and why was an utter mystery. The police had given up after a few weeks, all except Rhys. Some of his colleagues, she suspected, believed the whole thing was a put-on, that she'd run off to West Wales with a boyfriend and her mother's stash and freaked out and come up with this story about being abducted. She wished it was true. The not knowing had haunted her for years.

She suspected that Rhys knew more than he ever told her, that he was trying to protect her, but she never got any more out of him. In those weeks after she left hospital, she stayed alone in her room at home all day and night. Lying on her back, barely moving, staring at the ceiling. This was her only view. It was all she had trusted herself to see, all she felt safe looking at then.

She covered all the mirrors in the room. She couldn't bear looking at herself, she was frightened of herself, of what she might remember. She kept the curtains closed and the lights on, not stirring from her bed unless she had to. She kept her door locked from the inside. She'd listen to her mam come up the stairs, leave the food out for her, wait till she was gone, and then open the door to get it.

The only sound that reached her was Rhys calling after his shifts, talking to her mam. She strained to hear his voice. Something in it soothed her, made her want to follow him, gave her a small glimpse of peace. She began to call him, just listening to the calm lilt in his voice, not hearing his words. Always in the background there was Hope Sandoval on the stereo. 'Fade into You'. That's who he said she reminded him of. She didn't believe it but it was the first time a man had wanted to see the good in her.

Catrin carried on calling him for months, always her calling him. She called at the same time every three days; that way she knew if he wanted to avoid her he could. When she listened, his voice seemed to pass through her skin, massaging away her hurt. After eleven months of these calls she went round to his flat in that old block by the Arms Park and told him she was his. He had rescued her, given her life back, and now she was his. How afraid she'd been that he wouldn't want her.

She stood in the corner, too shy to meet his eyes. She unhooked her dress and let it fall to the floor. 'Do what you want with me,' she'd said. And he led her to the bed, spread her legs, knelt in front of her until she became half senseless with the pleasure. No man had ever done that to her before.

After that, he gave her a key. She came and waited for him in his flat. Sometimes for hours and hours, and he wouldn't come. He worked irregular shifts. Often it would be days before she saw him, before she'd feel whole again. Then that shrill rush through her body, as she watched him park. Inside her like a chemical. It wasn't a pleasant feeling. Like looking down from the high battlements of the castle, her throat dry, that sudden emptiness in her stomach and a small voice inside goading her to jump.

It was the same feeling she had in the dojo she went to in the early mornings: that moment before she began to fight. It was judo she learnt first, then karate, then tae kwon do and aikido. Behind the tinted glass Rhys watched her sometimes. He didn't think she could see him.

God, he'd been beautiful then, denim jacket slung over his shoulder, black Fred Perry tucked into his loose, frayed jeans. He wasn't like any copper she'd ever seen before. Snake hips, flat stomach, and head always bowed. The whole street could have been on fire, and he didn't look as if he would have noticed. That's how lost in his own world he seemed, and she'd loved him for that.

When she opened the door for him, he looked round at the bare hall slowly, as if getting his bearings again. Then would come the sudden, unexpected smile, that boyish dreamer's light in his eyes as he saw her face. How she'd loved him then. He could have done anything he'd wanted with her, she'd have let him, and sometimes he had, and she'd liked it. Through those first heady years her mind had held only one thought, that she'd never let anything take this away from her.

He was her first real love. He was the one that she'd thought would last. And when it hadn't, all the rest were just consolations and ways of forgetting herself.

Catrin moved away from the memories to a new, anonymous life in London. She buried herself in her work. Any overtime, she always took it. Any long after-hours assignments, she always volunteered. Anything not to be alone, not to be alone with her thoughts of what might have been. She found herself drawn to working under cover. It was a chance not to be that self that was half of something that could never be whole again.

The work they gave her seemed routine at first. She acted as a 'draw', a buyer planted in clubs to lure in local dealers. And with her tight leathers and tatts, she looked the part. The dealers couldn't resist her. Her MO was always textbook: once she'd scored a few times from one dealer, gained his trust, she'd float a bigger deal, get an in with his supplier. Then repeat the pattern, work her way up the supply chain to the bigger fish, the traffickers, the importers. Using surveillance work, she collected the evidence, built the case for the prosecutors.

The dealers communicated using public wireless connections, accounts with service providers in Russia and China, companies that wouldn't share information in a hurry. Even if they were only setting up a meet in the next street. To track them she had to hack the providers' firewalls, get in through the back doors of their security systems. She took the courses at Hendon, learnt how to play the RIPA laws. Like the Met's data officers, like the other listeners and watchers on the force. Without really meaning to she'd learnt to be a white hat, an unauthorised reader of other people's mail in the public interest.

After the courses she was assigned to the BDSM scene, fetish bars, bondage clubs. It was a sector no one else wanted, not even the officers who dabbled in it. She heard rumours of spiking and coercion on the scene, pain inflicted without consent, and tried to seek out their origin. She didn't care about the gossip she attracted, she thought only of those she could save. As the months passed she noticed that her brief from her DI was becoming increasingly specific. Normally an under got a fix on anything passing through the clubs – Es, meth, ice, whatever was in circulation. But she was briefed only to target date-rape drugs: Rohypnol, Mandies, incapacitants – and to focus only on the end users. It didn't take her long to understand why.

Her work was part of something much bigger, an op with far higher stakes than netting small-time drug rings. She thought her work would take her away from Rhys. But it didn't. It led her right back to him.

It was balmy weather the day she realised. A sun-drenched emptiness to the streets, a scent of hot asphalt. She's sitting in a pub, in the shade, watching the world go by. Except there's nothing much to watch. It's the middle of the afternoon, everyone in their offices or down at the park. A light breeze comes through the door. Then the air is still again. There must be a funfair down there, she can just hear the faint music from the rides.

Behind her there's a chink of glasses, the burble of the slot machine, just how an empty pub always sounds on a hot summer's day. She half closes her eyes, tries to let her mind go blank. Except something there's not right. She opens her eyes again, and looks around.

The barman has his back to her. He's drying glasses, putting them back on the rack. He turns for a moment, an old man, smiles at her. Slowly she is looking at everything around her, taking it in. The empty tables, the mirror, the slot machine. She needs to find whatever isn't right.

The couple by the door get up, go out into the sunlight. Smoke rises from the ashtray on their table, curling up through the still air. On the table, empty glasses. And there it is, the newspaper lying on the seat: what she's just seen and not seen.

Catrin picks it up and their eyes are staring back at her, those same eyes that had watched her through all the days of her youth. Stared at her from the school gates, from the hoardings along the overgrown railway banks. She'd tried to avoid them even then. The way they seemed to reproach her for not quite being one of them, for not being one of the missing.

Because she was the one who came back, after only four days. But it was months, sometimes years before the other girls were found. Out in the woods, somewhere wild and remote at the western edge of the country they'd turn up, left for dead in places they'd never been in their lives before. He always wore a hood or mask, they said, the man who'd taken them. Moved them about in a closed van, kept them, drugged, in cellars without windows. Even under hypnosis, after months of patient questioning, none had any idea where they'd been held, or by whom.

The only common thread – and it wasn't until much later that it came out – had made their ordeal even worse, if that were possible. The girls, it turned out, had all been in the small BDSM scene in Cardiff. Subs who got off on pain and degradation. But not that sort, nothing like what they had been put through. What had happened to them in captivity wasn't leaked. All that was known was that some had been burnt with acid, others hung from hoists for months by hooks worked into their flesh. They were disorientated when they were found, almost blind after the long periods in darkness. Most hardly knew who they were and no amount of therapy seemed to bring them back into the world of the living.

Because of the long periods the victims were held for, the worst was always presumed when any young person went missing in the area. The police went under-cover into the BDSM clubs, kept up surveillance for months. But they drew a blank. The months dragged out into years, the years into a decade or more. And still it carried on, every few months another girl missing, their faces on the hoardings, their doomed eyes staring out from the cuttings.

It had become a fact of life that just had to be endured. And then out of nowhere, as suddenly as it began, it was over. And all by chance, it seemed. Rhys, an officer with no connection to the case, busted a small-time dealer in Bute. From the dealer's house, he followed a grey van to a street behind the station. In the back of the van, he found a rack and shackles, a long cloak and hood. He followed the driver to a house nearby, found a trapdoor and below it a secret floor excavated into a warren of cells. He brought the house's owner out in cuffs. A loner, an out-of-work builder called Angel Jones. And after that the abductions finally ended; or at least they seemed to.

Catrin twists the tabloid, so she doesn't have to meet the eyes of the girls, feel their reproach again. *You were the lucky one*, they all seem to be saying to her, *we don't know why but you were*. Some of the victims had committed suicide afterwards. Most had shrunk away into a twilight world of antidepressants and tranquillisers, ghosts of their former selves. She wonders if it wouldn't have been kinder if some of them had died in his dungeons without knowing how the memory of pain can be many times worse than the pain itself, a life sentence more final and binding. And she can never forget that there but for the grace of chance, or something else she didn't understand, she too could have gone.

In the weeks to come, their eyes will follow Catrin again. She has no answers to the questions they put to her, to their mute stares. In the sidebar every time she opens her emails, on the news-stands as she walks down the streets, flickering on TV screens in the windows of shops. The case against Jones had finally got to court; the Angel of Darkness, the tabloids called him. But if he had taken her, why had she been released? Why did she remember several men in the car, when Jones had always operated alone? Nothing added up, and the only man who might have an answer – Rhys – had disappeared from her life like a phantom.

This time her work offered her no consolation, no protection. Due to a technicality Jones was still out on bail. And as the trial gathered momentum, within the London BDSM scene there'd been several copycat abductions. None of the missing girls had been found, but traces of spiking drugs had been found at clubs they'd disappeared from. So, undercover, Catrin found herself working the same case that Rhys had broken, following in his footsteps, a phantom following a phantom.

The terms of Jones's bail were as tight as legally possible, a curfew. He was under round-the-clock CID surveillance, under police guard in a safe house for his own protection. But in the public imagination, Jones had assumed near-supernatural status. Every copycat incident had brought speculation in the tabloids about the Angel slipping his captors, perpetrating further atrocities like some demonic being from Victorian folklore.

It was impossible of course, Catrin knew that, as did every officer in the Met working the copycat cases. But until the London copycat was caught, CID down in Cardiff and the Met were getting roasted in the press. Without Catrin knowing it her undercover work had been part of a major multi-unit operation to net the copycat and restore public confidence in the police. The bond with Rhys was there all the time, she saw that now, their purpose and fate still a shared one.

The day Rhys's evidence was due, she bought every paper, watched every newscast. But due to court restrictions his face did not appear, not even sketched by the court artists. It was as if his role was already airbrushed out. There were several pictures of others from Cathays Park – Rix smiling confidently at a news conference, DS Thomas posing in Jones's dungeons. But of Rhys there was not a single sign.

Of Jones himself there was also little to see. He was bundled into court under a blanket and taken out the same way. The pictures of Jones in the press had told her nothing about the man who might have been her abductor. Most were grainy shots of a man in a hood with long hair that covered his face. The arrest shots showed features blanched and flattened by the flashlights, eyes that were almost closed so they gave away nothing of the man within.

No one was in any doubt they'd got the right man. The evidence against Jones seemed airtight. There were IDs of the tattoo on his chest from every one of his victims. There were matches between drug traces in the tox reports of all the victims and those found on Jones's person and in his cellars at his arrest. The DNA evidence from the cellars and the van showed Jones had always acted alone. As everyone expected, Jones was sent down for life to Broadmoor Hospital for the Criminally Insane. The copycat incidents abruptly petered out. They turned out to have been no more than a stunt by a few opportunists wanting to sell fake stories.

Gradually interest in the case began to fade, and the Jones teams were disbanded. Catrin found herself assigned to more conventional roles, the standard routines of a drug officer's life. She had no idea what Rhys was doing, had no contact from him, and respected his wish that she never contact him. The man she owed her life to had withdrawn himself so completely it felt at times as if he existed only in her mind. The years had formed into a pattern around his absence, a discipline in forgetting. They passed in a blur of clubs and biker bars and stake-outs: in time she'd become almost one with the netherworld of dealers and users she snared.

Sometimes she picked up men in the clubs she worked. Sometimes she saw the same man for months on end, never taking him to her flat, meeting him between shifts at his flat and at hotels. The types she liked were lean and rough but with sensitive eyes, eyes she wanted to forget herself in, drown in. It was a way of seeing if men could still be trusted with her soul, and often they could be. She respected them for that. But it hadn't anything to do with love. It just helped her forget for a while. She knew she would never be loved like Rhys had loved her. A part of her wondered if she could ever love again.

Now he was gone forever, her rescuer, the junkie saviour. And still she had the nightmares. She lit another cigarette, drew deeply, then stubbed it out and fell back into a shallow, dreamless sleep.

When she finished the cigarette, Catrin did an hour of shen chuan, krav maga, jabs and kicks. She had a quick cold shower, drank her yoghurt and berries straight from the blender.

Then she sat on the sofa and looked again at the tapes.

She noticed nothing new. She ran the sequence with the money changing hands again. She wasn't even sure there was anything that significant to it now. It looked as if Rhys had only decided to strike after the money had passed hands, almost as an afterthought. He'd seen an opportunity to take the other man's stash, and taken it.

Like Pugh had said – snapshots of the law of the street. She watched it through one more time. It wasn't that complicated to read. The few ambiguities didn't really alter the overall picture.

She picked up her phone, called DS Thomas.

'Della Davies,' she said. 'What's she about these days?'

'Rich media dyke. Big fuck-off house in Llandaff, weekender in the Mumbles near Catherine Zeta-Jones's people.'

'Her money comes from?'

'Her agency mostly. Any hot story out of South Wales – celebrities, crime, politics. She's always involved somewhere.'

'Did Rhys ever work for her?'

'Unlikely. She only uses the best, pays top dollar – and she only ever uses women, fine ones preferably.'

She heard Thomas's yawn turning into a light burping noise. He was sniffling, he still had a cold. Jesus, Thomas, she thought, for a good-looking bloke you've certainly got some unattractive ways about you.

'Any chance Della could've kept up with Rhys?'

'No. He hadn't been in touch with her for years.' She nodded to herself, let him go on. 'About seven years back, Rhys went round once pestering her for money. She slapped a restraining order on him. He never went anywhere near her after that.'

Catrin smiled grimly. She was learning about Thomas: he was an arrogant, lazy sod, but he had a good memory. He rarely made mistakes, that was how he kept out of trouble, and got away with doing as little as he did.

'Any signs Rhys went out west recently or owned a camera?' she asked.

'Not that I know of.'

'Nothing photography-related in Rhys's room. Rolls of film, negatives. Old cameras?'

'No. Nothing. Anything of value like that he'd have sold years ago to buy his shit.'

She heard a bleeping noise. Thomas had started playing something on his hand console. It was his tactful way of telling her time was up.

'That second man in the CCTV film, any sign of him yet?' she asked.

'No.'

'You didn't want to talk to him before you closed the file?'

The bleeping increased in volume, there were some crashing noises. Probably Grand Theft Auto, just about Thomas's cultural level.

'Well, he wasn't going to be much of a witness, was he?' He was sniffling again. 'The one thing we can say for sure about him is he didn't see a damn thing.'

Catrin hung up. She knew Thomas was right. The second man was a dead end. Everyone was right, the death had been an accident. She had to accept that now. If she carried on like this her reputation would be in tatters.

She'd have to find another way of honouring

Rhys's memory. She shifted the file back into her PGP key and sent it off to an anonymous server in South Africa. Then she deleted all trace of it from her Mac. She wouldn't want to look at it again for a while. It wasn't how she wanted to remember him.

There were only four days left of her leave. She'd be wise to keep her head down from now on, stop calling Thomas; he might even begin to think she liked him. She had to build a life for herself back in the city, and that wasn't going to be easy with half the force probably thinking she was a few cards short of a full deck. The dead junkie's ex, it was hardly the best introduction.

Pugh was probably her safest starting point. He was a decent sort, even if he seemed to have turned in on himself. She could begin playing tennis again. She could check out the gyms and clubs, begin making new social contacts removed from the gossip in Cathays Park.

She remembered Pugh's words to her on the phone. 'There's one thing I've learnt from doing this job and that's to take care of the living. We can mourn the dead, but we should never let them pull us down into their graves.' He didn't know though, did he, he didn't know how much Rhys had been for her.

She took out her box, her papers, rolled a cigarette with a pinch of kanna in it. She put on 'Fire and Rain', the original Taylor version, the volume full up, the languid notes weaving with her smoke through the room.

It wasn't a song Rhys had liked, he'd said it was self-indulgent. Too close to the bone, maybe. She took down Pugh's guitar and strummed along to the deceptively simple chords. The music was haunting, pure still, but now she felt she'd moved on to a place beyond its reach. She closed her eyes, felt herself trying to drift gradually back into a period when it had still held some magic for her.

Over the music she heard the door buzzer going. She ignored it at first, but it carried on. She went to the window, peered through the nets. There was a car parked in the lane, a black Range Rover.

In the glow from the headlights she saw that Della was wearing a long, dark coat. Her high boots caught the glare. Her face looked very pale, no make-up.

What does the witch really want with me, Catrin wondered. She waited, silent, still as a statue, hoping Della would go away.

The buzzer went again, the noise building like a drilling in her head.

Catrin opened the door. Della's hair was soaked through, hanging down limply over her face.

'I just wanted to apologise for last night,' Della said. Her voice was weak, slightly tremulous.

Catrin watched Della reach into her pocket, but

leave her hand there. Her coat was soaked through. Catrin blocked her way.

'If this is another job offer, Del, you're wasting your time.'

'No, it's not.'

Della was leaning back on the windowsill, looking slightly unsteady on her feet. Her eyes were blood-shot, tired-looking. There was a hint of fear there.

'I shouldn't have lied to you about Rhys,' she said. 'It was wrong.'

'You hadn't seen him for years, had you?'

'No.'

Catrin moved forward to the door, held it open. The wind and rain were running down Della's face. 'Just keep away from now on.' *You sleazy crazy bitch* was what she really wanted to say, shout right into Della's face, then knock her to the ground.

Della made no move away from the windowsill.

'Look, what I told you about the photos,' Della said slowly. 'It's possible Rhys did have something to do with them.'

Catrin waited, saying nothing, her hand still holding open the door. Della was staring out into the rain.

'They came to me via that documentary maker, the one who's obsessed with the Owen Face mystery.'

'So what?'

'He told me he'd got them from an ex-copper, someone down on his luck.'

'That doesn't narrow it down much.'

'Someone who'd just died, he said.'

'He wouldn't say who.'

'No.'

Catrin took this in. Even if it was true it offered no real indication Rhys had been involved.

'That's all,' she said.

'That's all.'

Della was tapping her boots lightly on the floor. They came up above the knee, tucked into cashmere leggings that were a few shades lighter than the cashmere of her drenched Versace coat. All the rich tart's gear, she's sending me the same message as last night, Catrin thought. You come work for me, you can spend like I spend.

At last Della seemed about to leave. Catrin turned away, hoping the disgust showed on her face.

'So why bother to tell me this?' she said.

'I thought you'd find it interesting.' Della had begun to turn towards the door.

'The film-maker,' Catrin said. 'What's his name?'

Della just stood there with her back to her. Catrin waited, didn't really expect Della to answer. More than likely this has all just been another nasty little power game, she thought, leading nowhere.

'Huw Powell,' Della said.

The name rang a vague bell, but Catrin couldn't place it. Not at first, then it came to her. 'He was a copper himself, wasn't he?'

'Once, long ago.'

'In Drugs. Didn't he leave under a cloud?'

Della didn't answer, began walking back towards her car. Briefly through Catrin's mind had flickered the ghost of an idea, it wasn't more than that, just a ghost. She felt her pulse quicken, not with fear this time, but with something more like hope, and with it came an anger deeper than she had felt for many years.

'It was before my time,' Della called back.

'Corruption, wasn't it, something like that?'

Her words were lost in the wind. Della had started the engine. For a moment the air was filled with strains of some retro disco beat. Then the car was gone, and Catrin was left looking out at the rain and the night.

5

As Catrin reached the services on the road back to Cardiff, the weather was closing in again, visibility low, the rain turning to driving sleet. Her heavy bike was slipping in the slicks left by the trucks, her leathers soaked through by their spray. She decided to pull in, stay the night.

She parked and peered at her phone. She'd found Huw Powell's number the old way, in the telephone directory. She'd left two messages already, but still no reply.

The café area at the back was brilliantly lit up, but there was no one in sight. Next to the door, a jukebox – a replica fifties model – was playing a medley of Tom Jones hits. She'd heard them so many times it was like walking into silence.

She helped herself to a coffee from the counter, sat by the window. The dimly lit car park was empty. Down at the pumps, a single figure was filling a heavy-goods truck. The only other sign of life came from a television, the screen covered with weather warnings.

A notice showed that all ferry services out of Fishguard had been cancelled. On the ticker she saw the bad weather had closed many smaller roads along the coast in the far west.

The truck driver went over to a booth. She'd noticed the truck had come from the west, a Cardigan address on the side, its roof dripping with melting ice.

She caught the man's eye. 'How is it out in the far west?'

She could hear him chuckling under his breath, making the gurgling sound typical of a heavy smoker.

'That area's been cut off best part of a week already,' he said.

Next to the shop the door led through to a motel section, a recently built, no-frills Travelodge. Beside the empty reception desk, a swipe machine took her card details, then spat out a key into a plastic receptacle.

The maroon theme that dominated the reception area had been continued in the rooms. The furnishings looked barely used, but old all the same.

The lights along the walkway outside were tripping off automatically, the night closing in. All that was visible outside was a lone figure in a parka at the pumps filling an old van.

Sitting on the bed she opened the bag she used to store her CDs, the top covered with stickers from Spillers Records in Cardiff, now faded and peeling.

Though she'd never cared much for Seerland and Owen Face, she knew she still had some of their early stuff. Rhys had given to her the compilation way back in the mid-Nineties, the second year they'd been together.

She switched on her Mac and settled back on the bed.

The first track was one of Seerland's early numbers. She closed her eyes as she listened to the opening bars. First came the strumming of the balalaika, then the bass notes that drove the track forward. Then Face's cracked voice gradually filling the room like an ancient scent seeping from a broken bottle.

It was a song to be listened to in the depths of the night when even the world's insomniacs had drifted off to sleep. It'd been what Rhys liked to hear on night surveillance shifts, the trip-hop's unearthliness drifting out of his car stereo. She'd gone with him sometimes, to allay the boredom, getting her first taste for police work.

It had been the same routine every night, the same faces, every hour or so a runner bringing through the stones bagged up for sale by the boys on the corners. There wasn't much to do to pass the time except listen to music, or talk, or not talk.

She'd reach across and hold his hand, or lie with her face buried in his chest, nothing more than that, just lie there, forgetting herself in him, her shallow breathing merging with his until she could no longer hear her own breaths.

Sometimes she'd sense him shrinking away from her, the first sign that there were parts of him she'd never reach, bowing his head over the box where he stored his chocolate bars, the sheets of paper he used to make his origami birds. Acting as if she wasn't there at all.

She went to the track which had made Seerland famous, one of the small collection they'd released after they had signed with their first label. Typical of their early sound, she knew it had been a favourite with that tight-knit group of fans who'd followed the band before Owen Face disappeared.

The sound did not strike her as particularly original, there was something familiar, almost comforting in its trance-like beat. Over a finale of wailing feedback, the track ended with Face reading a poem. She could make out only one line – *I want to walk in the snow and not leave a footprint* – the rest was inaudible, lost in the feedback.

She remembered the same words playing on the radio the night of Face's disappearance. How she'd tried to shut them out of her mind by humming. Rhys had told her about Face's state of mind towards the end, his fierce intelligence, his tendency to self-harm with knives and razor blades. She'd thought he presented with all the tells of the classic potential suicide. But she knew there were many people out there who still desperately wanted to believe Face was alive somewhere, that he'd just needed time out and would return one day like a lost Messiah.

To his hardcore fans the Face had been more than just a rock star. He'd been their representative on earth, his anxieties and anorexia the outward signs of their own tortured souls. But his presumed death had forced them to move on and grow up. And looking back she could see now that his disappearance had coincided with the end of something in herself and the people around her at the time. Until then they'd all still nursed illusions of a successful career, a halfway decent marriage, a house in one of Cardiff's better suburbs, a couple of kids, a dog – a few pints before Sunday lunch with their mates at the rugby club. They'd still believed they could return to normal lives. But after he had gone these illusions had seemed quietly to slip away, and had gradually been replaced by silence.

Maybe a part of her still wanted to believe Face was out there too, that part of her that still remembered how to hope, that felt she owed something to all the missing ones. It was the oldest of human fantasies after all, healing time, bringing back the lost, the dead.

Her cigarette was almost burning her fingers. She let it drop into the mug at her feet. The CD segued on to Seerland's biggest hit. Over a backdrop of sitars and synthesised guitars the lyrics spoke of astral travel, the mind and the senses leaving the body to experience a world beyond the restrictions of the mundane. The sound reminded her of the Beatles in their psychedelic period – of 'Tomorrow Never Knows' and 'Strawberry Fields Forever'. It had a looping, slightly dazed beat, though as she continued to listen she had the sense there was some other more ancient ingredient that she was missing.

Looking out she could see through the trees beyond the pumps the dim flicker of headlights. She stopped the track and took off the headphones. The wind was stronger now, the sleet almost horizontal.

In the front pocket of her jeans she felt the vibration of her mobile. She looked at the screen: there was no caller's number visible. She raised the handset to her ear.

'Catrin?'

A crackle of interference was breaking up the voice. She didn't recognise it.

'It's me.' The voice sounded cracked, as if the man hadn't spoken for some time. 'Huw Powell.'

The static had gone, but the line was still poor. In the background she could hear what sounded like the crashing of waves.

'Huw Powell. The film-maker.'

The voice sounded weird, more mechanical than human. Like the voice of someone who didn't get out much. That's what these obsessives become like, she thought, they end up in their own worlds, cut off, barely able to communicate.

On the other end of the line there was a sharp intake of breath, as if the man was taking a drag on something stronger than a cigarette.

'Della called me last night, told me you might want to talk to me.'

The voice still sounded croaky, barely human. There was a long rasping noise, then a series of clicks and the line went dead. She pressed the 'logs' section to check for the number, but there was nothing there.

Then a text came through, just an address and a time.

The sleet had almost stopped now. If she pressed her face to the window she thought she could just see, through the dark row of trees and the lamps that lined the road, the orange glow of the city in the distance.

As Catrin rode through what remained of the western docks, she kept losing her way among the new buildings overlooking the quays. The area had once been a seedy but friendly enough cluster of reggae clubs, cheap guest houses and massage parlours. Now all this had been replaced by high-rise hotels and apartment blocks that seemed to have risen like a giant formation of shimmering crystals whole from the sea.

The address she'd been texted turned out to be a gleaming steel and glass tower, a needle-shaped structure that dwarfed the blocks around it. The door was opened for her by a uniformed guard, her name was entered on a clipboard, and she was directed towards the lifts.

In the transparent, climate-controlled pod, hidden speakers played Andean pipe music as it climbed the outside of the building. On her way up to the penthouse she took in the view of the city. Beyond a cluster of bars she could just make out the shopping streets of The Hayes and Queen Street, the turrets of the castle and the dim expanse of Pontcanna and the suburbs.

As the lift opened, Catrin saw a man standing in a lobby panelled in light, rather beautiful wood. He looked like a classic executive type, was dressed in a dark tailored suit and tie. As though he'd left the office late and still hadn't had time to change.

'I'm here to see Huw Powell,' she said.

He smiled warmly, confidently.

'That's me,' he said.

Her first thought was that she'd just been the victim of some kind of practical joke. The voice on the phone had suggested a crazy, a bong-smoking recluse, a one-man party. But the man standing in front of her looked clean-cut, conventional even, every inch the CEO of a major media company. It was the same voice all right, but levelled out now, quietly commanding.

He reached out his hand, but without moving. She had to come forward to shake it. That's how the powerful do it, she thought, they make you come to them. She looked closer at him. Apart from a slight redness around the rims of his eyes, there was nothing to suggest he'd been partying hard. He straightens up fast, she thought.

'You sounded as if you were having a good time earlier,' she said.

'I like to smoke temple balls after work,' he said. 'Helps me to unwind. They come from a little valley in the tribal regions. Best fucking dope in the world.'

He's not even denying it, Catrin thought. With money like that people soon stop worrying about what others think of them. He was an even six foot, somewhere in his late fifties, she reckoned. But looking well on it, broad shouldered and no sign of a gut. His black hair was shot through with silver, and there were fine crow's feet around his green eyes. Otherwise time seemed to have left him well alone. His features were dark, powerful. He looked rather like a lion, a green-eyed lion carved out of Welsh rock.

Powell was ushering her through a series of hallways, all panelled in the same rare teak, his hand placed very lightly on the small of her back. She felt a faint flutter in her stomach, and then it passed. She could see already she'd have to tread carefully with this man.

He guided her into a giant open-plan living space. It reminded her of the reception area in some high-tech City office, appeared to have been designed more for visual impact than for comfort. It felt pristine, unlived-in. On the walls, the only colour was provided by giant framed Seerland posters, some featuring Owen Face, others more recent.

He asked what she wanted to drink, then disappeared through a folding door. Through the gap Catrin could see the monitors of several large state-of-the-art editing suites, banks of screens flickering in the half-light.

'You've done well for yourself,' she called through.

He returned with two screwdrivers in tall glasses.

'The company runs itself,' he said. 'We know the formats that sell. We just give people what they want but are ashamed to admit they want.'

'What shows do you make?'

'The ones with big ratings. Reality shows, hidden camera shows. It's just a question of editing the raw material, holding up a mirror to nature.'

'It's a business that must have needed plenty of seed money?'

Powell was looking at her with a slightly disappointed expression. She couldn't read it exactly, somewhere between quizzical and suspicious, his head tilted to one side as if considering an object that had fallen off its axis.

'You're referring to the old rumours, I suppose,' he said, smiling now. 'That I left the force all those years ago on some kind of corruption rap.'

'These things get around,' she said.

'You're thinking I had money stashed away from my time at the force to start the business.'

'Did you?'

He was smiling broadly, almost laughing, appeared completely relaxed.

'Listen,' he said. 'I left the force because I had a good business idea, for no other reason. I may smoke a bit of weed, but I'm a straight shooter. You see what you get with me.'

The silence hung between them.

Then he motioned his glass towards hers in a wordless toast and gestured towards one of the sofas. Catrin took a swig of her drink. It tasted just right, as if it had been made by a professional barman. She wondered if an invisible army of staff waited just out of sight.

'Della said you might want to ask me some questions

about those photos?' He was looking faintly impatient now. He probably has far, far more interesting things to do than talk to me, Catrin thought. She knew she'd have to get in her questions quickly or she might not get another chance.

'Della said you'd got them from an ex-copper, someone who'd just died.'

He was nodding.

'That's right.'

'But you wouldn't tell Della who that was.'

He smiled. 'Well, she might not have taken the job if I had.'

'Why was that?'

She saw Powell wasn't about to answer her. Maybe this was going to be just another dead end. She glanced at one of the huge framed Owen Face posters on the wall, his face gaunt, his floppy hair hopelessly dated. It looked like an exhibit in a museum, already a piece of history. Then she saw his eyes, large and sad. Watching her, watching her as the eyes of the missing on the hoardings and school gates had. Mute, reproachful, as if she owed him something, owed something to the missing and all the time they had been waiting patiently to collect.

'I was thinking how Face's disappearance coincided with something that happened to the people around me,' she said.

'Oh?'

'It was like when Face went they noticed a part of them had already disappeared. After that they knew they couldn't be whole again, couldn't be normal again.'

He'd begun picking at his lapel, as if only half listening.

'But no one's life is normal, Catrin,' he said after a pause. She noticed how he'd said her name slowly, slightly dismissively but letting the sound of it linger on his lips. A shape moved across the large window, a gull: it hovered there a moment. She watched it dive out of view.

'You said if you told Della who the man was you'd got the photos from, she'd not have taken the job. Why?'

'She disliked him, thought he was a loser, a liability.'

Catrin thought about this for a moment. 'As long as there was money in it, I don't think Della would've have cared where the photos came from.'

'Maybe. But I reckoned she wouldn't risk her reputation getting mixed up in something that might turn out to be just bullshit. I thought it safer not to tell her where they came from.'

'The photos came from Rhys Williams, didn't they?' Catrin said.

He nodded. He seemed relaxed about admitting it

now, didn't hesitate for a moment. A straight shooter? Maybe he really was, she thought.

'Why did you hire Rhys?'

'I didn't. More like he hired himself.'

She caught his eye. He returned her glance unblinking.

'I ran into him one day, down the quay.' He jerked his head towards the window. 'It felt like he'd been waiting for me, was going to hustle me a bit.'

'And?'

'Rhys said he knew I was interested in the Owen Face mystery, did I want to hire him to do some research. I gave him four grand. Never thought I'd see him again.'

'Did you?'

'No. About eight weeks later the photos of those men in robes arrived. Then two days later Rhys was dead.'

Outside Catrin could hear the clink and whistle of the wind through the metal fastenings on the masts down in the marina. Powell had let his hand drop onto the leather of the sofa in the space between them.

'Rhys send any message with the photos?'

'Just that he'd got them from a very reliable source.'

'Nothing else?'

'Nothing.'

'And no indication I suppose who that source was?'

'No, none at all.'

He was gesturing vaguely out towards the water.

'Sad what happened,' he said.

'You don't think the photos are connected in any way to how Rhys died then?'

He didn't seem to have heard at first. She saw he was looking at her lips, as if waiting for her to continue. Then he shook his head slowly.

'They say it was just an accident,' he said.

She looked down at her glass.

'You must have known Rhys from the old days?'

'Not really. I left the year after he joined.'

Powell was running his fingers slowly over the sofa. His fingers were not touching her, but the ripples from their movements she could sense along her thigh. He was looking at her, not at her eyes but at her mouth.

'Perhaps we could see each other again,' he said. This time his smile was so brief that it disappeared almost before she registered it.

She wondered what this might lead to, what his interest might be. A man with his money could have almost any woman he wanted. What did he know about her personal life? She looked down at his hand moving steadily in a rhythm over the soft fabric. She remembered the slightly dismissive but lingering way he'd said her name and felt suddenly uncomfortable.

She pointed at the reflections of the Owen Face posters. 'You don't really believe Face is still alive after all this time, do you?' she asked softly.

'I'm not sure,' he said. 'The odds are against it.'

'Della said you've spent years on the mystery.'

'She's exaggerating a little. I've circled the case from every angle over the years, gone down a lot of blind alleys. And now I need to know what really happened before I can finish my film.'

He stood up, walked slowly across the room to the window that overlooked the marina. He appeared to be enjoying the view, but Catrin couldn't escape the feeling that he was turning his back on her in some more general way. He folded his arms and looked out again.

'You're not really that interested in Face, are you?' he said. 'Your main interest is in Rhys.'

'Why do you say that?' She felt Face's eyes watching her from every wall, waiting for her answer, that whole silent choir of Faces in the room watching her. She couldn't bear to meet the eyes and what they seemed to foretell. An image came to her of Rhys: he was walking away from her, white summer blossom swirling around him in the darkness. He turned back to face her for a moment, but his features were no longer clear to her. He walked on until he disappeared from view.

'I know you and Rhys used to be an item.' Powell moved back to where she sat, standing over her. 'Why else would you be here if it wasn't for Rhys?'

She didn't look up at him, her eyes on the seagull hovering outside the window. There'd seemed genuine sympathy in his voice, she noticed, and a hint of something else – anger, maybe even fear. In such a man the two emotions are probably very closely connected, she guessed.

'I'd like to show you something,' he said. 'Tomorrow over lunch.'

He was staring at her lips again, then down at her hips. He wants me to see that he's looking at me that way, she thought. He's used to getting his own way, and he's not even hiding it from me. She felt angry, wanted to give him a kicking, leave him with a nice big shiner on his smug rich man's face. Then the feeling passed.

'You said it was an accident,' she said.

'I said the police said it was an accident. I didn't.'

'So you think his death was connected to the photos?'

He said nothing, shrugged his shoulders.

'Stop playing games,' she said. 'If you know something, tell me now. You won't get another chance.'

She stood now, bending to pick up her bag from the floor, opening it to look for her keys. She was aware of his eyes on her as she did so. It wasn't altogether unpleasant, she had to admit. But still the sense of discomfort she'd felt earlier persisted.

'Let me show you something,' Powell said.

He was behind her, gently taking her arm. He led her up a spiral staircase to a large, almost empty room. It occupied the pyramid at the apex of the tower, the lights of the entire city spread out beneath them, on the other side the dark expanse of the channel.

He sat at one end of a table. On it was a small scale model of the tower, and some exotic fruits Catrin had never seen before. To either side of him were two young, well-built men. They were standing back at a respectful distance. The room was so large they couldn't hear what was said at the table.

Powell gestured for her to sit opposite him.

'You're going to work for me,' he said matter-of-factly, as if he was stating something they both already knew would happen.

'I have a job already thanks,' she said.

He pretended not to have heard, waved to one of the guards, who brought a square object to the table and two envelopes.

'By the time I've finished what I'm saying you'll have decided to work for me,' he said.

He was opening what looked like a backgammon box. It was rubber-sealed, Catrin noticed. Inside it was divided into small square airtight cubicles. In each was a small bag of what looked like grass or hash.

'This is for afters,' he said. 'To celebrate when we've signed our contract.'

The rich, she thought, they think they can buy us and use us at will. She got up, began backing away to the door. Powell made no attempt to stop her. He'd taken out what looked like a contract from the first envelope. He'd left the smaller envelope closed.

Then he took out a glass stem, a pipe, and several bags from the box.

'These are some of the finest dopes in the world,' he said. 'Temple sticks from the Manali Valley. The Dom Perignon of hashish, you'll like them.'

He picked up another bag. 'This is from Pakistan, Chitrali. So good the locals keep it for themselves. It's very rare to find it in the west.'

She'd reached the doorway, was about to go down the staircase. But she kept her eyes on him. He'd put his hand on the small, unopened envelope.

'It's in here,' he said. 'The thing that will make you change your mind.'

Catrin stopped, waited. He was opening the envelope, spreading some papers face down on the table like a deck of cards.

'Here's the deal,' he said. 'Three weeks of your time investigating the photos. In return, I'll show you something that may prove Rhys's death was not an accident.'

From the second envelope he'd counted out eight pieces of paper, face down, all identical except the last. She felt a flush of anger mingled with anticipation as she stared down at the papers.

He pointed at the contract. 'This is a confidentiality agreement, it's for your own protection. No one will ever know you worked for me.'

'Why me?' she said. 'You could hire anyone you wanted.'

'Because for you this will be personal. That could make the difference between a result and a lot of expensive pissing in the dark.'

'Three weeks to solve a mystery that hasn't been solved in twelve years? It doesn't sound like a very realistic proposition.'

'I'm not expecting you to solve the mystery.' His eyes were moving slowly down her body again. 'Though that would be nice, of course.'

'So what are you expecting of me exactly?'

'Just to find the source of the photos. That will be sufficient.'

Powell pushed the contract to the side of the table. She walked over, read it briefly. She signed it without even a moment's hesitation.

'All right, show me,' she said.

He paused for a moment. 'One thing you need to understand,' he said. 'What I will show you, it's not conclusive.'

'What do you mean?'

'I said what I have *may* show his death was not an accident, not that it did.'

He turned over seven of the papers. They were cheques made out to Rhys Williams, each for £500.

The eighth document was a bank statement, from a small private bank she'd never heard of. All the details had been deleted except the name and address of the account holder, and the cheque numbers.

The numbers of the cheques matched those on the statement.

'This was how I paid Rhys,' Powell said. 'A series of foredated company cheques.'

She looked at the dates: the cheques were dated one week apart.

'Notice anything?' he said.

'You paid him four thousand. But the final cheque was never presented.'

He moved the statement closer to her.

'Correct. You'll see he wouldn't have been able to present until the day after he died.'

She began to feel let down, this didn't seem to add up to anything.

'So what?' she said.

'No cheque was found on his person or at his room when he died.'

She sat back, stared at him. 'That means nothing,' she said. 'He could've just lost it.'

'Yes, and that would have been my assumption too, except for one subsequent development.'

He moved his finger over to the address of the account. A company registered on the Newport Road.

'The day of Rhys's death this small private bank's computers were compromised, but no moneys were stolen.'

'How do you know?'

'I am a part-owner of the bank. I was notified as a matter of course.'

'Okay,' she said. 'But banks get hacked all the time.'

He'd stood up, ushered her towards some binoculars set up on a tripod, directed towards the east of the city.

'Take a look at this,' he said.

'What am I meant to be looking at?'

He said nothing.

Catrin put her eyes to the sockets. She could make out the Newport Road in detail. She looked at the numbers on the doors of the buildings. She realised she was looking at the stretch of the street where the account of the cheques had been registered.

On the far side of the road, there was large gap

between the office buildings. She looked more closely. There had been a recent fire. What had once been a building as tall as those next to it, eight storeys at least, had been reduced to a single floor of charred rubble.

'Jesus,' she said. She stepped back, not quite believing what she'd just seen.

'That happened the night after the bank was hacked.'

She said nothing. She was waiting for him to go on.

'I was due there that night for a meeting,' he said. 'But fortunately I had a last-minute change of plan.'

She turned. He'd taken another document out of the smaller envelope. Two pages from a report by a private security firm. She recognised the name at once; it was one of the most respected firms of its type in the world.

He passed it over to her, keeping hold of one corner.

'Whoever breached the bank's firewall would have been able to see the address the cheque account was held at.'

She glanced at the report, saw enough to confirm what he'd said.

She felt slightly faint. What he'd shown her had an air of unreality and yet its implications were stark. Whatever Rhys had been doing while obtaining the photos had upset someone else a great deal, someone with reach and power.

She saw that Powell was looking at her with a quiet intensity. There was a genuine look of concern on his face, almost a look of tenderness.

'I need to go now,' she said. She began to go down the spiral staircase.

He followed her down. 'I'll give you all the background on Owen Face,' he said. 'Everything Rhys would have known. You'll be starting from the same point he did.' She searched through her bag, not stopping until she had her keys in her hand.

Powell guided her back towards the door, his hand on her shoulder as though the room was already dark and without him close to her she would lose her way.

As he did so Catrin noticed over the doorway a crucifix, made of the same wood as the panelling, almost two metres in height, all the details lifelike. The workmanship was beautiful. It must have taken years to finish, she thought.

It looked like something one might see in an ancient church but it had been carved recently. The lift was waiting and as she entered it she felt his hand again, barely touching, just the briefest of caresses over the nape of her neck.

6

Catrin dreamt that night she was standing with her mam on wet sand. She must have been young, barely knee height. It was raining and they were sheltering under a pine tree on the edge of a beach.

Out on the high waves there were two pale shapes skimming the surface of the water. Then they were lost under the crashing waves.

The rain eased, sunlight streamed through. Two men were walking along the shore holding surfboards under their arms. Their hair was long, dark, shimmering in the light.

One came towards her and she felt him lift her high into the air.

The other was paddling out into the churning foam. He rose up with the waves. She watched him glide down the cliff face of black water and he was lost in the breakers.

She waited, but there was no sign of him. Then she saw him, some way off, running away down to the rocks. His figure was as small as the birds circling in the sky. Then she couldn't see him any more.

From the back of her mind came the distant wail of feedback, then Face's cracked voice. *I want to walk in the snow and not leave a footprint.*

She sat up, wiping the fine sweat from her forehead. She remembered hearing the track as she'd lain awake in her old flat in Cathays. It had played on the radio-alarm, the red numbers of the clock blinking away the minutes as she waited for Rhys to return from his shift. She felt herself falling back into a shallow sleep.

Outside the motel she heard car doors slamming and voices, loud at first then dying away as they entered the diner. Lifting the curtain, she noticed that several of the parking spaces had been filled since the previous night.

She reached for the remote and the television in the corner flickered on. Images of snow-covered trees and huddled figures scraping ice from their windscreens were followed by high seas along the promenades at Tenby and the other resorts out to the west.

She checked her phone. There was a text from Powell. The address of his company in Penarth: he asked her to meet him there at noon. There were also three messages from Della's number. She deleted them without listening.

She called the switchboard at Cathays Park, got through to Occupational Health. Their line wasn't answering, so she left a message, telling them she'd send a leave extension form online via Human Resources. Her voice still sounded shaky, she didn't have to fake it. Next she called Thomas's mobile. He sounded half asleep. She told him she wasn't coming in yet. He made a grunting noise as if he didn't care either way, then hung up.

She did half an hour of kicks and jabs, based on the tae kwon do katas. She tried to push out some of the anger and sadness that was in her. But, as before, found she couldn't. This time she clung onto it, balled it up into a small place deep in her belly. Her whole body ached. She took a quick shower, laid some clothes out on the bed.

She wanted an outfit that would not look pliant and girlie, but not too hostile, not something suggesting she'd lost the habit of enjoying herself with men. She chose her black woollen suit, the jacket short, the trousers flared but tight; it was about the most conventional outfit she owned. It hid all her tatts. She pulled her weatherproofs over it, went out to her bike.

By ten-thirty she'd reached the lines of small industrial estates on the outskirts of the city. The rain had eased into a light sleet, the skies to the west filled with grey snow clouds. Before the flyover, she took a lane that ended on the nearside of the estuary.

The area was mostly derelict, with few buildings on either side. At the end was a small motorcycle repair shop. The windows above were blacked out. The only sign of what lay within was a sign with some Japanese characters on.

The door was open but Catrin couldn't see anyone inside. The air was heavy with the smell of oil and old leather. Against the brick walls several old Hondas and R90s were stacked. It didn't look as if the place had much work. At the back were steps going up to the floor with the black windows. She hesitated for a moment at the bottom, letting her eyes linger over the walls.

In dusty frames were pictures of biking champions from years past. She recognised Jarno Saarinen, Mike Hailwood, Giacomo Agostini. She looked round to check she was alone, kissed her finger then placed it against the handsome Italian's lips. She smiled to herself. It was what she had always done at the foot of those steps as a girl. As if she was reminding him to keep their secret. It was the same gesture she'd used with Rhys.

Rhys had no surviving family that she knew of. His mother had died the year before hers. It had been another bond between them. No family, no close friends: Rhys had been a loner, like herself. But Rhys had trusted the local sensei, Walter, to teach her what he knew. She wondered now if that trust had continued.

The dojo upstairs was almost empty. The glass screen

from behind which Rhys had watched her was still there. From the water pipes hung more scrolls with Japanese characters. The largest, she knew, translated as 'Unity, Spirit, Path', the smallest as 'Fear No Man'. At the end by a mirror, two boys were practising. The smaller, with a buzz cut, waited as the taller ran at him. Gripping his wrist, he threw him to the floor. The taller slid away over the mats into the wall.

She saw a third figure in the mirror, and swung round. Walter was standing at the door of his office. He'd put on weight and his hair had thinned. Across his hakama, his black pleated trousers, he wore a wooden training staff, tucked into his black belt. As she bowed he recognised her. His eyes glistened as he beckoned her into the office.

She went to hug him but felt awkward and stepped back. Behind the desk were photos of Kyoto from the years he'd worked for Sony. He'd been at the Bridgend plant, part of the cultural exchange programme with Japan. Next to the pictures was a shelf with a row of origami birds on it. She saw they were some of the forms Rhys had mastered. The perching owl, the crane with its upright tail feathers and long beak. All the figures were covered in a thin layer of dust.

'Cat,' he said, 'it's been a while.' He pointed at the top of the stairs. 'I can still remember the first day you came in here.' His eyes were almost closed in a rapt expression. She had the sense he'd been expecting her. She felt bad for not having called on him earlier. Now he'd think she had only come about Rhys.

She let him go on about the past until the talk dried up.

'Rhys kept in touch?' she asked.

'Nothing,' he replied quietly.

'You must've seen him around town?'

He shrugged. 'Occasionally,' he said.

'Anyone with him ever?'

'No. He was always alone.' He paused. 'He avoided me. I think he was ashamed.'

'Of what he'd become?'

Walter was nodding slowly, sweat beading under his hair. From next door came the sounds of the boys sliding over the mats. Catrin gestured down to the bike shop and asked how business was. He told her it was slow. He looked at her as if he didn't care. She knew she should be feeling more of a connection with the man. He'd trained her, taught her all he knew. But it wasn't there. Rhys was in the way.

She caught Walter's eye and saw what looked like guilt there. She reckoned he was thinking of all those times he'd seen Rhys and done nothing to help him. Now he blamed himself. Maybe he believed she blamed him also.

She touched his hand. 'It's not your fault,' she said.

'It wasn't the smack that killed Rhys.' She held his gaze. 'Rhys was working on something. Someone silenced him.'

There were questions all over his face, but she got up, hugged him quickly, then went downstairs.

As she stepped out to her bike she sensed someone watching. She looked into her visor as she put her helmet on. A reflection of the trees by the water spun across the perspex. She glimpsed someone standing between the black trunks. She turned but no one was there.

She got on her bike and started it. The Laverda was about the only thing she trusted in the world. It looked old, a classic, but she'd customised it herself part by part into a mean street racer. The front discs she'd fitted with state-of-the-art Brembos so it could be ridden hard, the handlebars shortened to give control at high speed. The tank was fibreglass, lighter than the original but more capacious. The 1000cc three-cylinders she'd tuned to make quieter but as rapid as the latest Ducattis and Dukes.

In a few moments she reached the line of trees. She edged the bike slowly in among them. On one side was an empty lot choked with weeds. On the other a stretch of rough ground with no cover. She stared at the spot where she'd seen the figure. There was nothing there, only some ancient rusted cans and ahead the wind over the empty waters.

She rode back and took the flyover to Penarth. A thick, icy sea mist had obscured the view of the old pier and the channel. The streets were deserted.

She found Powell's office in a narrow lane one block back from the waterfront. There was nothing ostentatious about it: just an old warehouse with a large, polished steel door. There were no signs outside, just the street number. She parked between two muddy vans, and rang the single buzzer.

The door swung open to reveal a large hall with a floor of varnished pine leading to stairs. The two guards from the previous night were seated behind a desk, looking bored.

Above on the landing Powell's tall figure was just visible. He was wearing a suit of the same cut as the previous evening, in a darker blue. He smiled thinly at her and gestured to her to follow him. She saw rows of technicians sitting bowed over editing units, their backs to the doorway. All were peering at blurred CCTV camera footage, most of it showing high streets and club entrances after closing time, the usual drunken brawls and young couples in clinches in doorways.

She recognised the material immediately. It was a popular show that had been running for many seasons. The format was a simple one and had been franchised to many networks across the world. Each week clips were chosen from across the nation's CCTV networks.

Most were crudely comic scenes of drunken antics, sometimes violent, occasionally intimate and erotic. If the participants gave their permission, and surprisingly they often did, the faces would be shown. But in many cases they were concealed.

Powell beckoned her over to one of the monitors. A couple of young lovers with hidden faces were framed in a shop doorway, the woman kneeling on the ground, her blouse unbuttoned, to expose a breast, pale under the street light.

'And some people actually give their permission to be shown like that?' Catrin said. Powell turned back to the rows of screens, as if noticing them properly for the first time.

'Of course,' he laughed. 'Though we pay them. That helps.'

'So the pieces are set-ups?'

'Never. That's what sets us apart from all the other reality shows. The people you see don't know they're being watched at the time. What you see always is raw human behaviour.'

He was still smiling, and keeping a few paces' distance between them. She thought of how tactile he'd been with her the previous night, and wondered what had changed.

'It must have cost, the contracts with all the CCTV companies?' she said.

'It all took time, like any business does.'

Powell's voice sounded calm, remote, as if he was talking about something in the distant past that didn't really concern him any more. They walked along a long corridor that led to a private office. There were no external windows, she noted, the place was like a bunker. The room was divided into two sections by a lacquer screen with faded panels. In one there was just visible the image of a pigtailed mandarin bent over a woman, her robe rucked up around her waist. Beneath the screen were several racks of DVDs and audio tapes in a locked, reinforced-glass case. Beyond the screen, the inner section of the room was filled with more of these locked cases fixed high on to the walls.

Some held early Owen Face posters, others signed and framed photographs of the band before Face's disappearance. The case at the end contained what looked like unpublished designs for the cover of their third album, 'The Lower Depths'. The overall effect was not unlike looking into a small shrine or chapel.

'You've got quite a collection,' Catrin said. Powell was looking slightly embarrassed, apologetic. The first sign he's shown me of weakness, she thought.

He'd shown her to a chair that was high off the ground, ribbed steel, not entirely comfortable. She sat, crossed her legs, aware of his eyes on her all the time.

'The fire,' she said. 'Any actual evidence of arson? Any traces of accelerants, fuels, telltale oxidisers?'

'The specialist Fires Unit didn't find anything.'

She knew most fires usually left some traces of their origin. The Fires Unit were among the most thorough in the country; that they had found no traces meant the starters had either been lucky or very professional.

'Any threats to your person since the fire?'

'None that I'm aware of.'

'But you've hired those two bodyguards in case?'

He was opening the box she'd seen last night, taking out a pipe, putting some bags in a line on the table.

'You look a little tense,' he said. 'I thought you might like to unwind.'

She shook her head.

'Tense is how I like it when I'm working.'

Smiling, he pointed to the first two bags.

'Normal hashish, Moroccan, Afghan, Lebanese,' he said. 'It's made from cutting, heating, and pressing the flowering tops of the plant with cellulose, or in Morocco henna.'

'But those?'

He opened the bags, dropped pinches of the contents into the bowl of the pipe. 'These are temple sticks, made from the pure resin. From Melana and Melani.'

She'd barely heard of these places. In India somewhere,

she wasn't sure. 'You're quite a connoisseur, aren't you?'

'Well, the police training all those years ago had its uses.'

He took a lump from another bag, held a long flame under it until it softened, smouldered, giving out a soft bluish glow.

'Bombay Black,' he said. 'Five parts hashish, one part opium.' He let a few thin flakes drop into the bowl.

With a long splint he was lighting the bowl, taking a shallow puff. The smoke drifted towards Catrin's nostrils. She was beginning to feel high just on the smell of it. He passed the pipe across. It was a situation she knew she should have felt very uncomfortable with. She was a serving officer, this was a man she hardly knew. A rich man, powerful, trying to get her high, possibly to compromise her. But strangely she didn't feel that way. Something in her suggested the man was on the level, wasn't trying to take advantage of her. He was interested in her, yes. But quite possibly for exactly the reason he'd given her: because for her this would be personal, not just another job.

He'd left the pipe smoking on a small brass stand, on her side of the table. For a moment she was tempted, then she shook her head. He poured her a glass of wine.

'Now down to business,' he said.

It was that weird voice she'd heard on the phone. He was holding the smoke down deep in his lungs as he spoke. He'd begun to take out DVDs and was loading them into the player under the monitor.

'This is some background for you on the Owen Face case.'

'Rhys would have known most of this before he started?'

Powell didn't seem to have heard. The lights dimmed, then a picture of the members of Seerland gradually appeared on the screen. This was amateur footage, filmed from the side of the stage, the picture blurred and shaky. At the centre of the stage Catrin could see a young Owen Face, the spotlight behind him. His eyes were invisible behind dark smudges of make-up as he screamed into the microphone.

Powell pointed up at the figure of Face on the screen.

'Look how distant he seems from the others, off in his own world.'

She wasn't sure what Powell meant. Owen Face just looked like a typical lead singer to her, full of undying love for himself.

'Distant? In what way?' she asked.

He paused. 'Despite all his rock god posturing on stage, in private he seems to have been a very reserved figure. Solitary, unworldly.' There was a sudden focus to his voice now. Surprising after the strong cocktail he'd just toked up. 'He wasn't at all materialistic and he liked isolation. Apparently he didn't install a phone or a sound system when he moved into his flat down in the docks.'

The camera angle broadened to show Face flanked by his band-mate, Leigh Nails, a tall gangling youth wearing a ruffled shirt. He was bent over his guitar as if praying to it.

'Leigh was the real musician of the group,' he said. 'Leigh and Face were childhood friends, then shared a bedsit at university.' As Powell spoke he reached down to fill her glass.

'This was filmed at Cardiff University at the time they released their first EP. Face and Leigh had just finished their degree courses – Psychology and Philosophy.'

'And the other two band members?'

'The other two, Teifi and Jonnie, had already dropped out. They spent their days in dead-end jobs, the nights writing songs together.'

The camera was focused on Face, with Leigh Nails moving in and out of shot. The singer and drummer were no more than blurred figures on the edges. The next piece of footage had been released by the record company, but the camerawork was no more sophisticated. Again the focus was Face, his right arm windmilling furiously over his guitar.

The camera zoomed in, revealing several horizontal scars on his right forearm. Catrin leant forward in her chair, then looked up at Powell. He seemed to have anticipated her question.

'As you know, Face had a history of self-harm. By the time they signed their first record deal, he was making no attempt to hide it.'

'He got careless?'

'The cynics claimed he thought it added to his appeal with his teenage fanbase. Seen enough?'

Catrin nodded, then told him to continue. She had already seen the video that appeared next several times. It had accompanied the first single released after Face's disappearance, which had hit number one in the charts on a wave of sympathy for the remaining band members. Leigh, Jonnie and Teifi were filmed in front of a backdrop on which a series of images of Face were projected.

Catrin picked up her wine and took a sip. Powell showed her an image of Face as a cowboy-suited toddler. 'Face's mother gave her permission to Leigh and the boys to use the personal family stuff.'

'I thought she wanted to keep a low profile?'

'She did. I suppose she thought if he was still alive this childhood stuff might push him into making contact again.'

He picked up another DVD from the pile.

'Now you might find this interesting,' he said.

In the centre of the screen, Powell's company logo faded from sight. Then out of the dark, as in an old-fashioned film, a silent black-and-white scene gradually flickered. For the first minute or so the camera was static, seemingly attached to a tripod. Face, Leigh, Jonnie and Teifi ran in and out of frame, waving directly at the camera, making grotesque faces and mouthing obscenities.

They weren't wearing uniforms and Leigh had already reached his adult height, but it was clear that they were still schoolboys. Face stood directly in front of the lens, his mouth forming unintelligible words, while a giggling Jonnie made bunny ears with his fingers.

She put down her glass. 'Teen spirits?'

'Most probably.'

The action was taking place at the edge of a wooded area. The boys were running in and out among the trees. Teifi, the shortest of the group, was taking a flying leap at an oak tree and starting to climb.

In the next shot the camera was clearly hand-held. Face, dressed in a cape, carried a thin wooden stick, on the end of which was a card with a swirling op art design. He displayed this to the camera, then spinned it with his hand in an exaggerated, theatrical gesture, like a magician's assistant. He moved in a circle, the camera keeping him constantly in the centre of the frame. The combination of Face's movements and the throbbing of the disc was making Catrin's head ache. It was almost a minute before she sat upright and opened her eyes again.

Powell was staring down at her.

'Who was behind the camera?' she asked.

'That's what I'd pay good money to find out. This piece of film was found at his flat during the investigation into Face's presumed suicide. When they showed it to his mother, she said she didn't know anything about it.'

'And the boys in the band?'

'Nothing. Old loyalties die hard, especially when it's the police asking the questions.'

The DVD played on, images of the disc replaced by another outdoor setting. The thickly wooded area could have been the same one as in the earlier scenes, the camera moving unsteadily through gaps between trees, a muddy path occasionally coming into view. Catrin had a sense of motion sickness, and she shut her eyes again for a few seconds. When she opened them, the camera was approaching a tunnel, moving down a leaf-covered slope. Patches of frost glistened in the grass. Whoever was behind the camera was half stepping, half gliding down towards the blackness of the tunnel's entrance.

The screen went black, and then faint light pulsed against the walls and roof. The camera tilted downwards, showing rings of candles on the floor in the middle of which there was a slumped form. Face was kneeling on the floor of the tunnel, his shoulders shaking. A figure that could have been Leigh stood over him, immobile, frightened. Beside him lay some paler shapes, four limbs neatly arranged, and perhaps a head in a pool of dark and on the far side, near another figure, was a hammer. Dark splashes were visible on the lower part of the wall, partially lit by the candles. Face's head was jerking as he vomited, a thin trail of liquid hanging from his lips. Behind him something was growing in stature, something large and feathered with a long hooked beak. From its beak dripped the same dark liquid as on the floor and walls. The camera was spinning now, the images no longer clear, the walls shivering with a weak light. As Face turned to the camera, his mouth curled into a strange smile, the scene cut suddenly to a van parked at the back of a club, then the screen went black.

Catrin was trembling; she clenched her arms around herself to stop it. The images had been no worse than in many horror films yet she was being drawn in. Just as the photos of the men in the woods had done. It was as if something deep in her memory had just been shaken loose. Was this what Powell had really brought her to see? Was what she had just witnessed, not Face alone, the true centre of his interest. She recalled the elaborate crucifix above his door, it was almost medieval or primitive, as if it was there as much to ward off evil as an object of faith.

'What was that then?' she asked softly.

'The truth is, I don't know what it was. Over the years I've placed a lot of small ads in the local papers, offering money for any Owen Face related material. The guy who sold it to me said he found it at a house-clearance sale. I pressed him and he said that the house had belonged to a photographer who'd recently died, name of Gerard Butcher.'

'So you think this photographer might have been behind the camera?'

'Doubtful. I looked into this Gerard Butcher, it turned out he wouldn't have known the band at that age. He didn't even live in Wales then.'

'So how would he have acquired the film?'

Powell shrugged. He was looking ashen, a little unsteady on his feet, though she imagined he must have watched the film many times before. 'Butcher was an early fan, collected memorabilia. He was involved with the band through much of their career. Maybe he picked up the film among some other memorabilia, not knowing what he'd found. It's impossible to know now he's dead.'

'Those shapes on the ground,' Catrin said, taking a deep breath, 'the limbs and the head. What are they? Animal parts?'

As Powell ran the sequence again, he was half looking away, she noticed. He paused at the frame of pale limbs, the head shape on the floor.

'I had a specialist lab, the best there is, go over it,' he said quietly. 'It's just too dark, impossible to see.'

He left the picture frozen on the image of the muddy path barely visible through the thick trees.

'Could you make me a copy?' she asked. 'I'd like to have a closer look at the woodland, compare it to what we can see in Rhys's photos. Try to get some matches on the vegetation types.'

Powell was staring grimly down at her. 'That was the first thing I did when I saw them,' he said. 'I had the botanical specialist from the university in. He said both scenes show a similar type of deep woodland, all the plant forms consistent with the types in the national park in West Wales. We're talking of hundreds of square miles of some of the most inaccessible terrain in the British Isles. He couldn't even be sure the photos had been taken within Wales, the woodland appeared almost too virgin, as he put it. What he meant was there are no foreign species of plants in either scene. Apparently that's quite unusual, like seeing a glimpse of the woodland as it used to be hundreds of years ago. There are still a few pockets of deep woodland that remain. But with the dimness, the poor picture quality, he couldn't be more exact about the location.'

'What about the specific plant types, couldn't that narrow it down?'

There was a light slapping sound, as Powell dropped a copy of the botanist's report beside her chair. 'He identified the same plant types in the background of both scenes. Rowans, goat willow, downy birches, among the larger trees silver birches, sessile oaks.'

'Any symbolism there? Those trees in conjunction?'

'Plenty. From Celtic lore, from Anglo-Saxon lore, Wicca, you name it. But all very contradictory. Some to do with warding off evil spirits, some with conjuring them up.'

'So the places in the woods weren't just random, they were chosen.'

'Or they had associations before the scenes were shot there. But when my botanist did checks with Cadw and the Forestry Commission, he drew a blank on the location. All the ancient woodland is monitored fairly closely, all plant types charted, particularly those areas with past religious or cultic significance. But none of the existing databases had matches for these plant types in this combination in any known woods. It looks like the place has never actually been mapped, or like he said, as if we're looking at snapshots of an environment that doesn't exist in that form any more.'

'So what about this Butcher character, the photographer, any leads there?'

'Nothing. As I said, Butcher may not even have known he had the film.' Powell reached over to an envelope that lay on the table. 'He just hung around the band a lot, maybe filched things now and then that he thought might later have value as memorabilia.' He pulled out a sheaf of photographs and handed them to her. 'He took these photos just before Face's apparent suicide. They were for a spread in one of the glossy music monthlies.'

Catrin had seen the pictures, they'd been shown on all the news channels the night Face had disappeared. Face was sitting on an old sofa, hands folded in his lap, his posture prim as a debutante at a charm school. He was wearing a pair of striped pyjamas, all his hair shaved off apart from a thin stubble on his pale cheeks.

'Two weeks after these were taken Face gave his final gig,' Powell said. 'A couple of hours later his car was found at the services near the Severn Bridge. The rest is history.'

'What made Face do it? Assuming he topped himself, that is.'

Powell thrust his hands in his pockets, raised his shoulders.

'The most common theory is that it was an unrequited

love affair with Leigh Nails. But don't let all the frocks and kohl fool you. There's no evidence either of them were the slightest bit gay. The band just flirted with a bi image on stage – camped it up – smart move if you're attracting an army of teenage girls. They love all that gender-bending stuff.'

He switched off the DVD.

'As you can imagine, there are plenty of other theories out on the fanzine sites. Most along the "he didn't jump, he was pushed" lines.'

From the desk he took out a wafer-thin laptop. Catrin stood behind him as he clicked to the bookmarked 'Official Seerland Fan Club' portal. On the site was a photographic collage of Seerland throughout their history. He scrolled down to the chatroom icon.

'The hardcore fans who were there from the beginning have their own theory about Face's disappearance. A lot of them sound like men in their thirties who've knocked about a bit, know something of the music business. Most of them seem to believe that Face was taken out because of some internal band rivalry.'

'Isn't that a bit extreme?'

Powell nodded.

'Sure, they argued from time to time like any band. But saying that one of the others would have considered offing Face is not supported by any evidence whatsoever.'

'There *were* differences within the band, though?'

'Not really. Only minor ones, and only ever artistic. In reality they all got on well. If you look closely at the interviews at the time you see that Face never took much of a position on musical issues. He seems to have been careful to avoid conflict. The band rivalry theory put about by the older fans just doesn't stack up.'

He had scrolled down the chatroom page so that he could point out the thumbnail pictures posted by the regulars. Some were hairy, roadie types, but others looked like sharp-suited businessmen.

'Then there's the predictable conspiracy theories about evil record companies.' He laughed, a sharp, derisive sound.

She could see he wasn't taking this line of inquiry at all seriously. 'So who were Seerland signed to then?'

'They were signed to Euphoric, this small independent label. But they were snapped up by Sony, just before they hit the big time. The word on the street was that the boys at Euphoric were less than pleased.'

'You sound sceptical?'

'The music business is pretty cut-throat. I know for sure Seerland wasn't the first band to bail out on Euphoric just before they made it big. And feeling vengeful enough to murder one of the band members? I don't think so.'

'But it's grounds for a grudge?'

'Except that Face had nothing to do with the decision to sign with Sony, and Euphoric would have known that.'

'How come? Face was the front man.'

'But Face was completely indifferent to financial issues. Everyone knew that. He was an unworldly figure, distant, as I said. He didn't have many interests outside the band, and even there his role was rather a vague one.'

'So no real suspects then?'

'None at all. The truth is, Face's life was quiet, almost solitary. It's difficult to see how he could have made any enemies.'

Powell picked up his pipe again. 'All these theories have one thing in common,' he said. 'They all assume Owen Face is dead.'

'You don't believe that?' Catrin saw he was rolling the pipe along the desktop, trapping it under his hand just as it came to the edge.

'I'm not sure,' he said. 'But I'm pretty sure that if he is, he didn't die jumping off the Severn Bridge.'

7

Powell wanted to leave immediately for the bridge, but Catrin told him she needed an hour alone first. She asked him to meet her at a café she'd passed on the seafront. It had looked empty on the drive in.

She told him curtly not to bring his dope box, that she'd do the driving. He said nothing, only smiled. He didn't seem to mind her giving him instructions or if he did, he hid it well.

She asked him then if he was bringing his bodyguards.

'You're trained in close protection, advanced level. I'll take my chances.' He was showing off a bit, she thought, showing he still had access to internal police files. It wasn't a surprise that he still had friends in the force, she let it pass. 'And call me Huw from now on,' he said.

She did a drive-by. The café was still empty. She parked the Laverda back at Powell's office, took an indirect route through side streets to the seafront. No one was visibly following.

She sat at the rear, away from the window and the counter. The first thing she did was to call a number in the west, the number of the photographic shop whose sticker had been on Rhys's photographs.

The answerphone message told her the shop only ran an automatic, drop and pick-up service in the winter months. This didn't surprise her. The towns in the far west were quiet enough even in the summer. In the winter, they were ghost towns. But if there was a drop-off service, someone must be coming in to check the machine.

She ran a Google map on her phone, found the shop opposite, some kind of olde-worlde arts and crafts place. She called the number. After an age, a gentle Pembrokeshire voice answered in Welsh. The line was bad, perhaps it was the storms.

Catrin explained she'd had a problem with some wedding photos. She asked for the home number of the owners of the photographic shop. The voice told her they were away on holiday for another week. They came down to the shop on Saturdays to empty the machine.

She scrolled down, put the date in her diary. Looking up, on the next table she saw Della's face, staring back at her.

Someone had left a copy of the *Echo* open at Della's celebrity column. Either Della didn't have much to write that week, or her vanity had got the better of her. The entire top third of the page was taken up by a picture of the columnist.

Della was lying on a lounger in a large Victorian-style conservatory. She was dressed in a flimsy trouser suit which looked as if it was made of silk. The jacket was short, the trousers cut low. The deep tanned flesh between revealed a belly stud. It was an old picture, Catrin guessed, probably airbrushed too.

The image triggered a half-unconscious memory, a connection with something she'd seen in a different context. But for the moment she couldn't place it. The piece beneath was a thin story about a married female marathon runner who'd been suspected of an affair with her trainer, a former Olympian and well-known lesbian. No loyalty, not even to the sisterhood. There was a picture of both women on a sunlit racetrack, arms round each other's broad shoulders.

Then a short article inset into the column at the bottom of the page caught her eye. *Face Photos Are Fakes*. It was a single paragraph only, the sort of thing most readers wouldn't even notice before they turned the page. It said little, only that some photographs that had come to the attention of Della's agency had been dismissed as fakes. There was a small reproduction of one of the photos Della had already given her.

Three men in robes standing in a wood. The details were barely visible. It was a space filler, nothing more. The article didn't even give reasons for dismissing the photos as fakes. Nor did it state the source of the photos.

Usually in pieces about fake sightings, the picture took centre stage. The alien, the Loch Ness Monster, the missing star. But here the image was barely reproduced at all. She wondered why Della had even bothered. The pictures had come to her from Powell. He was potentially a dream client for her, a cash cow. This kind of casual, unsupported dismissal of his evidence would only irritate him.

Catrin looked up and saw an old woman standing over her, waiting to take her order. She asked for a coffee, glanced out at the street as the woman went to get it. No sign of Powell yet, he was taking his time. She felt a faint tingle of anxiety. She hadn't seen anyone in the streets between his office and the front, but it had been misty. Five minutes more, then she'd go back looking for him.

In the background on the radio a local talk jock was going on about how soft it was in prison. 'There are so many drugs inside, lads are coming to the nick to score like,' the raised voice said.

'Right, and call girls are getting in, pizza deliveries, you name it.' His guest sounded croaky, as if he had a cold. 'Costs more to keep the buggers inside than in the bloody Ritz.'

'And when they get released, the paedos, the child killers, they give them a brand new life. For their own protection, saves them from the lynch mob like.' He laughed as if it caused him pain. 'New name, makeover, nice new pad, the works.'

'Wouldn't mind that myself,' the guest said, 'a new life.'

'Except for them it isn't a new life, is it? More of a new disguise. Underneath they're just waiting to come out to play again. Some even get plastic surgery from one of them top Harley Street surgeons, all on the taxpayer, you couldn't make it up.'

She'd heard all these stories before, knew them for what they were, urban myths, bar talk. It was true that a few notorious criminals, like the Jamie Bulger murderers, were released secretly, given new National Insurance numbers and identities. She didn't approve but she saw why it was necessary. But the rest was just Chinese Whispers, unsubstantiated rumours, paranoid fantasies.

Outside she could hear a horn, and some music blaring. Through the mist, she saw a Lexus saloon, long and silver, parked at an angle half up on the pavement. It was next year's model, she'd seen them in the ads but not on the road before. Powell had driven alone despite her earlier instructions. She could barely see him for the thick smoke filling the car. Jesus, she thought, the man is a complete stoner. Either that, or he's done this to piss me off. He's showing me he doesn't take orders.

She tapped on the window. 'Move over, big shot,' she said, 'I'm driving.'

By the time they reached the Bristol Channel the sleet had eased. They had hardly spoken on the journey. Ahead now Catrin could see the orange glow of the warehouses with access roads to the motorway, and in the distance the lights around the Severn Estuary.

'Which way, Mr Powell?' she asked.

'Didn't I tell you to call me Huw,' he said. He asked her to pull in at the services. The place was deserted now the traffic went over the new bridge.

At the far end of the empty parking lot she saw a raised viewing platform. Huw – she thought of him as Huw already she had to admit – was pointing towards it without speaking. Through the curtain of drizzle, the bridge behind them was barely visible. The platform had been built at the edge of the cliff and the drop was immediate and sheer. The railings would have stopped a toddler from getting too close to the edge, but not an adult. Huw was gesturing at a low wall under the platform.

In the half-light at the base of the wall, there was just visible the remains of a small shrine. Several sprays of drooping flowers, handwritten poems in plastic covers. Among them was a rain-soaked bear with a Cardiff City scarf around its neck, looking out towards the estuary.

Huw showed her the empty tarmac by the wall.

'Face's Honda Civic was found along here after the last gig.'

'Not your typical rock star's vehicle.'

Huw was looking at her as if she'd missed the point. She remembered what he'd said about Face's unworldliness; here was another sign of it. Perhaps for Face a car was just a car, a means of getting places.

'How was the car parked?'

'Square up to the wall, very tidily.'

She knew there was nothing odd in that. It was usual for cars to be left that way by suicides. It was very rare for jumpers to leave their cars badly parked.

A gust of wind through the window caught the collar of her jacket, batted it against her face. Huw took out a tissue, passed it to her. 'Face's car was found here only two hours after he left the gig.'

She vaguely remembered there'd been witnesses who'd seen Face driving. A couple had sold their stories at the time about seeing him wandering near the edge but she couldn't recall the details.

Huw seemed to have read her mind. 'Two pump cashiers saw him, also some roadside workers. There's no doubt Face was the driver, no doubt he came here alone. There was also his blood on the seat. Not a lot, but consistent with the self-inflicted bleeding on stage. That positively places Face in the car after the gig, as photographic evidence showed he wasn't bleeding prior to it.'

'And the witnesses saw him walking by the edge, right?'

'Correct. They did.'

'So all the evidence seems to support the suicide hypothesis. Face announces his intention at the gig, self-harms there dramatically, then drives alone to the bridge. No one ever saw him leave here alive. The simplest explanation is usually the correct one.'

Over to the right Catrin saw a man leaning against the barrier at the edge of the viewing platform. He seemed to be gazing down at them intently for a moment. His face was covered by the hood of his anorak.

She tried to make out more details, his height, his build, but couldn't see much through the drizzle. Then abruptly, as if sensing her eyes on him, he bowed his head. He strolled slowly away until lost from sight.

She looked back at Huw. 'You've checked the forensics report on the car carefully, I imagine.'

Huw looked a little sheepish. He didn't have to tell her nothing had been turned up. If anything interesting had been found she knew it would have been raised at the inquest, which had been detailed and thorough. The same went for the whole investigation into Face's presumed suicide. Catrin knew they were going over fallow ground.

'And the car went where?'

'To Face's mother.' He pushed his hands into his pockets, stared through the half-light. 'I tried to buy it via her lawyer, she wouldn't sell. It went to the band after she died.'

At the end of the car park the man in the anorak was getting into a dirty grey van. The vehicle remained stationary, no lights from it behind the railings.

Huw got back into the car, in the driving seat this time. She didn't try to stop him. He reversed across the empty forecourt, spun the car round into a narrower lane to the right.

It cut through a steep wooded outcrop, out onto a promontory about fifty metres above the estuary. They passed the driveway to a building with faded paint-work, a sign outside advertising pub food.

Huw got out, and she walked alongside him to the edge. The wind was stronger here than it had been at the services, the gusts pushing at their backs. She watched as he picked up a stone and threw it out over the edge.

Beneath them the waves were a deep mauve, the colour of the sky reflected in the water. She heard a distant splash as the stone hit the waters and disappeared. The horizon was already growing dark.

Huw was hunching his shoulders inside his coat.

'Did you know that the tides in the Severn Estuary are the second highest in the world? Only the tides in the Bay of Fundy off Nova Scotia are higher. So we're talking about some very strong currents here.'

'So bodies get carried off some distance?'

'It's not unheard of for bodies to end up as far away as Ireland – several local misper cases in the past have been closed with the help of the Garda.'

He still used the police shorthand for missing person. Once a copper, always a copper it seemed. 'In that case it's not so surprising the body was never found,' she said.

Huw screwed up his eyes, still focusing on some point in the distance. 'That's where you're wrong,' he said. 'The sea always gives up its dead.'

'So the bodies usually return whole, then?'

'Not always. There was a case of a builder who got thrown over the bridge by loan sharks. A few years later he started to reappear down on the mud flats, one piece at a time. First a tibia, then a femur, then a few ribs.'

A seagull skimmed the tops of their heads, making a squawking sound that seemed too loud for its size.

'Then a while back they found that skeletal foot in a trainer in Caswell Bay. Everyone thought it was Face. The press were all over it, but it turned out the foot belonged to some sixty-year-old alkie who'd jumped a year previously.'

'So what are you saying? No body, no suicide?'

'The laws of probability are against it. This would be almost the only case in twenty years where the body hasn't returned in some form.'

'Unless the body has already been recovered, by some hardcore fans perhaps, and buried secretly.'

Huw was already shaking his head.

'The bodies don't come back at predictable times and places. They'd have had to search hundreds of miles of coastline for months. Face's hardcore fans in those days were a scruffy, spaced-out crowd. They'd never have had the resources for an operation like that.'

Catrin remembered what had first bothered Rhys about the suicide story.

'But why d'you think Face came all the way down to the bridge from the gig? Why couldn't he have topped himself at the concert hall?'

'No one really knows. It may just be that he wanted to go by his flat first, collect something or drop something off perhaps.'

'But the team never found anomalies at the flat.

There was nothing left there or missing. It would've come out in the inquest.'

'No, there was nothing there at all.'

'No signs of a clean-up either, I presume.'

'The place was exactly as those who visited it remembered it. Empty apart from the basics.'

'Nothing weird in there that they would've ignored at the time but would tie in with the film? Dead animals, masks. That kind of thing?'

'Nothing like that.'

'Anything that would link with the photos in the woodland? Robes? Maps of the west?'

'No. And the flat was so bare, things like that would have been noticed. Nothing had been touched. His paperwork was all there, his passport, bank statements, bank cards and several savings accounts.'

'But no withdrawals in the months prior to the date of his going missing, no run money.'

'Nothing. The inquest showed royalties and fees from the band as his only source of income. He wasn't a big spender, as you can tell from the Civic.'

'And his flat, he owned it?'

'Correct. It's not there any more because of the docks redevelopment.'

'But there were photos of the interior at the inquest.'

'Only small-scale to support the forensic checks. He never had it redecorated, there wasn't even a single piece of art in there. He never splurged on drugs and partying, any of the typical rock star's trophies. He lived austerely. No television, no sound system, no luxury articles of any type. He didn't even have any girlfriends that we know about.'

'What about political interests, hobbies, private causes?'

'Nothing like that. He seems to have lived quite separately from the world around him.'

Huw took his briefcase from the car and went ahead of Catrin towards the pub. It didn't seem to get much custom now the new road had been built. Beneath the terrace area, the car park was empty. The path led up between barrels filled with black earth to an archway, one of the doors loose and fretting in the wind.

At the far end the doors opened onto a patio where piles of rusted garden furniture were stacked and chained to pillars.

The place was deserted. At a table in the corner Huw opened the case, took out two maps and spread them on the table. The first was a map of the world, the type that hung on the wall of schoolrooms, the different countries clearly demarcated by colour. The other was a 1:250,000 scale map of Wales. The maps were covered with dots in different colours. At the corners he'd placed ashtrays as weights to hold the paper down against the wind.

On the map of the world she could see clusters of green dots over Southern Europe, and blue ones in Asia. The barman brought a light to the table along with their drinks. It was a spotlight, on a stand, the type that might be used in a presentation.

He angled the beam over the maps, turned off the overhead lights, then closed the door and left them alone in the hall. Evidently the man had done all this before. It felt almost like a routine.

She waited for an explanation of what was going on. All the time Huw was smiling thinly, staring at the maps.

'Don't worry, I own this place,' he said quietly.

'This old pub?' Catrin glanced around at the dim surroundings.

'Right, it comes with all the land down to the bridge. I didn't want it going to developers, any potential evidence getting lost.'

She looked at him. 'You really are obsessed with this Face thing, aren't you?'

He didn't reply. He was running his fingers around the green dots on the map.

'These represent the cluster of sightings in the first years after Face's disappearance,' he said softly.

'Anything even remotely plausible?'

He was shaking his head.

'Most can be discounted. These areas, the Canaries,

Ibiza, Cyprus, were where a lot of Face's rank-and-file fans went on holiday. In most cases the sightings were late at night in bars. Too much sangria and the imagination starts to work overtime.'

'And the blue dots?'

'The ones in Goa and Kerala were reported by older, diehard fans, out on spiritual quests of self-discovery. It's known there was a culture of psychotropic drug-taking among this older fan group. So the reliability of these later sightings can largely be discounted.'

He began to point, more carefully and slowly this time, at the clusters of dots over the high-detail map of Wales. He told her these were the sightings reported in the last two years. There were fewer dots and they were less diffuse. Many of the sightings had been out in West Wales. There were several in Tenby, Newgale, the typical holiday spots. But the wild area to the north, the part where Rhys's photographs had been developed, this seemed almost clear of marks.

'None to the north. What could that tell us?' Huw cleared his throat.

'It's isolated, the boondocks. Either they haven't heard of Face, or wouldn't recognise him if they ran into him.'

The expression on his face told Catrin that she was missing the point. She realised he was reading a significance into the absence of sightings, presumably seeing it as a sign that the locals might know Face was there and were protecting him. She knew at once this was far-fetched, stoner's logic, not evidence of anything at all. She crossed her arms, sighed, looked at him hard and sceptically.

'Face's not even from there, though. His family were from further east. As far as I know he's never had any connection with that area.'

'Of course, you're right,' he said. Huw looked genuinely apologetic. 'I'm sorry, I've been lost in this Face mystery too long. The sad truth is I've gone down so many blind alleys, run in so many circles over so many years, I've begun to clutch at any shadows I can.'

'These sightings you've mapped, are any of the sources even credible?'

'Varied. Reports published in local newspapers, gossip in the band's chatrooms. Official, unofficial. There's a fair bit of speculation out there.'

She nodded, took out her iPhone and opened a couple of pages she'd bookmarked. 'I checked through them all last night,' she said. 'After I left your place I was up half the night. Nothing I found stood up at all to serious scrutiny.'

'Nothing?'

'No, not really. The ones out in the west mostly come from unofficial chatrooms. These characters seem your classic paranoid types, secretive, changing names, moving all the time. If they appear on the same site more than a couple of times, they get flamed. But there was something about the writing style that was similar. Maybe the same small group is behind them.'

She looked down at Huw's hands, noticed that they were clenched tightly around his glass.

'There are some strange ideas out there,' he said slowly.

'I noticed that,' she smiled, 'mostly stoned ramblings.'

He glanced out of the window, then back at her.

'Some of the weirder ones seem to be coming from an individual who calls himself Overseer. He uses that name on all the unofficial sites and he seems to command particular respect from the other users. He posts very irregularly. Months can go by before there's anything new from him.'

Catrin thought she'd seen a movement through the window. It was dark now, the shapes outside vague beyond the glass.

'So what does this Overseer have to say about Face?' she asked.

'Funny thing is, this character doesn't actually talk about Face much.'

'What then?'

'He seems to be peddling a strange theory, about

how some of the fans from the early days, who tried to find Face after he disappeared, have themselves now gone missing or died.'

She smiled again. 'Right, sure. Any actual names?'

'The only name I recognised was "Gerard Butcher", the photographer who was the source of that weird footage of Face in the tunnel.'

She put her hands up to her face, looked at Huw sceptically again. 'But this Butcher character didn't even shoot that film.'

'No, we don't know how he came by it.' Huw was starting to shake the maps, fold them back along their well-worn crease lines.

'Anything even remotely suspicious about this Butcher's death?'

'Not really. He'd been an alcoholic and a heavy drug user since he was a teenager. He died from a heart attack.'

Huw put the maps in his briefcase and locked it. He finished his drink in one swig. Through the patio doors Catrin could see at the bottom of the overgrown garden a row of yellowish lights, their faint reflections bobbing and glimmering in the waters. Outside heavy rain had started falling again. As they left, the barman was still standing by the windows looking out into the dimness. She wished him goodnight, as Huw pushed past him silently.

Down the driveway the wind was blowing twigs and discarded cartons across the yard. The dim shape of a van was just visible, parked under the swaying trees. There was no movement inside, no lights. Its snub nose facing out towards the waters it looked like the same van that had been up at the services. Catrin moved closer, trying to read the plates.

Huw had begun to cross towards the trees. There was a sudden flicker as the vehicle's lights came on, the whine of its engine rising through the wind.

For a moment they were blinded as the van swung forward, towards them over the uneven ground. It lurched straight at them, not stopping.

8

Catrin detached herself from Huw's arms. 'He was coming straight for us.'

'Probably drunk and didn't see us.' Huw was walking down to the Lexus. 'You know how they are out here.'

'No, not any more I don't,' she said. In silence they drove back across the bridge, along the road into town.

She cracked the window, kept a fresh stream of air around her face. She changed pace a few times, slow, fast, checked for tails. Nothing. There was no sign of the van behind or ahead of them.

Huw reached for a pipe hidden under the console. A small chillum, with carvings around the bowl, an antique by the look of it. He tamped it up and lit it. She didn't bother to try to stop him. He told her to go straight to her motel. His people would be waiting there he said, they would accompany him back to his office.

The pipe smelt strong, another cocktail. But when Huw spoke he sounded sober, focused. 'Anything I've told you sound like a credible lead yet?' he asked. She told him she'd run checks on Butcher and the Overseer, report back the next morning. But she made it clear to him that both lines of inquiry would likely end nowhere.

The footage he'd shown her seemed strangely still imprinted in Catrin's mind when she blinked her eyes closed, as vivid on her retina as if she'd just watched it. It was inside her now, like a bad taste that just wouldn't lift. Those dim shapes of the four limbs on the floor and the shadow rearing up over the wall. But as it was among Butcher's possessions at his house-clearance sale, she figured the photographer might not even have known he owned it. And this Overseer character, he was probably some online nut.

'You must think I'm just another eccentric recluse, clutching at the shadows of shadows, trying to draw you into the web of my obsession,' Huw said finally.

She told him she didn't know if he was or not. All she did know was that by obtaining the Face photos Rhys had put himself in danger, and now it was her duty to see the job through.

Huw asked her a few questions about herself, her career, her family. It was all very polite, very conventional. But he sounded genuinely interested in her answers. He wasn't looking at her in the way he had done, at her mouth, or down at her thighs. He became quieter, seemed increasingly lost in his own thoughts as they drove to the motel.

When they arrived she saw the two bodyguards sitting in the lobby, an identical Lexus parked outside. With them was a hard-faced man in his fifties, well-groomed like a news anchor, probably one of Huw's executives.

Huw got out, escorted her to the door. He was subdued as he shook her hand gently. He seemed genuinely sad to be parting from her, and strangely, she noticed she was feeling the same way.

Back in her room, Catrin called the photographic shop out in the west where Rhys's pictures had been developed but got the answerphone again. She then called all the shops in the same street, asked if the owners had left contact details before they'd gone on holiday. None of them knew where the owners had gone, and they hadn't left any contact details. She noted again the date of their expected return, in three days' time, and that they lived above the shop.

Then she booted up her Mac and ran searches on the National Criminal Intelligence Service database of aliases and gang names. She went into all the regional force databases. But as she was expecting, she came up with no matches for *Overseer*. A quick check on Butcher's Police National Computer record confirmed what Huw had already told her. The photographer hadn't moved to Wales until several years after the film in the tunnel would have been shot.

Then she clicked into the website of Huw Powell Productions. It all looked conventional enough. There were short excerpts from reality and clip shows the company was airing. She scrolled down into the section containing the company reports. Those for the last five years were all on file.

Remembering her forensic accounting at Hendon, she looked for the telltale signs. But everything seemed straightforward. The cost structure was exactly what would be expected of an independent production company, mainly salaries and the various production budgets. The company was making respectable seven-figure profits every year, mainly from its foreign rights sales. There were some write-downs relating to development costs for shows that had never been bought, tax-efficient donations to a series of academic and local charities. No unusual outgoings, no signs of any off-book accounting.

The only thing that struck her was how little Huw Powell himself featured in any of the material. He was listed as sole owner, but appeared to have had little hands-on role in the company's affairs for years. The executive type she had just met in the car park was listed as CFO, and directly managed all the sales and production teams. At most of the board meetings Huw Powell was not even listed as having been present.

It looked like Huw had had a lot of time on his hands, time to get high and indulge his obsession with the Face mystery and get a little lost, maybe. Catrin wondered if this had made him a man others were now trying to take advantage of. Her instinct was telling her that rich men with obsessions were often singled out as potential marks, as victims. She didn't think people were right to see Huw like this, but she could see why they might do.

She clicked to the site of the private bank the cheques to Rhys had been made out on. It was a tax-planning vehicle, incorporated in the Caymans, and used as a platform to re-invest the company's offshore revenue streams. There was nothing illegal or improper about this. The practice was common enough, and looking in detail at the company reports Catrin could again see no sign that Huw had much role in the bank's day-to-day management.

She did a few online searches on his name. There was no sign he courted publicity on behalf of the company, no sign he'd particularly avoided it either. There were photographs of him with Branson, John de Mol and executives from Endemol and other well-known media players. There were reports of his attending industry events, some old gossip pages linking him to various glamorous local women, a news anchor, an opera singer, an actress on a long-running S4C show. This last she noted was from the online version of Della's column. Most of these reports pre-dated his interest in the Face story. In the last few years, Catrin noticed, Huw had kept more and more out of the limelight, possibly as his interest in the mystery had increasingly taken hold of him.

Still, Huw seemed to have led a pretty charmed life, the only cloud over his head those old rumours about his resignation from the force all those years previously. Chances were this was in no way related to current events. But it was something Catrin knew she'd need to follow up on, if only to eliminate it.

She remembered now that DS Thomas's father had also been an officer at around the same time Huw had been serving. And immediately she wished she hadn't. Thomas's door was the last door she should be knocking on. But his father would have been a contemporary of Huw's at Cathays Park, might well even have served in the same unit at the same time.

The father was dead now, she knew that, but then Thomas had a good memory. That was how he got by, doing so little on the job, by remembering things others had to graft to find out. She phoned Thomas on his mobile, asked him if he wanted to meet for a drink. He sounded half asleep as usual, but he accepted without hesitating. He was acting as if he wasn't in the least surprised she'd asked, as if he'd been half expecting it.

'This isn't a date,' she said firmly.

She said she'd meet him at a car park off the Newport Road. That way she hoped she wouldn't have to depend on him for a lift back. She knew only too well what that could lead to.

She washed and changed quickly, then headed out with the Cowboy Junkies on her iPod. She didn't like to play music on her phone. A phone left a trace, an iPod used only in play function didn't. This was how she liked it when she was working: as few traces as possible.

She checked her phone before she switched it off. She saw a text from Della, just asking her to call if she needed help. She wondered what she knew.

She tried closing her eyes for a moment, but the image of Face over those shapes on the floor and that strange unearthly shadow on the wall were still floating there as vivid as before. She walked out into the dark.

At the car park, she got into Thomas's Audi, let him drive the rest of the way into town. She could tell it was a mistake from the start. She'd chosen an outfit that said she wouldn't be messed with. Her hardest biker boots, a short combat jacket over an army-issue

T-shirt. But his eyes were all over her. Everywhere except her face. He smelt heavily of strong cologne, never a good sign.

He played his fingers through the wires to her earpieces, following them down to the unit on her belt. He scrolled down the tracks silently for a minute, then just passed it back to her without a word but laughing to himself.

'Okay, so what have you got on yours?' She put it in her pocket, feeling angry already. '*Top Gear*'s all-time greatest tracks to take a dump to?'

Thomas said nothing, stared out at a few drunks walking past carrying bin bags towards an all-night burger bar across the street. He revved hard, pulling out fast and almost knocking over some of the drunks. To cool him down, clip his attitude, Catrin told him to take the street behind the station and to pull up outside a terraced house there. It looked like all the other houses in the street, but for her it had a special significance.

Whenever she'd had doubts about Rhys, she'd come to this house or pictured it in her mind. It was the scene of his greatest triumph, a place where he'd been brave and pure. That was how she always wanted to remember him, not as that low degraded figure in the CCTV.

'Know what happened in there?' she said. Thomas

was playing dumb, drumming his fingers on the steering wheel. He knew exactly what had happened there. She pointed down towards the cellar floor.

'That was Angel Jones's dungeon.' It was beneath them in cells below street level that Jones had kept the girls he'd raped and mutilated. The media at the time had played it as the city's greatest shame. He'd kept his victims there for years drugged out of their minds, then left them for dead in the woods, and it was Rhys who'd busted him, and he'd done it alone.

'But that was just a fluke. Everyone says that.'

She knew this was partially true, the bust had been a stroke of luck but in her eyes it didn't take away from the bravery of what Rhys had done. She noticed Thomas was smiling to himself.

'Rhys never made a big deal of it, did he.' He glanced at her knowingly. 'That's cos Rhys was shaking down the guy who sold Jones the drugs he used to spike the girls. Then he tailed Jones's van from there, blundered into Jones's house without back-up. Probably thought he was going to shake some other little guy.'

'Rhys still collared Jones, got cut doing it. That took balls, more than you'll ever have.'

Thomas was still looking his usual laid-back self, he didn't seem to have risen to the bait. She felt relieved. As they pulled away he slowly turned to her, caught her eye.

'But didn't Della have a thing with Angel Jones?' he said quietly.

'Come off it.' Catrin had to laugh, this was definitely a wind-up, his comeback for the detour. 'Della's shameless and twisted, but she's not suicidal.'

'No, for real,' he said in the same quiet tone. 'I heard Rhys might've busted Jones before when he went with Della, to get Jones out of the way like.'

She didn't believe any of this for a moment, didn't even bother to reply. She wondered how reliable the rest of Thomas's information was going to be if this was the kind of number he was trying on her already.

Thomas circled for a couple of minutes until he found a parking place. The building across the small, empty square had once housed the all-night club where she used to meet Rhys before she got to work in the mornings. In those days it had been patronised by hardened drinkers looking for a place to escape their troubles, a low place with threadbare carpets and beer-stained tables.

Now she could see the building housed another club on the ground floor, its lights raking over the pavements. Inside the place was dimly lit, the warmth due more to poor ventilation than to any heating system. At the back of the room the dance floor was empty apart for one couple moving slowly in a tight clinch. A bow-tied attendant, dressed like a relic from a Sixties

Soho sex club, showed them to a table in the corner. Catrin ordered a beer. Thomas asked for whisky, a double. He was looking around him as if only just aware of their surroundings.

'This place has gone upmarket.' He was still speaking quietly, she noticed, though there was no one else in earshot.

She glanced over at the couple on the dance floor. It was impossible to know whether the pair were amorous or just clinging together to stay upright. Thomas had closed his eyes, his head swaying back in rhythm to the trippy beat. She wondered looking at him how much he'd been drinking already that evening.

'Your father,' she said. 'He ever tell you much about his time on the force?'

He sat back in his seat, an exaggeratedly wounded expression on his face. 'Okay,' he said. 'I get this. Another pumping session.'

She was leaning back, out of his warm breath, trying to see what his eyes were doing in the dimness. 'Huw Powell,' she said. 'Your father ever talk about him?'

'Not much.'

'But he must have said something about him?'

'Powell was a career copper. A graduate, fast-tracked up the ranks.'

'Career cop doesn't mean good cop.'

'He was that also, apparently. A good officer, one of the best.'

Thomas was rubbing his palms together, shrugging. She took a sip from her drink, keeping her eyes on his. 'So what went wrong? There's been a cloud over Powell's name for years.'

'Just envy most probably. Powell leaves the force, does well for himself. Money always breeds envy.'

She could see from his face that Thomas knew more, but he wasn't going to spill without something back from her. What could she give him, apart from the obvious?

'Della Davies,' she said. 'I've got tight with her. I know she usually hires women, but she can also use a male investigator. She's a payer, as you know.'

It wasn't subtle, but it seemed to have worked. She saw his eyes narrow, his mouth resolve itself into a brief grin.

'I don't know that much,' he said.

'Give me what you've got.'

'Powell was a specialist,' he said. 'A watcher. Surveillance, hidden microphones, long-distance lenses, that kind of thing.'

She smiled to herself. 'I get it. So that's the link to those hidden camera and CCTV shows he does.'

'That was much later. In his day he used his surveillance skills on drugs gangs, on acid gangs using labs hidden way out in the country.'

'Which parts?'

'The far west, the wilds. Powell was from there originally, used his local knowledge. His family were yokels, from the back of beyond.'

Catrin waited for a moment; something Thomas had just said sounded potentially interesting. 'These labs Powell busted way out in the west country. Hidden in remote, dense woodland, would they have been?'

He was shaking his head. 'Doubtful, mostly they operated from out-of-the-way farms with track access for the equipment. This is all from way back, the pre-computer period. It's unlikely the details will have been retained except in court documents. Why do you ask?'

'It's only that among the materials Powell has on Face's disappearance there's a strange home movie set in remote woodland. I'm just wondering if there could be any connection between something Powell might've stumbled on all those years ago and his interest in Face.'

'Unlikely,' Thomas said. 'If he'd stumbled on something other than the labs out there, why wouldn't he have taken action at the time? Why wait several decades before following up on it? Doesn't make any sense.'

She nodded, took his point. He was right, it didn't really make sense. 'No suggestion Powell ever turned a blind eye, took hush money from the crews behind the labs?'

'No, Powell always played it by the book, he was methodical. He could conceal cameras and mikes in almost anything. He knew how to track chemicals and equipment up and down the underground supply chains. His skills took down some of the biggest illegal labs operating then.'

'So he'd have made enemies, rivals in the force?'

'Not really, he was more of a back-room boy. A nerd, a techie, kept his head down. He didn't get up anyone's nose.' Thomas had shifted a little closer to her and was staring down at the floor.

Catrin waited, but he didn't raise his head again. 'So how does all this connect to Powell's resignation?'

'Two or three years before he left, Drugs stumbled on a big lab in Heath Park, near the university.'

He was glancing at her lap, then lowered his eyes. 'An acid lab?' she asked.

'I don't know all the details. Just that it was a highly professional set-up, everything state-of-the-art. They had twenty-kilo Rotorvaps, the latest freeze dryers, self-cleaning vac-pumps, the works. The kit there was more sophisticated even than in the university's research labs. There was a long sting operation to catch the people behind it, and costs spiralled. At the time it was one of the biggest ops of the kind. The budget even needed special Home Office approval.'

'Who did the sting net in the end? Someone big?'

'No one, that was the problem. It ended up a very expensive failure.' He took a piece of paper from his pocket, a newspaper clipping now yellowed with age. Gently he unfolded it, and laid it on the table between them. Catrin could see a picture of a small nondescript building near the university, its few windows covered with closed black louvre blinds. Inset into the picture was a photo of a younger Huw Powell. His hair longer, his eyes brighter, filled with something that looked almost like inspiration.

She picked the paper up, looked hard at Thomas. 'What's this? You a mind reader now? How the hell did you know I'd be asking about Powell?'

She thought she saw a small glint of triumph in Thomas's eyes. *He wants to please me maybe, but for all the worst reasons.* 'It's a small town,' he said quietly. 'Word's already out you're working some gig on the side for Powell. It doesn't take a psychic to guess you'd be wanting to talk about him.'

She quickly read the article below the picture of the small, almost windowless building. The details were sketchy but the basic thrust of the piece was clear. An illegal lab busted near the university had triggered the longest and most expensive sting operation ever mounted by the South Wales Drugs Squad. When questioned, the press office at Cathays Park had refused to comment on whether the operation had justified the time and resources put into it. Next to this section appeared another small photo, of the new Chief Constable, a younger Geraint Rix. He was pictured walking down some steps, alone, his eyes down, looking into the distance. He seemed to be in a hurry, the shot was blurred. The article ended with unnamed police sources quoted as admitting the operation had proved a highly costly failure.

She looked up at Thomas. 'And you think Powell walked away with some of that money, used it to start his TV business.'

'No. I think that's unlikely.'

'How come?'

'Because my old man said he remembered Powell living in some bedsit down in the docks after he resigned, surviving on baked beans.'

'Powell could just have been playing it long, making it look as if he had come away with nothing.'

'Doubtful. He was broke for several years. His business started small, grew slowly.'

'So you're saying Powell was clean. It just looked bad. His resignation just happened to coincide with this huge spend by the unit?'

'Exactly. He left the force because he had a good business idea. No other reason. It was the dawn of reality TV. He had his surveillance know-how, got in on the ground floor. It was all hard work, there was no mystery cash injection.'

'Simple as that?'

'Well, you know what they say. Every surveillance man is a frustrated film-maker.' Thomas laughed quietly, said nothing more. He knew more, she suspected. Or maybe he was just stringing her along, hoping she'd put out.

She stared at him, prepared to wait him out. He let his hand rest lightly on her upper thigh. With a surge of anger she pushed it away. Then he arched his other hand to her shoulder, his mouth suddenly hard up against hers, his tongue trying to force its way into her mouth. She pushed him back, his chair fell against the pillar behind in the dark.

He put his hand up to his head. There had been something sharp on the side of the pillar, a nail perhaps. Blood was dripping through his fingers. He turned away from her and fumbled in his pocket for a tissue. She got up to help him, but he waved her away.

'You were always afraid to let go,' he said quietly.

He held the tissue to his head, and gestured her to come closer again. She shook her head; his smile appeared slightly pained now.

'You've got a top memory,' she said. 'All the time you've been pretending you'd forgotten me, I knew that was an act.'

'Perhaps you've changed?' he said slowly.

She glanced at him, then away towards the couple dancing.

'It wasn't me that needed to change,' she said.

He was looking straight into her eyes.

'That's not how I remember it. I was just a normal bloke, you suddenly turned on me.'

'That's crap. You got me drunk, then you took advantage of me.'

He was looking at her wide-eyed now, as if what she was saying was self-evidently absurd. The truth was she couldn't even remember that clearly. She'd only been used to Rhys then, only really known Rhys. Any other man touching her had felt like an act of violation.

Thomas was letting her keep her distance, his body slumping back in mock defeat. He reached across, through the struts of the chair, and touched her softly on her knee. In a tender way, not threatening.

'Hey,' he said. 'It was a long time ago. We have to work together. Let's not worry about it too much, eh?'

'You haven't given me anything on Powell,' she said.

He leant his head back against the pillar, his shoulders drooping, as if surrendering to her cold reasoning. 'Listen. Powell had always been a good officer, very diligent, quiet. But then apparently at the end he just freaked out a bit.'

'In what way?'

'Began smoking dope, not even bothering to be discreet about it.'

'He still smokes, big time. So that was the reason he resigned?'

'By then he was going to resign anyway, to start his TV business. If he left under a cloud, it was just a cloud of his own smoke.'

'Like a pupil who knows he's leaving flaunting the rules.'

'Exactly. He'd his big idea, knew he was leaving, didn't give a monkey's.'

She stood up now, concentrated on slowing her breathing. Thomas was staring at her, an expression of concern on his face.

He took out another tissue, dipped it in the whisky and held it against his head.

'Powell's a decent guy by all accounts,' he said. 'A head, sure, but solid.'

'Yes, I think he is too. In fact, I know he is. But I'd like to know more about that sting op.'

Thomas flicked the ball of tissue. It hit her jacket, bounced off onto the floor.

'I can look into it,' he said. He hesitated, smiling slowly. 'But I want you to treat me like the normal man I am, that's all.'

She jerked her knee away from his hand. 'That means something like you want me to give you head whenever you fancy some. But we behave the rest of the time like nothing's happening?'

It came back to her, but broken and blurred like a bad dream, something she'd always preferred not to remember: how when she'd been half senseless with drink he'd jammed her head under the steering wheel. What he'd done then, there hadn't been much gentleness to it.

'I should've reported you for assault,' she said quietly.

Abruptly he stood up, the action tipping his chair back, and moved towards her, his hands clenched into fists. The waiter was standing in front of the table but Thomas was still staring across at her.

The drunken pair on the dance floor stumbled apart as Catrin walked away along the edge of the floor. The place seemed suddenly much brighter. The colours of the neon pictures on the walls were merging with the blue light. A man further back was bowing his head, as if to hide his face, like the figure they'd seen on the platform above the estuary. The man in the van. Was it the same man? In the shaking light she couldn't be sure.

At the bottom of the steps she turned left. The sleet had stopped, the streets behind her were silent. She could hear no footsteps following.

Catrin glanced at the terraced houses on either side, some newly painted, others boarded up with faint lights behind the dark hoardings. Behind her now she could hear a light squelching sound. She recognised it immediately. The sound of high-soled trainers moving over damp pavements. She turned round. The street behind her was well-lit and appeared empty.

She moved on again, taking faster steps. Around one corner, then another. She stopped and listened. The sound was there again, nearer this time, just the other side of a row of high hoardings overgrown with ivy.

She waited, her eyes on the corner behind her. There, some way back from the road was a man in an anorak, his hood up. He looked very much like the man she'd seen at the service station, but in the half-light it was impossible to be sure.

Now she had her eyes on him, he paused, hesitated, neither moving towards her nor away towards the terrace of houses. She thought she glimpsed the flicker of something in his right hand, maybe a blade.

She turned, moved on to a gate that led through a small fenced area of public gardens. Once through the gate she began to run.

The ground beneath her feet was uneven, covered with broken paving and roots, and several times she lost her footing. She could hear nothing behind her, only the surge of her breathing and the blood singing in her ears.

On the other side of the gardens was another gate, beyond it an empty parking area. The gate was locked, there was no way through. She ducked down behind the wall and glanced back at the path.

At first it seemed nothing was moving there. But gradually she began to make out a thickening of the air between the trees. A man was walking very slowly towards the wall. His head was raised and moving from right to left, like a dog scenting the air. From his right hand came a momentary shimmer in the darkness.

She couldn't make out his face, just long dark hair drooping down the front of the hood that covered his face completely like a mask. Catrin had the strange sense that behind it there was nothing at all, just a pair of yellow eyes, no face. She moved silently deeper into the shadows. She reached down, dialled Della's number.

On the second ring the receiver was picked up with a dull clattering sound.

'I think I'm being followed, Del.' In the background she could hear music.

'Where are you?'

Despite the late hour Della sounded wide awake.

'At a car park. Round the back of the Hayes.'

'Keep walking down towards Queen Street. Someone'll be waiting for you there.'

Not looking back, she climbed the wall, pulling herself up on the squares of flint embedded in the bricks. On the top were shards of glass. She reached between them, hauling herself to a crouching position on the ridge. Behind her she heard a shuffling sound, then the wind hard on her neck. She dropped down on the other side. Her ankle hurt where she hit the pavement. She ran past the block-like façade of the Golden Cross, on towards the Hayes.

The clubs and pubs there had closed some hours before. The shopping precinct looked empty. Catrin leant down over the flower beds, catching her breath, then walked on towards Queen Street. A car flashed its headlights at her. It looked like a minicab, a small dark saloon. There were coloured beads hanging from the mirror, a silver plaque of holy verses on the console.

The driver's window opened a crack as she came alongside.

'For Ms Davies?'

She got in. The driver looked East African with a broad bodybuilder's chest and a long sorrowful face. The seats were covered with throw cushions, like a sofa, and smelt of sugared almonds.

The driver turned and looked over his shoulder at the hooded figure moving fast towards them from between two parked lorries.

'What are you waiting for,' she said, 'just fucking drive!' With a muttered curse the driver sped off northwards. A couple of minutes later she felt the car slow again. Outside she recognised the tall Regency terraces of St Andrew's Crescent, the polished brass plaques of city-centre solicitors and upmarket recruitment agencies.

The car had stopped at one end of the street outside what appeared to have once been a chapel, now converted, according to the developer's sign, into office space. 'Up there,' the driver said. Above the black railings there were lights on behind the stained-glass windows.

Although the car had pulled over, the driver didn't get out. Catrin walked up the steps, a camera in the fanlight swivelling towards her as the door clicked open.

Inside the large space was almost empty, a flooring of some greenish-streaked rock leading up to a mezzanine with desks around a seating area. At the top she saw Della bowed over a screen, her face lit by its pale glow.

'I was being followed,' Catrin said. 'When we went up to the service station to see where Face's car was found, we were tailed. Then when I left the club the same man followed me.'

Della was standing at the top of the staircase. The tapping of her heels echoed across the large empty space.

She didn't stand back so Catrin had to brush against her as she went past. She smelt of vodka and some very expensive scent. Catrin paused, stared at her until she backed away.

'You've been drinking. You're probably seeing things,' Della said.

'Speak for yourself, Del.'

Della held out a cheek, air-kissed her, then turned back to a couch shaped like a giant baseball glove that stood against the wall. Della's hair hung in limp trails over her face, and her eyes looked tired, bloodshot.

In the corner was a door, half-ajar, to another space, a large cupboard it seemed to be. Along the wall were packing cases filled with files and computer equipment. A framed spread from a magazine featuring a house with a large conservatory, Della's weekender in the Mumbles Catrin presumed. Beside the cases a filing cabinet lay on its side. The drawers were open, the contents lying in untidy rows on the floor.

'What's this, Del? Moving out in the middle of the night?'

Della turned away, seeming to ignore the question, and reached down to a bottle of vodka by her side. What remained in the bottle she poured neat into two tall glasses, passing one across the table.

The suit Della was wearing looked just like the one she had worn in the picture above her column. As she took the glass her hand was noticeably unsteady.

'What's wrong, Del? You seem edgy.'

Della glanced over at the empty space below the mezzanine.

'You think that man followed me here?'

Della had finished her glass in a single swig. She kept her eyes on the area downstairs. She didn't reply.

'Let me tell you what I think's going on here, Del.' She looked again at Della's suit, smiling to herself, then straight into Della's tired eyes. 'You hear about Powell's obsession with Face. You smell a big money opportunity.'

She saw Della wasn't reacting yet, no tells. 'You know people won't connect you with Rhys because you put an injunction on him. So you hire him to hustle Powell, bait him with some phoney photos.'

'Nice idea. And then?'

'Then Rhys gets greedy, tries to shake you down. You get into a tussle with him that gets caught on CCTV. You're wearing a slutty suit just like the one you've got on. Then later that night you get him offed down on the beach.'

'How do I do that?'

'Junkies are soft targets. They're just one fix away from death. You set him up with some strong gear, roll him into the sea.'

Della was smiling, seemed genuinely amused.

'Look, I did meet Rhys that night. I'd worked out

from what Powell told me the photos must've come from Rhys.'

'You're lying.' Catrin moved closer to the sofa.

'But I only wanted to find out where Rhys had got them. He took some cash off me, told me nothing. Except that he'd got the photos from a good source. Rhys said it was someone who knew you.'

'Knew me? The source knew *me*?'

'That's what Rhys said. He said it was someone who trusted you, Cat. Rhys said if anything happened to him, you would be the link to the source.'

Catrin looked hard at Della, tried to make sense of this, but couldn't.

'And you told Powell this, about the source knowing, trusting me?'

'I had to give him something, after all the money he'd put up.'

'*That* explains why Powell wanted to hire me, then.'

Catrin still couldn't make any sense of what Della had just said.

'Who the hell was Rhys talking about, who's the source?'

'If I knew that I'd already have sold it to Powell. That's why I wanted to hire you myself. You're the only link there is to the source.'

'That was all Rhys said?'

'Yes, and that was the last time I saw him alive.'

'You're lying.' Catrin slapped Della hard across the face. She didn't move, made no attempt to resist. Della was quivering, her mouth pursed open. Catrin slapped her again, saw she was bowing her head, her eyes glazing over slightly, her breathing fast. Della seemed to be waiting for more blows to fall. The bitch is actually getting off on this, Catrin thought.

She stood back. There was a slight smile playing over Della's lips, her cheeks were glowing. 'I shouldn't have lied to you about meeting Rhys,' she said. 'But I had nothing to do with his death.'

Della's dishevelled hair covered her eyes. 'And if I was trying to set up Powell, why would I have dismissed the photos as fakes in my article?'

She knew Della had a point there. She let her go on. 'Powell brought me those photos, told me to look into them, just like I told you,' Della said. 'I worked out they came from Rhys, so I contacted him and what he said led me to you.'

Catrin saw she'd made a mistake. Della had probably been telling the truth. The photos had come to Huw from Rhys exactly as Huw had described, and Della had known nothing about them until Huw had shown them to her.

She'd let her anger at the woman cloud her judgement.

Catrin felt bad at what she'd just done. She sat beside Della on the sofa. 'I'm sorry,' she said.

Catrin held her drink without sipping. She could feel Della softly touch her hand. She wanted to pull away immediately, but something stopped her. The anger had gone for the moment, replaced by a sensation that was calmer, more accepting.

She felt Della's lips brush hers, barely touching, just hovering there.

'You're drunk, Del,' she said. She turned away.

Tentatively Della reached her head up and tried to kiss her very gently again. Catrin didn't move her lips, but she didn't pull away. She let it go on for a moment, wanted to know what Rhys had felt. Maybe some flicker of him still lingered in what he had once felt for this woman.

'You want to know what we did, don't you,' Della was whispering.

Della was kneeling on the floor. She slipped the jacket off her shoulders, let it fall. She had pushed her trousers down to her ankles. It felt unreal, like some sort of bizarre joke, but Catrin could tell Della was serious.

She watched Della bowing her head, then crawling slowly across the floor, glancing back over her shoulder. Della suddenly lay still, like a puppet whose strings had all been cut. Her thighs were covered in thin, evenly spaced bruises.

Catrin crouched down beside her, but didn't touch her. 'And then, what did he do?' she said.

Della said nothing, just pushed her hand up to her crotch, began lazily clicking her fingers, as if calling for a waiter in an old-fashioned film or keeping time to some slow, half-remembered beat. Catrin saw now Della was just trying to taunt her. She pulled one of her arms up hard behind her back. Della seemed to be enjoying it, but Catrin carried on until she didn't any more.

'Angel Jones, did you ever know him?'

Della said nothing, so she pulled her arm back tighter, and she whimpered slightly. 'I met him a few times, that's all.'

'Why, Del? You got a death wish or something?'

'I didn't know what he'd done to those poor girls, I swear.' Della was sweating, the make-up smudging on her face.

'How did you know him then?'

'It was via a girl I met off a BDSM site, just a bit of fun, that's all.'

'Nothing Jones did made you feel he was dangerous?'

'No, he played strictly by the rules.'

'And the other girl off the site was one of his victims later, was she? Bet you got off on that, didn't you?'

'No, it wasn't like that.' Della sounded on the verge of tears now, but there was a note of genuine outrage in her voice. 'This girl had him eating out of her hand. She was dark, cloudy eyes, gorgeous, I fancied her rotten. I only went along because of her.'

This wasn't what Catrin had expected to hear. Jones was a monster, but here was a glimpse of another, more vulnerable side to him. Catrin loosened her grip a little. 'This other girl, what else can you remember about her?'

'Not much. She seemed a bit spaced-out, into Seerland, played their stuff constantly.'

'Like half the girls in the city at the time.'

'Right. I wanted to see her more. But she always wanted Jones there, so I just gave up in the end.'

'And Rhys knew you'd met Jones.'

'No, I never said anything about it to Rhys.'

'So how did DS Thomas know about it?'

'Because Thomas makes it his business to know nasty things like that.'

Catrin let go of Della's arm. She felt bad again for what she'd just done. Della was brazen and ruthless, but she probably wasn't actively evil. She briefly stroked Della's arm, and felt Della gently stroke her back. She sensed a calm again between them, an understanding of sorts.

Catrin noticed again the half-open door in the corner. She thought she could see something that looked odd inside, not right for an office.

She walked over to it.

She could hear Della padding across in her bare feet behind her, the tinkling of the pendants on her ankle chain the only sound in the large hall. Della was trying to steer her back towards the couch, blocking her path to the door. Catrin pushed her away.

'What's in there, Del?'

Della didn't reply, and she eased her way past Della's unsteady figure. She saw some broken blinds taped over the dormer window, a large mattress in the middle of the floor. Beside the unmade bed lay two open suitcases, a tote bag, several blister packs of pills.

'What's this, Del? Sleeping over at the office?'

Catrin walked over to the bed. Between the cases were some discarded dry cleaning bags, an overflowing ashtray, more pills. Xanax, zolpidem with an address in the suburbs on the prescription packets.

'Not sleeping well? Guilty conscience over something?'

Catrin could feel Della's breath close on her neck scented with the night's vodka. From behind she heard the clicking of a lighter, as Della lit a cigarette. She said nothing still.

'Something's not right here, Del. You're a successful businesswoman, but you're living out of a suitcase. You've moved out of wherever you live, hidden out here for a while, now you're packing up, moving on again.'

With a long sigh Della had sat on the bottom step, her shoulders hunched up under her jacket.

'Sounds like you're getting paranoid, Cat.'

'I don't think so. I call and you're wide awake. It looks like you're sleeping in different places every night. You've got Mr T outside on call at all hours. You're frightened of something. What is it you're not telling me?'

'I've told you everything.'

'No, Del. You're scared of something. I could tell it the other day when you came to see me, but it's stronger now.'

Catrin saw another laptop by the bed, some old copies of the *Echo*.

'That's why you wrote the piece in your column, wasn't it? You wanted it to look like you weren't interested in the photos.'

Della was standing behind her now, absolutely still. She seemed to catch her breath for a moment before she spoke.

'That night I saw Rhys.' Della's voice was weak, she wasn't trying to hide the fear there any more. 'I felt someone was watching us, someone was following him. Then the next day someone broke into my house, ransacked it. I've felt I've been watched, followed ever since.'

'Then?'

'Then I heard about the arson at Powell's office,' she said. 'I thought it best to hire some protection, lie low.'

Catrin sat down on the chair, taking this in. She felt suddenly very tired. A part of her wanted to lie back, close her eyes, fall away into a deep sleep from which she would not return until it was almost dark again.

'I think it would be safer for both of us if you stayed here tonight,' Della said.

'All right, but no more fun and games.'

Catrin rolled over from the chair onto the bed. She heard Della in the bathroom for a few minutes, the water flowing. Then Della came and lay with her back to her. She fell asleep almost immediately.

9

Catrin sat astride the Laverda in a back street off the Newport Road. She was smoking her second of the morning, trying to clear her head. The surrounding streets were quiet, everyone was already at work. She'd woken late to find Della gone. The office empty. No notes, no messages on her phone. From Della's she'd gone to Huw's office, picked up the bike. He hadn't been there.

She thought back to what Della had said about the source of the photos being someone who knew her, who trusted her, that if Rhys died she, Catrin, would be the link to the source. But it still made no sense. She didn't know anyone interested in the Owen Face mystery. She didn't even know any journalists or music business types.

She wondered again if Rhys had known she was back, remembered again how close he had been to her hotel when he'd died. Had her initial instincts been right, had he been trying to reach her that night? But why? What would he have wanted to tell her after so long? Or was it a warning of some sort? The more she thought about it, the less sense it all seemed to make.

The source was someone who trusted her, Rhys had said. But the list of those close to her was small. Her family were all dead. Her father she'd never known. Her colleagues were colleagues no more. Her lovers she met in clubs and online sites. She lived a life of deliberate, almost anonymous isolation. She trusted no one, so who would choose to trust her?

But there was another sort of trust, one not earned directly, but conferred by association. Surely this was what Rhys had been talking about. She would be trusted because Rhys had told the source that she could be, because after all these years she had been the one *Rhys* still trusted. She had no choice but to follow the same trail Rhys had followed, and see where it led.

Catrin looked at her watch: half an hour to kill before her appointment. She glanced at the navigator App on her phone, double-checked she'd come to the right place. During the night a text had come through from Huw, telling her he'd arranged for her to meet the remaining members of the band at a studio one block away. She'd deliberately got there early, to scope the surrounding streets before she went in. But there wasn't much to see, just the walls of warehouses, the few shops between them boarded up.

The tinkle of a radio floated out onto the street. She reached into her pocket for her iPod, but it wasn't there. In her hurry to leave Della's she realised she'd left it behind.

That wasn't the sort of mistake she usually made. She would have to go and pick it up later, not a prospect she relished. She still had her cigarettes and her phone, though. And the photo of Rhys, the one she'd printed from a still in the CCTV footage, in her breast pocket next to her heart.

She checked her rearview, then looked up the road ahead. No one had followed her. She left the bike fastened to the railings, walked round the block in the opposite direction from where she was going, then doubled back to the entrance of Shift studios.

She heard the chanting before she turned the corner. Three security guards stood close to the doors, a crush of teenage Goth girls jostling each other behind red velvet cords. They were chanting the names of the three surviving band members with one voice at the blind windows of the façade above.

Catrin pushed through the crowd, made her way up the steps to the guard in front of the smoked-glass doors. She reached into her coat and brought out her warrant card, held it close in front of his face. He spoke into the two-way radio clipped to his jacket, then held the door open for her.

He opened a second set of heavy doors in the hall just enough to let her pass. She smiled, and he led her over to the lifts. As they came out on an upper floor Catrin felt a vague sense of claustrophobia, and concentrated her gaze on the framed photos along the walls. At the end of the passage some heavily built men were pulling out large black cases from the mouth of the goods lift. All were dressed in black trousers and sweaters, their heads shaved, and on the back of their sweaters the crest of a London-based private security outfit.

As the men stood aside, the guard ushered her into a larger space with long glass panes facing back along the passage. The windows had been blacked out.

At the far end she could just make out the three surviving band members. Teifi appeared small and frail behind his drums, while Jonnie, almost as short, but stockier, was huddled in conversation with a petite blonde woman with a laptop on her knees. In the shadowy space behind them Leigh Nails was standing alone, seemingly in a world of his own, his Les Paul slung around his neck as he ran through chord progressions.

As the guard led her closer and her eyes adjusted she was surprised to see how much older Jonnie and Teifi looked than in photographs. Jonnie's hair was thinning, his brow creased with deep lines, while the shadows around Teifi's eyes belonged to a man many years his senior. Of the three Nails appeared to have changed least, his eyes were still bright and alert, but his prettiness was almost gone, his cheeks hollow but without definition. His plain trousers and shirt betrayed none of the extrovert glamour she had seen in the earlier videos.

The blonde woman's puckish features were creased into what appeared to be a habitual expression of irritation, which she made little attempt to hide. 'The boys are putting down tracks on the new album,' she said. 'They're busy. You've only got a couple of minutes, okay?'

Teifi put down his drumsticks, but did not step out from behind his kit. Jonnie had moved fractionally closer to him, their faces blank as children in a class too advanced for them. On the platform behind, Leigh slowly took his guitar from around his neck and rested it on the floor, not looking at Catrin.

'I suppose that none of you have heard from Owen Face?' she asked softly.

Jonnie and Teifi did not look at each other as she spoke, then Leigh slowly raised his head.

'Do you know how long we've known each other, Owen, Jonnie, Teifi and me?' Catrin noticed at once the weary, impatient tone in his voice. 'We used to play in the same sandpit when we were babies. Do you think we'd forget to pass on that we know he's safe and well?'

She held up a hand and nodded to show she understood. The expression on Leigh's face was a mixture of incredulity and hostility, but Teifi and Jonnie were more difficult to read.

'Any idea why Face might have been putting away money into several bank and building society accounts?' Catrin asked.

Teifi cleared his throat.

'We never talked about money, financial arrangements, that kind of thing. But Owen was never much of a spender, he was most likely just putting by the money he didn't spend.'

'He didn't spend, didn't have girlfriends, didn't like cars. Not exactly your typical rock star, was he?'

She could hear a vague murmur of assent from the shadowy space above her, but no one spoke. She stepped closer to the platform.

'He spent a lot of time alone, didn't he, when he wasn't with the band?'

The only sound from the platform was the tapping of someone's shoes.

'And when he got depressed he'd spend a lot of time alone?'

'So what? What are you getting at?' It was Jonnie

speaking now, in a weak, reedy voice that sounded both pained and impatient at the same time.

'Can you remember which rehab clinics he went to?' she asked.

'He didn't like people to know. He always kept that side of his life private.'

'So much of the time none of you really knew where he was?'

From the platform came another weary murmur of assent. Catrin continued. 'His flat's plain, not like a home, no pictures on the walls, not even a phone or a television. He spent a lot of time alone, but no one knew where he was. It sounds almost as if his real life was somewhere else, doesn't it?'

The three men were still looking down at their instruments. Nothing in their manner told her that they were the least surprised or interested in what she'd just said.

She let her heel rest on the edge of the riser, tried to catch the attention of the hunched figure behind the drums. He was looking over her head at something behind her.

'So you didn't notice anything different in his behaviour in the days before he disappeared?'

She could hear Leigh sucking in his breath.

'Look, no offence, but we've been asked these questions many times before. No, we don't know where Owen is, no, we don't know why he left, no, he hasn't been in touch. We've all of us shed tears for Owen but it's no good. He's not coming back.'

Behind the drums, Teifi was shifting his weight from one foot to another. He peered at her.

'We've just had to move on, as a band and as individuals.' She had the sense he'd had to use these same lines more times than he could count. He'd spoken to her in that soft tone reserved for the very old or very young, people who can't understand the obvious.

'So none of you heard from him after his car was found at the bridge?'

Leigh turned his back on her, picked up his Les Paul.

'No, nothing. He obviously jumped, didn't he,' he said in the same weary voice.

Teifi picked up his sticks again, and twiddled them in elaborate circles around his shoulders. Jonnie was looking down at some notes on his lap. Catrin knew that she'd have to be quick now.

She took out the image of Rhys, the still she'd taken from the CCTV footage.

'Any of you ever see this man?' She held it out. Jonnie took it, passed it to the others. They all looked, shook their heads.

'One final thing. Did Face have any connection with the far west, the national park area?'

Leigh looked for a moment as if he was giving the

subject some thought, but he might equally have been admiring his guitar.

'When we were starting out we did a few gigs over in Narberth. That's the nearest Owen ever went to that area, far as I know.'

'He never went there on a break, even a short one?'

'Not as far as I'm aware.'

She picked up her bag, stepped down from the platform.

'By the way, do any of your crew drive grey vans?'

'No, ours are white.'

Leigh had already turned away, his expression calm and far off. He walked slowly into the shadows, resuming his search for a lost chord.

The back of her throat felt scratchy and raw, her head sore from last night's drinking. The guard had disappeared, so she made her way back down the corridor alone, stopping in the empty hall. She found a machine that offered a selection of soups and hot chocolate and dug in her pockets for change.

'You should have used one of the others. Everything tastes the same from that machine.'

A lone figure was standing in the doorway. Like the roadies she'd seen earlier, he was shaven-headed and wore black trousers and a turtleneck. But his jacket looked worn, his trousers as if they hadn't been washed for a while.

'Here, let me.'

He fed money into another machine that offered only coffee. Catrin noticed that he did everything with his right hand, the lower part of his other sleeve hanging down in a knot, as if empty. When he spoke his mouth barely moved, his voice was a whisper. She removed the plastic cup from the dispenser.

'Thanks. You must be a veteran.' She eyed his jacket: 'You been with the band a long time?'

He said nothing, looked past her. The sound of foot-falls further down the corridor had distracted him. He moved away abruptly, making for the door. Catrin caught up with him, put her free hand on his arm in the doorway. He looked back at her, his anxiety obvious.

She managed to guide him back into the room. She stirred her coffee without taking her eyes off him.

'You were there with the band in the early days, weren't you?'

He nodded, glancing down the passage. Catrin saw that an old wound that ran from the corner of his eye along his jaw-line had been stitched clumsily. The brief smile he gave her came out as a grimace.

'You must have got to know Face then?'

'No. He wasn't someone you ever got that close to.'

As he began to turn away she put her hand on his arm. He looked towards the door again, motioned to her to keep her voice down.

'Nobody here knows anything,' he said. His voice was a whisper that she had to strain to catch.

'Who then?

'If you're serious about this Face business, there's only one of them left now who knows anything.'

'Who's that?'

He glanced again at the doorway. The corridor outside seemed empty.

'I don't know what his real name is, he used to be a late-night pirate DJ. He's used different names over the years. Nogood Boyo, Captain Cato, later he used the name Overseer.'

'How would I contact him?'

'He's gone to ground out in the country north of Pontardawe.'

'Where?'

'That's all I've heard. There was a fire in the pirate station where he was working. He ended up badly burnt. No one's heard from him for years.'

The roadie didn't say anything more. He walked quickly away through the doorway.

The rush hour was over, the streets cold despite the bright sun, and quiet. Catrin parked further up by the station. Huw had left another text, telling her to meet him in half an hour, in the main concourse. There'd be lots of people about there, dozens of cameras.

He obviously wasn't taking any chances. He'd chosen a safe location to talk, not a wireless phone connection. He was using a different number to text her from each time. She wondered if this was another precaution.

Less than a hundred yards along the street, she found an internet café. She walked past it a couple of times, in each direction, looking in the shop windows. No one was following her.

The café seemed empty. The neon sign in the window was switched off, the windows dark. At the back there was a bar area, a Gaggia machine and a line of juicers on a shelf under which an Asian boy sat reading.

Catrin ordered a coffee, sat at a computer away from the window. She found a site that contained Ordnance Survey maps of all the country north of Pontardawe. It allowed her to zoom into any area up to a scale of 1:25,000, and was detailed enough for her to see farm buildings. She panned the scale back, to see the area as a whole first, the lower peaks around the A4069 giving way to the wilder, sparsely inhabited regions of the Black Mountains and the Beacons to the north.

Saving the map, she clicked onto the internal access page of the only Severe Burns Unit in the region, the West Glamorgan NHS Morriston Burns Unit. The patient waiting-time stats showed an adult intake of approximately one thousand patients each year, and of those only thirty were severe burns cases: the in-patient files were held behind the standard NHS double password system, a single password for the unit and another for each authorised user.

She clicked straight over onto the initial patient admission files for the unit: these were low-security, the single password overridden by her last Tri-Service pass number. Searching by postcode, she brought up a young girl from Llandybie, the victim of a school arson attack who'd needed reconstructive surgery, and an elderly man caught in a house fire in the Ammanford area. But there were no other matches. After a few minutes she managed to access the National Burns Injuries Database and run the same postcodes, but there was nothing there either.

Next she tried a keyword search on 'Overseer' and 'Captain Cato' on the National Criminal Intelligence System database, then on Google, but again found no useful matches. She panned back to broaden the area, including the lower reaches of the Cambrians to the west. She keyword-searched the names of every farm, peak and feature on the map in conjunction with 'Nogood Boyo' and the other handles. But still no links came up apart from references to Dylan Thomas.

She noticed that one of the other characters in Thomas's play was called Captain Cat, only one letter away from 'Captain Cato'. Perhaps the old roadie had got the name slightly wrong. She tried a search on Captain Cat, and came up with links to a variety of fishing tackle shops and tourist souvenir shops to the west. She double-checked the addresses but all were in the coastal regions, with the exception of one. A fish restaurant called 'Captain Cat's in the rural Garnswllt area, north-west of Pontardawe.

The photographs on the website showed a large building located next to a minor road. On the walls inside she could make out several framed fish hanging alongside sepia photographs of old fishing steamers. The section entitled 'Who we are' showed a picture of the elderly husband and wife team that ran the restaurant. Both, the section said, were originally from the South London area. But when she checked the names on the NCIS, neither flagged up any form, nor did the pair have any connections she could see to the name 'Cato'.

Going back to Google, she typed in 'Captain Cat's restaurant' alongside the name of the nearest village 'Garnswllt', and was directed to a single link: the website of the *South Wales Evening Argus*. Their internal search facility revealed only one article on the place.

It seemed the original establishment had had some connections to the art deco style. There had been a short local campaign to save the building. It was shot from a variety of angles, showing the neon signs, the rounded corners and clean lines of the original structure. These were contrasted with more recent pictures, which showed the changes under the new management. These later shots had a grainy quality, presumably because they served no architectural purpose. Some were of the interior with its nets and lobster pots, the rest of the building's altered front. In the last two shots, the focal points were two signs, erected at each corner. Catrin looked from one to the other, but noticed nothing out of the ordinary. The flowers blooming on the verges identified the time of year as late spring or summer, and the trees on the drive threw deep shadows over the walls behind the signs. One of the signs just read 'Captain Cat's'. The other was identical, but with an arrow that would have lit up at night, pointing towards the door. It took more than a minute for her to notice what should have been obvious from a quick glance. Her brain had fooled her, making her see what she had expected to see, not what appeared in the image. The darkness on the white wall behind the letters was not a shadow, but the stain of soot from a fire.

The same blaze had warped the apostrophe and the 's' at the end of the name into a single rough oval, so that from the road the sign now read 'Captain Cato'. Catrin thought about this for a moment. She looked under the arrow of the sign to where the soot was darkest, but saw only a small, blackened shape, perhaps once a small statue of the captain, now barely human in form. As she peered closer she could just make out the face and the stumps of the arms visible in outline against the damaged wall behind. The thing reminded her a little of a voodoo doll, of something burnt in sacrifice.

She could imagine the place being referred to as Captain Cato's. There was a possibility the restaurant was where Overseer had picked up the name. If this was the case it suggested some connection or familiarity with the area. It wasn't that far from where the roadie said the man had moved. But she knew she was groping in the dark.

She clicked back to the detailed map. The restaurant lay several miles north of the village of Garnswllt, just at the start of the A4069, which wound through the hills to the small town of Llangadog. After this lay the Black Mountains. On either side of the road were small hamlets and isolated farmsteads. By the time she had made a note of all the relevant information her coffee was cold. She left her cup by the computer, and picked up her jacket.

Outside the sky had darkened. A thin, icy rain had begun to fall. Catrin fastened her collar, pulled it tight at the neck to keep out the cold. As she leant into the corner she noticed a tall figure in a suit walking between the rows of cars.

He was followed a few paces behind by a younger man carrying two laptop cases: a male secretary type with a brush cut, a shiny suit. A car was waiting, its back doors already open. With a gallant opening of his palm, the taller man ushered the younger one in. Then the man paused, glanced back at her. It wasn't Huw, though from a distance they looked a little similar.

It was many years since she'd last seen him in the flesh, but he didn't feel like a stranger. He'd appeared on all the late-night *Newsnight* shows, the ones she so often fell asleep to. His position as head of the Association of Gay Police Officers had made him a regular there. The chief was smiling but she wasn't sure at what. There was no one else near him. His suit had a fashionable herringbone pattern. His hair was full still, dyed jet black. He looked every inch the media player and politician-in-waiting he'd become.

She'd hoped he hadn't seen her, but he was coming towards her now. Catrin straightened up, held out her hand.

'Sir,' she said, 'it's been a while.' Immediately she felt stupid saying it. Maybe he made a point of greeting everyone now his business was to be popular. He looked down at his feet, seemed almost lost for a moment.

'I was very sorry to hear about Rhys,' he said quietly.

Apart from Pugh, it was the first time someone had said it to her like that. His eyes watered over, then as quickly the wind dried them.

'I'll always regret not looking out for him more.' He said this more hesitantly as if speaking his thoughts aloud. Catrin wondered if he'd been coached to sound sincere. Usually she could tell the real thing, but here she wasn't sure.

It was on his watch that Rhys had left. She remembered Rhys joking a few times how Rix had a crush on him. There'd been nothing in it, she was sure. If there had been, Rix would have intervened in the Internals inquiry that had spat Rhys out, but he hadn't. After the failed drugs tests, Rix had let the disciplinary procedure take its natural course. He could have saved Rhys but he hadn't.

Rix asked a few questions about when she'd be fit for duty. He said how much they were all looking forward to having her back. He held her gaze for a moment longer. He seemed to be weighing something up, but then he walked away towards the car, his brogues gleaming in the lights over the parking area.

She noticed Huw now standing by his Lexus. He was wearing a long black cashmere coat, and he looked much like the other businessmen coming out of the station. There was no sign of his bodyguards. Quickly she walked him into the station. Inside it was much warmer, the windows clouded by steam. She glanced back: it didn't look as if anyone had followed them in. She chose a table not exposed to the concourse.

Huw came back with the teas and was blowing on his, clearly in a hurry to drink it. He hasn't lost the common touch, Catrin thought, still likes a warm cup of builder's tea.

'You ever hear rumours about Rix having a crush on Rhys?' she said.

He raised his eyebrows. She knew what he was thinking, it was a rumour attached to almost every young male officer in the force at one time or another. If there'd been anything to it Thomas, who kept in with Rix, would have likely made an aside to her about it. She decided to let it go.

'So, what happened in the studio?' he asked, still holding the cup.

'Before I get to that, I need to tell you about something that happened last night.'

He waited, his eyes on hers.

'It was as I left a club. A man there looked like the one in the van. He followed me from the club to the Hayes. His face was covered by long hair.'

'Did you get a look at him?'

'No. None of his face was visible behind the hair. It was dark, and Della sent a car to pick me up.'

'How did she seem?'

'Frightened, very drunk. She was in some temporary office space in St Andrew's Crescent, sleeping on a mattress on the floor. She's been moving around for a while, living out of a suitcase.'

'What's her line?'

'She said she'd met Rhys the night he died. She'd worked out from what you'd told her that the photos came from him. She heard from Rhys that I was someone the source of the photos would trust, that I was a link to the source, that was why she came to me. And presumably that's also why you came to me?'

He nodded. 'Of course,' he said. 'But it doesn't seem to have led us anywhere, does it?'

Catrin felt her old fear of failure creeping back like a fever. 'You feel I've let you down?'

'No,' he said. 'Of course not. So what's spooked Della?'

'When she saw Rhys that night, she got the sense he was being watched. Then the next night her house was broken into, ransacked.'

'So whoever was following Rhys came after her also?'

'Seems that way.'

Huw sipped at his tea. He looked concerned, disconcerted. It was the closest she'd come to seeing fear on his face.

Suddenly she felt protective. She couldn't bear to disappoint him. Strange to feel this about a rich, older man, but there was something lost about him, something vulnerable there. Maybe his money had protected him from the world too long. Behind his stoned eyes she thought she could sense a certain innocence.

'I'll need to speak to Della again,' she said.

She sipped her tea, avoided his eyes.

'So what happened at the studios?' he asked.

'Face is history, it seems. They've all moved on.'

'Did you speak to Leigh Nails?'

'Yes, and to Jonnie and Teifi. The only person who would talk was one of the old roadies.'

Huw looked up over the table, questions on his face. She put down her cup.

'That Overseer character in the chatrooms. The roadie mentioned that he'd used other handles as well. No one has heard from the man for years. Apparently he used to be a pirate DJ. But he was seriously injured in a fire at work. Then he went to ground up-country. I did some digging online. He may be living somewhere in the Garnswllt area.'

'What makes you think he's out there?'

'One of the handles he used – Captain Cato – could come from the name of a local restaurant. The place is called "Captain Cat's", but one of the signs has been warped by a fire so the last letter reads as an "o". I just have a sense about it. It was the only reference I could find to the name anywhere. I don't know what connection he might have to the place, maybe a very casual one.'

'This character is too under-the-radar to have given a traceable address at any burns unit?'

'I checked. Nothing for that area either at the Morriston or on the National Burns Incident Database.'

He drained the last of his tea, looked across at her.

'But why "Cato"?' he asked.

'That I'm not sure about either. The historical figure, Cato the Elder, was a Roman statesman. He was firmly opposed to foreign influences, believed they would corrupt the purity of the Roman people.'

'No suggestion this Captain character is linked to any nationalist groups? You know, of the "Buy a cottage in Wales, Come home to a real fire" school?'

'Not that I'm aware of.'

'Some sort of code then, like the other names in the chatrooms?'

'Probably.'

She looked for a hint of excitement in Huw's eyes, thought she saw it there, but quickly it was replaced by something more guarded. This case had been his hobby, his passion for the last twelve years, a hobby that had suddenly become a dangerous pursuit, and here finally he thought he had a potential lead.

'Garnswllt must be a small place,' he said slowly.

He looked down at the silt of his tea, nodded to himself. He leant across the table, touched her hand, and smiled.

'If he's there, we'll find him,' he said.

She caught his eye. 'We don't know he's there. But odds are, even if we find him, he's just your average paranoid nut. This likely won't lead us anywhere.'

Catrin could see the disappointment in his face. It looked like the disappointment of a boy who'd been waiting many years for something, whose whole life had hinged on that waiting, and who was now beginning to doubt if what he'd been waiting for would ever come to pass. Then the expression disappeared again. He pushed his cup away.

'All right,' she said, 'I'm going to swing by Della's before she moves on anywhere else. This Overseer figure we can try to locate afterwards. Doesn't sound like he gets out much.'

She stood up and he ushered her to his car outside. He didn't seem that stoned, but she took the key fob from him, got behind the wheel.

About a block away, the cars ahead slowed, then came to a stop. The traffic was backed up to the bottom of the terrace. Almost immediately Huw got fidgety, ran through the radio stations, began tapping the stem of his pipe on the dashboard. Not used to having to wait, she thought, he's impatient, like a spoilt child.

She pulled over into a parking bay.

'Let's walk,' she said. 'It'll be quicker.'

She led the way past the line of stationary traffic. At the corner ahead a small crowd had gathered behind blue-and-white police tape. There were a couple of uniforms: she recognised the young PC who'd blocked her way at the tidal barrier.

He lowered the tape, without speaking, let them pass.

'Christ almighty.' Huw was pointing at something up ahead.

Between two buildings was a low, charred pile of bricks. It was the place where Della's office had been. A curtain of smoke, thick and black, still hung in the air. Through it she made out DS Thomas and Emyr Pugh, standing under a tree. They seemed to be sharing a joke, laughing under their white masks.

Pugh came over to her through the smoke. She felt the bitterness of it in her lungs.

'Della was in there?' she asked.

He nodded grimly.

'They got her out, but they don't think she'll make it.'

The smoke parted for a moment. Through the

charred bricks Catrin saw a melted tangle of girders. The heat of the fire had been intense.

'Anything suggesting arson at this stage?' she asked.

'Thomas said there are no witnesses,' Pugh said.

'Maybe he should look for some then.' She tried to curb the irritation in her voice. 'He's really saying no one saw anything?'

'The uniforms did the rounds. It doesn't look that way.'

Pugh turned away. Catrin felt a little unsteady, as if she'd just been winded. The smoke caught in her lungs, making it hard to take in air. She backed away, thoughts of Della unspooling through her mind. Her drunken crawl across the floor, her fingers clicking slowly to some half-remembered beat. In the past this was the kind of fate she might have wished on Della. It felt as if some part of her was to blame for what had happened. She bowed her head to retch, but nothing came out, just a thin trail of saliva.

As she moved into the clear air, Huw was staring into the smoke, looking dazed. She shepherded him back to the car.

'It's time we took that trip out west,' she said.

Huw waited in the motel bar while she packed, took a shower. She ran some checks on various police computer databases, including the National Criminal

Intelligence System and the new SOCA databases. Some she had authorised access to, others she could improvise access to without leaving footprints. She tried searching all known serial arsonists with keyword 'Face' or 'Seerland'. But nothing came up. She tried a number of other searches but quickly saw she wasn't going to find what she wanted.

All she knew was that anyone linked to the Face sighting photographs had become a target. First Rhys, then Huw. Then herself. Now Della. It was as if the pictures were toxic, endangering everyone who had contact with them.

She tried calling the photographic shop again, then the neighbouring shops, checked if the absent owners had been in touch since her last call. But they hadn't.

Next she made a call from the motel line to Captain Cat's. An elderly voice answered straight off with a south London accent, the owner she guessed. She asked him if he had any customers with burn injuries. He told her he didn't.

Catrin went back into the Ordnance Survey map of the area, looked at the wooded hills and tracks to isolated farmsteads. She did another search, made a list of pirate stations, those that had public contact numbers. Six calls later to a station in Port Talbot and finally she had a possible name, but not an address. She made two further calls, calls she'd have very much

preferred not to make, and as she hung up she reckoned she'd got the picture. She clicked into the South
Wales Police fires database and looked up the incident
report on a particular fire seven years previously in
Pontardawe. Then she pulled on her leathers, picked
up her bags, walked down to the Lexus.

They stopped at the station, where she got on her
bike and Huw followed her. She rode fast to the flyover,
then turned down the lane to the estuary.

She pulled up at the bike shop at the end. The shop
looked closed, the shutters down, but lights were on
behind the blacked-out windows above. She rapped
hard on the door.

After a few moments Walter appeared in his hakama
and white tunic. He looked dishevelled and his face
was dripping with sweat. She told him she didn't have
time to come in.

'Take care of her, will you,' she said. She threw him
the Laverda's keys, then gesturing to Huw to move,
got into the driver's side of the Lexus. She glanced at
the trees. The branches were shaking in the wind, the
first snowflakes drifting over the waters.

PART TWO

THE COUNTRY

I

The snow showers became heavier as they headed west, the wind funnelling between the cuttings of the hills, the flurries settling on the sludge along the hard shoulder. For over an hour the traffic had been down to a single lane, the tail lights ahead snaking in a long line into the dark horizon.

As they passed Port Talbot there were glimpses over snowbound fields and, in the distance, the glowing grids of industrial estates.

Throughout the journey Huw controlled the music, barely speaking. Catrin had expected nothing but rare Seerland recordings. But he'd played 'Endless Sleep' by Marty Wilde three times, and then the Shangri-Las' 'I Can Never Go Home Anymore'. He'd followed that by some mournful white soul she'd never heard before, and then Amanda Lear's haunting 'Follow Me'.

Catrin turned on the satnav and pointed at the dark patch on the right of the screen.

'That's where we're headed,' she said.

'Why doesn't the place show up on the satnav's map?' Huw asked.

'Maybe it was never registered for planning permission. Or it could be an ex-government facility of some sort. A lot of those places never get put back on the maps.' With one hand she pressed a mint out from the top of the packet, passing the packet across to him.

'The DJ's real name's Gethin Pryce. Or at least that's what he was calling himself when he worked the graveyard shift at the pirate station.'

'You checked the FDR1 reports on the fire there?'

'It was put down to faulty wiring in the lift motors. There was a policy on the place and the adjuster's report says the same.'

Huw looked at her. 'This is the third fire we know about, including Della's.'

She knew what he was thinking. She had thought the same as she'd checked the database of known arsonists. But neither the report on the pirate station nor that on the office at Newport Road had turned up any traces of accelerants or telltale oxidisers. And with Thomas in charge she knew the report on Della's fire could take weeks to come through. That avenue for the moment was a dead one.

'No evidence of signatures in any of them,' she said, 'so we can't cross-reference against known arsonists' MOs. We're blind.'

Huw nodded as if he already sensed this would be the case.

'How serious were his injuries?' he asked.

'Hypodermical and tissue burns to over seventy per cent of BSA. Most people wouldn't survive that. He needed extensive autographs and allographs.'

'He was registered at the Morriston?'

'Under an alias, but after initial treatment he transferred himself overseas for the graft work.'

She looked out of the window, but could see nothing through the snow and the thick hedgerows. There was only a single set of headlights following them but after a time they dropped back and disappeared.

Huw turned the music down. 'Must have had a hefty payout?'

'Enough to do up the place where he's been lying low, and live off it since.'

'How did you find him?'

'I managed to get his name from a former colleague at one of the pirate stations. The rest came from a DJ-cum-dealer I knew when I worked under on the BDSM scene.' She explained he'd known Pryce's name and story, but he wasn't the sort of source she wanted to owe favours to. He was what was known in that community as a rogue dom, the type who if he didn't get his favour returned might collect on it unilaterally. His idea of a discreet private hobby was to spike girls, use them in his dungeon for a few hours, then release them dazed onto the streets. If they were lucky they got off with no worse than a befuddled memory. He ran a sideline for a while in video nasties, usually of subs he'd gone a bit far with. His clients liked to watch the real thing, nothing faked. Nothing on the level of Jones, not even close to his stratosphere of cruelty, but still, not the sort you wanted to be in hock to. The Trainer he was known as; she didn't know his real name, just the handle, one of many no doubt.

'So what's the link between this creep and Pryce?' Huw asked.

'Not much. Trainer heard Pryce's story on the underground DJ scene, he never knew him.'

Catrin changed down to third gear, turning right up a steep, dark hill. A vehicle behind, too indistinct to make out, slowed for a moment then drove on along the lower road.

From the top of the hill, the lane curved between stands of tall firs. The snow had settled deeper in the hollows and was crossed by a single set of tracks. The firs gave way to high hedgerows, the darkness broken only by the occasional lights of distant farms.

She crossed a small stone bridge and turned into a track that wound slowly up a second hill. There was no indication of a house or any other building ahead of them. At times the track seemed about to peter out altogether into the muddy hillside.

Finally they came abruptly to a gate, and Huw got out to open it. She could see the upper floor of a small building with black window frames. As they came closer she saw that the structure had the simplicity of a child's drawing. The main door was framed by two windows, on the upper floor a third window in the centre exactly replicating the shape of the door. Though the cabin looked relatively new, the cladding over the porch had already begun peeling away in the dank surroundings. The porch was approached not by steps, but by a ramp leading up from the yard.

There didn't appear to be any bell outside, but after a few moments the door swung inwards to reveal the glare of lights. About halfway down the hall, a small girl was standing, her long chestnut hair framing a pale face. She was wearing a pinafore dress over white tights. She looked about six but her eyes seemed to have the confidence of someone much older.

Without speaking she led them into a room lined with paintings of Hereford cattle, at its centre a table with a bowl of russet apples on it. Pausing beside the table, the girl gestured to a ramp that rose towards a wide doorway at the back of the room. She took an apple, then ran off down the hall. They heard a low rasping sound from the far side of the room.

In the doorway was a man in a wheelchair. He was dressed in a baggy tracksuit, and covering his head was a black mask with slits at the level of the eyes and mouth. He raised a gloved hand, and beckoned them over.

'Come through,' said the man, and he prodded the keypad on the chair so that it began to turn.

They followed him down the ramp into a room with a single narrow window. The door was made from thick hardwood, Catrin noticed, and reinforced with steel cross-bars. Inside it was several degrees warmer than the rest of the house; tropical ferns had been arranged on shelves. As the chair moved ahead she caught a glimpse of something crimson under the lower half of the mask.

She turned away quickly. The images on the walls were of Seerland, and all appeared to be from the very early days of the band. In several of the photographs adolescent acne was still visible beneath clumsily applied layers of make-up.

Catrin knelt low by the wheelchair and took the masked man's hand. It felt strangely rigid, but there was a faint warmth there.

'So you must be the elusive Overseer,' she said. He didn't move, didn't respond. She wondered how strong his sight was, if he could see her clearly. He'd seen them over the twenty-foot length of the hall, judged them to be no threat, so she assumed his vision must still be sharp.

'I'm from the police,' she said. She took out her card, and then the still of Rhys, held them up to the slits in the mask. He still didn't react.

'This man,' she said. 'Do you recognise him?'

He said nothing, but the black mask shook fractionally.

'The name Rhys Williams mean anything to you?' she asked.

Again he shook his head.

'In any of the unofficial chatrooms,' she said. 'Have you heard talk of any recent Face sighting photos? Pictures that seem to show him in a wood wearing robes?'

The man in the wheelchair moved his head forward, as if what she had said might have interested him. But then he shook it again.

'Nothing like that,' he said. His voice was almost a whisper.

Catrin looked up again at the photos on the walls. None of the memorabilia was more recent than Face's disappearance. Huw was stepping from image to image, as if in a museum, studying each one closely then moving on. He'd stopped at a photograph of Nails and Face posing in a cemetery. Their rake-thin bodies draped over a gravestone, their eyes heavy with kohl, they seemed fawn-like, exotic, the Shelley and Keats of rock 'n' roll.

'I used to follow them in the very early days.' Pryce's mask was swivelling slowly towards the object of Huw's gaze.

His speech was slurred and slow. Through the open door of the cabinet in the corner Catrin could see tidy rows of diamorphine ampoules, blister packs of Demerol, other prescription medications she didn't recognise.

'It must have been a small group back then?' she said.

Pryce pointed his gloved hand at two photographs above the cabinet. The first showed a group of fans, mostly girls, who were sitting cross-legged in a circle. They were not dressed in the Goth black of the girls outside Shift studios, but in the baggy smocks and flares of the late eighties psychedelic scene. These images belonged to the very earliest days of the band.

The last photograph was a close-up. To one side was a girl, pale and dreamy-looking, with a pair of Lennon specs pushed up into her hair. Her head was resting against her partner, a thin boy with wavy, shoulder-length locks. They could have modelled for Burne-Jones or Rossetti, their eyes had the inward-looking, morbid appearance of the models of that period. They looked no older than eighteen, and had a close resemblance that made her wonder if they were siblings, possibly twins.

'So you must have known Face in the old days?' she asked.

Pryce was shaking his head, slowly.

'No, he was always distant with those he didn't know.'

'But it was a small group then, you must have got to know him a little?'

'Not really, he'd often leave the studio for days on end, come back moody, difficult to reach.'

Pryce's voice had grown even fainter as he spoke, as if the events came back to him now as from some dim, legendary past, like an ancient story from the Mabinogion. He was putting a tissue up to the mask which had darkened with some form of moisture coming from within. Catrin remembered that burns victims often suffered damage to their tear ducts.

'When Face went off from the studio, was it with the other members of the group?' she asked.

'No.'

'On his own?'

'No, a man would pick him up in a big car. He was older; I know that, because I caught a glimpse of him once. The rumour was that Face was his lover.'

'Who was he?'

'I didn't really see him ever. He had long black hair, down to his shoulders.'

'Anything else?'

'He never got out of the car, never parked up close either.'

Pryce was moving the tissue slowly over the slits in the mask.

'You don't know who he could've been?'

Huw had crouched down on the other side of the chair.

'No, but if you're looking for Face you may really be looking for this man.'

The surface of the mask around the mouth had puckered back into what might once have been a smile, or a grimace of pain.

'What do you mean?' Huw said.

'In the very early days of the band several of the fans close to Face went missing, just disappeared without saying they were moving on. But they were the ones into the heavy tripping scene, so no one made much of it at the time.'

'And you think this older man had something to do with this.'

Catrin had to bend down by the chair to hear his words now. She reached down and lifted the oxygen tube to his mouth.

'I'm not certain. All I can tell you is that when this man came on the scene, the inner circle around Face went missing, one by one.'

Pryce gestured for Huw to lean over the arm of the chair, so his head was close to the slit over his mouth.

'Then after Face disappeared, a group of us from the old days tried to find out what had happened.'

'Did you find anything?'

He shook his head, slowly. He was struggling to breathe and Catrin moved the tube closer.

'Nothing . . . but gradually we began to notice that members of the group looking for him were beginning to have accidents.'

'That's what you've been posting about in the chatrooms?'

This time the pause was longer. Pryce moved his head in the direction of the cabinet, and Huw brought out the diamorphine solution. Pryce filled the syringe at the side of the chair which was connected through an IV line to the rear of the mask. After a minute he raised his head, began to speak again.

'It was around that time that I heard from Ianto,' he said, haltingly.

They waited a few moments, then slowly he continued. 'That wasn't his real name, that's just what we used to call him. He was one of the diehards, had been there since the band first started to write songs together. He said that he'd learnt something important, sounded excited and worried at the same time.' Pryce's gloved hand brought the tube up to his mouth.

'He told me then that a couple of his mates looking into Face had disappeared, and he sounded scared.'

Huw bent closer again.

'He say why he was scared?'

Pryce shook his head slowly.

'I never heard anything more from him. I heard later Ianto died in a car crash abroad. I never knew his real name, so that was the end of it.'

Huw glanced out at the field, where the wind was whirling damp clothes round on a revolving dryer. For a moment Catrin thought he winked at her. He put his glass down by one of the monitors.

'Who looks after you?' he asked.

Pryce touched a button on his pad and a screen-saver flickered onto the monitor. Beside the screen was a framed degree in classics, half obscured by a small classical bust. The plinth beneath identified the figure as Cato the Elder, and in a square at the bottom was a line inscribed in a stone tablet. *Ubi facies omnium, facies bonorum personas gerunt.*

As Pryce pressed the pad, a collage of photographs appeared on the screen. All of them, from the earliest graduation portraits to the most recent, featured an attractive, dark-haired woman.

A sudden movement outside made Catrin look into the field. Two people, one large, one small, were walking up the path through the snow flurries. The young girl who had met them was holding the hand of the woman on the screen-saver. She looked much older than in the photographs, her hair grey, unkempt. She was staring up to the window, and she appeared to be shouting but they could not hear her words through the thick pane.

Pryce motioned with his head towards the door. 'Try to find Face's family,' he whispered.

Huw gently squeezed Pryce's shoulder in thanks, then gestured for Catrin to get moving.

As they crossed the yard, the woman's angry words were lost in the sharp wind whistling around the sides of the cabin. Catrin looked back at the mother and daughter. Their faces were full of fury and fear.

On the road into Ammanford, Huw pulled into the car park of a modern red-brick pub, the Drover's Rest. The sign said the place offered accommodation.

They took their drinks to a corner table, out of earshot of the bar. Huw took a deep swallow of his pint and sighed wearily.

'Well, that was jolly, wasn't it?'

Catrin tried to smile.

'I'm sure the medication has been working on his imagination. That stuff about the disappearing fans sounded like off-the-scale paranoia.'

Huw picked up his briefcase and put it on the table.

'Most of the early fans were drifters, travellers, underground characters. It would be next to impossible to verify who was there and what happened to them two decades on.'

'What about that older man he mentioned, the one rumoured to be Face's lover. He didn't sound like a drifter.'

'I don't think he got that right,' Huw said.

'Oh?'

'We know the band played up to a camp image. So if Face was involved in a gay relationship, more likely he would have publicised it, not hidden it.'

'How does this older man fit into the picture then? A behind-the-scenes manager?'

'But Pryce said he never saw this man with anyone else except Face. And it was Nails and Teifi who managed the band, not Face.'

'A dealer?'

'There's nothing to indicate Face had more money than the others at that stage. Why would a dealer with an expensive car be bothering to target him? It doesn't add up.'

Then a thought struck her. 'This mysterious older man, the disappearances around Face,' she said, 'this was all happening during the same period as the Angel Jones abductions.' She paused. 'I'm not saying they are linked, but it's interesting.' She glanced at Huw.

'We've no idea if there's anything in Pryce's story, but if there is we're talking a small locus temporarily and geographically for two sets of serial abductions to have occurred.'

'It's interesting, but unlikely to be relevant.' Huw smiled at her. 'Let's not go off on tangents here. Jones was into girls, focused mainly on BDSM. These fans who *allegedly* disappeared, they were both male and female, that wasn't their scene.'

'We can't say for sure that wasn't their scene. Della told me she met Jones way back via a BDSM site. Jones was with a girl, she said. The girl was spaced out, into Seerland, there's at least one potential connection there.'

She sensed in Huw a disappointment again, that might have been due to the quality of the Overseer's information but she felt perhaps it had spread out to herself and her approach.

He closed his briefcase. 'Della's not exactly a reliable source. This girl, do we even have a name for her?'

'No name. This was through a BDSM site, no one uses real names. But she made quite an impression on Della. I got the sense there was something unusual about her. Big cloudy eyes, a real beauty Della said.'

'Della kept any photos of this girl, trophies?'

'Unlikely. It's against privacy protocol to photograph

contacts from a BDSM site, they're strict about that, ban members who do.'

'So basically this is nothing, we're talking about a ghost here. A girl who exists in Della's memory, nowhere else.' Huw sipped his drink, lowered it slowly. 'And half the girls in the city were into Seerland then. This wouldn't place her among the inner fans. What about this Trainer creep, any connection with Pryce there?'

'No, he knew of Pryce through the underground music scene. Pryce wasn't into BDSM.'

Huw nodded. 'Okay,' he said, 'let's move on, I'm not seeing any other links to the BDSM scene and Jones from what Pryce gave us.'

Catrin looked into Huw's tired eyes. 'Unless Jones was a larger, more complex predator than was assumed at the time.'

'Apart from the dates, there aren't any matches at all with Jones. Jones didn't have any money that we know of, wouldn't have had a big car. He used some old grey van.'

'It was actually a similar grey van that followed us at the bridge.'

Huw raised his eyebrows. 'Sounds like you've got a blow-back from Pryce's paranoia. What are you floating here, some kind of Jones historical re-enactment society, a fan club?' He looked up at the ceiling, his eyes half closed. 'Forget about Jones. He's been buried in Broadmoor for years and he'll never get out alive. He's kept in seg, as high-security as you can get. Come on, it's a common model of van, that's why Jones used it.'

Catrin knew he was right. The reports in the press on Jones after he'd been sent down were of an entirely isolated figure, one who had chosen to remain silent, who never had visitors, never communicated with the outside world, and had no means of doing so. But it occurred to her now what else had troubled her about the figure with the van. 'Didn't Jones often use to wear an anorak? His hair long or a black wig to cover his face?'

'So what?' She didn't reply at first, tried to piece together those few fragments she'd seen of the man who'd followed her. Something in her mind seemed to be blocking off the memories, pushing them further out of reach.

She looked up, held Huw's gaze. 'Something's telling me we should look at a connection with Jones here. It may not be an obvious one, but let's stick with this for a moment.' She thought back to what Pryce had said. 'In some pictures, Jones's hair looked black, came down to the shoulders, as Pryce described that older man having.'

Huw appeared resigned now to having to eliminate

the direction she'd taken by argument rather than blanket dismissals. 'All right,' he said, 'but in some pictures Jones had black hair, in others short blond, in others he was shaven-headed. Jones was good at disguise. That is why fifteen years of surveillance in the BDSM scene failed to catch him.' He looked at her. 'Let's say for a moment Pryce was right, there was this older man in a big car, keeping out of sight. This doesn't sound like Jones's MO. Jones was unpredictable, he didn't lay down patterns of behaviour, but here we already have a pattern. The man always came in a big car, waited some distance away. Jones wouldn't have done it like that. He'd have approached in other ways, used different disguises.'

Catrin tried to work out what had first formed a link in her mind between the figure Pryce had described and Jones. She knew something must have done, but it was not something she could put a finger on consciously.

'Shut your eyes,' Huw said, 'try to picture Jones. Can you do it?'

She tried, and he was right, she couldn't. But that begged another question.

'At the trial, Jones's victims positively identified him. They were drugged, Jones masked all the time, so how did they do that?'

'Jones always covered his face, but sometimes his

chest was bare. He had a tattoo. No one was clear what its significance was, it seemed to represent a stylised raven's beak. It was a brand tattoo, not an ink job, one of those applied in a single go with a hot mould.'

Catrin's mind filled with the footage Huw had shown her. She saw the stains on the wall lit by the candles, on the floor the dark pool in which there was a paler shape, four limbs neatly arranged, barely distinguishable. Along the wall a shape was rising up, large and feathered, the shadow of some sort of apparel or mask. Dripping from its beak was dark liquid, the camera spinning, the images no longer clear, the walls shivering with a weak light. The shivering passed into her body, she felt herself grow suddenly cold.

'You're right, it was a raven. But isn't that what the shadow showed in the film with Face in the tunnel?'

Huw seemed impatient. 'Come on, that shape could have been almost anything.'

'But it meant something to Rhys also.' She'd pulled her jacket on but the feeling of cold persisted.

'What do you mean?'

'Rhys made origami ravens.'

'And other birds – swans and crows, all kinds.'

'Yes, I know, but he made ravens when he was under pressure. They had some significance for him. Like a talisman.'

Catrin took out her purse and from one of the

pockets some yellowed and creased paper. What it represented was immediately obvious, the stylised feathers, the long, hooked beak.

'This is one of them,' she said, 'Rhys dropped it the last night I was with him.'

Huw was barely looking at it. 'Shadows, Cat. Shadows of shadows.'

She felt embarrassed, began to put it away. Then she felt his hand on hers, its heaviness, its warmth, reassuring her, but of what? She raised her head and he was looking straight into her eyes. Briefly she felt he could see into her innermost thoughts.

'Cat,' he said quietly. 'I heard about how Rhys found you in the woods. You probably think Jones had something to do with that. And maybe you're right.' He paused, lowered his eyes, as if aware of their intensity. 'But you mustn't let your thing with Jones haunt this case. You mustn't follow lines that just aren't there.'

She nodded. She knew if she kept this up she'd confirm one of those doubts about female investigators that never seemed to go away: that however much they used logic and science, at some level they worked irrationally, followed fears and superstitions, not reason. 'Pryce suggested we find Face's family, but as far as I remember he never had much to do with them. You think there could be anything that was missed there?'

Huw seemed doubtful.

'Face was always a bit evasive in interviews about his family, but probably only because they were so normal. His father did a stint in the merchant navy, died of lung cancer a few years back. His mother used to be a nurse at Glangwili hospital. She died more recently. They sound like regular pillars of the community. Face didn't have much contact with them, but he didn't avoid them. There's no sign he had any strong feelings about them. Once he'd left for the city he didn't go back home much.'

Huw took out a road map from his case, pointed to the Glangwili area north of Carmarthen. The roads looked narrow, the area primarily agricultural.

'We could stop there tomorrow.'

He folded up the map and nodded at the buffet table. Catrin shook her head.

'I'm not hungry.'

Huw walked over to the buffet table. She was able to watch him for a moment unobserved, study how his body moved, the solid torso tapering into a pair of long, athletic legs. She had to admit, she liked what she saw. Despite the dope, he'd kept in shape, there was discipline there still.

- As Huw worked through his mixed grill, his eyes were half on the champions league match between Liverpool and PSV. 'You a football fan?' he asked.

'Yeah,' she said. She was beginning to feel quite drunk. 'Man U, as it happens.'

'Really?' he said. 'Me too.'

'Yeah, well,' she said smiling at him, 'it's not exactly an unusual choice, is it?'

'When I was a kid though, that was a hell of a team, Bobby Charlton, Georgie Best. You just had to support them, specially if you grew up miles from anywhere like I did. How about you, how come you're not a Cardiff City fan?'

'Oh,' she said, 'my dad was a Man U fan.'

'Right,' said Huw, 'you two bond over a match, did you?'

'No,' said Catrin, 'not exactly, he's not, well, he wasn't really around.'

'Oh,' said Huw, 'I'm sorry.'

'No need. It's not like I ever knew him or anything. He was just a fling my mother had. Then I came along and he left. That's what men do, isn't it?'

'What's that?'

'Leave,' she said, 'they fucking leave.' She was really starting to feel the drink now and failing to keep the emotion from her voice, struggling not to think of Rhys, the one who'd really left her, not the father she'd never known, the bass player for a band she'd never heard of, the father of whom she knew nothing other than he'd been another drifter through her mother's hippie scene.

'I'm sorry,' she said, and Huw just smiled and said something about it being a hell of a day.

As the players left the field she moved the conversation back to the Owen Face search, the quest for yet another man who, one way or another, had ducked out on his responsibilities.

'That inscription on the bust of Cato in Pryce's study, any idea what it meant?' she asked.

Huw made a search on his iPhone. 'It means something along the lines of – *In this land where each man's face is a mask, the true face wears a mask*. Originally it referred to Rome perhaps, or Carthage.'

'Couldn't it also be a pun on Face's name?'

'In what sense?'

'As in – where each man's "Face" is a mask. It's saying that Face wasn't what he appeared to be. Face's austere, reclusive lifestyle might have been some sort of mask – a front, that allowed him to pursue a double life. Maybe his real life was elsewhere.'

'It's possible I suppose.'

'That would also explain Pryce's own identification with the figure of Cato.'

'I wouldn't read too much into it. Someone in that condition and on that level of medication could be identifying with a lot of unusual things, no?'

The barman switched over to the local news. There was a short item on the fire, with an old picture of

Della. Then the shot cut to DS Thomas standing outside the charred remains. He'd put on a new suit for the interview, but there was no mention of arson, no mention of any other persons being sought in connection with the incident. He stared with a glazed look into the camera and seemed to run out of things to say. Catrin smiled again but inwardly this time. He was making an ass of himself. But then he was the sort who didn't really care what people thought of him.

She picked up a couple of rolls and some cheese and went to her room. The passage upstairs was lit by dim energy-saving bulbs. There was chipped paint on the dressing table, cigarette burns on the covers. Through the open curtains she could see the snow falling outside, swirling, grey and formless.

She moved closer to the pane, her nose almost up against the glass. Down in the whirl of flakes Huw's parked car was just visible. Standing beside it she saw a figure in an anorak. He seemed almost motionless, only his hands moving out ahead of him, as if in a silent act of supplication.

Instinctively she drew back from the window, reached down for her phone to call Huw but it was too late. Huw had seen the man and was already running from the bar. Through the snow Catrin saw that the man still had his hands outstretched. He backed away from the car towards the road. Huw went after him through the falling flakes, almost slipping, but the man disappeared behind the trees.

As Huw reached the place where the man had gone the branches shook violently, the snow rushing down in a thick sheet. Then he too disappeared. Catrin heard a loud cry then Huw staggered back into sight, his hands clasped to his face, his knees buckling under him. From the side of the building the barman rushed forward, put his arms around Huw's shoulders and guided him back towards the lights.

As she ran out Catrin could see Huw slumped at the bottom of the stairs. The barman held a bottle of water.

'What just happened out there?' She took the bottle and some tissues, then dabbed them over the end of the bottle.

'I'm not sure. The bastard hit me from behind.'

'Get a look at him?'

'Not properly. It was too dark.'

Gently she began to wipe away the sludge and leaves from Huw's face. His thick hair was matted with blood from a cut above his temple, but it wasn't deep.

'Did you see what he was wearing?'

'The usual. Hoodie, trackies, those air-sole trainers.'

'Get a look at his face?'

'No. He had long hair, almost covered his face.'

'It's got to be the man who followed me from the club. He's disguising himself as Jones used to. The hoodie, the hair over his face.'

Huw didn't seem to be listening. 'I don't know,' he said, 'it felt strange. Like if I'd pulled away the hair there would've been nothing underneath.'

'What do you mean, nothing?'

'Nothing, no face, just eyes.'

Catrin hesitated. It was what she'd felt too for a moment in the park. She took a deep breath. The barman had left the room, closed the door.

She walked with Huw to his door and waited outside until she heard the lock turn, then went down to check the windows. The bar was empty. She checked all the lower windows were locked, then went up to her room and turned the key.

Three hours later she was awake again. Her shoulders felt cold, numb. It was silent apart from the soft hum of the ventilation system.

She checked her phone. There were several calls from DS Thomas's private number, but he'd left no message. She tried his number but it was switched off, no answerphone.

She picked up her tobacco pouch from the bedside table. It was almost empty. Not enough left to roll a cigarette. Beside the pouch were her sleeping pills. She took two, crunching them in her teeth to quicken the effect.

Outside the snow was falling like feathers.

She stared at the window. Nothing else was moving there. She closed her eyes and let the rhythm carry her off to a dreamless sleep.

2

Catrin stood at the window and peered out into the feeble dawn light. During the night she'd got up twice, checked the locks on all the ground-floor windows. Nothing had been disturbed, and looking out over the layer of snow that had fallen overnight, she could see no prints.

She felt for her handset, punched in the number of Emyr Pugh the pathologist. It was his home number, the one he'd left on his card at the office, she'd memorised it. His voice was still groggy with sleep.

'Emyr?'

'Cat?' He still recognised her voice, she noted, after all these years. She heard him sniffing, some water running.

'Thomas is looking for you, wants to speak to you about something,' he said after a pause.

'I know,' she said. 'Last night his phone was off.' She heard the click of a lighter, a shallow intake of breath. She didn't remember Emyr smoking. She wondered if it was something he'd gone back to since his wife had died.

'Also, Della left a message for you on my work line. She must have left it the morning of the fire.'

'What was it?'

'Nothing, just that she was looking for you, couldn't get you on your mobile.' Catrin remembered she'd been interviewing the band that morning, her phone would have been switched off. She wondered why Della hadn't left a message as she had on previous occasions. Maybe because she'd never answered any of them. Maybe because she hadn't felt safe leaving one. Now she'd probably never know what Della had wanted.

'How is Della?' she asked quickly.

'In a coma still.'

She took a deep breath. 'Emyr, can you get into the force intranet, the archive section, from your home drive?' Under his breath Pugh muttered something about not being able to pass material without clearance.

She fumbled for her pack of Drum, remembered it was empty. 'The woodland loci where the Angel Jones victims were found. They'd all have been photographed by scene of crime officers, right?'

There was a low whirr as Pugh booted his system, 'They'd have swept for fibres and DNA within a fifty-metre radius of each body, so it's a fair bet.' A few moments of silence then, just a muted tapping in the background.

'The last six sites, from the late 1990s, are on computer,' he said.

'The woodland there, any trees visible in the shots?'

'The shots are of the ground cover.'

'What about leaves, foliage? Rowan? Silver birch, goat willow? Sessile oaks? Any of those?'

'Not that I can see, it's mostly mulch and mud. Looks like Jones used clearings, not tree cover, to dump his vics in.'

'And the locations of the woods he used?'

There was the soft tapping again, longer this time.

'No real cluster. They're spread at the edges of the national maritime park. St Dogmaels in the north, Mynyddog-ddu in the east. Pontfaen in the north, several in the woods around the Preseli hills.'

'Any symbolism, any patterning to the placement of the bodies?'

'None noted here. The SIO superimposed a number of geometrical shapes, hexagons, pentangles and so on. Nothing, it looks random.'

'So how was Jones accessing the park?' She cracked the window, still left the curtain closed, felt the cool air over her face. Outside everything sounded still, silent, no traffic moving yet beyond the trees.

'Seems he just drove up the B4313, the B4329, turned off when he saw dense woodland.'

'So he took his van up narrow tracks into the woods.'

'Unlikely. The assumption was he parked then carried the bodies on foot.'

She knew this was reasonable, it would have been an effort, but possible.

'His victims didn't weigh much by the time he'd finished with them,' she said, 'so Jones could've carried them in a mile or more, but further and he'd have needed help.'

'Right, the bodies weren't further in than a mile or so. No evidence of Jones using accomplices was ever found, as you know. In his cellars there was no DNA except his and his vics'. The vics' tox reports matched to the exact chemical footprint of the drugs found in his cellars. His vics said Jones was always alone with them. In the CCTVs he's alone in his hoodies and other disguises. They did biometrics on all the footage from the clubs, it was never anyone else but Jones in that gear.'

'You're right, nothing indicates he did use accomplices.' She looked down at the carpet, how dark the patterning was so as to hide stains. Something he'd said earlier had snagged in her mind.

'You said they searched for fibres at the scenes.'

She heard him tapping again. 'Within fifty metres, but as we're talking deep woods, there's not much here. The girls' clothes, his clothes, that's it.'

'And the fibres, they include hairs from that black wig he wore?'

She thought she could hear a door closing somewhere in the background. There was a longer pause this time before he came back on.

'Two samples here,' he said: 'both matched those found at his cellar. He used the wig to cover his face.'

'But the wig wasn't among the evidence taken from his cellars, right.'

'No, but then nor were some of his other disguises.'

She stared at a patch of damp on the wallpaper, thought about this for a few moments. The detail about the missing wig had not been released to the press. There had been the usual anxieties about fakes by pranksters contaminating the evidence chain if it had been revealed that some disguises were missing. But the photos taken by security cameras did show Jones with long, mask-like hair, so many people could have guessed it was a wig, or anyone imitating that particular disguise of Jones's might have chosen to wear a wig. It was another aspect of the hair disguise that interested her.

'Those hairs from the wig,' she said, 'they're jet black, or tinted in some way?'

There was a low snorting sound. It sounded as if Pugh was blowing his nose. This time the pause was so long she thought maybe the details weren't fully on file.

'They are tinted, some kind of yellow,' he said.

She thought back to the man who'd followed her in the park, the strange sense she'd had that behind the hair there was nothing at all, just a pair of yellow eyes, no face. She wondered how that thought had formed in her mind. The truth was it had been too dark to tell, she couldn't have seen anything under the hair. The harder she thought about it the more the face seemed to recede as it had before like an image in a dream.

'Any match to other wigs from shops or theatrical outlets?' she asked.

She apologised then to Pugh for taking up his time. He said he didn't mind, but she sensed his impatience mounting; she wondered what she was keeping him from. The tapping continued, quicker this time.

'No, they searched all known outlets, online, even internationally. They were hoping for proof he'd personally purchased the items. But they never got it.'

'And the hairs, what were they?'

He laughed briefly. 'Goat, it says here.'

'Goat?' She moved her feet under the radiator.

'Painted with a vegetable dye, they never traced that either. Sounds like a home-made job, that's why they never found a retail match.' He cleared his throat then coughed. 'He probably thought it was safer to make his own gear.'

She heard a click, the line had gone dead. It's the weather, she thought, these old country lines go down all the time in winter. She called back, just got a continuous beep. She left it a couple of minutes, staring out at the glare of the whiteness in the dark, tried again. The line was still dead.

Catrin sat in the gloom, listening for sounds from Huw's room. There was silence. She thought back to what Pugh had said. The security camera pictures of the wig in the press had been black and white. It was unlikely members of the public would have known about the yellow tint. She was almost certain that was what had made the yellow shimmer she had seen. Beyond that, all seemed darkness.

They drove west towards Pembrokeshire. The snow had thinned to an icy drizzle, the winds whisking the drifts against the hedgerows into blinding eddies across the road.

Huw was un-talkative, seemed lost in his own thoughts. Catrin browsed the in-car audio memory. She had expected some vast archive, but found only a small playlist. Some obscure medieval religious chants she'd never heard of. Then Allegri's Miserere and several other settings of the same psalm from the seventeenth century. The rest was all relatively modern. The Shangri-La's 'Walkin' in the Sand', 'I Can Never Go Home Anymore'. From the Sixties, Marty Wilde. Quicksilver Messenger Service 'Just for Love'. The Dells' 'Love is Blue'.

From the Seventies, Terry Reid's 'Stay with Me Baby'. The Motels. John Martyn, Little Feat, Gram Parsons. From the Eighties, only some early Seerland, and Amanda Lear. It was all melancholic, nostalgic music, felt like the music of someone in mourning for something, irrevocably lost.

'Sorry it's all old stuff,' he said.

'No it's fine,' said Catrin, 'you've got okay taste.'

Huw looked over at her then and she felt embarrassed, like maybe he thought she was flirting with him. It wasn't her style to give compliments, she wondered if in a small way she had been.

She decided on John Martyn's *Solid Air*, a record that never failed to lift her spirits. The title track, the song Martyn was meant to have written about Nick Drake, never failed to remind her of Rhys, as if Rhys's spirit was out there somewhere, moving through solid air.

The way up to Glangwili was slow going. For the first few miles she drove slowly behind the tail lights of the gritting truck. There were no lights of other cars behind them. They had to stop on the outskirts of the village to allow a herd of cattle to cross the road. Then the sky ahead began to clear.

The road twisted past a village shop and up a hill past several chapels and pubs. The place looked as if it probably hadn't changed much since Face's childhood in the 1970s. Through the hedges they could catch glimpses of the surrounding fields. In the lee of the trees the cows stood with heads bent low over the frozen grass.

Catrin followed a driveway that led round the back of the last pub on the hill. Hanging above it from a peeling post, a rusted plaque read the Sporting Chance. When they stopped, she tried Pugh again, on his office line this time. She got a pre-recorded message saying he'd be off for the week, annual leave. She tried his home line again, but it just rang without anyone picking up. No answerphone, no message.

Huw went forward and opened the door for her, then followed her through the entrance to the bar. Along the walls the mirrors were etched with images from playing cards, the character behind the barman a sour-faced queen of hearts. On the other walls roulette wheels and dice had been mounted under the light sconces, alternating with photographs of prize-winning cattle from agricultural shows of years long past.

About half the tables were occupied, despite the

early hour, mainly by elderly farming types with weathered faces. Huw walked over to a table by the door at which a morose-looking man was sitting opposite two women. The couple, she noticed, were already shifting uneasily in their seats. Huw smiled at them.

'Did you know the Matthewses? Their son was Owen Face, that one who disappeared a while back,' he asked. The old man looked uncomfortable, his wife tutting under her breath. The couple turned away from Huw, and began talking to each other in Welsh.

The barman had come out from behind the bar and now stood by the table.

'The locals don't like to talk,' he said, 'they're tired of all the journalists coming round over the years.'

Huw took out a couple of fifties and pressed them into the young man's hand. The barman spoke quietly now. 'Best thing you can do, is buy Rhonwen over there a couple. She might talk.'

They looked over and saw an elderly woman sitting on her own in the corner, two glasses in front of her, one already dead, the other half gone. Closer up, the woman's age – at a distance she looked nigh on seventy – was less obvious. She could have been in her mid-fifties but any attempts at grooming had long since lost out to the gin.

Huw's nose wrinkled briefly before he realised what he was doing, then he slapped his palms on his thighs, all business.

'So what are you having, Rhonwen?'

She didn't ask him how he knew her name, clearly she was already confident in her status as a local character.

'G&T please, love.'

Huw came back with the drinks, put down a double on Rhonwen's side of the table. 'Didn't you used to know the Matthews family?' he asked.

Huw waited while Rhonwen took a long, slow sip on her gin.

'Journalists, are you?' she asked.

Huw was nodding confidently.

'We haven't had many of you lot round for a while,' she said.

He put his glass down, out of range of her spray.

'Not many, you said.'

'That's right.'

'So there have been some round then?'

'Well, a couple of nights back, one came in.'

'How did he strike you?' Catrin asked.

'The usual sort. Polite, sounded like a Cardiff man.'

'How did he look?'

'He had a beard, long hair like one of those surfer types. I didn't really get a look at him. He was here one moment then gone the next.'

Catrin glanced at Huw, then back to the woman. 'What did he want to know?'

'Well, like yourselves he was asking if there'd been other journalists through.'

'That's all he asked?'

'That's all.'

Catrin was about to speak, but Huw was signalling to her to let him come in. The woman picked up her glass and Huw smiled reassuringly at her.

'When Owen was born, did you know the family then?'

She paused, the glass close to her lips. For a moment Catrin wondered if they were going to get anything out of her: she seemed too lost in the drink. But then her face slowly filled with a vague warmth, that warmth that comes from remembering better days. Huw pulled out another fifty, passed it over. Would anything they got out of her be reliable? Catrin thought. Inducements always tarnished evidence.

'I only lived a few doors down from them, *bach*,' the woman said to Huw as if she'd known him all her life. 'Owen was a beautiful child, so quiet, a little angel. He was born end of August 1972, I always remember it because it was during the Olympics: I didn't have a telly then, so Megan invited me over to watch it on hers.'

'What was Owen like when he was a bit older?' he asked.

The woman took a large gulp of her gin, held the glass against her chest.

'I didn't see him much then,' she said.

'Anything at all you remember?'

'Not really, no.'

Catrin caught the woman's eye. 'What about when he was at school, he get into any trouble?'

'No.' She paused. 'Well, I know Megan was worried about that, what with his father being away a lot, but no, nothing like that.'

Huw signalled to the bar for more drinks. Catrin pulled her chair closer.

'So Owen's father wasn't around much, then?'

'Well, no, he wasn't. But then it wasn't easy for him with his job.'

'He was in the merchant navy, wasn't he?'

'For years he was.'

Catrin looked over at Huw. He seemed slightly detached, as if he'd already written off the interview as a waste of time.

She turned back to the woman. 'Do you remember anything about the father's job? What ship he was on?' she asked.

Rhonwen smiled. 'The *Pembroke,* I remember because it's a local place.'

Catrin caught Huw's eye. 'Call up the Merchant Navy association archive site,' she said. 'The records are open to the public. I checked it last night.'

Huw pulled out his phone and called up various lists on the archive, a website he'd already bookmarked, scrolling down the pages. He ran his index finger over the screen, and pointed at a column of names and dates.

'If Sion Mathews was on the *Pembroke* he was away at work from September '71 until mid-February '72, calling at Lagos, Cape Town, Fremantle.'

It was what she'd been half expecting. She moved the screen over so Rhonwen could see it.

'Away from September '71 until mid-February '72. Might sort of rule him out of the running as Owen's biological father?'

She watched Rhonwen carefully for a tell that would reveal prior knowledge of this, but with the drink glazing the woman's eyes it was difficult to see what she knew. Finally she put her glass down.

'Well, maybe he wasn't,' she said neutrally.

Catrin put her hand lightly over Rhonwen's.

'Did you ever see Megan with other men? Bit of a one, was she?'

'No, never. She always kept herself to herself.'

'In what ways?'

Rhonwen sighed, sat back heavily and looked at

Huw. He put his hand in his pocket, waited to see what she'd do.

'She didn't really have what you'd call close friends.'

He looked at her as if he had all the time in the world. He kept his hand in his pocket, crinkled up a note so it made a slight noise.

'Well, you know how it is around here, we like to think of ourselves as hospitable. But Megan never used to have anyone in over the doorstep. If she met anyone down the shop she never had time to talk. It didn't go down well. People used to think she was stuck up.'

The woman stopped. He took out the note and looked down, as if just noticing it.

'Did she ever make trips away from the area?' he asked.

'No, only to her mother's occasionally.'

'Where was that?'

Rhonwen knocked back the last of her gin.

'I think she was living near Llan then. It's a small village out in the west.'

Huw clicked the screen onto a detailed map of the area. The village was where the woman had described it, an isolated place, far up on the coast of the national maritime park. Catrin panned down. The place, she noticed, was about twenty miles north of where Rhys's photographs had been developed.

'And now?'

'Up the road in Bancyfelin. She's like Megan was, keeps herself to herself.'

Huw stood, reached out his hand to shake Rhonwen's. Catrin got up, moved out from behind the table. She looked down at the woman, avoiding her eye. Huw had put the note on the table and was keeping his fingers over it.

'Did Owen ever go to his grandmother's out in the far west?' she asked.

'Well, he'd go there for visits with his mam when he was little. Sion was away at sea and Megan was doing night shifts at the hospital, so sometimes she'd leave him with his nan.'

Catrin nodded, then moved towards the door. Huw took his fingers off the note, the woman raised her hand in a farewell gesture.

Catrin waited as Huw stepped quickly after her. As he opened the car door she felt his hand briefly touch the small of her back. He stared out at the low, empty hills, narrow tracks petering out into small copses and beyond them the dimmer lines of more empty hills.

Bancyfelin lay about five miles west of Carmarthen. They arrived to find the area shrouded in mist, the frosted fields slowly regaining their deep greenness as the temperature rose, the bare sycamores along the roadside no more than blurred, skeletal presences.

Face's grandmother's house was one of a group of semi-detached properties on the edge of the village. Catrin began to think they had missed the place altogether, but as Huw slowed she saw a short tarmacked lane.

The houses all had immaculate lawns and tidily planted borders, as if a single gardener was responsible for the whole area. The one exception to this orderly scene was the front lawn to number 4a, which contained a high rockery topped with a statue of Jesus, a miniature well and garden gnomes.

They knocked on the front door. Up close they could see that, unlike its neighbour, the door had several additional locks, top and bottom. It seemed to be made, not from hardwood, but from some reinforced synthetic material. There was no response, no sound of radio or television from inside.

Through the thick net curtains and the concertina of security bars they could just make out the dim shapes of Victorian furnishings, pale antimacassars and religious pictures on the walls. To the side, the garden was blocked off by a high steel fence, its top covered with rusted barbed wire. Catrin knocked again, but still there were no sounds from within.

'She's old,' Huw said, 'maybe they've put her in a home.'

As they turned away they saw through the mist

a middle-aged woman standing in the doorway of the next house along. Catrin showed her card, and nodded to Huw as if he was a colleague.

'You two looking for Val, then?' The woman spoke in the gentle local accent. She ushered them towards her open door with the speed typical of a woman with too much time on her hands.

She had clearly already taken a liking to Huw. 'Just call me Gwen, love,' she cooed at him, smiling approvingly at his broad shoulders. She sat them down on a three-seater while she made tea in the kitchen, bringing it in on a tray with cream cakes on a rack.

Huw was staring out towards the garden.

'Val likes to keep herself to herself then?' His voice was low, inviting confidences.

The woman followed his gaze, gave a quiet snort of laughter. 'You'll not get in there,' she said, with an air of finality. 'She won't even have the delivery boy through the door when he needs paying.'

'Not a sociable type then?'

'She used to talk to me through the window sometimes when she saw me. Now she never comes to the front of the house except when there's a delivery.'

Huw put his plate down on the table. 'What sort of person is she?'

The woman settled her cup and saucer into her lap as if it was a favourite cat.

'Very religious. She got herself a special satellite dish so she could pick up those evangelical channels. And she has one of these old-fashioned record players and nearly every record she plays is Welsh hymns; in Welsh, mind, and at full volume by the sound of it.'

Huw bit into his éclair. 'That's not so unusual though, is it? The male choirs still mostly sing Welsh hymns around here.'

The woman picked up a paper napkin with a Santa Claus design from the tray and handed it to him. 'I used to be able to see in through the kitchen in the old days,' she said. 'And there was nothing on the shelves and walls there, no books or pictures, just crucifixes, row upon row of them. Now she's moved upstairs, taken to her bed or something. Anyway, she's gone quite peculiar.'

Huw put his plate back on the table. 'Did she ever explain to you how she'd first become so religious?' he asked.

'Not really, no.'

'Had she always been that way?'

'It wasn't like she was one of the regulars at chapel, and you get some real sticklers round here. But we never saw Val, not even at Easter or Christmas.'

Huw picked up his cup and hesitated. 'How was she with her daughter?'

The woman swallowed a mouthful of tea, shook

her head. 'They never had anything to do with each other. The daughter never visited.'

'But we've been told she used to visit. The daughter used to send her son to stay with the old woman out west.'

'Well, here Val's daughter never visited, nor did the grandson.'

'So something may've happened to cause a rift between the two women?'

Gwen shrugged.

'I honestly couldn't say, love.'

Catrin leant forward in her chair. 'Did the old woman ever mention why she moved back from the west?'

'She said it was because of the type of people coming into the area. That's what she said.'

'What type was that exactly?'

Gwen dabbed at a spot of spilt tea with one of the Christmas napkins.

'That was back in the time a lot of hippies and such were coming from the big cities to live out there.'

'Was there any group in particular?'

The woman sighed, rolled the napkin up into a ball, placed it in her teacup. It was something she didn't appear comfortable talking about. Catrin gave her most understanding smile.

'It's probably not important, but if you could try to remember.'

She had the feeling that the woman remembered perfectly well. She wondered if the hippie groups had offended her sense of what was proper. She glanced over at her again, as if to say she understood.

'There was one group, well, a cult she called them. She said all the members dressed alike. Their leader reminded her of that American man, you know from the Sixties, with the beard, the one they put in prison . . . Charles . . . Charlie . . .'

'Charlie Manson?' Huw put down his cup.

'Yes. Manson. That's right. Val said he was like him, an evil man, she said, a disciple of the devil himself.'

Catrin saw Huw smirking at this, covering his mouth with the napkin. She leant in closer so the woman didn't see him.

'But why did she think he was evil, apart from his beard?'

'Well, there was talk among Val's neighbours that the man had . . .' here the woman paused and lowered her voice, '. . . *relations* with all the women in the group. That sort of thing didn't go down well, as you can imagine.'

As Catrin put down her cup it rattled slightly. 'Did this group have a name?'

The woman hesitated for a few seconds.

'They weren't around for that long, no more than a couple of years, Val said.'

'But something she saw this group doing made her leave the area?'

Gwen hesitated.

'I don't know. The way she described it, this group were very private. They kept to their big house further north, so it's not likely she'd have seen anything they did.'

As if sensing Catrin's eyes on her, she looked down at her lap, where her hands were twisted tightly around each other. Catrin sensed that something the old woman had told Gwen had stayed with her, marked her in some small but indelible way.

'Her daughter was involved with them, wasn't she? That's what upset the old woman.'

'Well, she never said so.'

'But you suspect that was why Val no longer had contact with her daughter.'

Gwen sat motionless in her chair. Catrin watched her fingers, but they remained still. 'Did she mention her grandson Owen much?'

'Hardly, only when I asked.'

'Didn't you think that was odd?'

Gwen thought carefully before replying. She was taking deliberate, deeper breaths now.

'I'm not sure, maybe I did a little.'

'Because even if she'd fallen out with her daughter, she would have still tried to see her grandson. Yet she never mentioned him. That seems rather unnatural.'

Gwen seemed to be weighing this up carefully before commenting.

'Unless the grandson was part of the problem . . .' She said this hesitantly, as if fearful that Catrin would contradict her.

Gwen had started gathering the tea things together. Catrin waited for her to go through to the kitchen. Then she looked over at Huw.

'This leader, the one who looked like Manson, he sounds a bit like the figure who used to pick up Face.'

'Maybe. You're thinking Megan got involved with this group?'

'I don't know, but it sort of fits. Megan is alone a lot, lonely, gets with this group, maybe gets pregnant by one of the members while her husband is away at sea.' She thought it through for a moment. 'So by sending Face to see his grandmother in the west, Megan could've actually been sending him to see his father. When the grandmother discovers this it pushes her over the edge.'

'It's possible.' Huw glanced again at the fence in the back garden. 'All the security measures seem a bit over the top, though. I can't see why she'd be worried after all this time.'

Outside the light had subtly changed, the greyness of the day already taking on the deeper tones of dusk. The sky had filled with strands of pale mauve, signalling more snow to the west. The woman picked up the remaining cups, then stood at the front door, received their thanks for the tea.

'Do you remember the Angel Jones case?' Catrin asked softly. She'd waited for Huw to go on ahead. She was embarrassed to bring it up again in front of him, but something in her wouldn't let her leave until she'd asked the question. 'The man who held those girls in cellars for years.'

Gwen nodded, seemed only too eager to change the subject. Catrin looked the woman straight in the eye. 'Val never made any connections between this Manson figure and Jones, said that she thought it was Jones when he was younger?'

'No, never mentioned him.' The woman paused, her hands dug deeper in the pockets of her apron. 'Funny you mention Jones.'

'Why's that?'

'Well, a neighbour here.' She pointed to another house in the close. 'She was shopping in Aber the other day, swears she saw someone looking like Jones walk right past her, close as you are to me now.' She laughed slightly. 'Knew it wasn't him of course, but still, gave her quite a turn.'

Huw had come back into earshot. Catrin felt ashamed. She knew asking questions on the sly went against one of the basic rules of trust between investigating officers.

And he was still an officer at heart and abided by those rules.

The woman seemed subdued. Huw turned to face her. 'You said at that time this cult had a house up the coast. Did the old woman ever mention where they were based?'

'Not in exact terms, no.'

'But generally?'

'Somewhere up north of Abergwaun.'

'There aren't many villages up on those headlands. Any idea which?'

'Not really, no.'

The woman seemed eager for them to be gone now. Catrin didn't wait for Huw but pulled her coat tight around her shoulders and hurried down the path. While they were inside the temperature had dropped several degrees, and snow had begun to fall again. They sat in the car for a moment in silence.

'I'm sorry I did that,' Catrin said.

She knew Huw was aware of what she was referring to, but he said nothing, as if he didn't understand.

'Asking about Jones when you couldn't hear,' she said, 'it was wrong of me.'

He still said nothing. He looked disappointed and was trying to hide it and she hated seeing him like that.

'Should we go back to Pryce's?' she said. 'Show him

photos of Jones, just to eliminate Jones once and for all.'

Huw shrugged his shoulders, as if he didn't care either way.

'Let's sleep on it.' He started the heater, turned it up full. 'On all that medication, Pryce could just send us off after more shadows.'

3

The high winds nearer the coast and driving snow made the final part of the journey slow and difficult. By the time they began the descent into Abergwaun, strong gusts were pushing the car out to the edges of the sheer drops. They had to crawl down the cliffside road in second gear.

As they drove into the small town, through the snow-spattered windscreen Catrin could see the wind whipping the breakers into spiky, white-topped peaks. On the other side of the road was a row of boarding houses. Most were shut up for the winter, but one sign was still illuminated and some lights showed behind curtains in the windows.

In the narrow hall was an oak desk and an antique brass bell, which made no sound when pressed. On the window at the side of the door, the nets had been pushed aside. Someone had been standing there, watching the waves.

Under the sill was a half-drunk mug of tea and a copy of that day's *Western Telegraph*. No one came, and Catrin picked up the paper. The first pages were taken up by the weather stories. She leafed through them, only half looking at the images of desolate snowbound headlands and narrow tracks blocked by drifts.

'So what Gwen told us at least gives Face some connection to this remote part of the country,' she said.

'But she said that group moved away from here after a few years.'

'Right. Most of those alternative hippie groups moved away decades ago. It's difficult to see what could have brought Face back after all this time.'

'Unless the original group or some of its members were still out here?'

Catrin thought about this possibility for a while before answering. 'Gwen said the group all dressed alike, like a cult. In the photos, the men in the woods were all dressed alike in those robes and hoods.'

'But we're talking almost four decades since the woman saw this group. It seems next to impossible they could have been living isolated out here all this time without anyone knowing.'

She was looking over Huw's shoulder at the pictures of the heavily wooded snowy terrain. 'We know Rhys's photos were developed out here. So Rhys could have known about Face's old link to these parts.'

'Though we don't know where Rhys's pictures were taken.'

'Not yet.'

From behind a velvet drape to the side of the hall an elderly man in a neck-brace appeared. He wrote their names in the ledger in a neat, copperplate script. Then at Huw's request he showed them into the dining room. There was no one else eating. Outside the dark band of the sea was just visible beyond a pale ribbon of sand.

The food was brought through by a small, white-haired mouselike woman, the man in the neck-brace doubling as a waiter. As Catrin waited for the food on her plate to cool, Huw fastidiously put a piece of every ingredient on the plate on his fork before lifting it to his lips.

When he raised his head, she looked away towards the window. Down on the street an old camper van was parked under the shelter of the promenade, dim candlelight flickering behind its curtains. Two people, one holding a bottle, were walking towards the van. A side door opened. They stood talking for a moment in the small patch of light. Then they walked on towards the row of boarding houses and disappeared into the snow.

Huw had stopped eating and was looking out at the spot where they had disappeared. 'At first sight this would seem to be the perfect environment to hide out in,' he said.

'A large choice of cheap rooms, all the surf bums and other strays as camouflage?'

He put his fork down on his plate, shook his head. 'But in winter these towns have an occupancy of around a tenth of the summer season. Everybody knows everybody else's business. To hide down here you'd need the protection of a significant part of the community.'

The plates were removed and two steaming bowls of apple crumble and custard set down in front of them. Catrin ate in silence, aware of Huw's eyes on her mouth. How easy it is to forget, she thought, what a peculiarly intimate experience it is watching someone place things between their lips, then swallow them.

The television in the corner was showing a long-running soap, one she'd never followed. The two main characters were driving through the rain, which ran down the windscreen, covering their faces. Their car gradually disappeared down a long straight road.

Then the news came on. The top story was the weather once more. A reporter was shown sheltering in the entrance of a windswept ferry terminal. A sign showed that all ferries were still cancelled. The same reporter was shown beside a series of gritting trucks moving tentatively up narrow country roads.

Then she saw an image she recognised. Amid snow-covered fields there was a stone bridge, a track winding into wooded hills. The next shot showed the flashing blue lights of ambulances and fire engines. 'Christ,' she said. 'Look at this.'

Another reporter, an older man this time, was standing in front of the lights. In the background there was a glimpse of something low, dark and smouldering.

An ambulance was pulling away across the yard, followed by another. Black smoke drifted across the scene. The reporter looked calm, as if this was all just routine for him. In a neutral tone he said that all three members of the family had perished in the fire, that its cause remained unknown.

She thought of the young girl and the woman walking across the field. The little girl in her pinafore, her chestnut hair and searching eyes. Then through the smoke an image flickered over the screen, so briefly Catrin hardly saw it. In the foreground were charred timbers and blackened cloths, the remains of curtains flapping in the wind. Behind she saw a figure among the trees. The image was there for less than a second then it was gone. For a moment she thought she was going to be sick right there at the table. She began to push the chair back, meaning to go to the bathroom. She rose, steadied herself with one hand on the top of the chair, then slowly sat down again.

'Looks like we got out of there just in time.' She could hear the shudder in Huw's voice. His face was pale, drained of colour.

'Or we were followed there, more like,' she said. 'Look at the date on the film, the tone of the sky. That news footage was filmed yesterday, just after we left.'

'But you saw how narrow and quiet that track was. If anyone had followed us we'd have known about it.'

'They could have tailed us at a distance without lights. I thought I saw someone there in the trees.'

'How clear?'

'Not at all, it was just a flicker.'

'Worth getting the footage off the channel?'

'Doubt it.' Catrin took out her phone, searched for the channel's press office and after a wait was put through. She told the young press officer she needed a copy of the footage for an ongoing arson investigation, that there wasn't time to get a warrant. She gave her identity number, but not a whole number, she knew it'd mean nothing if there was a trace put on it.

The girl said she'd send it through digitally within minutes. Catrin gave her a private Gmail account as receiving address, then went into Gmail and registered the address she'd just given under a bogus name.

She turned back to Huw. 'They're sending it through. I think we must have been followed there by whoever did this.'

'But that track was too rough to navigate without lights, the country there was silent as the grave. Another engine would have been heard for miles around.'

'How the hell did they know we'd gone there then? A tracker?'

Huw looked sceptical. 'I had the car swept before we set out.'

'At the station?'

'My two guys had eyeball on it throughout.'

'At Della's office?'

'I never let it out of my sight.'

He's sharper than he looks, she thought.

'If we weren't tracked, then something weird has just happened here.' Huw stared at her. She stood up. 'I need some air, so I can think straight.'

He followed her out to the car.

Catrin checked the engine first, from underneath with a torch in her mouth, then went over all the components again from above. Then she worked through the interior, pulled out all the carpets, all the trim. Nothing. Then she went through the boot, the undercarriage.

Then she started again, repeated the whole process in reverse order.

'It looks clean,' she said finally.

'I told you.' Huw had been sitting watching at a distance, the glow of his pipe the only sign he was there.

She heard a bleeping from her phone. The footage from the channel had come. She ran it straight through from the beginning: the ambulances pulling away across the yard, the black smoke drifting across the scene, the glimpses of charred wreckage in the darkness. But looking at it again she couldn't see any shape in the woods any more.

Huw went inside to get his laptop. 'Mine has a high resolution,' he said, '1600 x 1200 pixels, if it's there we'll see it.' Soon he'd appeared again with his customised Mac, some hot chocolate and a bottle of whisky. They sat in the car and played the section through again. The drifting smoke, followed by the smouldering shapes in the background. This time there was a momentary view among the timbers of a wheel-chair lying there empty, then the blackened curtains. Then the woods behind. But there was nothing among the trees: there was no dim shape that matched what she thought she'd just seen.

'Shit,' she said, 'I'm sorry, there's nothing there.'

She could sense that Huw thought she'd been winging it, letting her imagination get the better of her. She took a quick swig of whisky, then started the engine.

'All right,' she said. 'It's time to check our only real lead so far in this case.'

Catrin drove fast, by a roundabout route back to a street only a few blocks from the hotel. She'd already studied the maps, so she wouldn't have to use the satnav. The satnav worked on wireless, she knew it was penetrable.

She kept the headlights full on. There was no other traffic on the road. There were moments when she could see only thick banks of snow. The winds driving the snow were pummelling the car. Along the roadside the ground dropped away sheer to the frothing peaks of the distant breakers.

The photographic shop was on a street so narrow they had to park the car on the street above. There were no lights on in the shop, but one in the flat above. Further down, an old Toyota was parked half up on the pavement. It was only covered in a thin layer of snow.

'If that's their car,' she said, 'it looks like the owners are back from their holiday.'

In the distance, through the fog, there was another pair of headlights. They were at the other end of the lane, not moving forward. They were high off the ground, as if on a four-wheel-drive vehicle or a van.

Abruptly, they swung away, and the vehicle disappeared again into the fog. Catrin heard the revving of the engine, then a high whining noise as the vehicle sped off, already too far away to follow.

She pointed into the bank of fog. 'That looked like a tail,' she said.

'Them or us?'

'Not sure.'

She picked up the envelope of photographs and ran down to the door. The tanned young man who answered was in his early twenties, with shoulder-length dreadlocks. He looked tired, hung-over from all the booze on the flight back.

'Can't this wait until the morning,' he said. He tried to shut the door, but Catrin pushed in past him.

She slapped the envelope down on the counter as Huw came in, allowing the door to slam in the wind. She reached into her coat, flashed her ID card. When he saw it the boy looked nervous, scratched his hair.

'Do you know a Rhys Williams?' she asked.

'Name doesn't ring a bell.'

She leant back hard against the stand of cheap digital cameras behind her. It began to rock. One of the cameras dropped, slid along the floor.

'It's just that he sent us these photographs and here's your name on the back of the envelope.'

The boy looked at the stand rocking, then down at

the gold sticker. She put out a hand, caught the stand before it fell.

'Yes, that's us,' he said. 'But this order came through our collection service.'

Huw leant forwards, putting his full weight on the edge of the till.

'How does that work then?'

The boy pointed to a box fixed against the outer wall of the shop.

'The customer puts in his memory stick, CD-ROM or film, then the machine provides a docket and a time of collection.'

'So you wouldn't have seen who collected the pictures?'

The boy shook his head.

'There's not enough custom to have the shop open in the winter. We just come down to fill and empty the machine.'

Catrin pulled one of the photographs from the envelope.

'Can you give me a date on this?'

The boy looked at the back of the photograph under the light, then balanced it in his open palm.

'This has been printed on our new chlorobromide paper,' he said. 'So it's been done in the last six months.'

'And the photograph?'

He looked at it again.

'It's digital, but the image is undated. It looks like the camera's dating system was disabled. There's no way of telling when the photograph itself was taken – it could be years old.'

'Wouldn't the customer contact details be entered with the order?'

The boy held up the envelope and pointed at its blank front.

'There's no name or number on the envelope, so it appears this customer never entered contact details.'

She brought out the rest of the images of the hooded figures in the surrounding woodland.

'Recognise any of this?'

The boy looked at the pictures, one after the other, and began shaking his head slowly, emphatically. Then just as he was passing them back, he looked at one again. She thought he'd recognised something, but then he just shook his head again and handed the photo to her.

'Could be anywhere around here,' he said.

'So it looks local?'

'Well, local covers the entire national park. We're talking hundreds of miles of woods and headlands that look just like that.'

Huw had already turned away, was walking back towards the door. Catrin was about to follow him when she had a thought and turned back to the boy.

'Your answer service,' she said. 'Get any odd calls on it the last eight weeks?'

The boy smiled. 'There was one,' he said.

'In what way?'

'Cardiff accent, asked me what times the box was filled up again.'

'So what was odd about that?'

'He sounded, well, weird like. Anxious, jumpy. He wanted me to call him back to a public box. Gave an exact time to call him.'

She looked at Huw, a thin smile on her lips.

'The box number he gave you, do you still have a record of it?' she said.

'That'd be the Dinas Island one,' the boy said.

'How do you know?'

'Because when I called, it was the pub phone. Seems it's the only public phone that works for miles up there.'

It was warmer back in the car. Huw shifted in his seat, turned towards Catrin.

'Did you think the boy was on the level?' he asked.

'Difficult to know. But if someone wanted to have photos developed and stay out of sight, this would have been a very convenient way of doing it.'

'You're sure it was Rhys, though?'

'Cardiff accent, sounded weird, anxious. Has to be worth a look.'

She drove back slowly through the falling snow to the hotel. There was a single light in a dormer window at the top.

Two shadows crossed the curtains. It appeared that the old man and his wife were turning in for the night. The sign and the lights along the short drive had been switched off. The two lower floors were in darkness.

She told Huw to wait behind her in the hall, and took the keys to the empty rooms from the rack behind the desk. She found the switches for the drive lights there and switched them on, so they could see anyone approaching from the street. Then slowly she went from room to room, turning on the lights, checking behind the furniture. She knocked on the door at the top, told the couple she and Huw were back and they'd lock up.

When she came downstairs Huw was already going down the passage to his room. He turned to her for a moment but said nothing, closed his door. Catrin still felt they were being watched. She switched off the light in the hall, then walked out, locking the door behind her. Nothing was moving except the stunted palmettos shaking in the wind. She got into the car, didn't start the engine. She sat there in the dark cabin, watching the street.

No vehicles passed, she saw no one out in the swirling confusion of the snow. The flakes were settling on the windscreen, she could barely see more than a few yards.

Catrin felt herself begin to lose track of time: her eyelids closing. She began to wonder if she was wasting her time, whoever was following them was not showing themselves, not yet anyway. She got out, into the cold air, and opened the boot where earlier she'd noticed the car alarm hardware. The system was top-end Bosch, retro not factory-fitted, she noticed. She set the touch-sensitive function, then the sensors on the mirrors and wings. The system could still be bypassed by someone who knew what they were doing. She'd check it again in the morning before they set off.

She went back into the hall, locked the door, then went up to her room. At the desk, she turned on her Mac, clicked into the aerial map of the national park. The boy in the shop had mentioned a small headland far to the north of the park. It appeared barely in-habited, connected to the mainland by a small causeway and like the surrounding areas was covered in deep woodland.

Catrin remembered what the woman in the village had said about the group living out on one of the head-lands. She zoomed in to maximum scale. There was a large house, but it was a care centre, a private clinic of some sort. The place has almost certainly changed hands several times since the group were there all those years ago, she thought.

She ran a few searches on the name, Dinas Island.

Little of interest came up. It was listed on a couple of ramblers' sites as a stopover on routes across the park. But apart from that, almost nothing. There were no residents' associations, no local forums that mentioned it. The place didn't seem to have any presence at all on the web.

Next she checked for historical links, but there wasn't much there either. She found references to a small Augustinian abbey, founded in the twelfth century, but by the sixteenth century the place had already been abandoned. Clicking back to the map, she could see no trace of it. She knew that abbeys were sometimes built on sites sacred to the old religion. But there were no signs of standing stones or other features that marked any ancient site. Almost all the small, club-like contours of the island looked to be covered by steep crags and dense woodland.

After a few more searches on local historical society sites the only links coming up were to a trial back in the early nineteenth century, and to the great storm of 1859. She glanced briefly at the link to the trial. It was to a site that judging by the graphics and lurid colouring was aimed at a younger audience, death metal fans and Goths. The material there had all been pasted from another source, a book by a pre-war American academic on historical witchcraft in West Wales. She clicked straight into an academic archive service she'd used before, and found the original book. The entry took up less than a page, and the details appeared rather sketchy. At the county assizes in 1837 a local landowner, Wyre Penrhyn, and his son Owen, had been accused of conjuration of evil spirits; there were no court records cited, only local newspapers. The account claimed other children in the same family and in the area had become possessed by spirits, and had disappeared into a cave which locals believed to be a mouth of hell. Both the men had escaped from prison prior to trial, so their trial had never been completed.

In a final brief paragraph the historian stated only that sightings of the older man, Penrhyn, had continued in the area for many years afterwards, as had the disappearances of local children. No sources for these later incidents were given. The entry ended by saying that the sightings had persisted long after the man would have completed his natural life, leading some at the time to say he had entered into some form of demonic pact or congress.

Catrin checked the next page, but there was only a small illustration. The drawing looked much older than the incidents described, from the sixteenth or seventeenth century. It showed a man wearing long black robes standing at the mouth of a cave. His arms were outstretched as in an act of supplication or worship. At the edge of the cave stood several young people, their faces distorted, as were their limbs, within a circle of what appeared to be black arrowheads or feathers. The man she thought must be intended to represent the witch, and those in the foreground the possessed children. The lines were crude and blurred, and Catrin suspected the author had included the picture because he'd been unable to find any later drawings to illustrate his material.

The story as it stood was evidently far from complete and lacked many details. The material she felt seemed to hint at another story behind the story. But whatever form it had originally taken, it was likely no more than another tall country tale, not relevant to the case except in one possible way: there was a chance it had been known by the cult leader, the Manson figure who had gone out there in the Seventies. Possibly this had even been the reason he'd chosen to locate there. She remembered other examples of this among cult leaders from the period. A cult set up on an island once owned by Aleister Crowley, another in an old manor in the Marches where a coven had once met. Maybe the witchcraft story had been used by the leader to inspire interest or fear in his followers. Maybe he'd deliberately identified himself with the figure who was believed to have made the pact. She wondered how this might connect to Face, and what Rhys could have found out there after all this time.

She clicked into the links to the storm of 1859. The

official records showed that a twelfth-century church, St Brynach's, along with fishing crafts and over twenty houses, had been destroyed at the time. None had been rebuilt and the small hamlet there had fallen into ruin. After that Catrin could find not a single further reference to the place. She turned off the lights, lay in the dark listening for footsteps or the whine of an engine but hearing only the sound of the waves.

Later when she couldn't sleep she went along the passage and knocked on Huw's door. The curtains hadn't been drawn, the light from the street filling the cramped room. The double bed was more like a generous single, the chest of drawers taking up the rest of the space.

She heard only the muted sound of the breakers outside. A large pipe with beads hanging off the bowl was sitting on the table, still smoking thinly, the close air heavy with its sweet aroma.

She sensed rather than saw Huw as she turned around. He took her by the shoulders. As his face moved closer she shut her eyes, feeling that old, familiar sensation of falling, not downwards but back into some distant, hollow space where nothing touched her.

There was a vague awareness of his hands running down her back, as she pulled his arms around her. She allowed him to continue, his movements slow, languorous. She kept her eyes closed, her flesh puckering in the cool air, her breasts swaying gently as she unhooked her bra, her nipples hard from the cold.

She turned her back to him, but kept her head half towards him, their lips still just touching. Do I want to control him, or let him control me, she wondered. Perhaps neither, perhaps I just want to protect him, as Rhys once protected me. It's the debt I carry in my soul. She felt him run his hands down her back and legs before kissing her shoulders, then his tongue across her nape, down her spine. She turned, pulled his head down between her legs.

'Come on then,' she said. 'Show me if all those years of experience have taught you anything useful.' The pleasure shuddered silently through her. She heard the waves breaking on the promenade outside, as she lay back almost still. He moved into her slowly while he stroked her, she felt herself being rocked like a child. She realised she was crying then, silently, and turned her head away so he wouldn't sense her tears. Then she felt his lips on her cheeks, gently kissing away the tears.

She felt him touch her hair, a vague, gentle movement, as if he was only half aware he was doing it. 'No women in your life, Huw?'

He didn't reply, rolled over towards the wall, one hand still loose over her thigh. When she looked down, he was glancing back at her.

'What about you, no men?' he said.

She didn't answer. No live ones, she thought, only a ghost. Huw ran his hand over her neck.

'You never said much about your mam,' he said.

'Not much to tell. She was a hippie, then an addict. Familiar story?'

'Did she tell you any more about your father in the end?'

Catrin took slow, deep breaths.

'I don't think she ever knew him that well. She was into free love and all that. A lot of men came in and out of her life.'

She let her head slip down onto his chest. She lay very still for a few minutes, then as she heard his breathing easing, she got up off the bed. By the door to the bathroom she paused, picked up her phone. There were several more calls from Thomas's number, but no messages. Huw lay face down, his eyes closed, his breathing deep and regular.

She picked up the packet of cigarettes on the dressing table, shook one loose, lit it with the book of matches in the ashtray. Outside the window three lorries were moving slowly up the road.

In the flickering pool of the headlights there was a sudden glimpse of yellow diggers, mounds of earth, tree roots and debris. Then all was darkness again, the shapes hidden by the outlines of the buildings and the high cliffs over the road north.

4

The fog closed in as they drove north along the narrow, cliff-top roads. Catrin had checked the car before they set out and found nothing. She kept the satnav off and they navigated with a map. At times they could see no further than a few yards ahead. It took several hours to cover only a few miles. There were no other cars on the road, no lights following. Several times she pulled over, waited, but no cars passed them.

They stopped at a pub along the way to find out whether the one road onto Dinas Island was still passable. A farmer said it had been that morning so they decided to press on. As they started their descent through the winding high-hedged lanes, she pulled the car over onto the roadside. They got out to try to get a better sense of what lay ahead of them. As their eyes adjusted to the dimness the unusual geography of the place gradually revealed itself. The island was not an island in the strict sense but a club-shaped headland several miles across and bounded on each side by cliffs.

The cliffs fell sheer to the churning breakers beneath them, this darkness broken only by the specks of foaming blowholes and a line of needle-shaped rocks rising to the north. The only link to the mainland appeared to be a lane running along a slender spit, a natural bridge between the opposing bluffs. It was visible as a thin black line rising towards a shelf cut into the cliffs that loomed out of the fog. Above on the thermals black-backed gulls and chough rode and through the screeching of the wind Catrin could hear the low, whining call of ravens.

Returning to the car, they drove slowly across the narrow spit, then down towards the headland across a plain of frozen winter bracken. The place seemed more extensive than it had appeared from the mainland. The road narrowed and wound through woods of ancient oaks, the way wide enough for just a single vehicle. Among the trees the only sign of habitation was a pair of black wrought-iron gates behind which glimpses of gables appeared among the branches.

From the gates the lane led through the woods until it came out at a cluster of cottages around a small, ruined chapel. There were no cars parked along the roadside. The cottages were empty, rotting shells, without windows and roofs. All the way down into the village the only sounds had been the cawing of the birds, and the crash of the breakers far below.

But now there was a sudden stillness broken by the distant note of a foghorn from further down the shore.

Nothing they had yet seen committed the area either to the twentieth or the twenty-first century. They drove on past a further warren of cottages, built close to the edge of the cliff. Catrin slowed beside a view through the fog to the same line of needle-shaped rocks they had seen from the mainland.

'A lot of people out here used to survive off smuggling and wrecking,' she said.

'And now?'

'Off not much, by the looks of things.'

Beyond the village, they saw ahead the lights of a larger building, and two smaller cabins at an unmarked junction. These looked as if they had once been craft shops, but now were closed, either for the winter or permanently. The shutters were partly down, the windows boarded-up. Through one they could just make out some dust-covered shelves of Celtic crosses and pentangles alongside pendants and earrings of the same elaborate designs.

They carried on to the larger building, where the windows on the lower floor were dimly lit, a trail of grey smoke rising from the chimney. In front was a gravel clearing, an old-fashioned petrol pump set up beside a hut. Two rusting camper vans were parked on a square of poured concrete, a ragged fence separating it from the drop to the rocks below.

'This must be the pub with the phone,' Catrin said and pulled in.

The high grass at the front obscured the path to the entrance. Under a weathered lintel the door was ajar, revealing a pub interior. Several men were standing at the bar, dressed in boots and fishermen's sweaters, the type of foul-weather gear that marked them out as locals.

It was dark inside. A bar counter stretched the length of the room. Behind it on the wall were photographs of different generations of a local lifeboat crew as its only decoration. There was a facial similarity between most of the lifeboat men, grandfathers, fathers and sons going down the years. Occasionally more than two generations appearing in the same shot. The barman had much the same features, was dressed the same way as the crews, but Catrin could not see his face in the pictures.

She noticed they were already attracting glances from the men further down the bar. She saw the phone now, and why Rhys had chosen it. It was the old-fashioned sort, with a long cord, so he could have backed into the passage behind to make his calls unheard. She went over to it, memorised the number. Later she'd try to get call lists from the service provider, see if any interesting numbers came up. But she didn't hold out much hope.

Rhys had probably not used it more than a few times. If he believed he was being tracked, in danger, she knew he wouldn't have used any regular call points. One of the reasons he'd been such an effective under-cover officer had been his unpredictability. Lay down patterns of behaviour, and you become predictable. Become predictable, you become vulnerable. It was probably one of the few rules Rhys had still lived by.

She approached two men at the bar and pulled up a stool. One man was short, with curly black hair. His companion was taller, his beard and sandy hair fading to grey. Putting her bag up on the bar, she took out the picture of Rhys from her wallet, another of Face cut out from a CD cover. She put them both on the bar.

'Seen either of these two recently?' she asked quietly.

The men looked over briefly and shook their heads. In the poor light she knew they could hardly see the photographs. But they made no effort to look more closely. She passed the pictures down to the men at the other end, who barely glanced at the shots and shook their heads.

'Looking for someone?' The voice was educated, probably English, definitely not local. She looked round. A young man in a long dark coat was standing behind her. She hadn't noticed him as she'd gone over to the phone.

He had thick fair hair, the even features of a romantic lead, somewhere on the borderline between handsome and bland. His cheeks were flushed, his eyes narrowed. Unlike the regulars at the bar he looked like a man with a purpose.

The man asked her again if she was looking for someone. He was keeping his voice low, so the others couldn't hear. His forehead, she noticed, was covered with a beading sweat. She nodded, showed him the two pictures. He passed quickly over the image of Rhys and looked more closely at the shot of Face.

'Isn't that that singer who jumped off the Severn Bridge?'

Huw was standing behind the man now, leaning an elbow on the bar.

'Why?' he asked. 'Has someone else been looking for him?'

The man's eyes were slightly glazed, feverish. His breath smelt stale.

'If there had been I'm sure I'd have heard about it,' he said. 'This is a small place, word would have got around.'

Huw was running his eyes over the man's well-cut coat.

'You don't exactly look like a local.' The man

glanced at the characters in waterproofs and heavy jerseys.

'I'll take that as a compliment,' he said drily.

'What brings you down here then?' Huw asked.

'The clinic. I'm the new psychiatrist there.'

'It's a psychiatric unit?'

'Just a rehab unit. Part private, part National Health funded.'

'So you'd know if any celebrities like Face had stayed?'

'I'd be the first to know,' he said, smiling. 'But we tend just to get routine referrals from the local NHS trusts.'

Huw indicated the men at the other end of the bar.

'When my friend showed the photographs around, the others here weren't exactly helpful.'

The man motioned Catrin and Huw away from the bar, the sheen of sweat over his face glistening in the half-light. He took out a silver cigarette case, tamping the tip of a cigarette briefly on the case before lighting it. His fingers were trembling slightly.

'You have to understand,' he said. 'The clinic up in the woods is just about the only employer here. Many of the patients stay on after their treatment, living in the community. They're given work at the clinic. They enjoy the peace and quiet and keep out of anything that smells like trouble.'

He signalled to the barman, who pulled a pint of Felinfoel and slid it along to him. A quick ripple of laughter passed between the men at the bar. Catrin put the photographs away in her bag. She waited for the young doctor to come back with his drink, then pushed the ashtray over to his side of the table.

'We heard there was some hippie cult here in the Seventies. They were led by a character who looked a bit like Charlie Manson. Anyone like that still around?'

The man smiled thinly, shook his head, tapped a worm of ash into the ashtray.

'No one like that.'

'Anyone still here from those times?'

'Not that I know of. But Old Tudor might know.'

'Old Tudor?'

'He works part-time as a nurse at the clinic. He's got one of those New Age shops on the road to the woods. It used to attract the hippie types in the summers. He came back here a couple of years ago. It's on my way to the clinic, I'll take you,' he said.

Outside the wind stung their faces. The man pulled a scarf over his face, eyes narrowed against the frozen grit being blown across the drive. He held out one gloved hand to Huw, then to Catrin, his back turned to the wind.

'Name's Doctor Smith by the way, Jonty Smith.' He

laughed briefly, nervously, began to cough. He got into a large pickup, and they followed him past the gift shop with its dusty displays, past the cottages and ruined church. He took a fork left, out along a straight road under an arching tunnel of birches and black alders.

Where the trees thinned there were brief views over the entire island. The place was much larger than it had looked from the shore. Through the fog loomed a long escarpment, an inland cliff face, that seemed almost to cut the island in half on the diagonal, running from south-west to north-east. They were driving along the lower half of the island and there was no obvious way to climb to the higher ground. There might be goat tracks, but it looked inaccessible by car.

Catrin took a pair of binoculars from the glovebox. There was no evidence of any paths up the sheer face. Above she could see only more dense forest and some further rising of the ground hidden by the steep, mist-shrouded cliffs.

About two miles along they came to a lay-by. On either side were thickets of hawthorn and piles of moss-covered logs. Set back from the clearing, a few yards down a frozen track, stood a prefabricated shed. It had been painted black, the twelve signs of the zodiac added in silver and glinting at them through the gloom.

Catrin pulled the car up a few feet short of the shop,

which looked deserted. No lights were visible, the door was closed and there was no sign to indicate whether the place was open for business.

'It looks closed,' she said.

Smith coughed again, opening his door.

'To the general public maybe, but Tudor'll be here. He kips on a folding bed in the stockroom summer and winter. He'll open up for me.'

The glass in the door was covered with faded papers advertising tarot card, palm and crystal readings. Huw pushed on the door. It was locked, but the movement was enough to cause wind chimes to jangle inside. Catrin peered through the gaps between the posters, saw several candles in tall holders giving out a weak, flickering light.

Smith banged his fist against the door. 'Open up, Tudor! It's the fraud squad!'

The man who opened the door to them was perhaps more than six and a half feet tall. He had a mane of long white hair, an extravagant beard, and was wearing the local uniform of waterproofs under a long black cloak. They trooped in, Tudor holding the door open, Huw ushering Catrin in ahead of him into a dark room filled with the scent of the candles.

Smith gave another of his dismissive snorts.

'Dear, dear. Forgot to pay our electricity bill again?'

Tudor led them back towards some seats by the till.

'What's all this about the fraud squad?' His deep voice betrayed no obvious anxiety.

Smith gestured at the arrays of tarot cards, crystals, bottles of homeopathic oils, dream-catchers, amulets, then at the shelves filled with black magic guides and histories of Celtic mysticism.

'Everything in this shop is a load of old bollocks, Tudor. We both know it. You're a bloody fraud, man.'

He barked another laugh, coughed, took out his cigarette case, ignoring the 'no smoking' sign that hung behind the till, and busied himself with lighting up. Catrin reached out to shake Tudor's hand, smiling apologetically.

'Get many visitors through in the summer?' she asked.

The old man pulled out the chairs around the low table so they could sit down. 'A few twitchers, ramblers from Cadw.' He spoke in a slow, wheezing drawl.

She glanced round the shop, there was a track through the dust from the counter to the table and chairs. Nothing else had been touched for some time. Tudor said nothing more, looking from Huw to the doctor as if checking everyone was comfortable in their seats, then slowly he turned to Catrin again.

'You remember how it was here in the early Seventies?' she asked, holding the old man's gaze. The man was looking to the back of the shed, a faraway look in his eyes. 'Do you remember a hippie group, a commune that lived in a big house at that time?'

The old man sat down beside the counter. Behind it were pictures of a young teenage girl, tanned with brown cloudy eyes, pretty, his daughter perhaps. The pictures were ringed with fairy-lights and more flickering candles. Draped over the frames was a garland of feathers, shells and small bones, a fetish, like one of the amulets on the shelves, but more elaborate. The girl reminded Catrin a little of the fan she'd seen in a picture in Pryce's room, but as she looked closer she saw that was all it was: a resemblance, an echo, no more than that. The combination of the girl's pale skin and thick coal-black hair was common enough in the area.

'Your daughter?' she asked. 'She's very pretty.' The old man made a noise that sounded pained. From the counter he had picked up a briar pipe. He had a slight tremor in both his hands.

'You asked if I remembered a group in a big house,' he said at last. 'There were a lot of hippie groups coming through at the time.'

'But this one was different, they had money. They didn't mix much. It was rumoured their leader had relations with all the women in his group.'

Tudor looked down at the floor, gave what seemed a wry smile. 'Their children dressed alike, the leader was the one with long hair?' he asked.

Huw nodded. The man pushed his hands under his weatherproofs. 'Like you said, they kept themselves to themselves,' he said.

Huw looked across at Catrin, then back to the old man.

'But they must have come down to the village?'

'Occasionally a couple of the older ones would come to buy provisions. But they never spoke to the locals or mixed.'

'You remember what they looked like?'

'Not really. It's a long time ago.'

Catrin pulled her chair closer to the old man.

'You said the children dressed alike, so you must have seen them?'

'Only from a distance.'

'But you saw them?'

'A few times I saw them playing in the wood above the hall, near the place where the villagers used to go to collect firewood.'

'How did they appear?'

There was a silence. Smith looked as if he was about to say something but Huw held up his hand. It was at least half a minute before the old man spoke again.

'Well-fed, well-dressed. Not like the other kids that I used to see hanging round with the hippie groups.'

'And what were they doing when you saw them?'

Catrin watched the man closely as he paused again. She had the sense, as she'd had with Gwen in Bancyfelin, that what he was remembering had unsettled him in some way that he didn't wish to share.

'I'd gone to collect hazel in the copses on the ridge,' he said at last. 'There's a view from there down through the ashes into a small glade. The edges are heavily wooded, it's not easy to see.'

'But could you see what they were doing?' Huw asked.

'They'd always be playing a game, like hunt the thimble, but with a straw doll. That's all I ever saw them doing there.'

'So you saw nothing that seemed unusual then?'

The man hesitated for a moment, and Catrin saw his hands were held tight between his thighs. 'Not really, no.'

'Either you did or you didn't,' said Huw quietly.

'It was rough, wooded terrain up there, with a ground cover of bracken. Like I said, it was difficult to see.'

'Could you hear anything?'

'No, just the occasional shrieking noise.' The old man was sucking his bottom lip in under his top teeth. 'The one looking wore some kind of costume. It looked like something home-made, with feathers on the arms.'

Catrin held his gaze. 'Any adults around?'

'The leader was there in the background, watching. No one else.'

Tudor had taken the pipe from his pocket, begun to fill it from a beaded pouch of tobacco. Huw took a lighter from his pocket, passed it over to him.

'We heard they used to live in a large house. Do you know where that was?'

'That was the hall up in the woods, where the clinic is now.'

The old man pointed up at something in a frame next to the pictures of the young girl. It was an old map which showed the club-like shape of the headland. To the north, some stylised stones marked the site of a cromlech. It hadn't been visible in the aerial map, so Catrin thought it must now be covered by the trees. Back then the northern part of the island, high above the escarpment, was unpopulated and there was no sign of any track leading from low to high. She wondered if the mapmaker had even visited the high ground. Certainly there was no sign on the map of any habitation there.

Tudor now indicated with his pipe a Celtic cross that marked the site of a large building. It was somewhat isolated, in a thickly wooded area just below the escarpment.

'But this group were only living on the island for a few years – in the early Seventies. Do you know who owned the hall then?' Huw asked.

'The place was derelict for years before the group moved in there.'

'Someone must have owned it?'

'The villagers say the same family owned it ever since there'd been an abbey there in medieval times. The Abbey was built beneath the cromlech – they built the religious houses then on the sites sacred to the old religion. After the old family died out it fell into ruin, until the group you're asking about began to renovate it.'

'Anyone else left in the area from that time?'

Yet again the old man took his time with his reply.

'There are one or two I recognise occasionally. They work at the clinic part-time. It's the only employer here. But I don't see them out and about much.'

He passed the lighter back to Huw who was standing up now, fastening his jacket. 'Do they live in the village, these old-timers?' Huw asked.

Tudor shrugged his broad shoulders, and got up to show them out. Smith had also risen; he seemed in a hurry to be gone now. 'There's a café a few hundred yards further up the road,' he said. 'That's where all the workers from the clinic meet after their shifts.'

Smith walked out to his pickup. Shale crunched under his tyres as he revved the engine then moved off fast down the lane.

The grey sky had darkened, the earlier snow had turned to a thin icy rain spotting the window. As the sound of the engine faded everything was silent. Over the windows Catrin noticed heavy reinforced metal blinds. Huw was helping the old man to edge them down. She glanced out past them. For a moment she thought she saw something glowing among the trees. But when she looked again it had vanished among the thick branches.

She went out and stood looking into the trees. The wind had dropped. It was still now. Further along she saw what looked like lights at the bottom of the escarpment, just a narrow glow between the branches. All around it the trees spread in a thick smudge more black than green, without clearings or paths.

'Look,' she said. 'Seems like there's another hut down there.'

Huw was standing at her shoulder. 'Well, some lights anyway. Could be anything.'

She peered closer but there was nothing more to see, just a thin strip of light. Behind her, old Tudor stood following her gaze out into the trees. Immediately he backed away inside.

She heard the heavy door closing behind them, the rasping of several large locks.

'Not very friendly is he, all of a sudden,' Huw said. The rain skated down the windscreen in fat droplets as Catrin turned the car down the lane. In silence she watched the outline of the headland slowly appearing through the sheets of rain as they made their way down again to the village. A shiver passed through her body.

* * *

Catrin told the barman she wanted to see all the rooms in the inn before making her choice. They were the only guests, so he had to show them almost a dozen rooms on each floor. She wanted to see the exact layout of the place.

All the ground-floor windows had been fitted with thick burglar bars and a recent alarm system. The only access to the ground floor was through the bar. She decided on two adjoining rooms on the first floor. They were dual-aspect, with windows overlooking both an inner yard, and the front. There were clear sight-lines down over the building's access points.

Catrin then went out and parked by the old-fashioned pump, an area visible from the windows. She chose this particular place, as it was the only area with a light, presumably placed there to deter locals from helping themselves to petrol in the middle of the night.

She told Huw she needed a couple of hours alone in her room. Once she'd closed the door she tried her mobile but there was no reception. Looking around she noticed in the corner one of the earliest generation ADSL points. It was covered with a layer of dust-coated cellophane, which made her wonder if it had ever been in use. She rummaged in her case for a cable, then plugged her Mac in. It was slow, but it worked.

Formal police applications for call listings from telecom service providers could take several days, sometimes weeks to process. They cost the force several hundred pounds each, more for fast-tracks. She knew she'd be unable to request them without making a formal SPOC application via operations at Cathays Park, and as she was on leave and no longer had pull there this was a non-starter. If she needed them later in any form as admissible evidence she'd jump through the hoops, but for now she knew more direct ways of acquiring the same data.

Within forty minutes she had saved several pages on her screen. The first showed all the in-calls on the phone in the bar during the last nine weeks, the second all the out-calls. A third listing, from the national PAYE data-base, showed all the employees at the clinic. The only names she recognised were those of the young doctor Smith and the old man from the shop. Tudor Mower he was listed as; the only Tudor, so she presumed it had to be him. He was doing three shifts a week as an assistant nurse in one of the private wards; no more details were given. She saw he'd started there eighteen months previously: this fitted with what the doctor had said about his returning to the area at that time.

On the line in the bar, there had been about sixty calls made during the last nine weeks. She noted the in-call from the photographic shop in Abergwaun made nine days before the photographs had arrived at Huw's address. Of the remaining calls about twenty-five were to or from the clinic's switchboard, another thirty-two to or from landlines in outlying villages.

Catrin could see that all but three of the calls had been to or from account holders with the same ten surnames as minor employees at the clinic who worked as cooks, cleaners and junior nurses. This suggested the calls were simply confirming arrival times back home and similar routine domestic matters.

To be sure she called each of the numbers in turn. As the phone was picked up she spoke in a heavy Cardiff accent. 'I'm a friend of the skinny bloke from Cardiff, you know who I mean.' In every case she was met with blank incomprehension. It was a fair, but not conclusive, assumption that Rhys had not made or received any of these calls.

This left only the three unaccounted for. All had been in-calls at various hours of the evening in the third of the eight weeks Rhys had been working the case. All three were from the same number. It was a public box in central Cardiff, and when she tried the number the line was out of order.

Then she deleted everything, unhooked the connection. She uncoiled the webcam and placed it on the windowsill facing outwards. Then she knocked on the door of Huw's room.

There was no answer. She opened the door. The room was heavy with smoke, she could barely see to the other side of it. In one corner the pipe with the elaborately carved bowl was smouldering, and on the bedside table, a small chillum lay upturned. Huw was lying back on the bed in a silk paisley dressing gown and a pair of salmon-pink pyjamas. Two laptops were open playing films, one a recent private Seerland concert. It was one he must have had filmed privately, she didn't remember seeing any reference to it on the band's site's official product listings. The other screen showed some obscure art-house film. But Huw wasn't watching either. His eyes were half closed as he gazed fascinated at a cobweb on the ceiling. She felt a sudden flush of anger, prodded him with her boot

'Despite the fires and the deaths, this is just a rich man's hobby for you, isn't it?'

He looked deeply hurt, and he bowed his head, said nothing. Immediately Catrin regretted what she'd said. He's as much a victim as the others in his way, she thought, he's given his life to this and he doesn't know where it's taking him.

He was smiling at her, pulling something out of a bag beside the bed. It was black, part sheer, part lacy, it looked exquisite. She knew of course he must have bought it before the trip. He'd already seen her as a sure thing, a done deal. Anger shot through her again redoubled.

'I'm not your whore,' she said, and slammed the door.

She changed into her trackies and Nikes, went down to the yard. Earlier she'd noticed behind reception an old wooden tennis racket, warped by the sea air, and some balls. She began pounding the wall under Huw's window.

'Sleep through that, you rich bastard!' she shouted. She went through the full repertoire of her strokes, forehand flat, backhand slice, then forehand topspin, her most natural shot. She knocked the ball shallow to the wall so it looped up for slams and volleys.

No one came out to complain. They were the only guests, and the bar was on the other side of the building. As the minutes passed the walls began to fade into a line of dim green shadows, resolve themselves again into the trees surrounding a court in summer. It was the park where she'd played as a girl, she was sliding over the hot shale, beating the coach. She could smell the mown grass, the syrupy scents drifting over on the light breeze from the ice-cream van. For a few moments she was back there and free again.

5

They are at the door, the two men again.

The taller is kneeling over her, he takes out her mask. She cannot move her hands. Its shadow under her, another long, pointed beak.

They're putting on the buckles at the back of her shorn head.

Their hands moving on her gently. In the shuttered half-light, she sees the two perching shapes on either side, shifting.

Over their eyes are mirrors. She tries to close her eyes, but she cannot. They are taped open. We will show you everything, the voices had said to her. Look into the mirrors, see yourself.

She sees herself in their painted arms. Her bound, open body, painted like theirs. She sees her oiled girlish limbs twisting under the long, hooked masks, under their vague flowing forms.

Was there nothing she hadn't seen then? Then the lights in the mirrors on their masks are blurring, blurring the edges of things like the memory of something that had long ago disappeared from the world.

Catrin woke, sweating. It was the old dream again.

She took deep breaths, letting the air out slowly through pursed lips.

She lit a cigarette, stared at the wallpaper for what seemed an age. Slowly she was becoming calmer, the sweat cooling. She looked at her watch. She'd been asleep a full seven hours.

She went over to her Mac. Before she'd gone to bed, she had placed her webcam on the windowsill, focused on the car. She'd run the feed into a certain obscure Welsh countryside webcam enthusiasts' site. It was one of the few that stored its contributors' feeds for up to forty-eight hours. The images would not be particularly clear, but she had to work with what she'd got.

She lit another cigarette and studied the feed, fast-forwarding through the images. Nothing. No one had entered or left the building. No one had been near the car.

Strangely, though she had slept deeply, she felt very tired, her limbs aching as if she'd hardly slept at all. She wondered if she was going down with something. She went into the bathroom, pulled back the curtain over the tub. The shower had a weak flow, barely more than a trickle. She ran it over her aching body.

As she got out, the room felt suddenly very cold. She towelled herself quickly by the one feeble radiator. She wasn't sure what it was, but she had a sense of something moving down below the window. This was a blind spot, out of range of the camera. She went to the curtain, drew it back fractionally, and peered down.

A tall, well-built man was walking along close to the wall. But there was nothing clandestine about the way he moved. He was striding away as if he didn't have a care in the world.

At first she thought it might be the doctor, Smith. The man was wearing a long, dark coat, similar to the doctor's. Then for a moment, he turned into the circle of light over the pumps and she saw he was much older.

He looked a somewhat eccentric figure. His hair was grey, but thick and long, still virile-looking, tucked into the collar of his coat. In one hand he held a long cane, with a carved handle.

Where had he come from? she wondered. Behind him lay only the cliff heads and the sheer drops below. He strode across the yard into the trees, and out of view. She waited but didn't hear the sound of an engine starting up. Only the silence of the early morning, then from far down the coast the distant plaint of a foghorn.

Catrin stared at the trees where he'd disappeared.

Something was still moving there, something spread out, low to the ground. She waited as her eyes adjusted to the dim light. She could see other figures now, threading in and out of the mist and the trees. They were moving in a single file, heads bowed, glancing back at her window. For a moment they seemed to be calling out to her. But no sound came from among the trees, it was too dark to see their faces. She was looking at children, she realised now, a column of children all dressed in the same old-fashioned black smocks. She remembered what the old man had told them, about seeing the children playing in the woods. But that had been four decades ago. So what was she looking at now, a trick of the light? The longer she stared at them the more they seemed to dissolve back into the darkness as if the trees were closing their branches around them. After a few seconds she could see nothing but the mist curling between the black trunks.

She dressed quickly, went into Huw's adjoining room. The bedside lamp was already switched on and he was standing at the window. Using his Bushnell bird-watching binoculars he was scanning the hillside above the village, but the grey band of the early morning sky was empty of birds.

His skin was cool to her touch as she took the binoculars. She peered again through the mist at the trees. Nothing was moving. It was difficult to believe she'd just been watching anything moving.

'You didn't just see something?' Her voice trailed off. It was obvious from Huw's expression he hadn't. He was raising his head slowly, kissing the lobe of her ear, the nape of her neck. She pulled herself reluctantly away, glanced at the lane snaking on towards the ruined rooftops. 'This is a small place, if Rhys was here, someone must have seen him,' she said.

Huw pulled on his coat. 'We've tried the pub, so that only leaves the café that Smith mentioned, where he said the workers from the clinic go after their shifts.'

As they went out to the car, Catrin saw a van parked close up against the wall. Some builder's tarps covered the rear window. Despite the cold, the driver's window was open. An arm was tapping on the outside of the door to a soft trance-like beat drifting out from the cabin.

The figure at the wheel was the same strange man she'd seen earlier. In the morning light she could see his face around his eyes was deeply lined. As she approached, she had the sense he'd been watching her since she'd come outside.

She raised her hand in greeting and it looked as if the man was about to speak. But then the window closed. The van started up, pulled away out of the drive.

As she watched it disappear from view the man turned his head and glanced back at her. All the time Huw had been watching the van carefully, an uncertain look on his face.

'I saw him from my window,' she said. 'And what looked like children up in the woods. They were all dressed alike in old-fashioned smocks. They reminded me of what Tudor said about seeing children up there all those years ago.'

'Are you sure?'

'Not really, I'd just woken up, was feeling weird. It was still quite dark.' She stared down the road at where the van had disappeared, then at Huw. 'You looked as if you'd seen him before somewhere.'

'A builder, maybe. Could be doing up some of those cottages we saw on the way in?'

'He wasn't dressed like a builder. His coat looked well-tailored and he was carrying a long cane, the kind of thing a nineteenth-century dandy might have carried.'

'Another of the doctors perhaps.'

'Then what's he doing driving a builder's van?'

Huw's eyes told Catrin she was over-reacting. 'It wasn't the same van that followed us at the bridge, if that's what you're thinking. This one was darker.'

She got into the car, turned the headlights on full. The wind was stronger but the mist still looked thick down the road. She revved, pulled out fast. There was no sign of the van ahead, no other vehicles on the road. On either side the lanes led off among winter hedgerows and the abandoned cottages of the village.

She turned past the ruined church and came into the road that ran under the tunnel of trees. A break in the canopy of branches allowed another brief view up towards the large house. But all they could see were the pointed gables they had glimpsed on the road from the mainland. The rest was hidden by high walls and the low, sullen mist that seemed as permanent a feature as the hills themselves.

Once past old Tudor's shop the road began to criss-cross the steep, wooded hillside, climbing through dense groves of oaks and beeches. At the crest of the hill they could see lights flashing around a small barrier across the road. A few branches had been torn down by the recent storms, but there was still enough room to pass. Catrin slowed about thirty yards short of the lights and looked down into the trees.

Then she cut the engine. 'It was somewhere down there,' she said, 'those lights we saw from Tudor's last night.' She got out, not hearing what Huw was saying behind her. The wind was stronger than she'd expected. She walked over, pushing against the fierce gusts to the side of the road.

At the fallen branches she turned and made her way into the cover of the overhanging bows beyond them.

Out of the corner of her eye she could see Huw following. He was opening his mouth as if to call her back, raising his hand, then dropping it, following her to the edge of the trees.

'It was somewhere here,' she said as he got nearer.

'How can you tell? These woods all look the same from a distance.' She could see he didn't want to go any further from the road.

Between the trunks a thin trail of slush led down the bank, zigzagging between the dripping branches. She could hear Huw shouting to her, calling her back, but she kept moving deeper in. The branches formed a canopy over her head so that only narrow streaks of daylight crossed the forest floor. It soon became difficult to know if she was following an actual path or just the gaps between trees. She looked back and saw rows of trunks, no sign of the path she thought she'd just taken. But gradually she began to glimpse more daylight through the branches. Ahead the trees were thinning into a clearing. To the nearside of it lay piles of newly cut logs. In the centre were two long sheds, each about twenty feet long, and raised off the ground on cinder blocks, the windows covered with wire netting.

The hut on the left had lights on inside. Their glow illuminated the patch of grass around it, turning it a brighter green. Although the door was shut, with padlocks securing it, Catrin waited silently to see if there was any movement on either side. Between the two huts a path wound up into the mist towards the escarpment. Stepping forward she got a foothold on the line of blocks and put her face up to the glass.

She could make out two rows of troughs, the pipes of a watering system between them, at each end a cluster of grow-lights between silver reflectors, but then the glass clouded over with her breath.

Huw was coming out of the trees, silently moving alongside her. She looked into the next window along. 'Someone likes their hydroponics,' she whispered.

'Mary Jane?' he asked.

'Not that I can see, but they've got some pretty peculiar stuff in there.'

She moved over to the next pane, rubbed her sleeve over the condensation and held her face back from the glass. Through the glare of the lights she saw several troughs of a plant with small, pointed greyish-green leaves, and beside it rows of pale green stems, about four feet high, with bright green leaves. Further down, low to the ground, were pots of a dark green herb with short stems and long leaves.

Among the plants she thought she recognised black henbane and jimson weed and mandrake, all members of the deadly nightshade family.

'Why would someone be cultivating these sorts of plants?' she asked.

'Their alkaloids were used in the old days by pharmacists to make painkillers and anti-spasmodics,' Huw said.

'But not any more?'

'Not likely. In the wrong doses they're potent deliriants that can cause psychosis, even blindness.'

She remembered what Thomas had told her about how Huw had been one of the task force busting the specialist labs. It seemed he hadn't entirely forgotten his pharmacological training from those days, though she wondered how dependable his knowledge was after so much time.

The other shed was in darkness. Huw produced a pocket torch that provided a narrow, but intense, beam of light. She gripped the window ledge again, found a foothold, shone the torch around the shed's interior.

Here deeper pots were filled with black earth, covered with the pale lobes of mushrooms and other fungi of various shapes and sizes.

'Someone likes a bit of magic with their mushrooms. They've even got those poisonous red ones with the white warts.'

'Fly agaric. We used to bust growers sometimes back in the Eighties. The others are psilocybin based, standard hallucinogens, but that stuff is quite hardcore. It's delirium inducing, could cause liver damage if you got the dosage wrong.'

'Like a paracetamol suicide.'

'Right. Wake up about three days later in scream-ing agony, and there's nothing they can do to stop it.'

She followed Huw back into the cover to the side of the clearing.

'Tudor could be selling to some lab on the mainland,' she said.

'I can't think of any sort of lab that would want that stuff these days.'

'This must all cost money, though.'

'Too much money for Tudor. That watering system and those lights were top-end imports, it all looked well beyond the old man's budget.'

'Unless Tudor isn't quite who he appears to be.' She looked at Huw, but something in his face seemed to say he'd already dismissed the idea. 'That shop of his isn't doing much trade,' she said, 'so maybe he has other interests out here?'

'Smith said he worked some shifts as a nurse at the clinic.'

'He does, I checked their PAYE register last night. That must mean he has pharmacological training. He'd know what he was doing with this stuff.'

Huw was shaking his head sceptically. Catrin glanced back at the path winding up into the mist towards the escarpment, but all was still.

'Then what about that figure dressed in the wig like

Jones? The one who's been ghosting us ever since we saw him at the estuary. This could be his shit.'

Huw still seemed unconvinced. He was making a low murmuring noise. She looked back at the sheds. 'This might explain why he didn't want the photos getting out. He could have interests out here which Rhys stumbled on. I seem to remember fly agaric and black henbane were used in witchcraft.'

Huw was crouching under the branches. 'Tudor had a lot of that black arts junk in his shop. But most of the stuff was covered in dust, didn't look like he actually used them.'

Catrin took a deep breath, saw her face reflected faintly in the glass of the window. 'Maybe someone's paying the old man to grow them. Could be the man in the wig. Rhys comes out here and so our man begins to close down anyone who knows about Rhys's pictures. Close down anything that might lead here.'

Huw was moving back into the branches.

'Come on,' he said, 'let's get out of here.'

Fat, heavy droplets of rain ran down the back of their necks as they walked to the car. They slid into their seats, Huw immediately starting the engine so that the heater would kick in. For a moment Catrin thought she could hear faint sounds like the cries of children higher up among the trees. She glanced back, but nothing was visible there.

They followed the road for about two miles, through the ancient woods until it reached the café. Like old Tudor's shop, the place was located behind a lay-by, a series of plain, prefabricated buildings. On each side they were hemmed in by the foliage of the surrounding trees.

The interior had white tiling on the floor and walls and rack lighting that gave the place a clean, aseptic feel. Men of indeterminate middle age in white trousers and jackets were seated in groups on steel chairs around small tables.

Catrin found a table at the back while Huw waited for service at the counter. A tall, cadaverous man was filling stainless steel containers with hot water and soya milk and arranging them on a tray.

Huw carried the tray over, placed it on the table with a grimace.

'It's camomile. Sorry, they don't do builder's tea here.'

He had also brought two small poppy-seed cakes, the colour and texture of brindled grey winter socks.

'They're supposed to be fat-free,' Huw explained, as he poured the tea into the cups. He was looking closely at the other customers.

'Do you notice anything?' he asked.

Catrin looked around again at the café's customers, hunched over their drinks, none engaged in actual conversation, although there were some sporadic exchanges.

Huw leant across the table and hissed under his breath, 'They're supposed to be attached to a rehab clinic, but these people all look out of their tree.'

The glare of the spotlights made it difficult to look directly at the faces further down the room. Instead she focused on a burly man on the table to their left who was dressed in the white trousers and jacket of a hospital orderly. There was a fine layer of sweat on his face. He was staring at a small ridge on the melamine table, his pupils as dilated as a frightened cat's. Catrin turned back to Huw.

'Rhys was a junkie, right?' Huw nodded. 'Small place like this, how many dealers can there be?'

She moved closer to him so she didn't have to raise her voice

'So if we can find the dealer, we've got a line on where Rhys was staying.'

She turned back to survey the room, focusing again on the table watcher to the left. They both rose, sat down on the steel seats on either side of him. He didn't acknowledge them at first, carried on staring. Catrin put her hand on his arm and he looked up slowly, eyes gradually refocusing. He blinked a few times, shook his head as though trying to clear it. Catrin's voice was little more than a whisper.

'You know where we can get some brown, love?'

He cleared his throat as if about to speak, but instead jerked his head to his right, indicating a man in a leather jacket by the doors through to the kitchen. On the table in front of him was a crash helmet next to several empty glasses. Catrin went over to him alone, while Huw hung back.

She flicked open her coat to give him a glance of the clutch of twenties she was holding. He stood up, nodded towards the swing doors. She was led through the kitchens into an enclosed yard.

Catrin took out three twenties and passed them over. He tucked them in an inside pocket, motioned her closer with his hand. She closed her eyes when he put his hand on the back of her neck. She knew what was coming, bent her head down as his tongue pushed the cellophane-wrapped package deep into her mouth in a king's cross kiss.

The dealer was already moving back towards the door to the kitchen. She spat out the wrap from her mouth into her left hand, took hold of his arm with the right. He had no option but to turn round and face her.

She flashed him her warrant card. 'You had a customer recently we'd like to talk about. His name's Rhys, but he may have been using another name.'

As she was speaking he tried to push past her, but Huw was ready for him. He held the man in an arm lock as she grabbed at his crotch. His lips curled back in a snarl, but the noise he made was no more than a subdued gasp. Catrin took out her wallet and showed him the photograph of Rhys.

The man tried to pull away, but she increased her grip.

'I served him two weeks ago, but he didn't look anything like that.'

'How do you know it was him, then?' asked Huw.

He moved a trembling finger onto the photograph. 'The dog-tags necklace, and that earring shaped like an Egyptian cross.'

'Know where he was staying?'

'In one of the holiday lets on Eglyws beach. There's only one finished, so it must've been that one.'

'Very helpful,' she said. 'Just a couple more photos for you to look at and we'll let you return to your busy schedule.' She brought out Rhys's mysterious photos of Face. 'You know who this is?'

'Course,' said the dealer. 'Do I win a prize?'

'Not exactly,' said Catrin, 'not unless you've seen him around here.'

'What?' said the dealer, a calculating look in his eye now. 'You reckon he's been in the clinic all this time, do you?' He considered it for a moment, 'Nah, I'd have heard. These fuckers,' he nodded towards the café, 'can't exactly keep a secret.'

'Okay,' she said, 'last question. Any idea where the photos might have been taken?'

The dealer took another look. Thick sweat was dripping down his junkie's puffy face. He shook his head, saliva dribbling from his lips.

'One more thing,' Huw said. 'In the woods, the grow-sheds. Whose gig's that?'

The dealer said nothing and again Catrin increased her grip.

'Tudor's?' she said, 'that funny feller with the cane?'

A look that was more than discomfort passed briefly over the man's face and he looked away. He was trying to shake himself free but Huw held him. 'Dunno, don't go into the woods, do I,' he said.

Catrin heard a clattering from the kitchen. She signalled to Huw and he released his grip, the man backed away then rushed to the door. By the time they got back to their table he had picked up his helmet and was starting his bike outside.

'Right, let's see if we can find Rhys's cottage then,' she said.

Huw nodded, finished the last mouthful of his poppy-seed cake, and they went outside. It was as dark now as it would be at midnight. The air was cool and damp, delicate scarves of mist slinking past with the promise of more to come. From somewhere down towards the cliffs came the distant shrieking of gulls, then all was silent again.

The village was deserted. They drove through empty streets. Most of the houses were in darkness, the only light along the way the occasional flickering of a television screen. For a moment behind the lines of houses the shoreline gleamed like a bleached skull as moonlight broke through the mist.

'It must be these,' Huw said.

A row of half-ruined fishermen's cottages stood where the road descended to a cove between the cliffs. They had been built into the small natural amphitheatre that spread inwards from the mouth of the cove. Their low slate roofs seemed to merge with the embracing body of the black rocks behind them. In high summer some might be occupied as holiday lets but now all looked uninhabited.

There were no curtains drawn. All the cottages appeared unfurnished apart from one near the end. It was as dark as all the others, the only sign that it had recently been inhabited a mug on a table close to the window.

Huw tried the handle of the door. It jammed briefly before allowing him the additional leverage to release the catch.

A bulb in the narrow passage offered only a faint

light. There was another lamp on a table near the door, but Huw did not switch it on, waited until their eyes had adjusted to the half-light.

The floorboards in the first room had been exposed and polished, covered in a large Bokhara carpet. The furniture seemed to be made from the same dark wood. Some looked antique and was inset with deep carvings. On one side was a large brick fireplace laid with twigs.

At the end of the central passage was a low-ceilinged kitchen. Its pine panels had warped in the sea air, some of the boards hanging loose. On the work surface was a wooden board on which rested half a loaf of bread. On a plate beside the board lay a slice of ham, an open jar of mustard.

At the end of the room, next to a large oak chest, was a desk in the same dark wood as the other furniture. Slowly, Catrin opened the drawers, but they were empty apart from some notepaper still in its wrapper, a packet of matching envelopes, some unused Biros.

She was about to move away to the other side of the room, but turned back to the oak chest again. It was about six inches deep and four feet square, the front decorated with a faded pastoral scene. She opened the door, and saw the shelves were filled with a series of small black shapes, row upon row of little paper figures of similar height and size.

She held one up for Huw to look at.

'A raven. It's a fair likeness,' he said. All the figures were identical: rows and rows of ravens all made from the same thick black paper.

Catrin stepped back, feeling tired, faint. The light from the kitchen seemed suddenly brighter, flickering in her eyes. Her fingers were tingling, cold now. She held onto the side of the desk, took deep breaths.

'I told you,' she said. 'A raven was a talisman for Rhys. He always made ravens when he was alone under pressure.'

Huw was opening the few drawers that were left. He didn't look remotely interested in what she'd said. He was standing near the window, looking out at the dim line of the beach. She stood behind him, one of the paper birds in her hand.

He lowered his gaze to a spot on the floor, near her feet. She wondered what was holding his attention. Slowly he reached down, picked up a splinter and put it to his nose.

He ran his hand along the wall panels, took his hand away, and sniffed it. Catrin too ran her fingers along the boards. They looked like the same wood from a distance, but up close the grain had been marked with something brown. She caught the faint, sweet scent of shoe polish.

'Maybe the landlord covering up some wear before letting?' she said.

They lay on the floor, checking the floorboards. There seemed to be no polish there. They worked their way back through the room, to the passage by the door but there was no scent of shoe polish there either. Then she checked the planks. Something didn't look quite right. There were gaps where the dust ended on the boards then began on the wall above.

'The floor's been pulled apart,' she said: 'the polish covers the splinters.'

They eased the panels up. Underneath were shallow dusty oblongs; no indentations were in the dust where anything would have lain. She lifted up one of the boards that had traces of polish on, peered down. The space was deeper but over it lay fine dust and grit that had not been disturbed.

'Rhys was good at hiding things,' she said. 'Whatever it was they were looking for, they may not have found it.'

Huw took the upper storey while Catrin stayed downstairs. Above she heard dull scraping, then tapping as he worked the boards up. She went back to the kitchen, looked in the rubbish. It had been emptied. She went back into the hall, stood there for a moment thinking of what they'd missed.

She knew most cottages would have a cupboard under the stairs. It took a few moments in the gloom before she could make out the door. A line, barely perceptible except at close range, led up the wooden casing. There was no handle. She looked closer, there was no dust there either. With a knife she levered a crack, large enough to grasp with her fingers, and it opened.

Inside a length of cord was attached to a switch in the ceiling. The space was so small that the light was, for a moment, blinding. Along the inner wall the shelves were covered by a thick layer of dust. It looked as if nothing there had been touched for many years.

She was about to close it, but she paused. She wondered if the searchers had done the same, opened it, taken a quick look, then gone. Any disturbance would have been apparent, but the dusty surface was completely smooth. She could just make out a few long-forgotten objects: a gas mask in its original container, a miner's lamp, a couple of old Latin grammars.

Catrin still felt slightly faint. She squatted down on the concrete floor, began to roll a cigarette but the lighter slipped from her damp fingers and rolled away. She reached her hand to her side and felt for it. Immediately the surface of the dust crumbled and left a finger-shaped hole. She noticed some dust a slightly different shade from the rest. It looked untouched, old, in a rough square shape.

She put her hand in and grasped what seemed to

be paper, and saw she was holding a mound of old newspaper. Behind was a canvas bag. It was at least the same age as the other items but the surface wasn't quite as dusty. She placed it on the floor, the zipper was stiff as she opened it.

She took out a cardboard file, and spread out the black and white photographs it contained. Some of the shots looked almost identical to the pictures that Della had given her, the dancers in a circle, the blurred, hooded figures among the trees. She felt her heart beat faster. There was another, much smaller snapshot of a young man that had been taken indoors. He showed no awareness that he was being photographed. At first she thought that it was Face, in the days when he seemed healthier, had a full head of hair, didn't have the look of a cancer patient losing the fight.

But a second glance showed she'd been wrong. The figure was similar in his colouring and looks, but it was someone else.

Huw was beside her now, looking at the photograph over her shoulder.

'I've seen him before. We've both seen him before,' he said.

Catrin looked at the face more closely. He did look familiar: it was someone she'd seen recently. But she couldn't place him.

Huw looked out into the dark hall behind them.

He was concentrating, listening for something, then he put his fingers to his lips.

'What's wrong?' She had tucked the folder into the canvas bag.

She hadn't registered the noise at first, the slow grinding sound close outside. It was followed by a tapping that seemed to be at the kitchen door. They'd closed the curtains at the front, but she realised now the lights at the back would have been visible from the cliffs behind. Huw moved into the hallway quickly and opened the front door a crack.

But there was no one there. Beyond the lights of the house, the darkness covered them like a blanket. They could hear nothing but the crash of the breakers over the rocks, as they went back to the car.

As they approached the village they saw that the windows of the bar were lit. Huw walked at Catrin's side to the door. She thought he'd want to talk about what they had found, but he said he was tired, went straight up to the room.

The bar was quiet, only a few of the regulars talking with the barman. She sat down at an empty table in the corner. Her hands were trembling slightly so she put them down on her knees.

The men at the counter seemed hardly to have noticed her. Most of them she recognised from the previous day. Sure that they were not watching, she spread the black-and-white photos over the table. The dancers were in the same poses as in the earlier set from Della, the blurred figures and background behind the same also. They looked just like prints from the same negatives.

Next she took out the smaller, colour shot of the young man, the one they had mistaken for Face. It was clear, looking closely, that this was an entirely different person. The boy had similar high, noble-looking cheekbones and heavy eyebrows; there was a resemblance to Face, but that was all. She had seen Face because they'd been expecting to see Face. But the boy, with his pale skin and black hair, definitely did look familiar, all the same.

It was hard to be sure, but the pictures looked old, she thought, twisted at the edges, indented where once there'd been frames. The sleepy eyes of the boy seemed to meet her gaze, blink back at her across the years. Catrin found herself thinking of the men who'd pulled her into the car all those years ago. They had been wearing ski-masks, but something in her mind had made a connection between this face and those men.

The masks had covered everything except their eyes. She could put her finger on it: just a sense she had, that she was finally looking into the eyes of one of them. She felt a sudden rush of fear mixed with confusion.

After all these years it looked like Rhys had not just been investigating Face, but something related to her own abduction, her own case. Could this be why Rhys had said she was the link to the source of the photos, why she'd be trusted by the source? Catrin took deep breaths, stared up at the ceiling to try to calm herself. The plaster there was crumbling, stained with damp. She singled out a square of it to concentrate on, shutting out everything else. In her ears the blood was pounding, the sound of the men by the bar gradually fading away.

She remembered again those weeks after Rhys had rescued her, after she came out of the hospital. She'd stayed alone in her room at home all day and night. Lying on her back, barely moving, staring at the ceiling. This had been her only view. It had been all she had trusted herself to see, all she'd felt safe looking at then.

All the mirrors in the room she'd covered. She couldn't bear to look at herself, she'd been frightened of what she might remember. She'd made her mam leave her food outside the door, which she locked from the inside. When she'd eaten, she'd leave the tray outside the door again.

The one who'd rescued her, Rhys, had left her his pager number, but she hadn't had the strength to call him at first. The only sound to reach her had been when he visited after his shifts and talked to her mam.

She'd strained to hear his voice. A part of her had wanted to lie with him in the dark, lose track of time, lose herself in his dreamer's eyes, make her bed an island on which they'd float away from that time and its harsh, bad choices. A part of her had wanted never to leave her room again.

6

Through the bedroom window the dull morning light fell across the ruins of their breakfast. Catrin held up a corner of the curtain, looked out into the rain. Down in the car park several men clad in bright yellow foul-weather gear were huddled in a circle. One had managed to light his pipe, which was giving off puffs of bluish-grey smoke. Above them the clouds were leaden, obscuring all views of the cliff heads and the hills.

On the tabletop, Catrin laid out the photographs again, the first set from Della's envelope beside the ones from Rhys's cottage. She looked slowly from one set to the other. She'd been right, they were identical, both sets printed from the same negatives.

Huw sat in his towel at the table. He looked briefly at the photos, then picked up the contact prints and held them under the lamp. They were enclosed in strip mounts from the same photographic shop in Abergwaun.

'No negatives here,' he said. 'Looks like these shots were developed digitally.'

'That would confirm what Rhys said to you, that the pictures came to him from a source. Rhys didn't take them himself.'

Huw was still peering closely at the contact sheets. 'They've been printed from a memory stick, probably. The originals would still be stored on the source's camera or on his computer.'

She looked hard at Huw. 'The source can't have been willing to send the images online. Otherwise why would Rhys have come all the way out here? He must have insisted on giving them to Rhys in person.'

'Unless Rhys met the source once he was out here?'

'I don't think so. To give Rhys the images digitally would require a significant level of trust. That sort of trust wouldn't have been built up in a couple of weeks. The source was more likely someone already known to Rhys.'

Huw sat beside her, nodding slowly. 'So then someone suspects Rhys has the images, and that leads to his cottage being turned over. And then they follow him back to Cardiff.'

'Rhys wouldn't have been able to go for more than a day without scoring,' Catrin said. 'So if the date the dealer said he last saw him is right, from here Rhys headed straight to Cardiff.'

'Back to home territory where he thought it would be easier to lose a tail?'

'Possibly. Della said they were being watched when she met him that last night, so by then whoever it was had probably caught up with him.'

Huw had picked up the canvas bag and now ran his fingers along the insides. 'There's something else in here,' he said. From a side pocket he lifted out a disc and loaded it in the laptop. There was only a single file. It was marked by the blue icon for a video package. He began to run the film.

Catrin couldn't see much at first, just some flickering, pale unfocused shapes among a confusion of shadows.

'What the fuck!' Huw suddenly backed away from the table, a look of alarm on his face.

She bent down and saw the interior of a cave or tunnel. The walls and low ceiling were glowing with the lights of candles in circles on muddy ground. Around the edges figures were crawling, three it seemed, though there could have been more, moving in a slow, uncertain circle. Every few seconds the screen went dark as the camera was jolted towards the ground.

As it pulled back briefly, the shapes gained mass and human form. Their heads were half bowed and all were naked, their bodies oiled and shining in the light. One of them was a boyish Face, his head shaved, his limbs pallid, emaciated. He was lurching forward into the lens, spreading his arms out on either side, his mouth dripping dark liquid onto the ground. On the floor was a puddle where there was some paler shape, four small limbs, a head barely distinguishable. Along the wall, what looked like more pale limbs lay in the darkness. All was black for a few moments, then the scene reappeared, at an angle. The camera was still now, placed on the rocks perhaps. To the side, someone was moving out from the wall, a fourth figure. It was taller than the boys, its back to the camera. Down its shoulders long black hair fanned out. One of the boys was crawling forward, head bowed, kneeling at its feet. Then the screen went dark again.

Catrin felt her heart thudding.

The piece didn't feel faked. She had a sense for these things. It felt more like a glimpse of something that had happened long in the past, in some savage, barely human time.

'You think that man is the cult leader?' Huw was looking closely at her in the dimness.

'Could be, he had long hair like the man Pryce saw in the car.'

The video had ended. There was just two minutes of blank footage on the file. She pulled the cursor back, rewound to the point where all three naked boys were visible. One of the boys' faces was averted from the camera. A second had his head bowed, as he gazed down into the puddle at his feet. She pointed at him.

'This boy, he looks like that one in Rhys's photos, doesn't he? The one we mistook for Face. He has the same pale skin and dark hair.'

Huw shrugged, turned away from the screen. 'In that light it's difficult to tell.'

Catrin put her hand on Huw's shoulder, felt him shudder. He glanced up at her, his eyes wide with an undisguised fear. 'What do you think it was in the film,' he said. 'Some kind of sick BDSM game?'

'I'm not sure. There's not much to go on, is there? It's difficult to tell whether those shapes on the floor are human or animal limbs.'

'They're small, they'd have to be animals.'

'Or children's? Dug up from somewhere maybe, to use in a ritual.'

Huw didn't seem to have the stomach to look again. She rewound, peered at the shapes, but it was too dark, they could have been anything. The closer she looked the more they became abstract disjointed lines. She turned back to the file in the bag, took out the snapshots of the young man they had mistaken for Face, the one she now believed had been one of her abductors.

The first looked like a school leaver's portrait in profile. It showed an adolescent with dark, unruly hair, his lips twisted between a smirk and a sneer. The other was a discoloured Polaroid, taken in a pub, arms and pints held by unseen companions framing the shot. In this second picture the man was a couple of years older. He wore fraying jeans, a T-shirt with a blue logo, his eyes half closed, a beatific smile spread over his youthful face.

At the bottom of the bag she noticed an inner pocket with more papers in. She laid them out on the table. They seemed to be copies of a standard Police National Computer Missing Persons Report. The name on the report was *Iolo Stephens*, from Fishguard. There was also a coroner's report on the skeletal remains of a body recently discovered on the coast north of Dinas Head.

The Iolo Stephens report contained all the usual information collated during the investigation of long-term missing person cases: the name, date of birth, distinguishing marks, GP's medical records, interviews with relatives, friends, past employers, known associates. The boy had left school without finishing his exams, drifted through part-time jobs in Tenby and other small seaside resorts, been reported missing by his family back in September 1998. None of the names on the report meant anything to her.

The last papers were a hastily made printout from the Police National Missing Persons Bureau, from the section specialising in cross-matching mispers with unidentified bodies. There were pages from the

Pembroke coroner's report of the previous month on the skeletal remains of a young man discovered by Dyfed-Powys police on Strumble Sands, three miles north of Dinas Head. A blurred photograph showed all the bones laid out like the last stage in an anatomy study on a stainless steel slab. The entry from the pathologist gave no evidence of external injuries prior to submersion in the water, and the coroner had returned a verdict of accidental death.

Catrin looked from the still of the second boy in the film to the two photographs of the young man, Iolo Stephens. There was no question they were one and the same person. She put her fingers over his clothes and hair, so only the face was visible. She recognised him now as one of the early fans in the pictures over the cabinet in Gethin Pryce's house.

She disconnected the chipped green rotary-dial phone from its socket and plugged in the laptop, while Huw looked over the photographs and the two reports.

'The boy in the first report, Iolo Stephens, he's in those photographs at Pryce's of the early Face fans,' she said, putting her fingers over the clothes and hair again.

Huw held the picture up to the light, a hint of recognition in his tired eyes.

'So it looks like Pryce's theory about the fans around Face disappearing when that man with long hair came on the scene has some substance.' Huw picked up the photograph of the skeleton. 'And the remains found in the Sands, it's the same boy?'

'I'm not sure,' she said.

She tapped in the address of the Dyfed-Powys Police database. After about a minute the force shield with the two red dragons in profile gradually filled the screen.

'Why not take the usual route to the PNC via Command & Control at the Met?' Huw asked. 'Or am I out of date?'

She shook her head. 'No, but the local force will often have more on their database than they upload to the PNC and the Police National Missing Persons Bureau.'

She keyed in the passwords and brought up the files. She put her finger under the case number on the original mispers report for Stephens.

'Can you see any follow-up on the Stephens case?' Huw asked

'There's nothing, only the routine six-month reviews by the DS.'

'Any other forces pulled the file?'

'None.'

The flickering light of the screen hurt Catrin's eyes and made her feel slightly faint. She stood up, opened the window a crack and breathed deeply.

She pushed the laptop over to Huw's side of the table. 'Here,' she said. 'I've already opened the databases of all the relevant agencies.' She brought out her Drum from her bag, quickly rolled a cigarette.

'Run all the relevant cross-checks,' she said. Huw remained bent over the keyboard as he worked his way through the PNC, the PNMPB and the National Missing Persons Helpline.

She lit up, drew deeply. 'Any links made between the Stephens file and the Sands body?'

'None by Dyfed-Powys. No cross-matches on the PNC, the PNMPB or the National Missing Persons Helpline.'

'Either case flagged on Scotland Yard's Kidnap-Ransom desk, or the Met's SO7?'

Huw pulled the keyboard closer and checked the files.

'No, no trace on either.'

She turned away, blew her smoke towards the crack in the window. 'Any match between Stephens's ante-mortem dental records, and those of the Sands body?'

'There weren't any dentals in the Stephens file. Is that usual?'

'Put it this way, it's not that unusual.'

'Because the investigating officer can't be arsed to collect them?'

'Lack of NHS rural dentists more like.'

She looked round for the ashtray, but couldn't see it. 'Height, build and age range match?'

'Height's one-eighty in both cases, pathologist's age range eighteen to twenty-five on the Strumble Sands body.'

Huw had stopped tapping for a moment, and Catrin turned her head towards the door. She could hear no sounds yet in the passage outside and no voices filtering up through the floor from the pub.

She passed the coroner's report over to Huw's side of the table. 'Anything in the Dyfed-Powys database that's not already in the pathologist's report on the Sands body?'

The dark reds and blues of the Dyfed-Powys portal poured out over the room as Huw went back into the local file.

'Nothing.'

'Did the Pembroke coroner run DNA tests?'

'Yes, but we don't have DNA for Stephens.'

'Did the coroner run diatom tests to see how long the body had been in the water?'

'There wasn't sufficient organic matter left on the bones to run a diatom.'

'Anything at all to suggest foul play?'

Huw bent over the report. 'Nothing at all. No abrasions, no broken bones. No signs of battery, laceration or external injury.'

She looked down again at the two photographs of the young man, then opened the nets, brought the bedside light onto the table. She stood under the window with the photographs for almost a minute, then passed them back to Huw.

'Look closely at the colour of the boy's skin. Doesn't it look slightly jaundiced?'

Huw looked over her shoulder for a full minute at the photographs. Then he opened the cardboard folder under the lamp, began looking at the photocopies of Stephens's GP notes.

'There's nothing unusual with the GP,' he said after a long pause, 'just the normal vaccinations, a broken ankle when he was seven. No blood work or other hospital referrals.'

'What about on the Dyfed-Powys file?'

He bent close over the screen again.

'They've scanned one inpatient record for Stephens from Withybush Hospital in Haverfordwest.'

'But they didn't bother to log it on the PNC or PNMPB?'

'That's probably because it's from January 1994, five years before Stephens was reported missing.'

Catrin reached over to the breakfast tray and tapped her long ash into a saucer.

'What was Stephens admitted for?'

'Acute liver failure.'

'At the age of sixteen?'

Huw was scrolling back through the notes. 'Recovery is recorded as complete, there are no follow-up outpatient records.'

He began to cough, raised a hand up to his mouth. Catrin was about to put the cigarette out, but took a final deep draw.

'Any history of hepatitis, drug use?'

'Nothing flagged here.'

Huw began to cough again. She stubbed out her cigarette in the saucer. 'How severe a case of liver failure are we talking about?'

'He was in intensive care for three weeks. Encephalopathy was three out of four on the scale. They were considering moving him down to the Morriston if there was any further deterioration in his condition.'

'Potentially life-threatening, then?'

'The notes show he required high doses of corti-costeroids and insulin, catecholamine support and continuous haemofiltration before he recovered.'

'Yet no follow-up treatment?'

'None recorded.'

'Which suggests he was not suffering from hepatitis or any other long-term liver condition. So what we seem to be looking at here is an isolated episode of extreme toxicity.'

'A suicide attempt perhaps, using a liver-toxic agent like paracetamol?'

Catrin reached back for the Stephens notes.

'I don't think so.' She clicked down, stared at one of the pages. 'Normally with suicide there's some incidence of depression or mental illness in the GP's notes, but there's nothing resembling that – no self-harming profile – in the Stephens file.'

Huw raised his eyebrows at her. 'Suicides can be spontaneous though, especially at that age. It's a vulnerable time.'

She stood by the window, began slowly to roll another cigarette. Something else had struck her. She looked at him.

'In the grow-sheds, those fly agaric 'shrooms, the strong hallucinogens, you said they were liver-toxic.'

'Right, like almost anything taken in the wrong amounts.'

She felt the damp air through the window, held her roll-up without lighting it. 'How long had that kit been there, d'you think?'

'It's more recent than his death, at least the lights and piping are.'

'There could've been previous grows, though.' She walked round the table and pulled her chair closer to Huw's. As he scrolled back over the file nothing was flagged.

'There's no tox report in the hospital notes,' he said, 'so looks like the medics didn't suspect anything like that or weren't alerted to it.'

'Go back into the PNMPB database,' she said. She watched Huw's heavy fingers moving quickly across the keys, the blue light washing over his drawn features.

'See if the system will let you cross-match drug-related deaths, mispers, unidentified bodies, and an age range fifteen to twenty-five – for the maritime park area?'

'Period?'

'Try '89 to the present.'

He pushed the screen to the left, so she could see it more clearly. 'There's thirty-seven matches in all.'

Catrin closed her eyes for a moment, the flickering light was making them ache. 'Now try the same search criteria on other isolated seaside regions, with comparable population figures: North Devon, North Cornwall, Antrim, North-Eastern Scotland and the rest?'

Huw was already tapping in the searches, scrawling a column of figures on the back of one of the photocopied pages.

'There's no significant difference,' he said slowly.

'What if you exclude DRDs, keep the age range, narrow the search to mispers and unidentified bodies?'

'Pembrokeshire's higher by a factor of about sixty

per cent, but on such relatively low numbers that's not statistically significant. Taking into account the legacy of alternative lifestyles in the area from the Sixties and Seventies it's probably what one would expect.'

'The overall figure?'

'Thirty-two.'

'How many of those have a connection to the north, the maritime park area?'

She watched him pull up the postcode chart, then tap in the codes. He looked exhausted, his shoulders slumped against the back of the chair.

'Twenty-nine.'

'But the national park's the most thinly populated part of the county – what's the population percentage in relation to the rest of the county?'

'About twenty per cent.'

She closed her eyes again, took deep breaths, the after-images of the light shivering still over her eyelids.

'How many of those mispers later matched to bodies?'

'Nineteen.'

She turned towards the wall, her eyes closed. 'I think we need to take a closer look at those nineteen cases,' she said finally.

As Huw downloaded the files there was a low whirring noise. She could hear the faint clatter of glasses downstairs in the bar, then there was silence again.

Catrin looked at the faces. Her eyes moved slowly from one to the next. There were none she recognised from the photographs in Pryce's room. But many were poor, overexposed. She ran her fingers over the screen, trying to read the foreshortened lives through the faces. A hatchet-faced youth standing in a muddy field whose thinness bordered on emaciation, a seventeen-year-old farmer's son from Martletwy, reported missing in June 1998, his body found seven years later lying on rocks near Cat Head. A twenty-year-old girl, a trainee teacher from Laugharne holding a wine glass, her wide blue eyes made owlish by large round spectacles, found floating in the sea off Crincoed Point. Next to her, ringed in a group photograph, a slight, seemingly bemused adolescent in a faded black Motörhead T-shirt standing in a crowded students' union bar. She'd been reported missing in February 1997 while reading Ancient History at Aberystwyth, her body spotted by a Stena Line employee and hauled out of Fishguard Harbour three years later.

'This one,' Catrin said. 'During the years of the Jones abductions, his reign of terror, I remember seeing her face in the papers as one of the potential abductees.'

Huw sighed quietly. 'But any girl who went missing in those years, the media always ran it as a Jones case.'

She looked more closely at the picture of the teacher. 'This one also. She was in the papers as a potential abductee. I distinctly remember her face from that time.'

'That means nothing. A girl would run off with her boyfriend for the weekend, it was put down to Jones. He was like the bogeyman. During the height of his abductions, the papers were running Jones scare stories every week.'

'That's true but there's something to think about here. These disappearances begin at almost exactly the same period as the Jones abductions.'

Catrin scrolled back to the first of the nineteen cases. The photo showed a boy just turned eighteen from St Dogmaels, to the north of the national park. He had the typical local colouring. Dark hair, wan cherubic features, shy downturned eyes. The file reported him as missing in the winter of 1989; unemployed, a school leaver, his family were travellers. 'The first case here's from February '89. That's within three weeks of the first reported Jones abduction.' She looked closer. 'There aren't many details, just a last sighting late at night at a pub.' She clicked into the end of the file, the coroner's report and the autopsy. 'His body washes up nine years later, down the coast here in a cove. Not a full skeleton, just the skull, a few ribs, a femur.' The screen showed dim sea-licked rocks, a small pale circle of bones.

Huw's eyes were bloodshot, half closed with tiredness, blinking rapidly.

'It's strange,' he said. 'The cases do begin at almost the same time as the Jones abductions.' Slowly he cleared his throat. 'But we know Jones was committed in early 2001. Yet the bodies have continued to appear.' He moved the screen so she could see the dates. 'Two years, four years, five years later. All during the time we know Jones was inside. And now, a month ago, there's another body found down on the Sands.'

'Stephens, the file Rhys had pulled?'

'Exactly.'

'The sea giving back its dead?'

'Most probably.' She watched as he enlarged the photo of the rocks at Cat Head where the farmer's son had been found, then brought up the picture of the locations of the traveller's bones in the cove. The fragments of bones lay in loose rings over the black rocks.

Huw pointed at the tideline further down, the seaweed crusting the base of the cliffs. 'Those look like atypical wash-ups.' He'd panned in closer to the images of the ribcage and the skull.

'Right, no ligaments or flesh still binding the separate bones.'

'That means they probably didn't wash up all

together like this.' Huw was sitting back, rubbing his eyes. 'Most likely these bones didn't come directly from the sea. There was some mediation first, a scattering agent, an animal, a beachcomber.'

She took a deep breath, held his gaze.

He clicked back into the screen, flicked through several pages. 'The local inquests didn't flag anything unusual, they're dealing with wash-ups all along this coast. There are strong currents, a lot of different wildlife that could've moved the bones about. There's nothing that suspicious in the bones being found like this.'

Catrin put her face to the window and gazed out into the mist over the yard. The air smelt of fires burning wood that caught in her nostrils. She felt faintly nauseous. She sat down very slowly, unsteadily at the table.

Huw pushed back his hair, sighing. 'Jones was Cardiff-based. He mainly targeted girls in the BDSM scene. I'm not seeing his hand here.'

'Unless he was a player with greater reach, as people thought at the time.'

Huw was looking at her, she couldn't see his expression in the dimness. 'But Jones was inside when these bones appear. A man can't be in two places at once. Jones was banged to rights on the drugs evidence, no question, they got the right man.'

Catrin thought back to how the case against Jones had been built. The prosecution had not relied on the victims' testimonies, as they'd been drugged, but the drugs evidence itself had been irrefutable. The drug they'd got him on was a homebrew scopolamine, effectively unique. Only his DNA had been found on the drug preparatory kit. The tox reports had matched the exact chemical fingerprints of the drugs on Jones's person and in his cellars to all the vics, so the case was airtight.

She knew Huw was right. A man could not be in two places at once. But still she sensed there was some aspect of Jones and what he was that she had somehow missed. For a moment the long hair of the figure in the hood and the sense of there being nothing behind it shimmered again before her eyes then vanished into the shadows.

'You're like all good cops.' Huw's voice was almost fading into silence. 'You want to find order, correspondences. But sometimes that order isn't where you think it is, and sometimes it isn't there at all.'

Huw had closed his eyes, as if in pain, his hands covering them. She heard his breathing, shallow and disturbed. She looked at the remaining pictures of the nineteen mispers. There were photographs of half-blurred faces in crowded raves, with red flash eyes. A sixteen-year-old boy from Trewidwal, his face barely visible in the candlelight of a house party. His bloated remains had been found by fishermen under the concrete causeway at Hobbs Point where the cars used to wait to board the ferry. A girl with long black hair in a half-empty dance hall, above her head a white arrow. Her skeleton had been discovered by divers near one of the coaster wrecks off Skomer island six years after her disappearance. Most seemed to have been drifters and runaways. In many cases there were only childhood photographs, in some no pictures at all.

She looked down the files at the accompanying details: the dates and places of birth, the schools they had attended, their parents' backgrounds. Some of the mispers had been privately educated, others had been children of the long-term unemployed and travellers. None seemed to have known each other, or appeared in each other's notes. She moved all the faces closer to each other.

For one fleeting moment she thought she sensed a faint resemblance between all the faces. But if there was some connection between any of the cases she couldn't see it. The weak light was making her eyes swim, the images merging, multiplying, swirling in the shadows, as at the onset of a migraine.

She reached down into her bag for her pills, pushed open the door to breathe the fresher air from the passage. She knew now she had to get out into the air immediately or she would black out.

The faces of the dead boys and girls swam before Catrin's eyes. At first, she walked blindly. The damp air had a weight and solidity that promised more fog. The sea mist was rolling in again from the direction of the cliffs. Through the low clouds came a hard, steely light, a watery glare that stung her eyes.

In the window of the first cabin a display of apothecary's bottles containing coloured liquids created a sudden brightness that she shrank away from. In the glass was a reflection of a vehicle parked behind her on the road. It was a van, its roof piled with a ladder and tarpaulins.

She turned and saw a man inside beckoning from behind the condensation on the window. The vehicle's engine was ticking lightly. Against the steamed-up pane, a hand was rubbing the moisture away in rough circular motions.

Catrin strained to see some details of the face but failed. He wore a dark coat and a scarf half covered his face. He had half opened the window and was waving. She looked around, but there was no one else on the road.

Now she heard a tapping sound. He was knocking something silver against the window. The end of a cane. It must be that strange man we saw yesterday, she thought. But why doesn't he just call out, why only beckon silently like that? She began to approach the van, but it moved away into the mist. Everything was still again, silent.

After about five minutes she came to the top of the hill over the high coomb, a natural amphitheatre of rocks that surrounded the narrow strip of beach. There were no cars parked out in front of the cottages and nothing on the road behind her.

At the edge of the sea the only thing she could see moving was a large brown dog, playing on its own near the rocks. It was crouching down with its nose almost touching the sand, barking at the waves as they came in.

She scanned the rocks and road behind her, but there were no other signs of life. For a moment she stood looking at the metallic tint of the sky reflected in the sea. Then slowly she made her way up to the path between the cottages.

The buildings had the same general appearance as moorland crofts. They were stocky, low to the ground, built from the same dark rock as the cliffs around them. All had the same slate roofs, the same dark plaster-work around the back doors. It was not possible to tell from where she stood which had been the cottage they had entered the previous night. The path led up above a shorter second row of cottages built back to back with the first, then stopped abruptly at a fence. From there a steep run of untended land stretched up between the rocks, the view beyond obscured by the overhanging heads of the cliffs.

It seemed there was no passable route to the cottages from the rear, the only points of access being from the road or the beach. As she climbed higher Catrin saw there were no yards or gardens behind the upper cottages. Their doors opened directly onto the path, and she felt increasingly as if she was walking through a tight crevasse, bounded by the cliff on one side and on the other by the blind backs of the houses. All sight of the road and the beach had disappeared, the only view down was through a series of narrow alleyways that ran between the cottages to the bottom of the bank.

She walked back in the direction of the road. As she looked down the first of the alleyways she could just see the outline of a boy wheeling a bicycle along the duckboards over the mud. At least it looked like a boy. From that distance she couldn't be sure. He wasn't tall, and had the frail, attenuated physique of a child in early adolescence. He had stopped and was staring straight up at her.

She put her head down, continued down the path. As she passed the mouth of the next alleyway she saw the boy had paused again and was turning once more to look up at her. At the next gap between the cottages she looked to her left, and the boy was there again. He seemed to be deliberately mirroring her movements, turning his head towards her at exactly the same time as she looked down.

Once she had moved back behind the cottages she knew that his sightline would be interrupted. This time she walked on only a few steps, then ran back to the point she had just come from. She held her breath, looked down the mouth of the alleyway she had first passed.

The boy was there again. But with him this time she saw a man, just a faint silhouette. His head was raised slightly, as if he was looking for someone or something particular but could not see it yet. He was standing back from the boy, in the middle of the pathway. Catrin could see little else of him but his long dark coat.

He was beckoning to her now, silently. The coat looked like the one worn by the man in the van. Why didn't I hear his engine? she thought. Her breathing was becoming rapid and shallow. Each time she reached the mouth of the next alleyway the man appeared. He was walking in tandem, beckoning her down, then she couldn't see him any more.

She turned, ran down as fast as she could towards

the seafront. Both the boy and the man had disappeared. The alleyways were empty.

Catrin thought she could hear above the cries of the seabirds the faint calls of children, but as she listened more intently the cries faded again like echoes and she heard only the wash of the sea. The dog had moved to the far end of the beach, no more than a vague shape now at the edge of the waves.

She looked out to sea. The wind had dropped but the waves were bigger than the night before, five or six feet high at their peaks as they crashed down on the beach in front of her.

She thought she could make out something shimmering above the waters. The dim light played tricks with her sense of perspective and at first she thought she was looking at a large bird, swooping low over the waves. It was only when the shape came nearer that she saw it was a man in a black wetsuit.

The surfer was bobbing in front of a rising cliff of black water gathering pace behind him. It seemed impossible that he would not be crushed beneath its bulk. Catrin held her breath. Then as the wave crashed around him he became one with its foaming spray and disappeared.

For a few moments there was nothing but the onward mass of the dark waters. Then she saw a slim form skimming down the front of the wave and crisscrossing it again. His wetsuit was jet back apart from a flash of silver across the heart. The wave was moving closer now. There were jagged rocks on either side of it and more, no doubt, unseen beneath the water. But the surfer made a sudden corkscrewing move that took him away from the rocks to where the waters were deeper. As a wave crashed over him its successor bore him almost gently into the shore.

He picked up his board and clambered carefully up the steep incline of the rocks. As he got closer she recognised the man with the cane and long greying hair. She felt suddenly disconcerted. A few minutes previously she was sure she'd seen him up on the road, and then in the lane. Now he was emerging from the waters in front of her.

She thought at first he was going to walk right past her without so much as a glance, but at the very last second he stopped dead in front of her. His eyes were the purest green she'd ever seen. He gave a quick low bow, then turned and carried on walking into the mist.

'Who are you?' Catrin called, and began running after him. 'Who are the children?' But there was no one there. As quickly as he'd appeared he had vanished again.

She spun around, scanned the rocks, the cottages. Nothing was moving. She stood for a few moments looking at the sky reflected in the windowpanes. Then slowly she made her way back up the road, back towards the inn.

Huw wasn't in the bar. He wasn't in the dining room at the back, nor in the small lounge next door where the curtains were still drawn, the chairs all lined up in front of the television. She went upstairs to their room. Someone had tidied it, removed the breakfast tray, made the bed, taken away the towels that Huw had left heaped on the floor. His cases were as he had left them at the end of the bed, the slim one for the laptop locked, pushed to one side under the table. The car was still where they had left it the previous night.

She went back down to the bar. The barman was alone with his back to her, wiping glasses. She coughed and he turned, smiled shyly, didn't meet her eyes. He looked as if there was something he'd just mislaid.

'Where's my friend?' Catrin said.

He looked out to the car by the old pump.

'Car like that, picked him up. He said to tell you he'd be away a few hours in Abergwaun.'

The man's accent was deep, he sounded as if he wasn't used to speaking English. Catrin wondered why he seemed nervous. He couldn't have known Huw had a second car the same. It sounded like Huw had left in the company of his security people. She wondered if he'd found something else in the missing persons reports, gone to check on it. She went to the payphone, but couldn't reach him on any of his numbers.

The barman was standing by the fridge. The rubber inside was perished, hanging down. He glanced nervously out at the yard. Through the dirty panes she could see nothing moving there.

She went down the passage and looked into the yard. It was empty. At one end were some beer barrels, at the other mouldering crates. The doors to the storerooms were closed. She looked up at the windows. On one side she thought she saw something moving, behind one of the curtains in the lounge.

She went back along the passage to the door. Inside it was dark, most of the curtains still drawn. She saw a tall man with greying hair standing in the corner facing out of the window. He was wearing a long coat that seemed to be made up of many different small animal pelts. Some were grey, others brown but most were black. It looked like something ancient, something tribal.

As he turned she recognised the man who'd just passed her in the mist, the surfer. His coat was open, and under it she could see his wetsuit, sleek and black, still glistening with patches of water.

If he was feeling the cold, he didn't show it. He

seemed completely at ease. He was smoking a cigar, a large one. It already looked half smoked.

'How did you get here so quickly?' Catrin asked.

'There's a short cut, by the cliffs.' His voice was deep, relaxed. It sounded local though overlaid with something more unusual she didn't recognise.

'I saw you coming past the other morning,' she said.

'Yes, I'd come the same way.' He offered her a cigar. She shook her head.

'No one seems to heed the smoking ban out in the country,' she said.

He didn't reply, but smiled at her as if she'd just said something faintly absurd. His features were dark, deeply lined as he smiled. They seemed as hard, as harsh as the black rock of the cliffs.

'But you're a smoker yourself,' he said.

She felt for the Drum and papers still in her pocket. She hadn't been smoking down on the beach.

He smiled again. His teeth were surprisingly white for a man of his age. His features seemed as timeless as the rocks and the winds. He took a book of matches from his pocket, lit one with one hand and brought it up to his cigar. He'd let the lit match drop onto some papers piled by the fireplace. Silently Catrin watched as the flame began to broaden, creep across the surface of the paper. She moved her foot towards the flames to stamp them out. But as the man glanced down at them, just as suddenly as they had spread the flames contracted, guttered out.

'You from round here then?' she asked.

'Was once, a long time ago.' She thought she saw a kind of reverie in his eyes, as if the man was running some old movie in his head that was infinitely more seductive than the world he saw around him.

'So what brings you back?'

'Just doing up a few ruined cottages, hoping to rent them in the summer.'

'You're a developer then?'

'A developer, you could say that.' He seemed to find this amusing, let out a brief, sonorous laugh. 'A late developer you might say.'

She showed him her picture of Rhys, pointed out his earring. 'Seen him about?' she asked.

He looked, shook his head. She wondered how old the man was, it was difficult to tell. Late fifties perhaps, though there was the vitality about him of a much younger man.

'You were here in the early Seventies?'

'Off and on,' he said.

'Remember a commune, up where the clinic is now?'

'Yes but they kept themselves to themselves, weren't here long.' These were the exact same phrases she'd heard before from Tudor and the woman in the village. They felt to her now almost like lines from a play, rehearsed, learned by rote.

'Any idea where they went?'

He was shaking his head again, blowing elaborate smoke rings out to the side of Catrin's head. He stepped forward and shook her hand. His grip was firm, lingering, almost painful for a moment

'Fransis,' he said. She waited, but he didn't give her a second name.

'Catrin.' Looking at his expression, she sensed she'd just given away more than those six letters.

He passed her his card, which looked cheap, the sort printed by a machine. There was a Cardiff address on it, and something scribbled on the back. The writing was slanted, very old-fashioned. She couldn't read a word of it.

She felt his gaze on her. She expected to feel uncomfortable with him looking at her like that, but she didn't. Her eyes were drawn to his wetsuit, the outlines of his muscles. The expression was still there on his face, one of knowing recognition.

'Do you think you know me?' She gave him her most direct stare.

He returned it, said nothing. She began moving closer to the door. He didn't try to stop her, but he didn't get out of her way.

'You've been trying to get my attention. Beckoning me?' she said.

Still he said nothing, didn't move.

'Up on the road, then from the cottages. What did you want?'

'I thought it was you,' he said.

'But we've never met before.' She glanced at him, half smiled at him this time. 'I'd definitely have remembered.'

'Oh but we have,' he said. 'It was a few years back. London, a club.'

She got it now. She should have known from the rubber and the macho posturing. He was the classic dom, their paths must have crossed back when she was under on the BDSM scene. Many of the doms wore masks, they could have chatted and she would never have seen his face.

Most of the doms she'd met were nothing like Jones or Trainer. They were professional men, sensitive, tender-hearted. They'd often started out as subs, that way they understood the sub's needs most intimately. It was like the best tango dancers, they'd train for several years first in the woman's role. She remembered how the subs she'd met told her how they only very occasionally submitted themselves to a man. They'd feel ashamed afterwards, barely able to look at themselves in the mirror. But something had always drawn them back. It had been the closest they had let themselves come to entrusting their soul to a man, and usually that trust had been repaid, for an hour or two in some hotel room at least.

'Isn't it a small world,' she said, almost to herself.

'Meet me tonight, a quiet drink,' he said.

Catrin saw him glance towards the window. A silver Audi was pulling up fast. DS Thomas got out, swaggering in his usual way, chest first, towards the door as if he owned the place.

She felt the surfer's firm grip on her hand again, then he was gone.

Thomas was standing in the doorway. He looked a little out of breath. On the floor at his feet lay a holdall and a padded Barbour.

He had dark pouches beneath his eyes, as if he hadn't slept. She wondered why he'd bothered to track her down when he could have been home with a few cold ones, it wasn't his style. He never left Cardiff and even there he did as little moving about as he could get away with

'How the fuck did you find me?' she said.

'Making unauthorised NCIS checks in a remote location, not exactly clever.' It had been a risk, she knew that, but one she'd had to take. He was grinning at her, a look of quiet triumph on his face. 'You're meant to be on sick leave, compassionate leave, whatever bullshit term Occupational Health call it now. But all the time you've been running round cowboying it.' She recognised his look now, it was the same look you gave a possession.

He pushed the holdall to one side, sniggered to himself. 'All your hacking, well, this won't look good for you if it gets to Rix.'

His eyes hardly moved as he gave her his lazy, lopsided smile.

'All right,' she said. 'You got me, so what do you want?'

He sat down opposite her. He wasn't looking half as pleased with himself as she'd expected. His eyes were wide, anxious-looking, his legs jerking with an edgy energy.

'This is how it works,' he said. 'You tell me what you know. If it stacks up, I'll tell you what I know. If it doesn't, I'll bury you.' She'd expected him to tell her she'd have to go back to town but it seemed his focus was on the case. She never thought he'd care, but looking at him now she saw she'd been wrong. He had enough to bury her already, what did she have to lose.

'I found the cottage where Rhys was staying,' she said. 'The place had been turned over.'

Thomas brought out his packet of Embassy, smiled his lazy smile again. 'Typical junkie, probably hid his stash and forgot where it was.'

Catrin moved the ashtray to a mid-point on the table between them, tried to smile, found she couldn't. She took out her tobacco, her mind still filled with images of the beach, the surfer, the grey light there.

'At the cottage I also found details of an old misper case from '98, the name of the misper Iolo Stephens. There was also a coroner's report from last month on an unidentified body washed up on Strumble Sands.'

'Cause of death?'

'Accidental, but hospital records showed an admission for liver failure five years before the boy was reported missing, at the age of sixteen. But curiously there was no evidence he had ever had hepatitis, suicidal tendencies or had been an intravenous user.'

Thomas sat forward and rested his arms on the table.

'Any connection to Face in any of this?'

So Thomas knew Rhys had been working on Face. He might have guessed that from knowing she was working for Huw. Catrin paused, trying to gauge what part of her suspicions she should disclose.

'There were other fans around Face into a hardcore tripping scene who'd also gone missing. A photograph identifies this misper as part of that same scene. He looks like one of the group who abducted me when I was a teenager. I can't be sure of course, it's just a sense I have. We know that Face's mother was involved with some strange cult here at the time Face was conceived. Stephens was about the same age as Face, his family from the same area.'

'So this tripping scene around Face, this cult. They are the same group?'

'Looks that way. A man who looked a bit like Charlie Manson seems to have been in control of both scenes. My sense is this figure's behind what's been going on out here.'

Thomas was watching her closely. She noticed he didn't seem particularly surprised by anything she'd just said.

'And this figure is?' He asked this very slowly, his eyes narrowed at her.

'I think it could be Angel Jones.' She paused. 'Or if not Jones himself, someone close to Jones.'

He laughed, a rasping, hollow sound. 'But Jones is like the bogeyman,' he said. 'He gets blamed for every-thing. One minute he's abducting, the next torturing in dungeons. The next he's leading some cult. He can't have been everywhere.'

She wondered if she'd told him too much already, but then, she didn't know what he already knew. With the records of her hacking he was holding enough to end her career, maybe put her inside. She knew she was playing a dangerous game if she kept too much back from him.

'Any other cross-matches to this Stephens case?' he asked slowly.

'There's a higher proportion of mispers of similar age during that period for the maritime park area against comparable coastal population segments. Of those, nineteen were later found dead, all their bodies found in water. Apart from that, no obvious connections between any of those nineteen cases.'

'You're thinking some were down to Jones?'

'The disappearances begin about the same date Jones began operating.'

Thomas looked hard at her. 'But?'

Her throat felt dry. 'But some of the bodies appeared after Jones's imprisonment. So if Jones was involved and these youngsters were being held somewhere, someone else has been the captor, and for many years.'

Thomas said nothing at first, just stared at her.

'Maybe Jones's city dungeon was no more than a sideshow, a satellite, the main event was a much larger country operation.' Catrin wanted to mention the strange figure who'd been following them, the one who dressed like Jones but couldn't be, but something held her back.

'People have been disappearing,' he said, 'I give you that. There could always be more innocent explanations of course.' His cheeks were cracking into a humourless grin. 'Yet you seem to determined to choose the blackest one.'

She looked out of the window. The wind had picked up again. A piece of polythene was blowing across the car park, cracking as the wind caught it.

'But nineteen young people missing in the same rural area within a few years of each other,' she said hesitantly. 'And no one comments, no one starts an inquiry, no one seems to notice. It doesn't feel right somehow, does it?'

Thomas looked deep into her eyes, his expression unreadable. 'Who says no one noticed?'

He took out a carefully folded piece of paper, which was almost coming apart in his hands. It looked like an old newspaper article, slightly yellowed at the edges; it smelt musty. The top of the page confirmed this, the date was from the late 1990s.

'When I picked up your unauthorised searches on NCIS, I saw you were going into all the missing person cases in this area.' Thomas spoke more quietly this time as he passed her the paper, keeping his palm under it so it didn't fall apart. 'So I did some digging of my own.'

Taking the paper from his slightly clammy hand, she had a sense of déjà vu. That night in the club, how she had come to ask Thomas questions about Huw, but Thomas already had the article about Huw's lab sting with him. It had felt unsettling, as if Thomas was always several steps ahead of her, as if he'd been reading her mind. Or the next best thing, hacking her.

It was an old article from the local paper, the *Western Telegraph*, dated just after Face's disappearance at the bridge. PARK RESIDENT MOURNS DAUGHTER'S DISAP-PEARANCE read the headline. Catrin recognised the photo of the resident in question immediately. It was old Tudor from the shop. Next to it was the picture she'd seen over his counter framed by fairy-lights and candles, a picture of a tanned, smiling girl with deep brown eyes. Catrin saw she was right: the girl was the old man's daughter.

The article spoke of other residents of the area mourning their missing children. The first paragraph dealt with anxieties about Jones, who was referred to only as the Abductor or the Man in the Mask. But the main body of the piece focused on a discussion of the phenomenon of suicide clusters in rural areas. Many of the names she recognised from the other misper files. The farmer from Martlewy whose boy had been found on the rocks at Cat Head, the family of the sixteen-year-old discovered under the ferry crossing, the parents of the girl whose body had been found floating off Crincoed Point. The assumption among the community was that all the young people had thrown themselves off cliffs and high places along the coast; though none of these suicides had actually been witnessed.

Some of the same pictures from the missing person files, she saw, had been duplicated in a row at the bottom. She wondered if these were the only images that survived of these young people. In the files some had appeared only as black silhouettes denoting male or female, like shy members of a dating site. How soon a life is diminished into a few small unremarkable signs, she thought, how soon it can fade from view. She looked again at the images of the young faces, at the dates under the pictures, trying to see if there was anything she had missed before.

'But these nineteen young people were missing for long periods,' she said, 'sometimes many years, before their bodies were found. They all disappeared somewhere first. This doesn't fit a suicide cluster.'

'I know.' Thomas sounded unusually nervous, tentative. 'That's because there's another possible explanation of why these young people disappeared.' His lazy smile had vanished now. He looked as tense as she'd ever seen him.

'There's something you need to know,' he said quietly. His knuckles whitened as he squeezed her hands together.

'When I was new to the force, I worked with Rhys on a case. We were both still in uniform then.' She saw a thin sweat appearing above Thomas's upper lip.

'This case was?'

His eyes glanced at the door, as he lowered his voice. 'Three suspected ODs, otherwise healthy young men, all had died of liver failure. All three bodies had been found on beaches up here.'

'Just like the Stephens case?'

Thomas was nodding slowly.

'No one looked at this from a profiling angle?' she asked.

'Of course, but no profiles fitted.'

She paused. 'But Jones? He was into abduction, spiking, torture.'

'It looks like Jones at first, I agree. But Jones was never a known killer.'

'What he did was worse than killing. His victims emerged like the dead, barely recognisable. When they returned it only spread more fear. He left them in the same area these other bodies were found.'

Thomas was moving his hand impatiently. 'Yes, there are parallels. But when you look closely there are also differences. The liver damage, none of Jones's known victims had it. All these bodies were left in water – water destroys evidence. But Jones used woods, dumped his victims alive.'

'There were those old rumours that Jones killed, hid the bodies. Maybe he had a different MO out here. Used his victims as accomplices in group activities, rituals, then disposed of them.'

Thomas held up his hand, cut her short.

'No. This case didn't fit any existing serial matches or patterns, not a single one. They sent the data to Europol, Interpol – no matches, not even any precedents. So a special task force was set up in-house by Drugs to investigate the deaths.' He paused, took a deep breath. 'Then a couple of months later traces of synthesised tryptamines on two of the bodies led Drugs to a lab near the university medical faculty at Heath Park.'

'That same lab which triggered the big sting op you told me Powell was involved in, the one that needed Home Office approval?' Catrin felt her chest tighten. Everything was beginning to connect now but in a way she had not expected.

Thomas nodded. 'It was a highly professional set-up, as I told you, everything state-of-the-art. They had twenty-kilo Rotorvaps, the latest freeze dryers, self-cleaning vac-pumps, the works.'

'No connection to the university?'

'The university denied any knowledge of it, though they said that it was as sophisticated as anything they had. All the equipment was top-end, research grade, but there was no evidence any original research was being done there. It was a drugs lab, pure and simple. All the chemical precursors were set up for the production of exotic tryptamines, Belladonna alkaloids and

5-MeO-DMT. These were some of the strongest hallucinogens on the scale at the time. But the strange thing
was that these drug types were too exotic to have
much market value. So whoever was responsible for
funding the lab would never have recouped their capital
investment.'

'If there was no market, then why go to the trouble
of setting up such a lab?'

'That's what everyone was asking themselves at the
time. On the face of it the enterprise didn't have any
obvious commercial rationale. Yet this was the most
high-end drug lab anyone had come across.'

'Couldn't traces be put on the orders for the chemical precursors and hardware?'

She heard a noise in Thomas's throat that sounded
something like wry amusement.

'We tried. For a while it looked as though a San
Diego biotech company was in the frame, but this
proved a dead end. The paper trail led through a maze
of offshore shell companies and blinds. Then that big
sting op was launched, the team posing as synthetic
drug manufacturers in competition with the Ukrainian
and Thai labs. By acting in the same way as the target,
as the competition, they tried to draw in the same
buyers to get a fix on the distribution chain, on who
the end users were.'

'How close to a result did they get?'

'Not even a whisper: after two years the op hadn't even netted a single potential buyer. By then the whole situation was getting a bad smell. Rumours began to circulate that some of the officers were taking kickbacks from the hardware suppliers, stringing out something that was going nowhere to build up retirement funds.'

'Any substance to these rumours?' she asked.

'None. That was the thing. It felt like a deliberate whispering campaign. No one knew where the rumours were coming from, but the longer the op went on the worse they got. The word was the new chief Rix wanted heads on plates, the whole business wound up as quickly and cleanly as possible before Complaints got wind of it.'

'Was anything ever proved?'

'Nothing. Fingers were pointed at the three officers who had initially requested the expenditure. That was myself, Rhys and the officer in charge, Powell. They crawled all over us, but never got anything.'

Thomas was swallowing hard, putting a hand to his mouth.

Catrin looked out into the passage, then back at Thomas. 'So you believe there was a deliberate smear campaign to hobble the investigation into the lab?'

'If so, it worked. By the time they climbed into Rhys and Powell and myself, the op had already been wound up. There were a couple of small articles by the Insight Team in the *Sunday Times*, some follow-up pieces in the *Western Mail*. But after a couple of months the press lost interest and it looked as though everyone had forgotten about it.'

Catrin looked into Thomas's eyes again, thought she saw a flicker of some deep and long-standing fear but it was there so briefly she couldn't be sure.

Thomas leant forward slightly, his eyes dropping for a moment to Catrin's neck.

'Yet all these years later, it looks like Rhys may still have been working the same old case.'

Thomas stared down at the blank space ahead of him. 'Rhys always believed that the lab and the deaths were all linked to a single figure out here,' he said.

'What made him think that?'

'He would never tell me. But that's why he was out here around the time he found you in the woods. It's all one case,' he said quietly.

All was still outside. Through the nets Catrin saw the hazy, tired light that had already a tinge of dusk about it. She remembered how Rhys had always seemed preoccupied, how she'd sensed a pain there, something he was keeping locked away, that she couldn't reach. She'd open one door to it and another would close and now she knew why. All the time he'd been protecting her from the darkness the case had spread inside himself.

Thomas stood up. 'There's something I have to do,' he said. 'Wait here, I'll be back.'

She watched the door close behind him, turned to the window and pulled back the curtains. The afternoon light was fading behind the low, incoming banks of fog, the weather closing in again.

Catrin woke to a light knocking sound outside the door. She raised her head, looked at her watch. She'd been asleep for almost an hour. The temperature in the room had fallen. The headache that had been with her all day had eased, in its place a dull, tired numbness. She got up from the chair, stretched. Padding over to the door, she opened it a crack.

Thomas was standing back in the narrow passage. He was hanging his head slightly, not looking at her directly.

Catrin didn't move from the doorway at first. Then, still not fully awake, she stood back, let him through. As he edged past her his steps seemed unsteady. His breath smelt heavily of drink.

By the window was a counter with a dusty stand of tea bags and coffees. Catrin emptied two coffee sachets into the mugs, switched on the kettle. He must have gone back to the bar, she thought, or brought a bottle of something in the car.

'You didn't used to drink so much,' she said. 'You're

troubled by something aren't you, something you're still not telling me?'

Thomas didn't reply. She felt his hand reach up, touch her shoulder.

'You should come back with me, first thing.' His voice did not sound slurred now, but quiet and clear. His eyes were bloodshot, but the level emptiness in his gaze did not come from the drink.

She wondered if he knew Huw was with her, if he had contact with Huw still. Probably not, she thought. He was looking away from her towards the window. But there was nothing to see there, the curtains were still closed. She saw in his eyes just apertures over a void. She couldn't read them.

Gently she removed his hand from her shoulder, let it drop to her side. His eyes softened as she did this. She thought she glimpsed a loneliness there.

'I'm sorry for what I did to you. In the car, all those years ago,' he said.

'So you admit it now.'

'I was drunk. The truth is I don't remember what I did,' he said.

She poured in the water from the kettle and used a Biro to stir the coffee.

She wondered what had got into Thomas. All his usual cockiness seemed to have evaporated. He'd come because he needed information from her, but once he'd got it, he'd wanted to share with her. Thomas and Rhys went way back, that was something Thomas had kept from her. This might explain his sudden openness with her, but it also troubled her. And there was one thing he'd told her almost nothing about, something he'd claimed not to know when she'd first asked him back in town. Now she wondered if he'd be more open with her.

'Those drugs you were talking about earlier, the ones at that Heath Park lab. How would those differ from the standard hallucinogens?'

His lips had parted into a vague, unfocused look of disapproval.

'With the usual hallucinogens, magic mushrooms or acid, a part of the brain, however small, always knows that what it's seeing is an illusion.'

'And with those other types?'

'That part of the brain is suspended. The illusion is absolute. You enter a parallel reality. You see a demon, that demon is there with you, real as anything you've ever seen. They're deep trance drugs, the type ancient shamans used to enter the spirit world.'

In her mind's eye Catrin could see again the path winding through the dark trees, at the end the two sheds, under the glare of the grow-lights the troughs of plants, and far above them through the woods the looming shape of the escarpment.

'But could such weird drugs ever have any practical uses? Something that could justify the expense of a high-tech lab like the one at Heath Park?'

'I'm not sure.' He paused, seemed about to go on but didn't.

'But whoever's behind all the disappearances clearly used them in some way that's somatically dangerous. That must be why those three bodies all exhibited liver damage.'

Thomas didn't seem to be listening to what Catrin said. She moved closer to him before she spoke again, glimpsed a ring of sweat on his collar.

He was reaching to the window, pulling the curtains to. His body was closing out the light from the corner. She felt his breath on her neck. 'The liver damage,' he said, 'it may not have been the only factor in the deaths.' His voice sounded faint, just a murmur, as if he was half speaking to himself.

She wanted to step back, but didn't.

'What else?' she said.

'Those first three bodies also had some facial damage. The eyeballs had been picked away, apparently by birds, the noses and ears, the tongues.'

She stepped back. 'But soft-tissue damage in wash-ups is common from exposure to gulls and other coastal birds.'

'Yes, that's the obvious explanation.'

She waited but he didn't go on. She felt him reach up, his fingers brush gently over her cheek. She backed away against the wall.

'You didn't ask about Della.' He said this in a neutral, deliberately level tone.

Somehow she saw Della as indestructible, she couldn't imagine the world without her. But of course she had been very vulnerable. They all were. 'Well, how's she doing?'

'She's still in a coma, her brain was deprived of oxygen.' Catrina felt relieved to hear that Della was still alive, still had a chance. 'She left a message for you on my line, the morning of the fire. She didn't say anything, just to get in touch.'

She remembered what Pugh had said, about the message Della had left on his line. She wondered again what Della could have wanted, and why she hadn't left a message on her own line. She sensed Thomas's fingers rising to her neck, just lingering there as if afraid to touch.

'Come back with me,' he said.

She shook her head. Then he lowered his hand and walked to the door, not looking back. Catrin heard his boots clacking out over the gravel to the cars.

For a brief moment he looked back at her, then disappeared. The place where he'd been standing seemed a deeper black than the space around it, as if he was still watching her. Thomas had just told her so much, and yet she felt she no longer knew who he was. Maybe she'd never really known him at all.

Catrin waited. The only movement outside was that of the birds, circling high above the empty square of tarmac, drifting away into the fog. Over by the rocks she saw a pinprick of light, a cigarette perhaps, then all was dark.

Gradually she noticed another vehicle by the rocks. It was parked near Thomas's car, an old van. One of the doors was opening, a figure standing behind it.

It was the surfer, wearing the same long fur coat. He waved slowly at her, then got up onto the rocks and looked past her into the room.

He's seeing if I'm alone, why else would he be looking past me like that? Catrin closed the curtains, ran back into the passage. The air was filled with the voices of the men in the bar. She went to the door, looked in. There was no sign of Huw there, nor of Thomas, just the usual bearded figures nursing pints.

Through the coloured glass in the outside door she saw the outline of a man in a long dark coat. He doesn't want to be seen talking to me, but why? she wondered.

She ordered a drink, stared at the pictures of the lifeboat crews behind the bar. When she turned back to the door, the man was gone. She finished the drink in a single gulp and went back into the corridor.

There were no overhead lights on. She ran her hand along the wall, feeling for a switch. The wall felt cold, rough under her fingers. She leant back against it, breathed deeply, tried to get her bearings. Through the door behind her came a band of weak, fan-shaped light to the foot of the stairs. She reached for the banister rail, but grabbed the edge of a picture on the wall. Another lifeboat crew perhaps. The picture fell and she felt herself tumbling forward onto the steps.

She heard the glass crack. A shuffling, behind her. The man was standing in the doorway, blocking the light.

'What do you want?' she said. Her voice came out as frailer, more tremulous than she would have liked.

'I'd like to meet,' he said. 'Just the two of us.' His hand grasped her arm, pulling her up.

'No.' She tried to call out, but his hand was over her mouth. It smelt sweetly, of some expensive cologne, not like a builder's hand at all.

She felt herself falling backwards and jabbed hard at his eyes. He didn't react. His face felt strangely stiff as if it was not made from flesh at all. He was strong: with one arm he pulled her down the passage, through a doorway, his hand still over her mouth.

He closed the door, flicked the switch. They were in what had once been the tack-room of the inn. Old saddles and racks were hanging around the walls with dusty stirrups and bits.

He pulled her over against the rack. She tried to stamp on his instep but he anticipated her move. She felt his hand harder over her mouth, his fingers pushing apart her lips and forcing themselves between her teeth.

She bit down hard and kicked at him. It felt as if she was kicking something inanimate. She was falling again, but he held her back against the rack.

'Who are you?' she said. 'You're one of them, aren't you?'

He'd taken his hand from her mouth. There was a look of almost tender concern on his face. 'One of who?' he said.

She had her left arm free now, and hacked at his windpipe. He didn't flinch, just moved closer, his breath slow and level. She drilled at his face in a series of fast, hard punches, moves she'd practised many times, trying to unsight him. He stepped back out of range, and she broke free and ran for the door. She could hear men coming out from the bar, moving down the passage. Before she had time to shout for help, he rushed forwards at an almost inhuman speed. She expected him to grab her, but she heard his leather soles darting out over the gravel into the darkness.

She went up the stairs, to the room, locked the door. She waited, listened. But there were no sounds outside.

She took out the card he'd given her and held it under the light. FRANSIS SERAFIM. FRANCIS SERAFIM LTD. Then a Cardiff address. She booted up her Mac, ran his name and address on the PNC. Nothing came up, he had no record at all. She went into the Companies House site next. It was a new company, just formed, hadn't even filed its first accounts yet. He was listed as a sole trader, no associates.

She ran a few more searches: there were a couple of listings in Cardiff and London gyms, a surf club membership, an earlier membership to a house builders' association. It all seemed banal enough.

Catrin got up, went through to Huw's room. He wasn't back yet. Under a bottle of whisky he'd left on the table was a note, saying he'd gone into Fishguard to use a teleconferencing facility. She called his mobile from the landline.

'You've got your guards with you?' she asked.

'They picked me up.'

'Don't bring them. It will attract too much attention. Come back alone.'

She poured some of the whisky, drank it neat. She still felt tense, rolled a cigarette. She reached into Huw's dope box, picked out one of the baggies and crumbled some in.

It was strong. A couple of drags and she felt light-headed, slightly giddy. She picked up the surfer's card again, noticed the old-fashioned writing on the back. She held it under the light again. There was a single name. *The Wing*. Then the web address of a popular BDSM site, not the most fashionable but one of the largest.

She clicked onto the site. It was the usual dom's profile. She'd seen dozens like it over the years when she'd worked that scene undercover. A couple of shots with bare torso and leather mask. Then some shots of him in civilian life, standing with his surfboard, to show his face, to show he was just a normal guy.

She took a closer look at his interests: conventional enough in the context – spanking, whips, bondage, role play. Nothing that heavy, no mention of edge play or any of the more extreme areas. Many doms would show off their dungeons if they had them, or their arrays of toys and whips, but despite his obvious experience there were no pictures of that sort. She noted the site worked like most of the other BDSM sites, on a rating system. The contacts would score each other out of five. This way members could check if another member was trust-worthy, worth contacting. It wasn't foolproof but it seemed to work.

He was an active member, he'd had over a dozen encounters in the last three months; all had given him the full five stars. This was unusual, subs could be notoriously choosy. Normally it would take several encounters before a sub built up the requisite trust with her dom or found a match for her needs.

Intuitive, she thought, good at reading people. That usually comes with having started out as a sub. Usually there would be some negative feedback along the line, but Catrin could see none at all.

She did next what prospective subs would do. She checked the profiles of his various encounters to see what kind of members had attracted him. The photographs were all characteristically coy, but there was enough detail to see they were good-looking girls and women between late teens and early thirties. There were different types, different hair colours. There didn't seem to be any clear common denominator, except that where they were visible all seemed to have brown eyes. Deep brown eyes, just like hers. Oh fuck, she thought, just my luck.

She looked carefully from one profile to the next. There were the typical poetic self-descriptions, talk of empty souls and voids and a returning, irresistible need to submit their will utterly to another, of the paradox of freedom through enslavement. Like most subs they were quite articulate. She clicked from one text to another, then back again. Something wasn't quite right. She looked carefully at the syntax, the punctuation.

Then it struck her. All the profiles had been written by a single person.

It felt like a set-up, a trap. He could be that thing subs fear most, a rogue dom. Once someone was shackled, they were helpless. If the trust wasn't there, anything could happen.

7

Catrin woke late, after eight. It was still dark outside. She could see Huw in silhouette at the window. On the table lay rows of printouts. The laptop was open over on the dressing table, its screen glowing with the blue and white of the Glangwili Hospital portal.

Huw was staring out at the weather. Catrin could see the tendrils of mist moving past the window, the deep grey sky that probably wouldn't lift all day. Huw pointed at something outside.

'Whose car's that?'

Sliding down the bed, she peered over his shoulder. The boxy shape of Thomas's Audi was just visible through the mist. Beside it she could see the distant outline of a man sitting smoking on the rocks. It didn't look like Thomas; someone older, his head turned away, staring out to sea. She thought it might be Tudor from the woods, but couldn't be sure. For a moment the man seemed to raise an arm, as if acknowledging her gaze.

'That's DS Thomas's. He must have stayed overnight,' she said.

'A fishing expedition relating to the fires?'

Catrin felt Huw pulling her into his warmth. She knew immediately she didn't want to talk to him about what had happened with Fransis. She didn't want him to know about that side of her life, her undercover selves; however she tried to explain it, she knew it would come out all wrong.

'How much did you give Thomas?' he asked.

'I told him about the Stephens file, that Stephens was a Face fan, maybe linked to some cult out here, maybe one of my abductors. That what looked like Stephens's body had washed up on the Sands only a month ago.'

'And?'

'He thought the case had similarities to a suspected serial OD case Rhys had been working back in the Nineties.'

She exhaled slowly, feeling calmer than she'd expected. Huw had stopped kissing her, but his lips were close to her neck, his breath warm on her. 'And these similarities were?'

'The case had centred on three bodies of previously healthy young men that turned up on the coast here, all with acute liver damage.'

'Did he say if Rhys had fingered any suspects?'

'No, he said traces of synthesised tryptamines on the bodies led to that state-of-the-art drugs lab in

Heath Park, and after that the trail went cold. A sting was launched, a mirror lab set up to draw in the buyers, get a fix on the distribution chain. But as expenditure spiralled without any results the whole op got a bad smell, got closed down.'

Huw was still staring out at the lone figure out in the mist. 'I was part of the team that devised that sting,' he said without looking at her.

'Thomas told me.'

'That lab was a dead end. We never found out who was behind it.'

Huw put his arm around her waist as he spoke. Gently she pulled herself away. She'd had an idea, something vague, a sensation as much as an idea, but now she felt it slowly gathering momentum inside her, like a desire, a hope. 'The drugs from that lab had no known commercial value, right. They're deep trance drugs, Thomas said, the type used in some forms of witchcraft and by ancient shamans to enter the spirit world.'

Huw seemed dubious, perhaps not following her yet. She thought back to what Thomas had said, that all the time Rhys had been working a single case. She ran the chain of events once more in her mind. The first three bodies with liver damage had led Rhys to the lab in Heath Park. Then the trail had led Rhys back to the island, and he'd found her drugged and senseless in the woods. In Rhys's mind whoever had abducted her was behind the lab, behind the nineteen disappearances, the nineteen dead. He was the man with the long hair, the man in the films.

This same man behind everything, all right, but who was he? She thought back to how the abduction dates coincided with Jones's. Two prolific serial abductors wouldn't have been operating independently, not within the same small area and time frame. So everything pointed to that figure being Jones, and Rhys had evidently been of the same view. Rhys arresting Jones no longer seemed a chance event. Rhys had arrested Jones because he'd already been looking for him.

But if Jones was the man, then how to explain why bodies were still turning up? This was what had drawn Rhys out again to the area, and had led to his death. Slowly Catrin drew a shape in the condensation on the pane, a stylised bird's head, watched as the shape dissolved back into the moisture.

'The type of drugs made in that lab, the trance drugs, Thomas said you're transported into a parallel reality, one that seems as real as this one. This was why the shaman would believe, when he took those drugs, he would meet his spirits and gods.'

Huw was staring at the ghost of the shape on the pane.

'Or his demons. Much of the imagery of our devil has been taken from what was witnessed during the trances of ancient shamans. You think the abductor has been using these drugs to conduct seances, necromancy. That's what we're seeing in those films?'

'I'm not sure.' Catrin put her hand over his, held it tightly. 'Did you ever encounter drugs like those in any other busts during that period?'

Huw seemed hesitant. She watched him click into what looked like a secure private email account. There was some text encrypted there in PGP and another encryption system she'd never seen before.

'This was some research I did, at the time we found the lab.' He paused. 'It didn't make much sense to me then. Still doesn't, really.'

Catrin looked at the text. Most of the first part was a series of chemical formulas. She recognised only some from her drugs training. The main formula was for a synthetic variation of something called dimethyltryptamine. DMT, a very powerful hallucinogen, one of the most powerful and dangerous ever discovered. Usually the hallucinations were short and intense, no more than a few minutes before the chemical was metabolised by the body. But what she was seeing on the screen shocked her. There were formulas for prolonging the experience, blocking metabolisation with harmaline and other inhibitors. This would enable the intense hallucinatory effects to continue for days, maybe weeks even.

'Dimethyltryptamine,' she said. 'It's known as the soul molecule. It's plant-derived, but also intrinsic to the human brain. It's found in the pineal gland, that's where up to the time of Descartes philosophers located the human soul. It's the chemical associated with near-death experiences, crossing over to the realm of the dead.'

Huw nodded. 'Also with witchcraft,' he said, 'and ancient Celtic shamans would use fungi and other plants that contained it to travel into the underworld. Like the plants in those sheds. If the figure we see in those films is the abductor, then what the hell was going on there?'

'I don't know.' She put her hand over his fingers, felt how cold they were. Gradually letting go she bent over the keyboard. She cross-searched the names of the drugs with the words 'witch' and 'shaman' and confirmed what Huw had said. She looked up to where she had drawn the bird's head; only the faintest outline was left of it now. She keyed in the word 'raven' and a long list of links to various anthropological studies came up. It seemed the raven had symbolism for many ancient religions. She narrowed the search to Celtic significances. The raven she saw had been a symbol of hidden knowledge, of death and departed souls, and the costume worn by shamans making the journey into the underworld had often been that of a raven.

Catrin sensed something tugging at her memory. She went back to the account by the American academic of witchcraft on the island, and read it through again. The account claimed children in the area had become possessed by spirits, and had disappeared into a place the locals believed was a mouth to hell. Sightings of the older man, Penrhyn, had continued for many years afterwards, as had the disappearances.

The piece still felt sketchy and incomplete. She knew she couldn't read too much into it and looked again at the small illustration of a man wearing long black robes and standing at the mouth of a cave. His arms were outstretched and at the edge of the cave stood several young people, their faces distorted, as were their limbs, within a circle of what appeared to be black arrowheads or feathers. She thought of what Tudor had said he'd glimpsed in the woods, a child playing in a cloak made of feathers. She touched Huw's hand and noticed it was cold.

'From the beginning of this case, I've had a sense that everything's been happening for one purpose, for one specific but terrible purpose. And Rhys understood that purpose, it was a burden he carried within him, that ate away at him. He became a junkie to cope with the pain of carrying it. That was why Rhys was still working something related to that old case after all these years. Once it was inside him he could never let it go.'

Catrin felt for her roll-ups. 'And at the end, when Rhys had no one else to turn to, when they were hunting him down, he was trying to reach me. He had to pass the knowledge of the case on to someone, and he chose me.'

'So where does his source fit in?'

'Rhys made sure his source knew who I was, knew I could be trusted. That's the way Rhys kept his secret knowledge of the case alive.'

'Yet the source never came to you. Rhys said the source would trust only you, so why has that source not revealed himself?'

'I don't know.' She moved away from the middle of the room, sat down on the bed, laid the pouch of Drum on her naked thighs.

She heard the sound of water pouring from the bath taps. Then Huw came and sat at the table, his fingers moving over the outlines of the faces he'd printed out. In the flickering light from the Glangwili Hospital portal his eyes had that deep-set, hollow look of someone who had been staring at the screen for hours.

'Yesterday,' he said, 'the teleconference, it gave me a chance to check on something.'

'Something you didn't trust me with.' Catrin stared hard at him, steadied herself on the chair and felt a surge of anger rise through her. All the times Rhys had not told her things came back to her, those nights she'd waited up at the flat, drinking alone until sleep came. At least I must really feel something for him, she told herself. If I couldn't I wouldn't care what he did.

'This thing,' he said, 'it was about Emyr Pugh.'

'Ah, I get it, you know Pugh and I go way back, so on this you kept me out of the loop.'

She thought he was smiling, trying to hide it. 'No, I didn't want to use the phones here.'

She didn't see why he found it funny. 'Bollocks, you've been haunted by this case for years, like Rhys. I'm just a means to you, a tool.'

Catrin got up, went into her room, slamming the door, then realised she'd left her tobacco behind and felt even angrier. She needed to know what the connection with Pugh was, and if she sat in the dark fuming she wasn't going to find out.

She opened the door a crack, stood there silently. Huw threw her the tobacco, smiling sheepishly up at her.

'Pugh,' he said. 'If I'd really meant to keep that from you, I'd not have mentioned it, would I?' He looked down, no longer smiling. 'Think about it.'

She knew he had a point, began to calm down a little. 'So what was it?'

'I wanted to know if Rhys had ever mentioned the case to Pugh.' He paused. 'I know you said Pugh sometimes saw Rhys around town, usually down the riverside where his body was found.'

'But Pugh's had plenty of occasions to tell me if Rhys had said anything to him, and he didn't.'

'Right, so I wondered, well if maybe it was something he didn't want to tell you, because he didn't think there was anything in it, didn't want you chasing after what he thought was junkie bullshit.'

'So?'

'So I left a message, told him if there is, to get in touch but not by phone. But he's away on leave.'

Catrin laughed. 'I could've told you that anyway.'

She came back to the table and sat down at the screen beside him.

'Any other acute liver conditions in the mispers not uploaded into the files then, the type that might've been caused by these extended trance drugs from the lab?'

'I checked the GP notes, the NHS inpatients records at Withybush, Glangwili and the Morriston hospitals for all the other mispers we've pulled, and drew a blank for any liver or toxicity-related admissions on any of them.'

'Anything else come up?'

'Just the usual pre-teen, early teen issues – routine

fractures, asthma, suspected meningitis, nothing that ties into the Stephens file.'

In the half-light, she began to roll a cigarette by touch.

'Something doesn't feel quite right about that.'

'In what way?'

'Mispers, runaways tend to have fairly active medical records. One would expect some incidence of teenage pregnancy, self-harm, psychological or drug-related problems.'

'But the more sensitive issues – teenage pregnancies, self-harm episodes – these often get handled in the private sector at the request of the parents. That would explain their not showing in the NHS databases.'

She opened the steamed-up window a crack, felt in the drawer for a lighter.

'That might explain the cases from middle-class backgrounds, but about half of them, like Stephens, were the children of long-term unemployed and travellers or were in care.'

'But we know those are just the types that can slip out of the system altogether.'

When she sparked the lighter, the flame was too long. She could smell her hair singeing. She blew the smoke up towards the window.

'Another explanation could be that someone deliberately wanted some of those medical histories off the radar, either by paying for the youths to go private, or by wiping the files.' She watched the smoke drift out into the mildewed air.

'So why did the Stephens admission still show then?' Huw asked.

'That admission was over five years before his disappearance. You said that the cases had all the usual records up to early teens. Maybe the wipe-out only went back five years from the disappearance dates, so the Stephens notes got through?'

She had the sense suddenly that Huw was no longer listening to what she was saying. He went through to the bathroom and turned off the taps.

She switched on the lamp, started to gather up clean underclothes, jeans, a sweatshirt. Then she sat on the edge of the bed, just as she used to with Rhys, waiting for her turn in the bathroom.

Huw stepped out of the door, a white towel wrapped around his waist. He put his right hand up to her face, pushing a stray hair away from her lower lip.

Unfastening the towel, she began to dry him. He was still, head bowed, lifting his arms as she ran the towel down his chest. She worked quietly, methodically. When she had finished she put the towel on the bed, her arms around him so that she could rest her head in the warm, salty groove of his collarbone. He was kissing the top of her head, so softly she could barely feel his breath through the strands of her hair. She felt an unexpected moment of emptiness and calm.

Huw moved away from her towards the table. Catrin carried her clothes through to the bathroom, leaving the door open so they could still hear each other.

'Those cottages at the cove,' she called through the steam. 'I got another look at them. Most have been done up in a similar style to Rhys's. It looks as if they're all owned by a single company?'

She could hear Huw working the keyboard.

'You're right,' he said. 'Eglwys Beach. It's owned by a company registered to an address in Cardiff.' He repeated the address to her. She heard more tapping. 'But on the registry that address is listed as derelict.'

Catrin let the warm water course down her tensed-up back. Through the door she saw Huw lying on the bed, staring up at the ceiling.

'In the village, have you seen any other cottages being refurbished?'

'None.'

Through the steam she could see nothing clearly now. 'That older man with the cane, I asked him and he said he was doing up some holiday lets near the village.'

'Must be those then.'

'So Rhys was staying in one of his cottages,' Catrin

said. The steam was stinging her eyes, making her sweat. 'But when I asked him if he'd seen Rhys, he said he hadn't.'

'Maybe he didn't recognise Rhys from the picture?'

'I pointed out Rhys's earrings. They're not the sort of thing you'd forget. Fransis Serafim he calls himself, unusual name for a local man.'

'Rhys could've asked this Fransis to keep quiet about his being there?'

'Or Fransis chose to keep quiet about it.'

She went and sat in front of the small dressing table by the window as Huw called the barman to ask if he knew where Fransis's place was.

'And?'

'He thought he might be connected to the clinic in some way.'

Catrin cast her mind back to the staff register she'd run, didn't remember his name there. 'He's a patient?'

'The barman didn't seem to want to talk about him.'

'He seemed all on edge yesterday when the man was here. Like that dealer, he seemed uneasy when we mentioned him.'

She pulled on the band that held her hair out of her face when she did her make-up.

'Call him again, ask him which room Thomas is in,' she said.

Behind her she heard Huw's calm professional tone,

a pause, then the click of the receiver dropping back onto its cradle. Huw got up, stood by the door.

'Thomas didn't come back to his room last night.'

'How did he know that?'

'When he went in this morning the bed hadn't been slept in. He said he saw Thomas leaving the building last night in a van with builder's tarps on it.'

The bar looked closed, the doors shut. Glasses lay on the tables, uncleared from the previous night's lock-in. A fug of stale smoke hung in the still air.

The young barman was crouching at the back, painting a long, old-fashioned surfboard. The wood had been sanded down and he was applying to it a thick coat of some pungent metallic paint.

Huw cleared his throat. 'Sorry to bother you again,' he said quietly.

'That's all right.' He'd directed towards them that cautious yet curious expression of people from country parts for whom any stranger seems an object of fascination.

'The man who didn't come back last night.' Huw was standing over the board admiring the barman's handiwork. 'We're friends of his. We'd like to take a quick look in his room, if you don't mind.'

They followed him upstairs to a room opposite the first landing. It was smaller than theirs, recently repainted in the same muted primrose as the landings. Near the ceiling the damp was already showing through.

'There's nothing here, as you can see.' The surfaces in the bathroom were still wet where they had been wiped down. Catrin went and had a closer look, ran her fingers along the gaps between the tiles.

She could see the remnants of a dark stain, but it had all but disappeared. She lifted her fingers, smelt them. It wasn't a smell she recognised, something sharp, chemical.

'You don't think that's odd?' she said. 'He books a room but doesn't use it?'

The man closed the door and led them downstairs again. 'Well, that's what happened before,' he said.

The doors to the yard were still closed, the lights off, a feeble glimmer filtering through the dirty panes.

'How many times has Mr Thomas stayed here?' Huw had followed the man into the narrow passage where the old board was leaning against the wall. Catrin waited a little way behind as they spoke.

'He's stayed maybe half a dozen times over the last year.'

She wondered what to make of this. 'Know what he's been doing here?'

'No idea. He never talks with any locals.'

The man was moving his brush quickly over the board, some drops of paint falling to the floor. She glanced further down the passage. Stacked against the wall were what looked like antique children's toys, next to them some small dolls made from reeds. 'This gentleman with the van, Fransis, know anything more about him?' she asked.

The barman shook his head. Catrin thought she'd take a chance now. 'I heard this Fransis was seen up on that escarpment above the woods,' she said. She was a good liar, she'd kept her tone almost indistinguishable from her previous questions. The man stopped moving his brush in mid-motion, and only when the paint began dripping on the floor did he look down at it.

'That's not likely,' he said. 'No one on the island ever goes up there.' He didn't look round at her, but continued brushing the same small square of board. 'It's not safe. You have to know the paths.'

'So what do they go up there for?' she said.

'How do you mean?'

'The people from the island, you said they know the paths.'

He kept his eyes on the board. 'It's nothing,' he said. 'Don't worry about it.'

Huw thanked the man, then led the way back along the passage to the day room. The curtains were still closed, the ashtray on the floor unemptied from the previous afternoon. He shut the door before speaking again.

'What do you make of that? Thomas has been coming down here on the quiet. Then he leaves with this Fransis character, doesn't come back.'

'I'm not sure.' The room felt cold. The radiator in the corner gave out little heat. Catrin sat on top of it, began to roll a cigarette. 'The barman said Fransis was connected to the clinic. But his name wasn't on the staff register.'

'An outpatient?'

'Maybe. Let's check there, see if we can get more details on him.'

She flicked her ash into the fireplace. 'There's something not quite right about this whole place, don't you feel that?'

'In what sense?'

'It's as if the place is hiding something. It's there, but just out of sight all the time.'

Huw was leaning closer to her, his eyes flicking over to the door. Catrin could hear the sound of the birds far out over the waters.

She threw her half-smoked stub into the fireplace. In the distance a figure out on the rocks was moving slowly away into the mist. She reached for the binoculars, but it had disappeared into the dimness. As the cries of the birds faded, it was difficult to believe anyone had been there at all.

'That looked like Tudor,' she said. 'He was there earlier, watching us.' She looked out into the half-light.

'It may be nothing, but Tudor's daughter, the pretty one. She was one of those youngsters reported missing, but she was never matched with a body.'

Huw had already turned, picked up his coat. 'She may have run off to London or somewhere. But Tudor must have known something about those grow-sheds, his place was the closest habitation, there was nothing else near.'

'Except the escarpment.' She lowered her eyes from the window. 'You don't think Tudor's who he appears to be?'

'I don't know, I'm not really sure any of them are.' He paused. 'Like you said, this whole place feels wrong.'

As Huw reached the door, it was already opening. Standing there was the barman and another man, their broad shoulders blocking out the light. Catrin saw that the barman was staring at Huw, not moving, as if he wasn't going to let him pass.

The second man stepped forward. She recognised him as one of the regulars from the bar, the one with the beard and sandy hair fading to grey she'd seen on the first day.

'Your lady friend,' he glanced past Huw to where Catrin sat. 'A gentleman wants to speak to her.'

The barman was still blocking the door, his arm across the gap.

'This gentleman,' she said, 'who is it?'

The bearded man stepped back into the shadows.

The barman was still there, watching. 'He's waiting for you, the gentleman, at the clinic.'

There was silence. No one moved. She knew she had enough space to land a kick on the throat of the taller man. But she could hear a shuffling further in. More men were behind them; how many it was difficult to tell.

'We just wanted to make sure you got his message, like,' the first man said in a slow drawl. 'There's no hurry or nothing.'

She thought she heard a nervous laugh from one of the men, then there was silence.

'This gentleman,' she said, 'he's the one who's called Fransis Seraphim. The one you're all afraid of.'

There was a dull murmur from the passage. She glimpsed the men she'd seen before in the bar, standing in a line along the wall. They made a narrow gap for her to pass.

'Who is he really?' she said. Her eyes moved from face to face, the weathered features impassive. 'Who are you all really?' She could smell the damp fishermen's jerseys, the close scent of male sweat. All the faces were looking at her blankly, expressionless, and no one said a word.

As she glanced back, the men's shoulders were closing around her. Huw had disappeared from view. She felt hands suddenly drawing her forward towards the light.

8

The pickup felt cold. As the engine started, the air filled with the sound of trance drumming. Then all was silent again, just the soft whirring of the heater.

As they drove out of the village, the coastline was visible only as a bank of murky greys and subfuscs as vague and insubstantial as the low clouds covering it. The road climbed through the oak woods Catrin had passed the first morning, then past tall birches to the drive down to the clinic. Through the intricate trefoil of the gates she saw in the distance a building made from the ancient, dark rock from which the cliffs were formed.

The men with her said nothing, kept their heads straight ahead, not glancing at her once. The barman was driving, and on her other side was the tall man with the grey hair, with next to him a younger man she'd never seen before. Throughout he kept his face averted, hidden behind his baggy hoodie.

On both sides the drive was bordered by hedge-rows that had long ago lost their shape and become overgrown, the branches raking the side of the vehicle. Soon she could no longer hear the calls of the seabirds and the waves breaking on the cliffs behind them.

The barman now slowed almost to a crawl. Catrin peered out at the trees. 'This must have been planted when the house was first built, perhaps earlier. Blackthorn doesn't normally grow above fifteen feet, but this must be nearer twenty.' She wanted them to think she was relaxed, let them ease off their guard. The man in the hoodie put his hand out, ran it gently along the hedge.

'Isn't the blackthorn sacred to the ancient Celts?' she asked.

'Clever girl.' It was the man in the hoodie. His voice was low, cracked, barely more than a murmur, yet vaguely familiar to her. 'In the old calendar it represented the Waning or Dark Moon.'

Through her mind for a moment flickered the trees in the first film. All had had their significance, she was sure of that now. She said nothing more, stared into the dark thickets receding far into the mist. The trees on either side of the drive hung low, making a deep tunnel over the track until abruptly it opened into a paved area in which a crumbling ornamental fountain doubled as a bird-bath.

The building that housed the clinic, on the far side, was more extensive than she had anticipated. The high brick façade was inset with columns of black rock, but was otherwise plain, unrelieved by decorative effects. The windows were intersected by the gangways and ladders of old, rusted fire escapes, shrouded with a thick layer of ivy. There was a faded coat of arms over the entrance. The place looked like an old boarding school run to seed. There was nothing to identify it as a clinic, no ramp for wheelchairs, no signs apart from a wooden arrow pointing to a parking area. Beside several trailers resting on bricks in the long grass Catrin noticed a van with builder's tarps on the roof.

The barman braked abruptly, spun the pickup round at the entrance to the clearing. He threw the door open, but did not get out. 'The gentleman who wanted to speak to you will be in there,' he said. She wondered why he wasn't going any closer. There was still over thirty yards to the main building.

'What are you so frightened of?' she said.

He just pointed at the doorway. She could see reflections from the trees, maybe camera lenses. She knew she was probably being watched.

Catrin looked through the branches. Just visible in both directions as far as the eye could see a razor-fence ran down into the woods. Threaded through the fence were black, tear-shaped nodes and lengths of slim, transparent wire almost invisible against the frozen leaves. It was classic stealth security, discreet but effective. So the only way out was back along the drive, and that was closed off by the gates.

The barman slammed the door behind her and revved his engine. 'Look,' his voice was muffled by the sound, 'we're just the messenger boys. Around here when the clinic shouts, we have to jump.'

'What about my friend back at the inn?'

'Don't you worry about him.' He closed his window, began to pull away. 'Just do what they tell you, and he'll be safe.'

There was a spray of gravel as the car fishtailed into the mist. Catrin was left standing alone, looking up at the building. She could see no lights on, no signs of life within it. She moved towards the builder's van which was coated in mud. She ran her finger along one side. A damp sliver came free; beneath was a lighter grey. It looked like the colour of the first van that had followed them.

She heard a crunching sound and turned. A lone man was coming round the side of the building. He wore the same white trousers and jacket she had seen on the men in the canteen in the woods. His lips were moving, but his words did not carry through the mist. As he got closer she saw that it was the young doctor, Smith, who'd shown them the way to Tudor's place. He looked very pale, the blood drained from his face.

As he saw her he seemed deliberately to pull himself upright. He was carrying some cases that looked hastily packed.

'Are you the one they call the gentleman?' she said. He pushed the cases into the back of his large pickup. He said nothing, seemed reluctant to move away from the car. Catrin waited. There were still no lights or movement inside the building.

'No, it's someone else who's expecting you,' he said at last. His tone was professional, almost cheery, but there was an undertow of tension in his voice. She looked at his car, wondered if it was strong enough to ram the gates. The bull bars on the front looked more for show than for business, and she decided it probably couldn't. She saw they'd now been joined by two other figures. Maybe the two had been there all the time in the mist. They were standing back, wearing white smocks, and both were shaven-headed and well-built. Orderlies, by the look of them.

'Just follow me, please.' The doctor quickly shut the door to his car, locked it. It had a series of additional retro-fit locks, Catrin noticed. Without speaking he led her inside, the other two men following close behind. The first room was a large hall that seemed to function as a security checkpoint. At the back were the rubberised arches of what looked like a large metal detector.

Ahead of her the doctor turned left, past a shallow cupboard crammed with cardboard boxes. She looked back. Behind her the two men in white were standing silently, arms crossed. One of them glanced at her, sniggering under his breath.

The doctor gave her a thin-lipped smile but said nothing. As he moved along the corridor she noticed a line of smoked-glass camera domes mounted on the ceiling, some covered with fine wire mesh.

'The security here seems rather tight for a rehab unit,' she said.

'Yes.' The man was trying to sound relaxed but failing. She got the sense again that he'd have preferred not to be have been going back into the building.

'Any particular reason that you know of?'

'Measures had to be taken to ensure that no one tries to bring in drugs, potential weapons that might be accessed by more vulnerable patients.' The doctor was watching her closely now.

'Like who?' she asked.

'Well, like most rehabilitation centres we offer withdrawal programmes for the standard spectrum of addictions – alcohol, opiates, cocaine, amphetamines.' The doctor paused; the sound of his own voice seemed to give him more confidence. 'We've also occasionally had patients with conditions that result from abuse of hallucinogenic drugs.'

'You mean acidheads?' she asked.

'Not always. Some with conditions resulting from the more extended forms of hallucinogenic experience, those involving misguided quests for spiritual knowledge. This part of the country, as you know, has had more than its share of psychoactive experimentation in the last few decades. Some members of the alternative community seem to have taken a trip that they never came back from.'

There was a rattling behind them, a sound like a trolley being wheeled down a long corridor. Catrin looked round, but could see only the two men following, nothing else, just the bright light and empty space. She couldn't see their faces clearly in the glare.

She moved closer to the doctor. 'Why didn't you mention this when we asked you in the pub? You said this place was just a standard unit for NHS referrals.'

The doctor said nothing further. He led her in silence up the stairs to the second floor. He kept glancing out of the narrow windows at his pickup parked at the front. The first door on the right opened into a small, overheated room. Once inside he blocked the door and stood in front of it. Catrin could see the window ahead had bars over it. Outside she heard the two orderlies laughing nervously.

The doctor stared over her shoulders, not catching her eye. Suddenly he moved his hand towards her and she backed away. She saw the outline of a row of syrettes in his coat pocket.

His young face looked tired, anxious under the fluorescent lighting. She heard the door locking behind him. On the far side, the small window let in as much brightness as the mist allowed.

She reached over for the ashtray in the middle of the coffee table. It was balanced on a stack of magazines and Twelve Step leaflets, the edges curling and yellowed. As she moved it towards her she noticed that an undisturbed layer of dust covered the surface of the papers.

'Looks like no one's been here for a while.'

As she ran her finger over the tops of the magazines, small clouds of dust drifted out into the air.

'Not the cleaners anyway,' the doctor said.

His eyes kept being drawn back to the wall behind her. But as he saw her watching him, he quickly looked away. She swung round but there was only a large square noticeboard behind. On the top half were anti-drug leaflets, cartoons with simple stylised figures. The lower part of the board featured photos of the staff arranged on a diagram of a tree.

The supervisor was placed on the top branch, a middle-aged man with a well-tended beard over hollow cheeks. To the right of the trunk were several young men with thinning blond hair, who could have been brothers. She recognised the men from the canteen in the woods.

The doctor had moved away from the door towards the board. As he saw her looking closer he edged nearer to it, but Catrin had seen what he was trying to hide. The picture was not as faded as those above. Situated in the lowest section of the diagram, labelled 'Facilities Management and Security', it showed a man in a charcoal suit, with a high forehead and long grey hair.

Immediately she recognised Fransis. 'That man,' she said, 'he's working here under another name.' She looked more closely at the board. *Archie Molloch* was the name there, it meant nothing to her. She stared hard at the doctor. 'He's the one who's asked you to hold me here, isn't he?'

The doctor avoided her eyes. She could see a barely concealed tension in his face. He moved quickly towards the door and tried to get out before she could reach him. But Catrin was too quick for him, she had her fingers round his throat, his arm in a lock behind his back. He tried to swing round, kick back at her, but she was ready for him. Her fingers dug deeper into his larynx. He couldn't move, couldn't yell.

She heard the two orderlies moving their weight from foot to foot outside. She edged the doctor back to the far end of the narrow room.

'This Mr Molloch, he's the gentleman who was expecting me,' she whispered, 'isn't he?' She saw fear on his face, his eyes narrowing. She'd never seen someone look so terrified. Suddenly he lurched towards the window. The drop was at least fifteen metres but he attempted to butt his way through the glass. Catrin held him back, pulled him to the floor, keeping her fingers on his throat.

'What is it about him that spooks everyone?' She'd put her mouth to his ear as she whispered.

He shut his eyes tightly, shaking his head back and forth violently. *Just like a small boy who thinks if he closes his eyes bad things will go away*. She grabbed a bunch of Twelve Steps leaflets, bunched them together and stuffed them in his mouth as she eased the pressure on his larynx. She reached over to the light, worked the cord around his hands and legs, then his neck. He was hog-tied now, like one of the show subs she used to see in the clubs. She peeled down his trousers, then unbuttoned his jacket and his shirt. She put the tip of her boot on his buttocks, pushed him gently away from the window until he was facing the large mirror on the opposite wall.

'Look.' Sometimes, she knew, it was shame that could break the strongest spirits. He'd kept his eyes shut, but she prised them open so he could see himself in the glass. She had her iPhone out. 'Smile!' The flash went once, twice, bouncing back from the mirror. 'It's going to go viral,' she whispered, 'might even make the tabloids as you're a doc, is that what you want?'

He shook his head violently; fat tears were running down his cheeks now. She prised his eyes open again and took the leaflets from his mouth.

'He just asked me to bring you here,' the doctor said weakly, 'I don't know anything more.'

His eyes moved to the door and she held his throat tighter. She could tell he was holding back on her still. She held the screen of the camera to his face so he could see how it looked for him, then asked him in a quiet but insistent voice why he was so frightened.

'It's nothing, just a rumour, that's all.' His voice was weak, breathless. 'One of the orderlies here used to work at Broadmoor, he started it.'

'And?' Catrin drew over the dead flowers from the corner, raised the vase so he could sip a little. She lowered her ear to his mouth but kept her fingers on his throat in case he tried to bite her.

'The rumour is that's Angel Jones, it's the same man.'

She snorted a low, derisive laugh, tightened her grip again. 'That's bullshit, impossible. Jones is a lifer, his sentence is indefinite.'

'I know,' he said quietly. 'But they're saying Jones

was de-sectioned, released after an appeal a couple of years back. The whole thing was hushed up by the Home Office, one of those secret releases, like the Jamie Bulger killers, no press coverage.'

Catrin didn't believe this for a moment, it sounded like some crazy rumour that had got a grip on everyone, had made them all hysterical with fear. She knew things happened like this in small communities. She also knew it wasn't possible. Jones was about as likely to have been appealed as the Yorkshire Ripper. She moved her face close up to the doctor's, her tone soft now, tender. 'But they must've got that wrong, the evidence against Jones was airtight. They got him on the drugs he'd used to spike the girls he held in his cellar. I know the officer who busted his dealer, that's how he came to bust Jones.'

'They say that officer retracted his testimony at the appeal. Then Jones was cleared by the Broadmoor psychiatric panel and walked.'

'What?' She was trying to keep the fear out her own voice now. There was a certain disturbing logic in what the doctor had just said.

There had been positive IDs of the tattoo from every one of Jones's victims. But it was the drugs that had made the case airtight: the exact chemical footprints on all the vics' tox reports were in Jones's spiking agents, only Jones's DNA on the drug kit. That's why

Rhys's evidence, the linking of Jones to the drugs, had been crucial.

She bent closer to the doctor. 'This orderly from Broadmoor, is he credible or like those other stoners in the canteen?'

The doctor said nothing so she exerted a little more pressure. 'He's left,' he said quickly. 'He didn't want to work here with Jones around.'

Her thumb dug into his windpipe. 'Any proof this man is Jones, apart from this rumour?'

The doctor was moving his wrists, trying to loosen the wire. She reached down to tighten it.

'Ever see this man with anyone from outside?'

'No one sees him much.' He said nothing more. She waited, her face close to his, gently released her other hand's grip on his throat again. 'He's with a girl sometimes, looks like a club girl, she has tattoos and that.'

'Always the same girl?'

'Seems so, I've never seen her up close. She doesn't live in the village, maybe in the woods somewhere. They say she's his regular sub from way back, a seriously hardcore case she must be to stick by him all these years.' The doctor seemed to be trying to get her trust now. Catrin could see it in his eyes, he was begging her to let him go, but she had to stay strong.

Catrin turned all he'd said round in her mind. Her first thought was that this girl sounded rather like the one Della had met on the BDSM site, the spaced-out one who was into Seerland. She remembered how Della said the girl had Jones in her thrall. Jones having a girlfriend had never been mentioned in the press. It still seemed unlikely he could have had one and that all this time she'd remained out of sight. Huw had said the girl was no more than a ghost who existed in Della's mind. 'They say what Jones's connection to this area is, why he's come here?' she asked.

'No.'

Catrin took a deep breath. She looked back at the door, listened. The men were still pacing outside. Soon they'd begin wondering why the doctor hadn't come out. There wasn't much time. She glanced up at the mirror, thought she saw vague shapes behind the glass, the outline of something low and long. She eased the paper back into the doctor's mouth and pulled him gently into the corner. What he'd just said had confirmed her worst suspicions. But elements about the story were still bothering her. Surely Jones's release would have reached the press? Even with a Home Office shut-down, a closed court throughout the proceedings, gagging orders, the whole shebang. Then after the verdict anonymity orders, a new identity, new National Insurance number, new past, new everything, like Maxine Carr. Even then, word still usually crept out. But in this case it hadn't.

It was just the sort of dirt Della usually got hold of. This story would have been a big scoop for her. Della had a network of sources throughout the criminal justice system. That was why everyone left her alone. Maybe that was what Della had tried to reach her about that final morning before the fire. Then she thought about Rix, about Thomas: both must have known Jones was out. It would have been flagged for Rix's attention as chief of the neighbouring force to where Jones had been released. Yet he'd kept it quiet. And Thomas was part of the original case team. He must have been called as a witness at the retrial, or at least known about it. Yet he'd told her nothing. It felt all wrong. Like all along a lot of people, powerful people, had been protecting Jones. But why protect a monster?

Catrin attached the flex binding the doctor to the radiator, which she checked was cold. His eyes still pleaded with her, but she looked away. The doorknob turned. One of the orderlies was calling something. She didn't have much time. She looked at the mirror again, the shapes inside it. It must be a two-way, she thought. They used them to watch disturbed patients in the old days. She worked her fingers under the rim, made a small gap and got a glimpse of a dark space on the other side.

The mirror was now loose in its moulding, and

she was able to squeeze head first through the gap. She dropped down into the darkness on the other side, and peered around her in the half-light. The space was much larger, higher than she'd expected. She couldn't see the full extent of it. The object on the floor looked like a long sofa. Behind it were more chairs on a stand as if in a small theatre. In the corner was a door, ajar. Light was seeping through the doorway and across the floor.

She crept over and looked out. The corridors and the stairwell were deserted. There were no sounds from the floors above or below. At the far end, she could see a long passage, and a nurses' station.

She moved tight against the wall towards the nurses' cubicle. Beyond it were stairs covered in some sort of thick rubber. Below them another passage veered off into darkness. According to the diagram, officially Jones was in charge of security, but she felt his connection to the place must be much deeper. It seemed that all the time she'd just been stepping through Jones's labyrinth. All she really knew for sure was that she had to get to him before he got to her.

One of the doors ahead was wedged open by a flat-bed trolley. The stairwell had been covered with a wire mesh, where a number of small objects had collected, shards of broken plates, papers and tin cans. Behind the wire were several rows of strip lights, some old and flickering.

She heard the muted sounds of trolleys being pushed along the passages above, and a low keening sound.

She edged forward to the edge of the nurses' station. Partitions of reinforced glass enclosed two office chairs and a desk, on top of it a computer screen, phones, mugs. She could see no signs of photographs, postcards or other personal touches, but what looked like a site map was stuck on the glass.

There was a floor plan for a ward of twelve beds surrounded by four service passages, a series of bathrooms and consulting rooms. Slowly Catrin moved up the stairs and saw the layout was similar. A nurses' station, connecting service passages and a ward beyond. It all looked conventional enough.

She looked around: most of the wards appeared hardly occupied. A few gaunt, lethargic-looking men in dressing gowns were sitting round tables, playing cards and watching television. They looked up at her briefly without interest, then lowered their heads.

It must be a break between shifts, she thought, no sign of any staff. As she went down the stairs again, she stopped at each nurses' station, glanced at the drug charts. Every rectangle represented a patient, and the grid of lines within contained the types of drugs administered, dosages and dosage times.

The first lines showed entries for Ultram, naltrexone and a series of other opiate agonists routinely used in the detox of heroin and methadone addicts. The second line showed dosages for standard SSRI antidepressants, Librium and other long-acting tranquillisers. The rest of the chart was given over to the results of daily saliva, nebuliser and urine tests for the main drug types – opiates, cocaine, amphetamines, benzodiazepines.

All the medications listed were of the type that would be given to patients with conventional addictions. None seemed to relate in any way to the more extreme hallucinogen-induced conditions alluded to by the doctor on their way into the building. Most of the patient profiles looked like those of standard long-term addicts referred on by the local NHS trusts, just as the doctor had first told her.

As she put back the charts Catrin thought she could hear from deep in the building again the high, keening sound, like the sound of a long-abandoned child crying. At the same time she was aware of a slight shuffling noise much closer at hand, a reflection moving, in the glass – something behind her.

She felt a large hand cover her mouth, pull her head back. Her head began spinning. She closed her eyes, tried to get to her feet. But the figure was strong, pinning her down against the side of the cubicle so she could not kick out.

Then the hand brought her head down out of the lights and its fingers prised open her eyelids. Looming over her she saw Huw's face.

'Don't move,' he said softly. 'Those cameras are motion sensitive. We're in a blind spot here – rise above a certain height and we'll trip the alarm.'

Catrin squeezed his hand, to show him she understood. Then she followed him back along the edge of the room and down into a narrow gap between some trolleys. He put his arms around her narrow shoulders now, stroked her damp hair.

Huw smiled. 'I bribed them. It wasn't cheap. They were scared half out of their wits. But in the end they came round.' He gestured down at the fading light. 'They dropped me at the gates, then ran like bats out of hell.'

He was wearing walking boots, and a padded green jacket. His binoculars rested against his chest.

As she told him she was looking for the man the orderlies believed was Jones, she saw a look of bewilderment cross his face, felt him grip her shoulders. 'It seems there was a mistrial,' she said. 'Rhys retracted his evidence against Jones in an appeal held in closed court. Looks like the whole thing was kept under wraps. One of those executive decisions by the Home Office? It seems some powerful elements have been protecting Jones. He's been here all this time on one of those secret release programmes, covered by an anonymity order.'

'Anything else not right about this place?'

'The doctor mentioned patients who have conditions resulting from extreme hallucinogens, the ones who never come back from their trips, but I haven't seen any.' Catrin held his hand tighter, more for his benefit than hers. She sensed a potential link with the extreme trance drugs in the Heath Park lab, and those in the grow-sheds. If Jones had been the elusive figure behind it, if all along he'd had political or criminal justice protection, this would explain how he'd evaded arrest for so long.

She pointed up at the smoked-glass dome. 'All these cameras. There has to be a central monitoring room that covers the entire complex.'

Catrin led him to the window and pointed to the high gable looming above them, its windows facing the mist-shrouded outline of the escarpment. 'That's the highest point. It has sightlines over the entire area,' she said. 'The monitoring room should be up there under that gable.'

She told him that the route there would be through the service passages, that when the place had been a private house those had been the routes the staff used. The staff always slept in the attics, so these passages would lead to the spaces under the gables.

As they moved beyond the wards, the corridors became narrow and shadowy like a passage backstage in a theatre. In places there was not enough room to walk two abreast, and Catrin led the way using a torch.

Along the inner side of the passage were unused offices, most of which now served as storage rooms. She noticed a row of old gurney beds, some lounge chairs covered with twists of stuffing. Through the windows on the far side of these rooms she could make out figures in white coats, following them at a distance.

The way ahead had been blocked off; they had no choice but to descend by a narrow back staircase. The glimpses through the windows showed an inner yard stacked with rusted railings. To its left were the windows of what looked like a long refectory or staffroom, more figures in white inside, the tables scattered with styrofoam mugs and spent coffee filters.

She looked up again at the jagged crenellations along the rooftops. Before Huw could stop her, she took off her coat, wrapped it around her hand and picked up a length of rusted railing. Crouching, she moved nearer to the wall.

The hallway was lit with strip lights wedged below lengths of chipboard casing. At certain points the boards had come loose, warped by the damp sea air, and through the gaps she saw coils of heavy cabling.

Lifting the bar above the strip lights, she forced it through the half-perished rubber, sparks flying back into the darkness as the circuits fused.

'We've probably got less than a minute before the emergency generators kick in,' she called back to Huw. 'Follow me.'

Catrin ran across the dark hallway and up the flight of stairs. The banisters were thick, knotted with elaborate carvings. The shapes of the carvings snagged on her jeans, but within seconds she'd reached the upper landing.

Through the open door she saw the silhouette of a man with a shaven head. Running down into his collar were the leads of earpieces, his head was bobbing to a trance-like beat. He rose from his seat, moving with muscle-bound steps across the room.

His arms outstretched in front in the dark, he was feeling his way to a door in an inner wall. As he half turned, she recognised him as the man they had sat next to in the canteen, the table-watcher.

'He doesn't exactly look on the ball,' Huw whispered at her shoulder. 'But we'll need to move fast, get out before he returns.'

The emergency power had come on in the stairwell. On the desk were monitors, several baggies, over-full ashtrays and crumpled twists of silver foil. The monitor opposite the chair was showing footage from a porno webcam, in grainy black-and-white, pale limbs pulsing in a staccato rhythm across the screen.

The screen was partly hidden by the coils of a water pipe. Huw shifted it out of the way. His head was bowed now over the image on the screen. Catrin approached until the image became clearer.

A man and a woman were lying on a black, plasticated sheet, their bodies shiny with oil. The man was bending over some attachment on the back of the woman, who was out of shot. He wore a black leather mask and on his chest was a tattoo, a raven's beak. Strands of grey hair came out of the back of the mask. She knew immediately the man was Jones.

In the lower left-hand corner of the screen was a digital clock which showed that what they were watching was happening in real time. Emerging from off-screen, hands were pushing the woman's buttocks wider apart. Further up her back was a black shape, another raven. The rest of it was covered with welts and bruises. As they skewed to one side of the bed, the sweat-matted hair that hung down over the woman's face parted for a moment. Catrin caught a glimpse of young bruised eyes, half senseless, staring vacantly out ahead of her.

Then they moved out of view. Catrin was left looking at the empty, ruffled sheet, the heavy wooden panelling around the bed carved with satyrs.

'That girl,' she said, 'I've seen her before.'

'In one of the misper searches?'

'No, more recently.' It didn't take her long to get it. It had been on the BDSM site, one of the girls among Fransis's contacts. She recognised the features from photos of several of his other contacts. He's been using the same girl, she thought, to model for the profiles he'd invented, just altering the make-up and camera angles: that was clever – safer than scanning images from other sites.

'That's Jones's girl, I'd bet on it,' she said. 'His willing sub, his accomplice.' The camera stayed on the elaborate carvings around the bed. Some showed warped grotesque faces, ancient deities, horned beasts. In the background was a larger space, almost in darkness. From some points deeper in came a flickering that might have been an arrangement of candles on the floor. Catrin felt she was looking at something familiar.

'Let's see if we can find that place on other cameras. That way we can get a sense of where he might be,' she said.

Huw sat in front of the bank of screens, his hand on the control that worked the cursor. Each of the eight screens divided into grids of eight smaller pictures, so they now had sixty-four distinct views of the complex above their heads. Most showed stretches of empty corridor, half-lit hallways and landings, the storerooms and yards they had passed through earlier.

Occasionally orderlies could be seen crossing the empty spaces, sweeping torch beams along the passages and into ventilation shafts.

'They're out looking for us,' Catrin said.

On one screen were images of the wards she'd just visited. Huw scrolled through several of the first ward, then the others lower down. The men in their dressing gowns were still slumped in front of the television. The rest of the images showed the outside of the clinic, seemingly endless shots of barbed-wire fences and black wooded hillsides.

'There's nothing else here.' Huw moved back to the original shot. Unlike in other cameras, the lens position was fixed. The subdivisions in the screen merely showed the same flickering space. It was windowless, empty, just the old panelling, the bed in the centre as in a film set, the cave-like space receding into blackness.

He slid the cursor down the sidebar until he found the zoom function. The image of the panelling expanded and a small section of the wall now filled the entire screen.

Under the surface of the paint Catrin saw tiny craters and crevices, but she could not see a single hair or speck of fluff on the dark surface.

'It looks like the place has been washed down,' Huw said.

Huw moved over to the stack of DVD-R players beside the desk.

'All the players have been disconnected,' he said. 'They've upgraded from DVD to DVR. That means there are no discs, no coaxial cables, everything's stored digitally on a hard disc that could be miles away, secured behind passwords.'

'But those cameras in the empty ward aren't motion-sensitive.' Catrin had got up from the desk, moved out of the sightline of the doorway. 'They're continuous. So anyone watching from here might have seen what's been going on there.'

Outside the door they heard heavy, stumbling movements. She pointed urgently to a pile of cardboard boxes behind the door. As one, they rose and hid behind them. The orderly was entering much the way he had left, his arms feeling ahead of him in the dark, his movements slow, unsteady.

But he wasn't completely gone. He'd noticed that the link to the old panelled room had been replaced by images of the empty cell. He lurched over towards a glass case on the wall.

As the man reached the panic button, Huw came at him from behind, a length of cable pulled tight between his fists. He wrestled the man down onto the floor, the wire cutting across his windpipe. The man couldn't move, he couldn't cry out.

He groped blindly for the button. But Catrin pushed him back, her boot slamming hard in the centre of his chest.

'It must get lonely up here all on your own,' she said.

The orderly was gasping for breath as Huw tightened the wire round his throat. Catrin kept the weight of her heel on his chest.

'So you've been a bad boy, jerking off over Jones in action. Bet you've been enjoying that.'

She used the tip of her boot now to raise his head, so that he faced the screen image of the bed. At first the man didn't seem to want to understand. He had opened his eyes wide, was pulling his head away from the screen, as if there was something there they couldn't see.

'What has Jones been doing in there?'

The man let out a high, screeching sound. Huw pulled the cord, silencing him, then gradually released it to give him air. His head was shaking from side to side, then abruptly he grew stiller, his eyes blinking rapidly.

'I don't know,' he said at last. His voice was strangely high, reedy, like air blown through a broken pipe. 'The camera gets turned off sometimes, then afterwards the room has been cleaned up.'

The man started to lose consciousness. He sank back into Huw's lap. Catrin kept on scrolling through the different cameras. There were only more images of empty corridors and the black hillsides.

'Where is Jones?' she asked softly.

The man's head lolled to one side; he was breathing weakly through his mouth, unevenly. 'No one knows that,' he whispered.

'Don't worry, we believe you,' she said. 'But where did you last see Jones heading on the other monitors? The man isn't invisible, he must have appeared somewhere.' She put her lips close to his ear.

His lips were moving but it took a moment for the words to form.

'Up the top.'

He was out now, his pupils staring blindly up at the ceiling. She slapped his face, but he wasn't coming round. She let him slump back into Huw's arms. They could hear noises down in the stairwell. Huw pulled the man under the pile of boxes behind the door, nudging them forward with his feet until they covered his body.

Catrin felt Huw drawing her close to him, so the weight of his body was shielding her as he moved towards the door.

9

The footfalls behind them died away as they ran outside. What light there was came from the sickle moon, hanging like a gash in the blackness. Each time Catrin lost her footing, Huw pulled her upright again, keeping her moving into the woods.

Somewhere up ahead lay the escarpment. It was barely visible in the dark, but she could just make out its outline jutting out from behind the trees. There were glimpses of a clearing between clusters of hazel and holm oaks. Steps had been cut into the earth and covered with rough planks of wood. Catrin looked back now, noticing a sunken area at the edge of the clearing, above which the land rose steeply. Lights had fanned out behind them from where the clinic lay hidden in the mist, but were not moving forward.

'Why aren't they coming after us?' she whispered.

Slowly Huw moved into the open space ahead. No pathways led to the place, yet it seemed to have been preserved from the encroaches of the surrounding woodland. She could see a series of objects lying among weeds that had grown up through the shale. Most appeared to be small buckets, the sort that children might play with in a sandpit, though there was no sand anywhere in sight. Others were in simple symmetrical shapes, stylised crosses and waves and stars, their bright colours dulled by the mud.

But Huw was no longer looking towards the play area and had raised a hand up to her mouth. Following his line of sight along the ridge, Catrin saw a figure partly hidden by the trees. He was no more than thirty yards away, head bowed in a play of torchlight. He was holding small binoculars, the type bird-watchers use. But there were no birds visible in the dark sky, nor could any calls be heard; only the wind and the insistent patter of the rain.

She edged through the trees towards the figure. The man was not moving away, just standing still, silently beckoning to them. As Catrin got closer she saw he was wearing green farmer's weatherproofs, and around his neck a string of furs and small bones. She recognised him as old Tudor, and was sure now that he had been the one who was watching them earlier from the rocks outside the inn.

Huw rushed past her and pinned the man down. 'You're one of Jones's people –' his words seemed spat out with anger – 'you're a lookout, aren't you?' In the faint glow of the moon Catrin saw dried mud on the man's forehead and his grey, uneven teeth. He looked frightened but said nothing.

She eased Huw away and touched the man's arm softly. 'We heard about your daughter,' she said and lowered herself slowly. 'I'm sorry. She looks a lovely girl in those photos.'

She thought she saw tears welling up in his rheumy eyes. 'She wasn't my daughter,' he said softly, 'but I brought her up as my own. Her mother was a traveller, a wild child. I looked after her girl when she was off doing whatever she did, until one day the girl just disappears.'

'Her name?'

'Caris. She took my surname. Mower.' He was glancing into the trees.

Catrin followed his stare, but saw nothing. Around them there were no sounds other than the drumming of the rain and the muted hum of the wind. The old man was gazing out into the darkness as if he had already forgotten they were there.

Gradually a realisation struck her, one that had sat half formed at the edge of her mind ever since they had visited the shop in the woods. 'Your daughter – you came back here to look for her, didn't you?' Old Tudor leant back on his heels so as not to disturb the branches in front of them. He said nothing but he nodded fractionally. She thought of the girl the doctor had mentioned seeing from a distance with Jones, of the girl they'd just seen with Jones on the screen. The old man seemed to smile at her, the moonlight filtering behind him through the branches.

She moved closer. 'Caris, she's the one the orderlies spotted with Jones, isn't she?'

There was fear in his eyes. He squatted low on the ground, motioning for Catrin to do the same. His gaze was on the clearing now, the coloured shapes floating in the black pools of rainwater, the steps no more than a dim smudge against the trees.

'This place,' she said, 'what is it?'

'It took me a while to find out,' he said.

Some of the star-shaped and other objects had begun to roll in the wind, back and forwards on the sodden ground. Huw glanced nervously towards the ridge above them.

'Spit it out,' he said, 'we don't have much time.'

The man stared intently into the mist. 'It's Jones,' he said quietly, 'sometimes I've seen him here, and sometimes children playing.' Catrin kept her eyes on the man. 'The children are always silent. They play with a straw doll or old-fashioned toys. One wears some kind of costume, with feathers on the arms.'

Old Tudor had spoken in a measured, calmly emphatic tone. Catrin felt Huw touching her sleeve. He was looking down to the edge of the clearing, scanning from side to side. 'But that's what you said you'd seen them doing all those decades ago,' she said.

'That's right.' She watched for hesitation, any tell that he was lying, but she couldn't see one.

'So how do you explain it?'

He shrugged. 'I took some photos, but they came out badly. I sent them round to universities, asked them if they recognised anything.'

'And?'

'Nothing. But then a few months later a graduate from Aber calls me, says he's found a picture that looks like mine. It was from some academic psychological journal from the early Seventies.'

Huw glanced at Catrin, then looked closely at the old man. 'But how could that be?'

Tudor was smiling slightly. 'It wasn't exactly the same, just the same place, the same costume. It was all odd stuff. It was a study into some cult from way back.'

Huw had half risen to get a better look around. He crouched down again uneasily.

'Okay,' Catrin said, 'I get it. So this cult they studied, the one into all this weirdness, it was the one here in the Seventies. Jones's group?'

The old man turned, his eyes hidden from them both, as he watched the trees. 'They may have had older roots.'

'How do you mean?'

He stared out between the branches. 'The author of the article claimed their leader to have been a member of an occult order founded a couple of hundred years back.'

Catrin thought through what this could mean. Most organised occult groups had died out long before the war, but perhaps this one had carried on in isolation, avoiding publicity up until the point the academics studied them. If Jones had been the group's leader, and the group had other influential members, in politics maybe or the criminal justice system, this could explain why Jones had been protected all the years until his arrest and then released. But where did Face fit in? And Rhys? Something was warning her not to write off other explanations yet.

'That article give the cult leader's name? Jones, Serafim, Molloch or any of Jones's aliases?'

'Penrhyn.'

She turned to Huw. 'That's the name of a man who along with his eldest son was accused of witchcraft out here in the nineteenth century. Another alias, maybe.' She tried to catch the old man's eye. 'Any other details about him?'

She caught the stale scent of the old man's breath as he moved closer. 'Not much. All it said was that he came from an old family from this area. One of his ancestors had been a radical figure in the occult revival of the nineteenth century. His group was expelled from the main occult movement.'

The darkness of the place was like a fist closing around her. 'And the reasons for this?'

'It didn't say. It seems this group viewed Crowley and the other Satanists as mere showmen. Its members focused on going back to the roots of witchcraft in the old Celtic religion and in shamanism. After they were expelled from the occult movement, they went further underground.'

'So what happened when the academics came here?' Huw asked, his voice barely a whisper.

'It's not very clear, the study was never completed.'

'Why's that?'

'Some of the academics were threatened. Dead animals were left at their homes along with photos of their children. They backed off.'

Catrin followed the old man's eyes out to the clearing. Nothing was moving there, the shapes lying still in the tall grass. The moon had gone in between the low clouds, the ridge above barely visible now. Lights were threading through the trees towards them. Moments later they had disappeared, and everything was dark again.

She felt her stomach clench, her legs tensing, the sweat cold on her shoulders. Her hand reached out, scraping over a trunk's rough surface as she steadied herself. We are close now, she thought, and I need to stay clear, strong.

It seemed as if the lights in the trees were moving towards them, but then they turned and started to gain altitude. Whoever was carrying the lights was ascending the slope, heading for the escarpment. Huw stared intently after them, trying to make out the path they were taking.

Catrin put her hand on the old man's shoulder. 'That track up there where we can see the lights, it leads to the top of the ridge?'

'Yes, but there's nothing up there, just the woods.'

Huw seemed in no hurry to get up. He was crouching against the bank. The leaves around them were quivering, but the wind had dropped. As Catrin rose, she felt Huw's hand on her arm. She pulled her arm away, stood up. For the moment, she felt no fear.

'No,' he said, 'we can't just go up there blindly. There's no mobile coverage, no chance to call for help. Much better we try to get back, contact the police.'

She could see the anxiety on his face. He touched her arm again, more gently this time, but again she pushed him away.

'In case you've forgotten, I am the police.' She was angry now. 'I'll go alone. Do you know where the path up the hill starts?'

'I do.' The old man spoke quietly.

'If you can point me in the right direction I'd be grateful.'

'I'll come with you.' Tudor got up, stiffly shaking his long legs.

Huw was standing back from them. Behind him, Catrin heard a rustling, close in the branches. Something was moving towards them through the trees from where the lights had been.

She heard the branches cracking, a sweeping sound low along the ground. Huw had heard it too and turned back to look.

'Don't,' she said. 'This way.' She reached out and tried to pull Huw back, but he lifted the branches and then she couldn't see him any more. The air was filled with a sudden screeching, and a rushing as a dark shape swept past. She ran straight into the branches where Huw had disappeared, the wet leaves brushing over her eyes. In the blackness she sensed the movements of feathers all around her and at the edge of her vision lights were flickering. She shouted out Huw's name but there was no answer.

Something was pulling her back. She turned and saw Tudor's face behind her. 'This way, quickly,' he said. 'It's too late for him now.'

The old man pulled her after him into the deeper brush. They made their way on hands and knees through cover so thick that there was no knowing what lay above or beneath. She was surprised by the muscles bunching up beneath her grasp on Tudor's arm and the ease with which he moved. His strength seemed that of a much younger man, as he led her upwards.

Through the trees a single path ahead led up the steep face of the escarpment. This was where the lights had been moving. A crude gangway had been built from black-painted planks, clinging to the edge of rocks higher up. Over the planks a length of rope hung, frayed and loose, shuddering in the wind.

The sounds were heading this way, not back towards the clinic. Whoever had closed in around Huw, they were somewhere ahead. There was still a chance he was alive. He was strong, resilient, she had not heard him cry out. She sensed his presence up ahead, silently calling to her.

The blurry form of a mound was occasionally visible through the mist. The trees were dark walls on either side, many dead, their branches black and rotting. They climbed into a hollow, a dark, hunched thing that merged with the dimness. In the moon's weak light, a muddy path led on, bordered with what might have once been hedgerows but were now overgrown and shapeless.

The old man had begun to move on into the trees,

but Catrin stopped him. Ahead was a steep leaf-covered slope, patches of frost glistening on the surface of the grass, and beyond it lay a blackness that could have been rock or the mouth of a cave. The place looked familiar. Catrin thought of the old print of the witch at the mouth of the cave. She thought of the scene in the first film of the approach to the tunnel, the person behind the camera half stepping, half gliding down towards the blackness of the tunnel's entrance.

Beyond the fallen rocks and tall grasses she saw a heavy stone lintel over a rusted hatch. The rocks were covered with thick moss and weeds and overgrown. The place looked long-abandoned.

As she moved up to the hatch, she thought she could make out the scent of Huw's expensive cologne. She pushed on the metal, but it didn't move. She stood back. Deeper under the lintel she could make out a sill, covered with cobwebs, over it an ancient length of chain-link wire. It looked like it had once been an opening of some sort.

Climbing onto the ledge under the door, she peered down but could see nothing within. Her fall was broken by something soft and smelling of mildew. As her eyes adjusted she saw the floor was covered with feed sacks that had once contained straw. In the corner was a rack of old, rusted farm implements, hoes and scythes.

As Tudor landed beside her dust rose into the air. In the beam of his torch she saw a low passage ahead, broken plaster and brickwork.

She pulled a scythe from the wall, held it ahead of her in the darkness. Calling out for Huw would only reveal their position. Better, she thought, to get a sense of the place first, to find out where the others were and create a diversion. The torch lit up the walls of the passage. On the ground below were shallow puddles of rainwater, some black feathers floating on their surface.

Tudor was beside her now, and they had reached a rotten wooden door. Behind it were no sounds or lights. The space seemed shallow like a cupboard. Catrin could hear hangers along an empty rail, as he felt his way inside. He brought out a long, pointed object and set it down slowly on the floor. He moved the beam along its length, revealing a black mask that would cover all the face. From the back, strands of raffia sprouted in a stylised imitation of feathers, while the front formed a long beak.

As he lifted the mask to eye level, the buckle on the chin-strap made a muted tinkling sound, and the mask's shadow suddenly reared up on the wall behind him. For a moment Catrin felt she was back there again in that room, in the shuttered half-light, the web of the mask over her eyes. She saw the two perching shapes on either side, their feathers shifting, spreading. She felt a sweat over her neck, down her back. Her nerves were tingling, alert to the slightest move in the air.

She gripped the scythe tight. The pain focused her, she clung on, waves of anger coursing through her. She let it burn in her now, screwed up her eyes, tried to see what was ahead.

As the beam edged hesitantly forward it picked out another door. Again she thought she could smell Huw's cologne, fainter this time. She closed her fingers over the scythe and tried to make out any movements or sounds further in, but there was nothing. As the light spread again she got a glimpse of a large cavernous space. From far within she thought she heard the low whining call of ravens. If there are birds here, there must be another route in from outside, she thought, but peering ahead she could see only more blackness.

'This must be the place the locals used to think was a mouth to hell,' the old man whispered.

She took a coin from her pocket and threw it out in front of them. There was a dull clattering sound, then absolute silence.

Catrin moved forward slowly now, feeling the ground ahead with her scythe before putting her feet down. On either side the space had broadened significantly and it was impossible to tell how far it extended around them. The beam spun upwards and caught a ceiling covered with tapestries woven with images of the planets and constellations, their colours faded, and the tattered linings hanging down.

Then it illuminated a wall painting, about twenty feet high. In the centre was an oak. On the upper branches were the stars and the planets and a woman with long golden hair.

'This must be where the occult order met,' the old man whispered. 'This is all ancient Celtic imagery. That's the tree of life, the figure at the top must be the Great Earth Mother Goddess.' He moved the beam down over the moon and stars. 'This is the Upper World, realm of stars, celestial beings, the dwelling place of the spirits of the air.'

As the light moved down, abruptly the imagery changed. Catrin saw black tangled roots and flames and strange, distorted faces. Sitting in the centre was a giant with the head of a stag and long curved horns. At his feet were horned beetles and snakes, and on his shoulder a large raven with a crooked beak.

The old man kept the beam on the image of the raven. 'That figure is the Lord of the Lower World, where much of our imagery for the devil comes from. The raven is his servant, the spirit of the dead.'

The beam moved over the giant horned figure, down

to his cloven feet. In the low light she could make out some huddled shapes over against the far wall. The old man was bending over something under the horned figure. It looked at first like a low wooden altar, or shrine. On it were tall vessels resembling censers in a church, their silver dulled by the years.

Catrin ran her hand along the back of the altar. At the bottom of the hollow, her fingers touched pieces of card, some slick and bending, others hard, slightly grainy. She reached in further, and lifted them out.

She nudged Tudor to keep a watch, as she drew them into the light. They were photographs, several dozen of them, and she spread them out in a semi-circle on the ground. Most were of figures wearing long, flowing robes, similar to those in the photographs from Rhys's source. They had joined hands and were dancing in wide circles. All wore hoods, deep hanging cowls that half hid their faces.

Holding the torch closer, she could make out a boy with long curling hair down to his shoulders, his eyes shadowed with kohl. She recognised him immediately as one of the boys in the photographs in Pryce's room. Another showed a girl of about fifteen squinting in strong summer sunlight. She had long, jet-black hair, just like another of the fans in Pryce's room.

Catrin pointed at another photo of a young girl, the

side of her face emerging from deep shadows. 'This is one of the nineteen mispers. Her bones were found on rocks up the coast. She also looks like one of the fans in the scene around Owen Face.' This confirmed to her what she'd already suspected. The early Face fans who'd gone missing and the nineteen youngsters who'd gone missing from the area over the years were all one and the same group of people. The common element was the cult, that's where the young missing persons had disappeared.

She took the torch from the old man and looked more closely at each of the pictures, shifting them into different combinations, bringing some together then moving them apart. She was seeing echoes between some of the younger faces and those of the figures in robes. It was not the echoes between two ages of the same face, but something vaguer, more like a mirroring of certain inflections in the same features across different faces and ages.

Many of the faces had the same high cheekbones, the same heavy arched eyebrows, which the older girls had tried to pluck and disguise, the same high noble-looking foreheads, like Face's. The same large brown eyes. Catrin put down the torch and closed her eyes. The faces were swirling, spinning, but merging in the darkness into a single compound face. She knew now what it was she was seeing, but part of her mind was telling her that this was something too unnatural to be possible.

It looked as if the missing persons might all be related by blood. They had features in common, but with all their different backgrounds she knew this couldn't be. She felt her mind groping for explanations, but none made sense. Tudor was shifting his place behind her. He looked anxious to get out now. Quickly Catrin reached her hand in, pulled out the remaining photos. In these ones the people looked older than those she had already seen. She recognised some of the same figures, but as younger children.

One showed a girl in a tie-dye T-shirt and broad-rimmed sunglasses sitting on a bench by a pier. A boy on a tricycle, staring at something out of shot. At the bottom a girl of about seven. She stood on a coastal path, huddled against the cold, looking away. Behind her was the black, glassy surface of the sea, bathed in a muted winter light. Her thin dress gave little protection against the wind. Her feet protruded beyond the swoop of her skirt, sockless. For a moment Catrin felt again the whip of the wind against her face, her toes in the icy grass.

She tried to focus on the picture, but couldn't. Her fingers had gone clammy, and the photo slipped to the floor. She took deep breaths, but the air felt close, stale, like the air in a tomb. She didn't remember the picture being taken. That meant it had been taken without her knowledge, by someone watching her. She looked at the other pictures: all had been taken from a distance. The other youngsters had disappeared, their bones washing up years later along the coast. She wondered why they had all been chosen, why she had been chosen. A part of her wondered now if she'd live to find out.

Catrin picked up the photo and put it with the rest in her pocket. The old man had crouched beside her. She felt him pulling her down behind the altar. He was pointing deeper into the cave.

She could see little at first, just the flickering of tapers. Far down in the darkness were a dozen or more figures, wearing long robes and hooded. She thought she recognised the gait of some regulars from the bar and the older men who had smoked their pipes out on the rocks. All carried burning tapers that threw long shadows over the ground.

Gradually in the feeble light she made out more figures. Some were short, barely waist-height to those on either side and some were holding hands. These must be the children, the ones she had seen down in the woods. Their eyes glimmered in the dimness.

At the edge of the group something was being drawn along the ground. It was a man's body, the hands and legs tied, and it was masked and hooded. Over it a cloak seemed to shudder and long coloured ribbons hung down on either side. Something about the outline of the body reminded her of Huw, the broadness of the shoulders, the long thin legs.

Then as the body moved into the circle of tapers she saw the cloak was made up of the wings of ravens, and the ribbons were trails of bloody flesh, and suddenly the caves were filled with the birds' screeching. The hood over the eyes was dark and wet with blood. The body jerked in the rush of beaks and claws, then disappeared into the blackness.

She felt a rush of anger mixed with crushing fear. The place was closing around her like a curse. She tried to think rationally, logically. All those little moments she'd shared with Huw – his tenderness, his vulnerabilities, that sense she'd had that he'd needed her, that she'd needed him as much, maybe more if she'd let herself. If she survived she knew these thoughts would never let her go. She prayed death had come to him quickly.

The tapers receded quickly into the cave. One of the men seemed to turn, beckon to her. His head was featureless under his mask, then she could no longer see him. The central space was empty again.

Hesitantly she edged forwards, Tudor close behind her with the torch. He moved the weakening beam over what lay around them. The space was made up of large rough boulders coated in moss. On the walls were elaborate carvings, warped faces and ancient horned gods. This was the area she'd seen on the screen. In the centre was the bed, sheeted in black plastic. Deeper in, the space was lit with candles, as it had been in the two films.

She turned to check they were alone. It was impossible to tell. The shaft further in was covered with lines of small bones, glowing in the light. At the end between torches stood a stone statue with cloven feet and a stag's head. The bones were too small to be adult and had been cleaned, as unnaturally white as those in an exhibit. Heaped under the statue were feathers and smaller animal bones that might have been those of birds or rodents. A sense of death clung to the place.

Tudor had moved further in. On the far side the wall was higher, made up of more rough stones coated in moss. Between the stones were metal rings from which chains hung down, and below them piles of old mattresses. From somewhere among them came a rustling, that might have been the sound of a small animal. A shape slipped away into the darkness. For an instant, Catrin caught sight of a human head, its forehead a sickly pallid colour. Whoever it was seemed in a daze like a sleepwalker, staggering this way and that in the gloom.

She saw the veins on the person's arms were covered with black scabs and abscesses. It looked like a young woman; for a moment her eyelids fluttered, diaphanous against the torchlight like trapped moths, her pupils staring blindly up into her skull.

Tudor drew the girl gently back by her shoulders, wedging the torch into the brickwork. One of her wrists was attached to a metal chain. Her face was slack, saliva running down onto her breasts. He cupped his hands and brought water from a drip above to her lips.

The girl looked like the one Catrin had seen on the bed from the monitoring room, but she couldn't be sure. Her face reminded Catrin of some of the faces of the children in robes. She took the pictures from her pocket, looked at them under the beam. Then the pictures of the same children at earlier ages, taken from a distance. Among them was the picture of herself by the sea: she watched Tudor as she put it under the light. He didn't react. She moved her fingers from one similar feature to the next and peered up at him, waiting for a reaction.

'They're all his,' he said quietly, 'all of them. They're all his children.'

She took this in, shivering now, trying to shut away one part of what it meant so she could still think clearly. It fitted with the rest of the dismal picture.

Jones or whoever he was had had children with various women in the area. Then when the women had drifted away, he'd stalked the children. Later he'd drawn them back into the scene around Seerland. It would have been a good cover, the band had a reputation for attracting drifters, lost souls, suicides waiting to happen. When they'd started going missing, no one would have been that surprised.

The old man was still smiling his cracked smile. She'd expected him to be nervous but he seemed calm, almost serene. She touched the girl's wrist where the metal had chafed it. Along the forearm, under the scabs and dried mud were the lines of an old tattoo, a long, hooked beak. It looked like something half buried under the skin, she thought, something that had scratched its way in and was waiting to be woken.

Gently she put the girl's arm down and looked up at Tudor. He was staring into the centre of the room where there was nothing but dust and the shadows. He nodded slowly, looking at her as if she must already understand. 'To gain favours from his master, the witch believes he has to make the greatest sacrifice of all. He must sacrifice to him his own children.'

Catrin was feeling faint. Through her mind spun images of the elaborate crucifix carved above Huw's door, the crucifixes in Face's grandmother's house. She sensed they must have already known some of the horror of it.

The old man had stepped back into the dimness. She could no longer see him clearly. Around her the wind was rustling through something hanging near her; what, she couldn't tell. Then the old voice, or an echo. Each time Tudor's words began again she felt the horror closing in around her, a sudden vacuum, shutting away her breath. She was shaking her head, trying to make the words stop, but they wouldn't.

She couldn't hear his words now. Though he was near, only a few feet away, his voice seemed at a distance. There was only one thought in her mind, one question which everything seemed to have been leading up to, a question that seemed to be at the black heart of it all. She knew it was one of the most ancient human beliefs: the greater the sacrifice, the greater the power that emanated from it. This was the law Jones had lived by, he had sacrificed more than his soul, he had sacrificed something far more precious, the souls of his own children. He had always known they would die. But what did he believe he had received in return for such a sacrifice? What could have been worth such a price? Immortality, a secret power too terrible to name. She wondered if she'd ever live to know what it was.

She looked for the beam of Tudor's torch but could

no longer see it. The girl had gone too. She heard a low rasping sound then muffled screams. Picking up the scythe, holding the blade out ahead, Catrin inched forward.

There was a shuffling noise behind her, and when she looked up she saw a man with his face hidden behind the long hair of a wig. Slowly he peeled it off and put it down. She thought she could hear Jones laughing to himself. As she was about to cry out, he put his fingers gently to his lips.

'Nothing's what it seems,' he said quietly.

He looked tired, his eyes bruised and reddened. He pointed at a chair opposite. 'I've been waiting for you,' he said.

She said nothing at first, reached over with the scythe, held the blade against his neck. But he didn't move, he seemed almost oblivious to her presence. 'Where's the old man,' she said. 'And the girl?'

He looked blankly at her as if he didn't know what she was talking about and then he smiled.

He'd put his head in his hands, his fingers pushing up the thick grey hair so that she could no longer see his face. 'I'm not who you think I am. I'm a friend.' The weak, cracked voice was hardly recognisable. 'But not a very useful one, I'm afraid.'

'You killed Rhys because he finally got too close to you, didn't you?'

'Rhys was a good cop, a good man.' His shook his head, his hands still covering his face. 'He was not long for this world, he was in the last throes of addiction. He knew he only had a few months left to break the case that had haunted him all his life.'

'The case of those nineteen young people who had disappeared.'

'Twenty if you count Face.'

'Twenty-one if you count Caris, Old Tudor's girl. Yes, Face was just part of a much larger pattern of disappearances. But his fame obscured that fact, and there were those who wanted to keep it that way.'

'Face was never Rhys's main interest. Face was just a way of getting finance from Powell for tracking down the man behind the disappearances.'

'You, Angel Jones.'

Past the frames along the wall she got a brief glimpse into a further stretch of the tunnel, lit by low-watt strip lights. Rows of narrow bunk beds lined the walls.

'I'm a very bad man, Catrin.' He hesitated. 'But not as bad as you think I am.'

'So you tricked Rhys. You knew he was obsessed with the case. You gave him a lead, but you wanted something in return. You wanted your freedom.'

'He perjured himself, yes, made it look as if my conviction had been unsafe. So I got out. But it wasn't a trick.'

She pushed the blade tight up against his neck. 'Of course it was, you were able to give him a lead in the case because you yourself were the man behind it all. But what you gave him, it was too much. It led him to you, so you killed him before he could expose you.'

'No,' he said. 'You're looking at everything the wrong way up.'

She waited but he said nothing further. He'd begun to play his thick hair through his fingers, staring out into space, his face blank.

'You see,' he said, 'it was Rhys who came to me, not me to him.'

'Why?'

'Because he'd heard something, something vague but to him tangible enough to make him take the risk of releasing me. It was just a rumour really,' he said quietly. 'Almost a legend, going around the scene. He must've picked it up on the streets.'

'That was?'

'About this girl I knew, an underground figure, hard-core, into extreme edge play. How one night she'd got high on meth and told a strange story about being a member of a cult. About how they wore masks, went on heavy trips and how all the members had disappeared, one by one.'

'So Rhys wanted you to find this girl. He saw her as a lead in the case, that was why he got you out.'

He was nodding, peering out at her from between his fingers.

'Rhys owned me, he gave me back my life, a chance to do something good, but he could also have taken it away again. I was his man, I got the job here because this was where the girl was. I got close to her again. That was how I found those photos.'

'The girl Della saw you with way back. The girl you used in all the profiles?'

'Caris, Tudor's daughter,' he said. 'I loved her, but she used me, her cult used me. I was their scapegoat. They needed a bogeyman figure as a cover for all the disappearances back then, so through her they fed me, fostered my myth.'

'You knew this and still loved her, still branded yourself with her cult's sign?'

'You don't stop loving someone because they're using you. She let me do to her what I could only do to others by force. Rhys knew that I loved her, that was why he knew I had to tread a careful line. If I exposed myself openly as the source, then I'd have lost her.'

'But he told you to trust me, why not reveal yourself as the source?'

'I tried. I asked the doctor to hold you, I followed but you were always with Powell or Thomas.'

'You followed me from the club?'

'All the time I was trying to reach you Catrin.'

'And down in the village, the inn?'

'The whole village is bugged, there's constant surveillance.'

She thought about all the cameras she'd seen, the units around the wards; what he was saying had a ring of truth to it. 'That was why you gave me your handle, to contact via the site?'

Jones nodded weakly, his hands still covering his face. She knew she couldn't let her guard down. He'd deceived many before her, this was probably all part of the game for him, winning the trust of his victims before taking them down.

He was silent for a moment. She sensed him watching her carefully from between his fingers. He seemed to have read her mind. 'You're not exactly in a position to bargain, Catrin – if I'm who you think I am, the witch, why would I bother to feed you a line?'

It made a certain strange sense, but several things still weren't adding up. If what he told her was true it begged another more disturbing question.

'But if not you, then who is he?'

'He always wears a mask when he comes here.'

Jones handed her a photograph, a tall man in robes, his hood pulled up over a long, beaked mask. The image could have been of anyone. It told Catrin nothing.

'So you're saying you don't know who he is?' she said incredulously.

He shook his head very slowly. 'No one here knows. Some do what they do because they're paid, others out of a mixture of superstition and fear. They think what he's done to his children means he's protected by the devil.'

She looked around. There were no sounds from further inside. The only movement was that of a small black bird that had been perching on the wall gliding away into the tunnel.

'And Rhys never told you who he thought it was?'

He moved his hands over his face very slowly, like someone who'd been in pain for a long time. 'No, but I think Rhys was close to finding out before he died.'

'What makes you think that?' she said.

Jones had shifted closer and was looking down at the picture. Through the space ahead she could detect a slight movement of air, bringing with it the faint scent of the sea. She stared into the blackness.

'Rhys didn't know who it was,' he said softly. 'He did know about the nineteen drifters and dropouts from the scene around Face. But the rumours he'd heard of someone else in the background were always too sketchy to follow up.'

'Penrhyn. It was the family name of a man once

accused of sacrificing his children to the devil. This man seems to have been doing the same thing.'

'Rhys said he rarely heard any name used. In fact, he wondered sometimes if we were pursuing a myth, a phantom.'

'And Rhys thought he was here on the island?' Catrin asked.

'Rhys thought he only came occasionally to the island, that he had another life on the mainland.'

'Why?'

'I'm not sure. In those last weeks at the cottage, Rhys was in a bad way with the heroin. He'd become paranoid, incoherent. He'd stopped trusting me. He'd go off for days on end. Then before he vanished that last time he said he was on the edge of something, some sort of breakthrough, but I never got to hear what it was.'

A weak smile flickered across Jones's face.

'It certainly all makes a pretty story,' she said.

Jones didn't look as if he cared what she believed. His cigarette dropped from his fingers, rolled onto the table. The smoke drifted up into his eyes. He stared into it as if at something alien.

She didn't know whether to believe him or not, but the tiredness that seemed to grip him matched her own, made her feel that in this at least he was a kindred spirit – not a saviour, not a solution, though perhaps as close to it as she was ever going to find in that place and at that hour.

'You say Rhys was "on the edge of something" before he disappeared. Did you form any idea of what that was?'

He shook his head. 'His mind was so confused by then,' he said.

'But what was he working on prior to his telling you about this "breakthrough"?'

Catrin sensed he was listening but not to her, to something she couldn't yet hear, but he remained motionless. 'How can I trust you?' he said slowly.

She lifted the scythe to his neck again.

'Because Rhys told you to,' she said.

His eyes gave nothing away. 'Rhys ended up dead, maybe he told me to trust the wrong person.'

She pushed the blade into his skin, drew blood. He didn't flinch.

'He had a lot of international law pages bookmarked on his old laptop. The floor of the room where he worked was covered with notes on all the equipment and chemicals ordered during the Heath Park lab sting. Something about the whole operation was still worrying him. He kept saying that the internal investigation into the failed sting had been looking at the operation from the wrong end.'

'Meaning?'

He glanced at her as if expecting her to know only too well what he was about to say. 'Well, the investigation had always assumed that all the big orders of lab equipment and specialist chemicals were designed to generate kickbacks for the officers in the sting. But they never turned up a single piece of evidence.'

'So?'

'So all the focus was on locating traces of a money trail from parties acting for the supply companies back to the officers. What was never explained was why so much – all the precursor chemicals and the top-end lab equipment – could not be accounted for when the sting was wound down.'

'One of the officers had been selling the materials sideways?'

'But no market had ever existed for such chemical exotica – for the precursor chemicals for tryptamines, belladonna alkaloids and DMT, the ancient deliriants. Yet what Rhys noticed was how the requests on the order forms to the Home Office had always been surprisingly specific. None of the officers had a formal background in chemistry, but the precision of the orders seemed to imply the guiding presence of someone with advanced narco-pharmacological training.'

'So maybe one of the officers was consulting with a chemist? That doesn't add up to much.'

'No, it doesn't, not in itself.'

'So why was Rhys interested?'

He smiled as if the answer was only too obvious.

'Timing,' he said, 'that's what interested him. This was the era of the international crackdown on all the MDMA and acid labs – remember – when precursor chemicals and large-volume lab equipment were becoming very hard to obtain by anyone outside government or the large pharmaceutical companies. If someone had wished to obtain these chemicals in volume, and remain undetected, the infiltration of a police sting would have provided an elegant mechanism for achieving this.'

'So what you're saying is that the lab sting in Heath Park wasn't to provide kickbacks for some of the officers, but simply a supply platform for the materials and chemicals? That the whole thing was a set-up from the very beginning.'

'It's the only explanation.'

'But surely the Internals would have found traces of a money trail?'

'No traces of any payments were ever found.'

'So you're suggesting one of the officers in the op may have been under the control of those who were sourcing the chemicals, answering directly to the cult?'

There was a long pause.

'There may be a simpler explanation,' Jones said, reaching into his inside pocket and producing some pieces of paper, pages from the *Western Telegraph* that had been tidily folded many times over. The first showed a scene Catrin recognised: an open, snow-bound field, in the centre of which stood the charred remains of a cabin. In the foreground, an electric wheel-chair lay on its side in the sludge.

'The man who died in that fire, Gethin Pryce, was the last of the early group around the band. He'd been out of sight for years.'

The second page unfolded into an image of a tidy close of Seventies-style semis. The front of one house was blackened with soot, its windows charred hollows.

'That house belonged to Gwen Evans,' Jones said. 'She'd lived next door to Face's grandmother in Bancyfelin for years. She died in a domestic house fire a day after Pryce's house was torched.'

Seeing the pictures Catrin began to feel dizzy, so she lowered her head, took deep breaths. 'It was Gwen who led us to this island. But the weather was bad that day. The roads were empty. We'd have noticed if anyone had tailed us to her house.'

'Who could have known your itinerary?'

'No one,' she said.

'Except one person, of course.'

She felt a slow lurching sensation, a spreading empti-ness in her stomach. Nothing felt certain any more, not the room in front of her eyes, not the words that Jones was speaking to her.

She heard a noise behind her and spun round. Little was visible in the light of the tapers, their soft glow barely illuminating a foot from the walls.

She moved to the nearest one, dipped the scythe into the oil, and held the flaming blade up above her. Jones was no longer at the table, she could no longer see him.

She heard the distant sound of the waves crashing against the rocks. She called out, her cry echoing far below her. But there was no reply. Behind her she thought she could sense something moving, brushing low against the ground.

Then the lights went on and she saw that Huw was standing at the end of the chamber. On either side were his two bodyguards, and two more men behind.

'I hired you to find the source of the pictures,' Huw said.

Catrin looked around, tried to see where Jones had gone. In the brighter lights she caught glimpses of the tunnel ahead. The walls were shivering with the black wings of the ravens.

'Now your job is done, my child,' Huw said.

Beside him she saw more men standing around Jones's slumped form. His head was bloodied, and his eyes were bleeding slits. He was being dragged among the birds, and they closed on him from every side until he disappeared.

She felt the tingling of something sharp puncturing her arm, a needle. Lights pulsed around her. Along the walls the birds looked vast, they seemed like messengers from another world. They were carrying her down, and silhouetted on the wall above her were other long, beak-like shapes.

Now she saw it as if for the first time. The dream had been a memory, she had been one of his, one of his many children. Her mother had been one of his group. Those were where the other dreams had come from, the dreams of the beach and the rocks and the man with long black hair running round her in a circle.

Later they had come and reclaimed her, taken her by force, the men in the car. Rhys had found her, freed her. He had protected her, from the cult and from the truth of who she was. But she knew now this place was her fate, and it had been waiting for her all along.

She feels the hands touch her again. Some are calloused and knotted with muscle. They are Huw's hands. They have always been Huw's hands. The men's bodies are shaved, damp with paint, the masks cool as they brush across her skin.

They drag her down into the darkness. The smell of the sea strengthens as they pull her towards its sound. The place around her now is a nesting cave high in the cliffs. Against the rocks the birds are clustering over something on the ground. Their wings seem

not black but a colour she has never seen before, irides-
cent in the spray from the waves far below, rising and
falling like the wings of angels.

Impressions swing dizzyingly in and out of focus.
Something is drawing her towards them, telling her
to give herself to them. The only way forward is to
wade through the rock pools and as she does so, her
legs numb in the water, she realises that the shape is
a body, bound in sacking. She knows it's the man
that she'd seen being dragged into the cave. He seems
to call to her. As his fair hair moves with the water,
she makes out the face of the young doctor. His eye
sockets are empty and the place echoes with the cries
of birds.

As she looks up she sees a raven's mask leaning over
her. She wants to cry out, but the words are frozen in
her throat. In their place a metallic taste, ice cold, cuts
away her breath.

The robe beneath the mask parts to reveal a painfully
emaciated torso, the raven's head entirely out of
proportion to the skeletal frame beneath. Each limb
is lined with the elaborate stigmata of track marks, of
blackened veins and lesions. The man's breathing rasps
again through the mask, the long beak distorting the
sound.

Strength, she thinks. From nowhere, she finds the
energy to reach up and grab the mask, tearing it off.

The man makes no move to stop her. The face beneath seems barely less dead than she feels.

She knows at once it is Face, that he was her second abductor in the chamber. Face, the favoured son, the heir. He grabs at her with stick-like arms as she moves back towards the edge, grasping at the air. Under his scars, the raven wings scored into his chest seem to beat, as if about to rise into the air. His breath smells of death. She cries out, pushing him away.

Suddenly he is on her, mantling her in his cloak as he bares his teeth over her face. He is looking at her eyes, not into them. She knows then he is about to bite.

She rolls back towards the edge. Ahead far below lie the churning waters – she pushes towards the gap. But the others are close, their hands touching and scratching at her body. Her legs are lifted, and she feels cold rock cut into her bleeding skin as they drag her.

She reaches out, holds onto the rock. He moves his mouth over her face, pulling up her skin with his teeth.

He weighs no more than a child, but the drugs make him powerful. She holds his twisting shape above her, but it is like fighting a tree, or a living root, and she hasn't the strength. She can feel his animal teeth nipping at her scalp, biting through her hair. When she pushes him back, she succeeds only in bringing his eyes before hers, then he is at her again, his teeth digging into the skin of her cheek.

Briefly their eyes meet. His expression is dull, cold, inhuman, he is looking at her as if at something already dead.

She sees Huw striding forward now, his hand outstretched. Deep inside her, rage boils up and turns to white-cold anger. She pulls Face in towards her, clasping his head beneath her arm and catching the first flicker of emotion in his eyes. If I go, you go, she thinks, and reaches out with her other hand for Huw, pulling him forward with his own momentum. As Face bites at her hand, she pulls them both towards the edge and steps out into the void. For a moment, she hangs there. And then all three of them fall. Strange that it is so peaceful, she thinks, and then nothing.

When she came to, she was aware only of the contrast in feeling between her left side, cold and exposed to the elements and her right, warmed by something firm and soft. The smell of Huw's cologne was everywhere, vetiver and lime. Her feet were dragging beneath her through the mud.

No, Thomas, she thought. It was Thomas who was pulling her to the far side of the mudflat. Moments later, he laid her gently down, turning her head away from the ground. And then he was gone again. She watched him move further along the beach, and thought how strangely like a baby she felt, calm and motionless as he began to move an inflatable out from the rocks.

Everything was playing out as if on a distant screen. In the weak light she saw him moving back towards her, but far away still.

There was a shuffling sound nearby. Dazed, she turned her head to see a hooded figure standing on a rock a few yards behind her. There were others behind him, up on the cliffs.

The man wore a long robe of coarse cloth, and held in front of him the long and bright blade of a sword. He lifted it high above his head.

Thomas ran, dropping the dinghy behind him, only a few feet away as the figure came down towards them. He held out the sword in front of him, stroking the air between them, gesturing that she should move away towards the rocks.

Everything was happening as if in slow motion, Thomas hesitating, brushing the hair from his face. The man striking out towards them, sparks rising where the blade struck. Now he'd ripped the front of Thomas's jersey. The blood was spreading over the wool. Thomas was reaching out and wrestling him for the handle of the sword.

Above, the figures stood silent, watching. Then the air was filled with a rushing and a hollow rasping sound, as Thomas broke away and drove the blade into the man's heart, and then a second time. With the second thrust the robed man slumped into a heap on the rocks.

Catrin found an unknown secret reserve of energy, and raised herself from the ground. She walked over to the body and pulled back the cowl. There was mud on Huw's cheeks, and his greying hair had matted close to his scalp. His eyes stared back, level and lifeless, and his robe was open to the thick, silver hair of his chest.

Thomas was standing over her, hand to his belly, his face still flush with colour, betraying no pain. She felt him pulling her hand, her feet dragging in the pebbles.

He pulled the dinghy down to the edge of the water. Another figure was there, walking as tall as a giant against the tide. It was Old Tudor, carrying what looked like a child in a blanket across his chest. They pushed the boat down to the foaming wash.

As Thomas knelt over it the outboard spluttered into life. The wind had slackened and mist hung thick over the water. There was a cold, dark crossing ahead.

SOME MONTHS LATER

It was almost silent on the tennis court. All Catrin could hear was the distant chug of a motor yacht far out past Mumbles Head.

She bounced the ball at her feet, then looked up to see where her opponent had positioned himself. Thomas was wearing baggy beachcomber's shorts and a Lion-of-Judah T-shirt. He hadn't dressed the part, nor did he look anywhere near ready to return service.

She served hard down the centre, the ball catching the inside of the line. It was a good, precise serve, but not quite hard enough. From nowhere Thomas returned the ball surprisingly deep to her backhand, a clean winner.

That was the thing about Thomas. He played like he worked and lived, never seeming to have his eye on the ball or anywhere near it. But it was all mis-direction. When he reached the ball he knew exactly what to do with it.

She still had match point. She served again, hard at his body. This time she ran behind her serve to the net, volleyed his return deep. His return down the line missed by inches.

They sat on a small bench at the edge of the court. Thomas had brought some beers and smoothies in a cooler down from the house.

'The first rule in any game,' she said. 'Always play with someone better than yourself or you'll never improve.'

He took a sip of beer, his eyes half closed against the late afternoon sun. 'That's exactly why I play with you,' he said.

She gave him a quick smack with her strings. He was looking back up the staggered lawns towards the grand Victorian house ringed by small, spiky palm trees. At the back, facing them, was a large conservatory, to one side of it a pool, black-tiled in the shape of a heart.

'I thought you hated Della,' he said. 'So why use her court?'

Catrin glanced up at the upper windows, their curtains drawn, and thought she glimpsed Della watching them.

'We seem to have a strange understanding now,' she said. 'The fire hasn't changed her. But she never goes out now, just sits in that big house on her own, won't talk to anyone. I feel bad if I don't come here.'

Thomas looked at her carefully. 'You think if she's given the chance she could change?'

Catrin didn't answer, wasn't sure if she could. She wondered if Thomas could tell how difficult and how new everything now felt. Even the smallest things, leaving the house, taking a walk, deciding what to wear. The enormity of what had happened still weighed on her chest, making it difficult to breathe at times. Sometimes she still woke sweating in the night, had to run to the window and gulp down the cold night air. Remind herself she was alive: not free of it, she would never be that, but alive, able to try to live again. She clung to what little hadn't been contaminated. Her bike, her exercise routines, she strung them out all day, or played chess online, over and over again. She wanted to be too tired to think. No therapists, no counsellors. She never kept the appointments Occupational Health had made for her. If there was a way for her to live now, it would be her secret. She didn't know what lay ahead there out in the light. She didn't know quite who she'd be. Someone different certainly, maybe someone she wouldn't entirely recognise.

She looked up, saw Thomas beckoning her, a second beer in his hand. She followed him down steps to the bottom of the garden, where a gate opened onto the beach road. Her Laverda was chained to the railings. Down on the beach a small café decorated like a surfer's shack had been set up under the promenade.

It was still early in the season, and the place looked

almost empty. Inside, a school leaver with spiky hair showed them to a table. Thomas pointed to the glass counter. Under it were the usual array of sticky buns and flapjacks.

A single black fly was buzzing, drawn by the sweet things under the glass.

'Watch the flies,' Thomas told her. She watched as the fly made its way to the counter. But then, as it was about to enter, it paused. Something else had caught its attention, higher to the right of the counter.

It flew up in that direction, and into a small black box. There was a frantic buzzing from inside the box. Then all was still.

'Powell's operation,' Thomas said. 'It was meticulous from the start. Being a drugs cop gave him the ideal cover, a supply platform for precisely the specialised drugs he needed for his occult practices. By using the ancient trance drugs and that ancient place of sacrifice he thought he'd tapped into a reality lost to us down the ages.'

Catrin didn't need to be reminded. She understood only too well how his infernal machine had worked. 'Powell must've believed in his primitive, psychotic mind,' Thomas continued: 'that only by sacrificing his own to his master could he achieve what he wanted to.'

She stared at him. 'Yes, but I'm still not sure I know

what that was exactly. What did he believe he was getting in return for such a high sacrifice? Money, power, a crack at immortality – or was it something else?'

A dubious look crossed Thomas's face. 'We'll never know. But strangely I don't think Powell wanted much. You'd think he'd expect something vast in exchange for such a high price, much like Faust. But I don't think he did. I suspect he just saw it as protection money. He believed he'd got what he had the way he had, and to keep it he had to keep on placating his master in the same way.'

Thomas shrugged. 'I may be wrong,' he said. 'It may have been something conventional, or something too terrible to describe. But I somehow doubt it. Every man has a desire they believe can only be granted by a power greater than themselves. Powell believed he'd found a radical and effective way of achieving that desire, but that same desire is there in all of us.' He glanced at her, squinting in the sun. 'I mean, what price would you pay if you believed it would buy you what you wished? Can you say for sure that you'd know what to ask for?'

She turned away. To have Rhys back. Is that what he thought? She suspected he had been drinking before they'd met for tennis. No smell, but she just knew. She'd heard he'd been reporting for work later every morning, and sometimes not coming in at all. Hiding what he was going through, playing the lad. But that was his way and she knew whatever she said wouldn't help. Of course the therapists all said sharing helped, but if they didn't they'd be out of a job, and for some things she knew it didn't, it just didn't. Talk about the outside stuff all you want, she thought, the logistics and reasons of it all, that helps, but not what's really going on inside. Not what you see when you're alone. He'd do it in his own way and his own time, just like her.

'Angel Jones,' she said, 'at what point d'you think he realised Powell was the hidden hand protecting him all those years?'

Thomas took a sip of beer. 'Maybe the night of the fire at Pryce's? Once Jones suspected it was Powell, he'd have known his chances of surviving were slim.'

She knew Rhys had taken a significant risk in freeing Jones, releasing a big evil in order to snare an even greater one. She'd no doubt he'd put safeguards in place, Jones had hinted as much, probably a statement and evidence left with a commissioner for oaths so Jones could have been tried under double jeopardy laws if he hadn't kept to the deal. Rhys had gambled on Jones preferring to bite the poisoned hand that had fed him, to die a free man than live on as a puppet. But she wondered if the safeguards had actually been necessary. She knew now that on the final night Jones had come to Thomas, not knowing if he could trust him and told him where the dinghy was. Surely that had limited his own chances of escape. That he'd also directed the old man and his girl Caris to the boat had diminished those chances yet further.

She looked at Thomas. 'Building Jones up into a bogeyman provided the cover for the disappearance over the years of Powell's children, the nineteen half-siblings,' she said quietly. 'Of course Powell played it safe, never showed himself to Jones. He used Caris as his main connection. He made sure Jones never knew too much about his cult, nor his cult about Jones.'

'Right, and Powell's eldest son Face's underground following provided a way to draw the children back into Powell's web without anyone noticing. The island was his sacred ground, his killing ground. But the younger children, no one knew of their existence, so he didn't need a cover for them.'

Thomas was looking closely up at the black box above the glass counter.

'All right,' Catrin said, 'so what's your point?'

He was pointing up at the fly-trap. 'But when Face himself disappeared, Powell knew the press and every conspiracy theorist around would be all over the case.'

She watched as another fly flew unwaveringly up from the counter and after a short buzzing inside the box was silent.

'Powell devised a clever defence mechanism,' Thomas went on. 'By setting himself up as a Face obsessive with big money, he ensured that any investigation into Face or the fans who'd disappeared – his nineteen children – always went through him.'

'And Rhys walked right in.'

'Yes, but not entirely.'

'Because Rhys wouldn't reveal his source?'

'And that's why Powell needed you, because you were the only person named as trusted by the source. And as you were the final child who'd escaped the cult, you suited Powell's purposes perfectly.'

Thomas finished his beer. She glanced at him; he was still smiling his lazy smile.

Slowly he nodded. 'When Rhys was killed, I already suspected the island was at the centre of it all. That's why I'd begun to focus there.'

'But why didn't you use back-up?'

'Because that way I'd never have found out who the leader was. Powell was a surveillance expert, the place was always monitored closely. Any big operation and Powell would have known it was coming. Out there, on his own terms, he was always a step ahead.'

The surveillance, all the contracts with the CCTV companies, she knew that was how Powell had been able to destroy any footage that might have shown Rhys being drowned. The companies might have also removed footage of the second man, the one in the hut, who Rhys had attacked because he knew he was one of Powell's men. Foiling the surveillance may also have helped Powell to protect Jones. But there was much she might never know. Who Powell's associates were, for instance, and how far their influence reached. The unknowability had been designed in from the start, so any associates might survive him. Rix, for instance, had kept a lid on Jones's release, which served Rhys's purpose. It had made her consider again those old rumours about Rix having a crush on Rhys. Perhaps there was something in them after all, or maybe Rhys had had something on him. Though she knew Rix could have acted for other reasons, and if he had he was someone she would have to watch in the future.

Thomas was moving closer. 'Face's body, they still haven't found it.'

'But I saw it there in the mud.'

'The islanders must have moved it before the uniforms arrived.'

'So Face is still officially missing?'

'Yes, the case remains open.'

She didn't ask about Caris and Tudor, she'd checked in with him every week. His girl was still in a secure clinic in London, not talking. Tudor visited every other day, but months had passed without her breaking her silence. Thomas pushed the window wider and the salty spring breeze passed over their faces.

Catrin felt Thomas touch her hand under the table as she looked out. The boat she'd heard earlier had crossed to the far edge of the horizon, almost out of sight now.

When she stood, Thomas made as if to follow but she gestured him back and walked out onto the beach on her own. She didn't look at the boat. She closed her eyes. She felt very alone. Maybe that's how it would always be now. If there was a way to carry on, she would have to leave Rhys behind.

ACKNOWLEDGEMENTS

Thanks to Geoff Mulligan, Alison Hennessey and Briony Everroad for their painstaking editing and proof reading; Patrick Walsh for keeping it all on track, Jake and the rest of the team and John Williams for his invaluable advice.

My hat off to KJ for her input on Pembrokeshire, the band and much else; to Paul Powell for his advice, Richard T for those discussions way back; Maruja K for Spain; HTR and Valerie Demat for their unknowing but significant support, and the Valley Commandos for their unique friendship, companionship, and protection.

www.vintage-books.co.uk